TOR BOOKS BY DIANA MARCELLAS

Mother Ocean, Daughter Sea
The Sea Lark's Song
Twilight Rising, Serpent's Dream

Twilight Rising, Serpent's Dream

DIANA MARCELLAS

TOR®
fantasy

A TOM DOHERTY ASSOCIATES BOOK
NEW YORK

This is a work of fiction. All the characters and events portrayed in this book are either products of the author's imagination or are used fictitiously.

TWILIGHT RISING, SERPENT'S DREAM

Copyright © 2004 by Diana Marcellas

Maps by Ellisa Mitchell

A Tor Book
Published by Tom Doherty Associates, LLC
175 Fifth Avenue
New York, NY 10010

www.tor.com

Tor® is a registered trademark of Tom Doherty Associates, LLC.

ISBN 0-812-56179-1
EAN 978-0-812-56179-1

First edition: August 2004
First mass market edition: March 2006

Printed in the United States of America

0 9 8 7 6 5 4 3 2 1

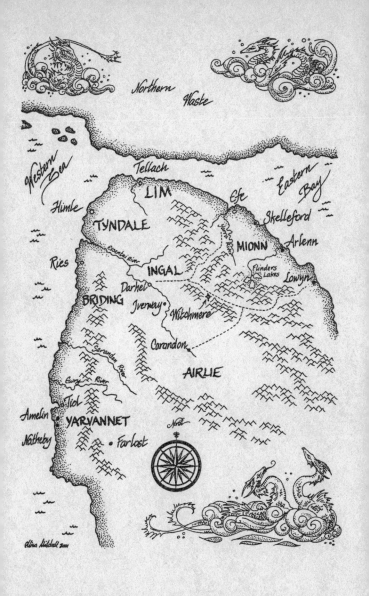

Twilight Rising, Serpent's Dream

*T*he Daystar edged above the trees that shaded the narrow ravine where the forest house stood above the tumbling brook, surrounded by everpine. The sun's mellow golden light glanced downward, lighting the upper edges of the ravine and not yet penetrating its shadowed depths. Already the dawn's light was tinged with blues and lavenders as the Companion, the world's second sun, began its own dawning close behind the Daystar. In a few weeks the Companion would complete its steady winter's advance on the Daystar, and the suns would Pass in the sky, worsening the storms of early spring for Mionn's bay shore and mountain plateaus. But today, on this late-winter morning with the air fresh with the tang of winter cold, today the dawn was still and clear.

Ashdla Toldane and her twin brother, Will, sat cross-legged on the house porch, watching the dawn. Yesterday afternoon they had walked the several miles to the cabin from their father's house on the outskirts of Ellestown, the largest of the towns by the Flinders Lakes, and had spent the night in comfortable privacy. Here in this hidden ravine north of the lakes, secure from discovery by the Allemanii townsfolk, it was safe to work their forest magic, the traditional shari'a chants that summoned the power of the forest, the rites that wove the patterns of life and strength for all who lived nearby, both human and four-footed. In the eastern Allemanii earldom of Mionn, on this isolated plateau high in the interior of the mountains, a line of forest witches had handed down the forest gift from daughter to daughter for generations, and, occasionally, to her brother when the daughter was twinned with a son, as Ashdla was twinned with Will. For three centuries, ever since Allemanii butchery had nearly ended the shari'a witch-folk, a forest witch, called *shajar* in the ancient language, had safeguarded this cabin and the caverns nearby, waiting for the Finding promised by the shari'a dragon-spirits, the Four, who had guarded the shari'a people since their beginnings.

The Allemanii had once been a sea folk from lands beyond the Western Ocean. War and blight had driven them to voyage in their longships over a thousand miles of ocean to seek a new home. Led by two nobleman brothers, Aidan and Farrar, they had come first as invaders, but had quickly settled peaceably along the coast and rivers of the shari'a lands. Aidan had become their duke, a new principal rank of High Lord not known in their West, and Farrar had become earl of Mionn, the easternmost of their new earldoms and counties. The native shari'a preferred the upland valleys and forested plateaus of the mountains, and so for a time the ancient shari'a lands had room for two peoples, one new, one old, very different from each other but for two generations becoming almost friends. The peace had not lasted: eighty years after the Allemanii's Landing, their third duke, Rahorsum, had suddenly attacked the shari'a fortress of Witchmere and had slaughtered every shari'a he could find. Thereafter Rahorsum and then his son Bram had pursued the shari'a survivors with sword and fire, hunting the shari'a until no more could be found. Bram had then turned on his own Ingal folk, invading the Allemanii villages then dying from the Great Plague loosed by the shari'a, murdering Allemanii women and then their men who had tried to defend them, calling any woman witch for the mere guilt of her sex. And so the Disasters that Rahorsum had loosed on the shari'a had turned back on the Allemanii, decimating Duke Bram's people. In time the earls of Mionn and Yarvannet had intervened, invading Ingal to catch Bram and end him. For four more years the Allemanii lands had been convulsed by civil war, but in time Bram was caught and grimly executed, then a new duke was elected by the High Lords, a better duke, a thoughtful and high-minded lord whose new laws had reestablished the peace. By then, however, the shari'a had vanished, every last one apparently put to the sword or pyre.

But not all had died. Some shari'a had fled into exile across the Eastern Bay into the East; a few others had vanished into hiding in the Allemanii towns and the nearby forests to live under peril of the Allemanii's shari'a laws that proscribed any shari'a witch from living. Those laws still existed, as did the Allemanii legends of the shari'a as a folk to be feared and hated as evil. For three hundred years every shari'a survivor in the Allemanii lands had lived in constant fear of discovery, of when the hunt would begin, the murder accomplished. After so long a time, Ashdla wondered, how many shari'a still survived in these lands? A dozen? Perhaps as many as a hundred? More? Who could say? The Mionn witches did not know. The Four had long promised a gathering of those shari'a who had survived, a Finding of all shari'a folk that would bring the long-awaited renewal. How many would come for that gathering? The dragons would not say; perhaps even they did not know. The shajar of Ashdla's line could only wait, chanting the old chants, making the old rites, preserving what had been for what would come.

On a wide branch of an ever-oak across the stream from the house, the forest dragon, Amina, settled to listen to the chant, as she always came to listen. The dragon's golden eyes flickered in the shadows of the sheltering branches, as gold as the light now glancing downward through green laceries, blending gold with the green-scaled shadow of her sinuous body, a living and shadowed light. Only the shari'a-born could see the Four; since the twins' earliest memories Amina had been their comforter and guide and, since their mother's death five years ago, their teacher, whenever Amina would consent to teach.

Good morning, children. The dragon's mental voice resonated with the rustle of leaves, the quiet movement of cool water, and was underlaid with the warmth of her unswerving affection, with the steady patience of the land that had endured the ages. *The dawn approaches.*

Yes, it does. Ashdla smiled, happy to see her. *Good morning.*

Good morning, Amina, Will sent. He glanced inquiringly at his sister. *How about the "Call to Spring" for the chant today? It fits the season.*

Ashdla nodded. *You lead, Will.* Will shifted his seat slightly and then relaxed, his hands loose in his lap as he waited, his face lifted toward the suns still hidden behind the forest canopy. The leaves of the surrounding trees stirred in a slight breeze, whispering. The water below the porch laughed softly, slipping over stone and moss in its endless tumble, cool and playful, the never-ending music of water, the sound of renewal. A nearby bird greeted the dawn with a sweet cry. Ashdla sighed softly, yielding to the Patterns of Life that now gathered around them. Leaf and bole, fur and feather: life took shape within the morning, beginning the day, weaving life. As the dawn light strengthened, the Patterns wove around Ashdla and Will like spiderwebs, bringing an easement of night fears, bringing the newness of the day. Birds caroled, leaves whispered, and all was alive, moving, moving, and hope rose again with the morning, lifting the heart. As the Daystar rose above the branches, glancing down in golden shafts of light, Will raised his hands.

"Ta'ala bin kora ishar'at," he sang softly, chanting the ancient shari'a greeting to the season, the first of four seasons that now impended. *Raw and cold is icy spring.* "Birandi kitir ta'latin ginah, bin naali sahari nadif na'far." *The storms come on the eastern wind, the teal on the watery ponds raise their cry.*

Ashdla raised her hands, palms lifted toward the dawn, and chanted the response. "Naali shar shimal daray, ta'fria madani, ta'fria timaas." *Birds awaken from meadows, out of the wood, out of the green grass.*

"Sun climbs to sun, at the zenith soon to Pass," Will sang in the old words, his voice lifting high into the morning, "Turn upon turn, year upon year, / Soren, dragon of air, rises to new life / And the suns dance."

They lowered their hands to their laps again and waited,

listening. Beneath the cabin porch, the water tumbling in the stream seemed to chime in softer rhythm; the faint shirring of air through leaves fell to a near-whisper, hushed and stilled. The Patterns wove around them steadily, tracery upon tracery, building new connection and renewal, the promised renewal of the coming spring. Soon these trees that now slept in winter, all naked of their leaves save the everpine, would put out new buds on every branch, followed by a great canopy of new leaves and spring flowers, beginning their cycle to summer, when all was warm and shadowed within the forest: soon, when the spring came, soon now, and with the summer to follow, warm and welcoming. The Daystar's brilliant sunlight glanced more strongly into the ravine, tipping every branch with golden fire, and sparkled upon the lingering snow of late winter.

Slinkfoot nudged Ashdla's hip with her sharp-muzzled nose, wanting attention when Will would not, and Ashdla dropped her hand to the ferret's sleek head for a brief caress. In Ashdla's tunic pocket, the tiny shrew family who lived there squeaked faintly; and above their heads, on a rafter of the porch roof, she heard a mock owl's faint fluffing of feathers as Owree, too, watched the chant. Their animal friends often attended the dawn chants, for what reason Ashdla couldn't say, only that they did, for whatever meaning they found for themselves. Perhaps they liked only to be near Ashdla and Will wherever they might be, and found meaning enough in that. She patted Slinkfoot a second time and then pushed the ferret away. "You know better, Slinkfoot," she chided softly. "Don't interrupt chant." Another push earned Ashdla only a limp-bodied sprawl, a happy show of sharp, white teeth. The ferret waited a moment, just long enough for Ashdla to look away again, then began to edge back, as slow as sludge sinking down a slope, thinking Ashdla wouldn't notice if she did it s-l-o-o-ow. Ashdla tried to ignore her.

The dawn light strengthened, filling the ravine with a golden shimmering light, stronger now. When the time was right, a moment both felt when it came, Will raised his hands again.

"A good season for long journeys is summer," Will sang into the morning. "Quiet is Amina's tall fine wood, / And green the plumage of the canopy. / The light dances on green leaves, moving with the wind."

"In Basoul's autumn," Ashdla answered, chanting the old words they both knew, "Ferrets steal through the high grass, hunting. / The birds cry, soothing, and eddies swirl in the stream. / The waves mount upon the shores, / And good is the warmth of the land."

"A good season for staying is Jain's winter," Will continued, and the suns' light struck down brilliantly, filling the world, "Fire is roused on the rim of the world, / And the stars, cold fire, burn in the True Night. / Memories are gathered and the heart is kindled, / And all is safe."

They lowered their hands to their laps and listened, bound into the forest Patterns, a part of the greater whole, the whole a part of them. Ashdla closed her eyes against the Daystar's dazzle and sighed, then felt Slinkfoot again press closer to her thigh and then the sharp nip of teeth, pricking through the fabric of her trousers and disrupting her mood. She looked down and frowned at the small animal.

"You know better, Slinkfoot," she chided again. "Where are your manners?" Slinkfoot bared her white teeth, undented, then companionably laid her narrow snout on Ashdla's leg, hinting for another caress. Ashdla heard the small sigh of contentment, then the first small snore, more comment than real. Not even Slinkfoot could sleep that fast, whatever the ferret pretended.

"What'd she do?" Will asked, turning his head toward her. The sun made a halo around his head, and his eyes were still distant, lost far away in the depths of the forest. He blinked, then looked at her with more connection to the day.

"Wanted attention, as usual. I guess she gave up wheedling you." Ashdla pushed at the ferret, got another soft snore. "Here, Will, take her. She's your ferret."

"*Our* ferret," Will corrected mildly. "You keep her."

Ashdla wrinkled her nose, then gave up and pulled Slinkfoot into her lap to cuddle her, which is what the ferret wanted all along, of course. Slinkfoot sniggered softly in triumph, then chewed amiably on Ashdla's fingers as she petted her. Ashdla looked up at her brother and smiled. "That was nice, Will. You're always good at leading dawn chant."

"Dawn's my best time of the day," Will said lazily, uncrossing his legs to stretch his knees. "Maybe I'm a dawn witch."

"There's no such thing as a dawn witch," Ashdla reproved, then shook her head as Will smiled even more lazily, as undaunted as the ferret. Sometimes Will voiced the most amazing ideas, usually to poke at tradition and make Ashdla bristle. "Shari'a gift follows the four elements," she instructed loftily, "not the time of day."

"So you say," Will retorted. "If I want to be a dawn witch, why not? The books say that when the Finding comes, the four shari'a gifts will change to six or seven. We'll be more than air and fire, sea and forest, but something else, too, probably a combination. Maybe the Change is here. Maybe a dawn witch is one of the new gifts."

"Combination of what?" Ashdla asked skeptically, narrowing her eyes.

Will frowned slightly, considering. "Well, dawn fills the air with light, and it's the beginning of the day's cycle, just like the forest has a cycle of life from spring to winter. Maybe a dawn witch combines air and forest." Ashdla snorted, and Will looked at her with open irritation. "Either you believe the books or you don't, Ash," he said. "The books say what they say. You can't pick and choose what to believe. The books say that combination gifts will mark the Change, that the gift would first divide and then combine. You've studied the texts just like I have, and combination gifts are expressly prophesied in the *Lists of the Change*. So why not a dawn witch?" He stopped himself and looked away from her at the trees, a small muscle working in his jaw. "Amina's gone," he said then, and Ashdla looked, too, and saw that the ever-oak branch was empty. Will sighed heavily. "So is what we made with the chant." She heard the regret in his voice, and bit her lip.

"I'm sorry, Will," she said contritely. Sometimes she knew she pushed too far and ended up hurting Will's feelings, the last thing she wanted to do. Forest twins always tussled, or so the books said, but she liked to talk to her brother. Will always had interesting ideas, even if some of them were uncomfortable for a traditionalist like herself. At least I think I'm a traditionalist, she amended. "I really *am* sorry, Will," she said, and then saw him relax.

He gave her a wry smile and shrugged his forgiveness. "It's all right. After all this while, I've gotten used to you."

He stood up to stretch, then put his hands on his hips and looked out at the ravine. His face glowed in the suns' light, smooth planed and untroubled. At fifteen Will was often impatient with the world, anxious to finish growing into his manhood, and then to take charge of whatever he should; but in chant Will found a different purpose in living, one more suited to their witch-blood, and perhaps more natural to himself. He was a shari'a witch like Ashdla was, and shared the forest gift with her, as had all the male twins of the cabin witches. His witch-gift was more erratic and not quite the same as hers, although the difference was hard to define; but he heard the forest like Ashdla did, knew what she knew. The day was colored the same for him; the trees spoke in the same voices. He was Ashdla's second self, as she was his.

"Forest witch is better," Ashdla suggested mildly, not pushing it, but not letting go of it either.

"So you say," he retorted, then turned his head to grin at her. "The chant *was* good, wasn't it? All the chants are working better since Amina told us that Brierley Mefell is coming to Flinders. I wonder why? Maybe believing is what makes chant work best, not the words or the gestures or the other things the books say."

"Chant words aren't important?" Ashdla asked incredulously and frankly goggled at him.

"Oh, stop it," Will said. "I'll say what I like, Ash, and maybe you should listen when I do. Maybe you'll learn something." He put his hands in his pockets and slouched comfortably, looking at the morning. "When do you think Brierley will get here?"

"Now how would I know that?" Ashdla asked reasonably. "Amina won't say, and I haven't a clue. 'Soon' is all we get." She dumped Slinkfoot rudely out of her lap, and the ferret rolled on her back and playfully batted at her hand, then tried to bite again. Ashdla got to her feet, brushing at her trouser legs.

"You can at least guess," Will suggested. "You like to pretend you know everything. I just handed you a chance to prove it." Ashdla bared her teeth, copying Slinkfoot's most common comment. Will laughed, and Slinkfoot's laughing snigger echoed near their feet. The ferret always took Will's side, every time; and Will thought it hilarious that Ashdla even minded, which she did, although it wasn't smart to admit it. Slinkfoot did a lazy roll and a toothy yawn, then batted her feet and squeaked pleadingly at Will, wanting up.

"You don't win arguments with Slinkfoot." Will bent to scoop up the ferret, then draped her comfortably around his shoulders. "Or with me," he added playfully.

"All I said was there aren't any dawn witches," Ashdla said. "And no, I don't know when Brierley will get here. Dump it, will you?"

"I'm just trying to get you to think creatively. It's what a male twin does—that's also in the books, by the way, so don't sniff. 'The male forest gift, although erratic,'" he intoned, quoting, "'touches the edge of the unknown, evoking new patterns that take half shape and then dissolve.'" And so the books say, whenever they admit we brothers have a gift at all." Will looked out at the forest again, and his expression softened. "Do you hear it, Ash?" he asked, and she heard the yearning in his voice. "Do you hear the Promise?"

Ashdla turned her head to look, too, as the suns' light streamed down on the forest, touching every leaf, every branch. Birds called to each other in the trees, and beyond them a distant sound moved, the beginning of a wind at the far edge of the forest, moving toward them. "The wind is changing," Will murmured. "It's finally changing. Can you hear it?"

"Yes, Will," she whispered. "Yes, I hear." She sighed. "I wish Mother could have lived long enough to hear it," she said sadly. "She waited for the Finding all her life."

"Every forest witch in this cabin has waited all their lives—except us." He turned his head and smiled. "Except us. We will see the Finding, Ash. We will see the gathering of the shari'a, and with it the new dawn and the rising light of our people. The darkness is ending at last."

She shook her head. "The danger isn't, Will. The Allemanii still proscribe us from living. They still hate."

Will slipped his arm around her waist and pulled her close, then kissed her lightly on the mouth. "But the darkness is ending," he said, his voice filled with joy. "I can feel it, Ashdla. Truly." He turned his head and looked again at the forest rising before them and on every side, and his face was exalted. "Listen! Do you hear them coming?"

The distant wind moved toward them, shaking the ever-pine branches, sighing past leaf and twig, ruffling the icy grasses of the meadows, stalking every glen. It moaned and cried, then shouted and blew its fury through a thicket of ever-oak, and sighed to nothing again, a bare whisper to stir the leaves. It rose over the far edge of the ravine and plunged into it, tossing a fine mist off the water of the stream and rattling the bushes, then swept down the ravine toward the cabin. Will tightened his arm around Ashdla's waist as the air dragon, Soren, flared into view, a misty golden figure driving the wind. Behind him, tumbling figures of red and blue and green, the other dragons hurtled joyfully in his wake. Soren's wings snapped like thunder, booming off the sides of the ravine; and the passage of his coming swept a cascade of dead leaves onto the planking of the porch, tugged and flapped at their clothing, tossed their hair, and he was a clean and fresh wind, newly come, the harbinger of spring. The Four soared past the porch, and Ashdla and Will watched as they disappeared around the turning, hurtling onward down the ravine toward the lakes.

"Maybe it's a sign," Ashdla said. "Maybe in the spring

Brierley will come." Will nodded, and they smiled at each other.

"And spring is nearly here," Will said happily, then looked up at the Daystar. "Three weeks and the suns will Pass, and spring will be here."

"Three weeks," Ashdla said and sighed deeply. "That's too long, Will."

Will laughed and hugged her. "But soon enough. Come on, we have to get home. Da might be worrying."

~

Michael Toldane's smithy stood on the far edge of his Flinders town, next to the forest edge but near enough to the marketplace for convenient business by the folk of Ellestown. This morning had been busy, enough to put a lancing pain in his back when he moved the wrong way, but Michael stolidly ignored it. No doubt he'd pay a price tomorrow with a stiffened back and uneasy movement, but that was part of a blacksmith's trade, long accepted. He straightened from nailing the shoe on the yearling mare's hindfoot and patted her neck. She was a good beast, patient and gentle, but nervous to be shod for the first time, and not at all sure she liked it. The bay mare nickered at him worriedly, then swiveled her head to look at him.

"A fine lady you are," he said to the horse, "I agree. You stand easy a bit, sweet beast, and then we'll do the next one."

The folk of Ellestown brought Michael their horses to shoe, their tack and bridle leather to mend, plow tools to sharpen, an occasional sword to forge, although the Ellestown folk rarely had need for swords. Count Charles's local factor, Hinton Witt, maintained a small force of soldiers to keep the peace, but aside from occasional drunken brawls at festivals or short-lived conflicts between young hotheads, the soldiers rarely had need of their swords. In the centuries since the Allemanii came to these Mionn shores, the people of the Flinders Lakes had never known war or invasion: their good earls had kept Mionn safe from the tumults of Allemanii politics, allowing their folk to feel comfortable with living. The forests gave the Flinders folk a steady market for their timber, the lakes abounded in fish, and the dark soil of the broad mountain valley brought good harvests every autumn, not enough to make the Flinders folk as rich as the merchants and Mionn nobility who lived in Count Charles's bayside capital of Arlenn, but none were poor.

Forest gift, Michael thought contentedly. The Flinders folk thought their prosperity and their comfortable lives were a blessing of the inland mountains, the lakes, and a happy combination of good soil and abundant water, with the safety of distance from the bayside's harsh weather; but Michael knew differently. The forest witches of Mionn had made their home in this broad valley since the Disasters three centuries before, living secretly among the Flinders folk, and the land prospered because they did. It was the special gift of the shajar, the shari'a forest witches, their blessing of the land and all that lived within it.

Michael looked out the smithy's wide door at the lake, where a light wind ruffled the waters, then walked a few steps to look up the lane toward town, hoping to see his children; but they still wandered in the forest, no doubt, as was their way. It had been their mother's way, too, her wild, shy way that had caught his heart and still held it, although Dani had gone into her grave five years before. He took a deep breath of the cold winter air, then for a time watched the wind move over the lake.

He was a large man, black-haired and handsome, with rippling muscles and a broad chest, strong enough to handle any willful horse. In his youth he had won the heart of a local girl, Dani Kindelay, not for his strength of body, but for the gentleness that often graced large men who had nothing to prove. They had been married for two years, with the twins just starting to crawl across the wooden floor of their small house at the edge of the town, before Dani had dared to tell Michael her secret. Fearful she would lose him if she told, she had delayed those precious two years, lived with him and loved him, believing her life with him would end when she told. Allemanii law proscribed Dani's witch-kind, and she had known Michael Toldane was an honorable man, a man who believed in laws, and in truth.

For two years, for her love of him, Dani had avoided the forest house in the deep ravine north of the lakes, had forsaken the chants and the hope of the Finding, had given up her charge of guarding the Star Well left by Thora Jodann, the last of Witchmere's great adepts. For two years she had pretended a normal life, wistful that it might last forever, but with the birth of her daughter and son, both born with the forest gift, she had bowed to necessity. No Flinders witch had ever abandoned the Well, as she could not, and she could not deny her children their shari'a heritage. Indeed, that heritage would mean their safety when they grew old enough to understand the danger and must learn to guard themselves. And so, on that summer day early in the third year of their marriage, Dani had left the twins with an indulgent neighbor and suggested a walk in the meadows beyond the lake.

"A walk?" Michael had protested. "I have two horses to shoe."

"Please, love. The day is beautiful, and I want to walk with you."

And he had relented, putting up his work for the day, and they had walked through the town, her hand tucked under his elbow, and then wandered far into the meadows beyond the lake. At the edge of the forest leading up to the ravine, she had kissed him, then pulled him down onto the soft grass, delaying just a little longer for one last time in his arms, one last time to love him.

Far up the ravine they reached a small house, its ancient timbers weathered into dull grays and browns and nearly invisible in the shadows of the forest. Dani led him past the house to a narrow path and then to a cleft in the rocks and the narrow tunnel behind it. He followed, wondering, his footsteps echoing hollowly on the stony floor of the tunnel.

She said nothing to him and glanced back only once, her face pale and bereft. But why? Michael had wondered with the first sharp pricking fear of whatever now troubled his Dani, whatever it was. Ahead he saw a dim light, and followed Dani into the cavern at the end of the tunnel.

In the shadows of the Star Well, Michael had gawked at the four ghostly figures ringing the mortared circle of stone at the center of the Well, unmoving shades of four witches caught in time, as Dani later told him, waiting the centuries for the Promise Thora Jodann had left here. When Duke Rahorsum had turned on the shari'a, killing all he could find with his soldiers' thirsty blood-drenched swords, Thora and three other adepts, one each of sea, fire, air, and forest, had built the Well in Mionn, hiding it safely within the forest for the future time the Well might summon the shari'a who had fled the Disasters across the bay into the East. With that Finding would come the Change, a transformation of the shari'a not even Thora had fully understood.

Many centuries ago the Two had become the Four, profoundly changing the shari'a people and the dragon-spirits who guarded them. When the Allemanii had invaded the shari'a lands, a second Change had impended, a promise that Four might divide into Six or even Seven, but the Change had been cut short by the Disasters and the scattering of the shari'a. With the summoning of the Exiles by the Star Well, a Finding long promised by Dani's books and her forest witch tradition, the Change could begin again, transforming the shari'a gifts, awakening new possibility in living. For three centuries the shajar who guarded the Well had yearned for the Finding, as Dani yearned and now dared to reveal to her husband, knowing he would not tell the Allemanii townsfolk about what she showed him, but unsure of all else.

Michael had cautiously circled the Well cavern, stepping with great care, and had peered at the disintegrating books on their shelves, the odd artifacts in the alcove. Finally he stopped by the shade of the forest witch and studied her, then looked at the hawk on her shoulder, the ferret peeping from beneath her hem.

"She has your face, beloved," he decided. "Not in the features, but in the spirit." He turned and looked at his wife gravely. "What does this mean, Dani? Why did you bring me here?"

Dani hesitated, her hands clasped tightly in front of her skirt, and her eyes filled with tears. She opened her mouth to speak, but no words would come. Michael tipped his head and smiled at her, waiting, and she could not bear his smile. In agony she bowed her head, and struggled to tell him, but she could not. "I love you, Michael, more than you know," she managed in a strangled voice.

"And I love you, dear heart, more than living itself." He had looked around at the Well again, then looked up at the shadowy greens of the trees visible through a hole in the cavern ceiling. "Is this a shari'a place? Is that what you're trying to tell me?"

"Y-yes, Michael."

"Then that explains it," he said.

She raised her head, confounded. "What?"

"How you caught my heart, never to lose it. I was ensorcelled, plain as that." He spread his arms, inviting. "Ah, well," he said cheerfully, "too late now." And Dani had breathed again, and then could move toward him, and found herself tightly within his embrace, against all accounting.

Dani and her Michael had lived eight more years together, gentle years to teach her children what they must know, and, one summer season, to travel alone to Witchmere, the ancient shari'a fortress high in the Ingal mountains, seeking answers. But then Dani had drowned in a boating accident, leaving a great void in Michael's life, a void he could never refill. His silences had grown longer, he knew; and he often sat on the front porch of their house, his cup forgotten by his side, or stood in his smithy door, as he did now, and watched the wind ruffle the lake. Dani was there in the ruffle, in the teasing touch of the air on his face, her very fingers, and there in the soft whisper of the trees overshadowing the house—her touch, her voice. Forest gift it was, a shari'a gift deep enough to leave him something of her, Allemanii though he was, to leave the comfort of a touch and a voice because he had loved her and she had loved him, and together they had loved the valley she had guarded.

After Dani's death Michael had continued his blacksmith's trade, and had cared for his children with gentle solemnity, but he had not invited his children's talk of witchery, did not ask to visit the forest cabin or the Well. When he found a mock owl perched on Ashdla's bedstead, he ignored the bird, as he also ignored the ferret prowling in Will's room nearby. He permitted Ashdla's visits to the forest cabin whenever she asked, and welcomed her cheerfully when she returned, but did not ask details. Only once had his daughter begged him a favor, to take her to Count Charles's bayside town to hunt for other shari'a, and Michael had consented, as he had consented for his wife years before.

The wind shirred across the lake, raising sparkles from the suns' light on the water. Dani was there in the sparkles, too, he thought. Beloved, he thought wistfully, and yearned for her, as he always yearned. The light danced on the water in answer, and he smiled. Beloved, he greeted her happily. Years before, when he was young, a witch had touched his heart, caught it, held it, and he did not mind the keeping, even now.

Michael took in another deep breath of the air, fresh with mist off the broad lake, then turned back to his shoeing of the mare.

~

It was near noon when Ashdla and Will arrived home. Will went into the house to hide Slinkfoot under his bed, and Ashdla found their father at work in the smithy, as usual, bent over a horse's hoof. The heat from the forge bathed the stable, allowing their father to work bare chested, as he often did. She waited in the stable doorway, watching her father as he took the next horseshoe from the hot forge and plunged it into a cask of water, raising a cloud of hissing steam, then inspected it a moment before laying it on the anvil. A powerful blow with an iron hammer erased the slight defect, and he inspected it closely again before walking back to the yearling black mare with the white blaze on her nose. As Michael approached her, the filly snorted and rolled her eyes dramatically, then sidled a step away from him.

"Come, lady," her father said patiently, "no need for alarm. When the fourth is on, we're done."

The horse thought about it anxiously, for all that the first three hammerings hadn't hurt her a bit, then looked an unhappy appeal at Ashdla standing in the stable doorway. It was the young mare's first shoeing, Ashdla sensed, and the sweet animal still hadn't decided quite what she thought about it. So far not much, that was plain. Ashdla spread her hands encouragingly. *No help for it, dearling. He'll just keep trying until you give in. I should know.* The mare nickered anxiously, edged away another step, her eyes rolling white. *Go ahead. It won't hurt.* The mare snorted and bobbed her head violently twice, then quieted and stood still. Michael lifted her hind foot, then fitted the shoe to the underside of her hoof and drove in the nails, one by one, his arm muscles rippling. When it was done, he straightened and patted the mare's flank, then turned and saw his daughter watching him.

"Well, there you are, my girl," he said in mild surprise.

"Hello, Da." Owree winged down from the stable roof and would have landed on Ashdla's shoulder as he liked to do, but she quickly motioned him up to a rafter. Michael squinted at the mock owl as he settled high in the stable, and Owree blinked back with huge golden eyes, then happily ruffled his wing feathers, glad to see Michael, even if Michael did not share the pleasure.

"Best not to let the townsfolk see you have a pet owl, Ashdla," he rumbled, and turned back to the forge.

"It's not that strange, Da," Ashdla blurted, startled that her father chose to notice Owree. He usually ignored her mock owl, and Slinkfoot, too, whatever they did inside the house.

"Strange enough, sweetling," Michael said. "Will can hide that ferret of yours inside his shirt and you can keep shrews in your pocket and no one's the wiser, but that bird's too hard to miss."

"He's my friend," she objected, more sharply than she intended. "I'm sorry, Da," she said contritely. "I just meant—"

Her father turned and smiled. "You meant he's your friend. I know. Your mother kept friends, too, even more than you and Will do. When you and Will were toddlers, I thought our house more an animal burrow than a home for people. Her pocket shrews liked to sleep with us in our bed and she allowed it, however they wriggled and climbed my spine. Later she relented her extra bed friends, but for a while I had a hare and his wife in the bread box, a teal duck and her hatchlings waddling my parlor, and, yes, a mock owl who blinked at me from the rafters, thinking he owned the place." He looked up at Owree again. "Like that one does. What's his name?"

"Owree," Ashdla said shyly. "And Will's ferret is Slinkfoot."

Michael nodded. "Good names, suiting them both. But I'm serious, dear girl. Remind your owl that he's a night bird, to wait on a branch until you open your window after the Daystar's setting, and not a thing to fly about in daytime when the townsfolk might see. That tale about Brierley Mefell in the duke's dungeon has put Ellestown to talking about older tales, and our townsfolk like their gossip far too much. I don't want you to catch their attention. It's not safe."

"Yes, Da," Ashdla mumbled.

Michael untied the mare from the post stand and led her into a nearby stall to await her owner's arrival, then filled the hopper with grain and checked the bucket of water by the stall gate.

"Da—" Ashdla said hesitantly.

"Yes?"

"Brierley Mefell is coming here to Flinders. Amina said so." Her father turned, his eyes widening in astonishment, and Ashdla tumbled out her words. "She's not dead. It's the time of the Finding, when shari'a will come here and we won't be the only ones anymore. Amina says—she's the forest dragon, you see, one of the Four—Amina says that the time the Well's shades have awaited is coming now, that Will and I will see the Finding. Da—" Her father was staring at her, deeply appalled. "Oh, Da, please!" Ashdla lifted her hands and took a step toward him. "We don't want to hurt you with memories you don't want. We don't want to remind you of Mother, but what can we do? Amina says—"

"Memories I don't want?" her father interrupted, his voice husky. "Is that what you think?"

Ashdla nodded miserably and hung her head. "I'm sorry, Da," she whispered. "I'm so sorry."

"Don't be ashamed of what you are, Ashdla," her father told her sharply. "Never that; I won't have it. Your mother had the same problem with doubting herself, thinking the Blood was a taint of some kind. She even thought I'd stop loving her when I knew. It took me a while to persuade her, and when I did, it earned me animals everywhere for a time, but finally she believed me." Her father crossed the stable floor and laid his palm against Ashdla's cheek. Ashdla looked up at him, bewildered, and her wonderment made him smile.

"Forest gift has a lack, you know," her father said mildly, "your liking animals more than people. It blunts your insight, even limits your witch-gift in some ways. It would have been easier if your mother had had a twin like you do, someone like herself, a second self to share thought with her; but even with a brother a forest witch has trouble hearing Allemanii minds. We used to practice, she and I, having her listen to my mind, trying to guess what I was thinking. But, sadly, I haven't a trace of witch-blood, full-blooded Allemanii that I am, and so she had no advantage there. She never did quite get the knack of it." He gave his daughter a mild frown. "Obviously neither have you and Will. Not want her memory? How can you think that?"

"But you never talk about her or witchery—"

"Truth, I don't." He tweaked the end of her nose. "I thought it good caution to pretend we had a normal house, no more and no less than our neighbors. But I was wrong in that, I see, making you and Will worry. I know all about your Finding, dear girl, for your mother gave me all her true hopes once she fully believed in me. I've read most of the books in the cabin, and I watched with her in the Star Well many times, wondering about the ghosts that stood there. I even watched her chants until she started taking you and Will up to the cabin to teach you her craft. I often wished I could hear what she heard when she listened to the Patterns, but all I could do was watch."

"But it hurts you to talk about her," Ashdla said quietly. "I'm not wrong about that."

He regarded her for a moment. "No, you're not wrong. I'm half a man without your mother, and always will be." He bent to kiss her forehead. "But that half a man often sees your mother in your face, darling girl, and hears her voice in your voice, and is comforted." Then he clucked his tongue. "Does this Brierley Mefell have to come here? I'm not liking the danger it'll bring."

"Well, it's not really something you stop—" Ashdla said uncertainly, then saw her father's smile broaden as Ashdla completely missed the tease he intended. She tsked at him, stepped up to wrap her arms comfortably around his broad waist, and then laid her ear on his muscled chest, listening for the slow heartbeat, sure and steady, that was always there. "I love you, Da," she murmured, and his strong arms came firmly around her, hugging her close.

"If only love always turned the star tide, dear girl. Where's your brother now?"

"Inside the house."

"Well, let me finish up here and we'll have our noon meal. It's your turn to cook, not mine, as I remember."

"Yes, Da."

Michael looked up at Owree, who looked back with great interest, blinking golden eyes. "And you stay up there on that rafter, Sir Bird, at least until nightfall. You can entertain yourself watching me do things you don't understand. Better yet, take a nap. Daytime waking isn't proper for an owl." He frowned, then looked down at his daughter. "Is he often awake during the day?"

"Not usually, but Will brought Slinkfoot home with us,

and Owree always comes along, too, when Slinkfoot does."
She wrinkled her nose. "I think I'm territory, Da."

"Well, of course you are," her father said with a snort.
"What else, when it's an owl and a ferret? Go along now. I'll
be in soon."

⌒

Will helped with the meal, taking the dishes to the table and
fetching in the pitcher of cool milk from the ice shed beside
the house. As he filled the glasses, Ashdla felt him look at
her and turned around to look back.

What? she sent.

I wish you'd have asked me before you told him, Will
grumped. *It might have gone badly.*

*It seemed the time. Owree trapped me, and it sort of hap-
pened.* Ashdla shut the pantry door, and brought cheese and
a half loaf of bread to the table. *He knows all about the
Finding, Will. He knows everything.*

But he's never said so, at least not that we remember.

They worked their eyebrows at each other, amazed that
their father could still surprise them, and then Will blew out
a breath. *Do you think he can see Amina?*

*I doubt it. He doesn't have the Blood. Only shari'a can see
the Four.*

*But he said he can see the shades in the Well. How can I
see them and not see Amina?*

Maybe Allemanii can see the shades, too, she answered
uncertainly. *Not that I want to test that, so don't think of
borrowing one of your friends to find out.*

Will made a face. *Of course I won't. Do you think I'm
stupid?*

Well . . . Ashdla trailed the thought, then skipped away
with a laugh as Will started around the table. When he kept
coming, she ran for the door, but he boxed her escape neatly,
then pinned her against the wall. She squirmed in his grasp,
giggling.

"Take it back," Will demanded. Ashdla stamped on his boot hard. "Ouch!"

"Take back what?" she teased. "The truth?"

The front door opened and their father stepped in. "This is fixing the meal?" he asked, lifting an eyebrow. Will let go and stepped back, then glared at Ashdla when she sniggered. Michael calmly took off his coat and hung it on the peg. "Well?" he prompted.

"Sort of, Da," Will said, not relenting his glare at Ashdla. "I have to keep her in line."

"I'll keep *you* in line," Ashdla retorted, and poked Will hard in the ribs, then dodged as Will instantly retaliated.

"Children, that's enough," their father rumbled.

Ashdla skipped around the table and sat down, then watched Will seat himself across the table. *I'll get you later,* he promised darkly.

In your dreams. She wrinkled her nose at her brother, got a disdainful sniff back.

"Seems to me you're evenly matched," Michael commented, taking his own chair. "Seems to me you might give up this tussling. You're old enough."

"Yes, Da," Will mumbled.

" 'Yes, Da,' " Michael echoed mockingly, then gave both his children a mild glare. He picked up his knife and reached for the slab of cheese. "I keep hearing that and nothing changes. Why not?"

"Nobody ever gets hurt, Da," Ashdla protested. "Forest twins always tussle: the books say so."

"Just because the books say so, girl," Michael said, "doesn't mean you must."

"Yes, Da," Ashdla replied meekly, but it didn't deceive her father a whit. She giggled at his expression.

"Why do I even try?" Michael asked the open air. "Just don't break the crockery, at least not much of it. And pass me the bread, daughter, if you please."

Ashdla did so, and watched as her father cut the bread. She twigged the first slice and gave it to Will, then added the next to her own plate and reached for the crock of butter. They ate in a companionable silence, then Will went out to help their father in the stable. The customer came for his mare, and another of the townsfolk brought his wagon harness for mending, followed by another with a horse to shod and a plow blade to sharpen.

At midafternoon Ashdla watched her father and brother through the window as they talked with Hinton Witt, the count's factor, their voices muffled by the windowpane. A few minutes later the three disappeared into the stable, and Ashdla suddenly remembered Owree perching in the stable's rafters. Factor Witt had authority in the town as the count's local man: as part of his duty to the count, he collected the lake tolls on the fishing, published the count's occasional decrees in the town square, and kept the peace with a small troop of soldiers. An affable man in his forties, Witt had been Count Charles's factor in Flinders for fifteen years, and was well liked by the Flinders folk, for all that he came from the bayside town of Arlenn and still considered himself more Arlenn folk than Flinders. Years ago he had married a local girl named Sigrid, pretty enough in her youth but now the worst gossip in town. Their daughter, Emilie, had followed her mother's habits, poking her nose into every business of the young folk in the town, flouncing her skirts and batting her eyelashes at all the local boys. Lately Emilie had developed an avid interest in Will, one of the very few local boys who still chose not to pant after her. In Emilie's assessment of her due as the factor's pretty and only daughter, Will's indifference simply wasn't allowed. Emilie wanted *all* of them.

Ashdla sighed feelingly. Someday, and maybe sooner than she feared, she'd have to face Will falling in love, then getting married. It wasn't fair to Will for Ashdla to resent it—indeed, Ashdla herself might find someone, too. But when Will did find somebody, would she lose a part of what they shared? She feared so. Was it wrong for Ashdla to want all of Will forever?

Maybe you're just as bad as Emilie, she scolded herself unhappily. Maybe there's not much difference at all.

She craned her head to look out the window, but the men were still inside the stable. Surely a mock owl in the rafters wouldn't strike Factor Witt as odd, Ashdla thought anxiously: the local owls often borrowed high places in the town's barns for a day's sleep. Surely not. But what if he told his wife? Ashdla winced as she imagined what Sigrid's tongue could do with even that slender fact. Sigrid Witt had created the most amazing rumors from practically nothing at all, and everyone had to listen, her being the factor's wife and all, even though they knew what a horrible gossip she was.

Does Sigrid notice when Will and I go across the meadows? she wondered. Do the other townsfolk notice when I'm gone a day or two, and then talk to each other about it? Ashdla suddenly felt herself watched by dozens of Flinders eyes, the same townsfolk who had watched her grow up, who knew her as only Michael Toldane's daughter, an ordinary girl if too shy for her own good. If Count Charles ordered her arrest as a witch, it would be Hinton Witt who brought his soldiers to take her. Ashdla stepped back warily from the window, then stamped her foot that she had. Don't be silly, Ashdla, she told herself angrily. Nothing's changed: it's all the same as before. Her own assurances mocked at her: as her father knew, as she knew, the danger never faded; and it would be the Ellestown folk who raised the cry when they knew.

Ashdla bit her lip and watched through the window until the factor emerged from the stable, chatted affably with her father a few more moments, and then strode away, a square and stocky figure, confident in his authority.

That evening at dusk, as the Companion spread its blues and lavenders across the sky, Ashdla found her father seated on the porch, watching the lake. She sat down in front of his chair and leaned back against his knees, then sighed contentedly. His hand touched her hair and lingered there, and she brought his fingers to her lips for a kiss, then held his hand against her cheek.

"I'm worried, Da," she said softly.

"About what, dear girl?"

"Did Factor Witt see Owree?"

"Not to worry, girl. All that interested him were his new swords." Michael paused. "Don't take what I said about your owl too much to heart, Ashdla. A little more prudence with your bird, and all will be right."

"If the town finds out about me and Will, what will they do to you, Da? They'll think you knew and punish you for it." Harboring a witch bore severe penalties under the shari'a laws, with a scale of punishment matching the degree of offense. Occasionally Allemanii were burned with the witches they had defended, or so the cabin books said of times long ago. Ashdla felt a sudden rush of fear for her father, her strong and capable father who loved and protected his shari'a children, as he had loved and protected their mother.

"No one's finding out anything," her father said firmly. "Don't be anxious, girl."

"I still worry, Da, but I'll try." She pressed his hand tighter.

A breeze ruffled the surface of the lake, dancing the last glow of the Companion's twilight into broad lanes of blues and lavenders across the water. The breeze shirred across the lake toward their porch, stirring a slight dust on the shore, rustling the grasses in front of the house, then lifted over the porch railing and teased cool fingers across Ashdla's face. Then, far out on the lake, a gleaming blue dragon rose slowly from the depths, the twilight shimmering on her scaled body. The sea dragon spread translucent wings, and bowed her neck gracefully. From the blue fire dancing all around her, a second dragon took form, rising in muted reddish flames beside her; his jeweled eyes gleamed in the twilight. *Patience, daughter,* Jain said, his voice a deep-rumbling croon. *All will be well.*

Patience, Basoul echoed, bringing comfort like the touch of cool water, a fall of refreshing rain.

The errant breeze swept back across the porch and out onto the lake, and again took misty shape as a golden dragon spiraling upward into the sky. *We are coming.* Soren soared still higher over the lake water, stirring the air with the turbulence of his passing. *It is the Finding,* he called, and his cry was exultant. *Wait for us.*

We are coming, my beloveds, echoed Amina's soft voice from deep within the forest behind the house, a voice Ashdla had known all her life. *Patience—*

The next instant the Four were gone, and Ashdla saw only the broad lake and the fading light of the evening. She took a deep breath, and for a moment could not fill her lungs deeply enough. The Companion's twilight moved slowly on the water and vanished in a last flash of lavender, bringing the clinging darkness of the True Night.

"Did you see, Da?" Ashdla whispered, hoping that he could, just this once.

"See what, dear girl?" her father asked indulgently.

"Never mind, Da." Ashdla sighed and kissed his hand, then cradled it against her cheek. "Never mind."

2

*L*ate that night, by the river road that led upward from the Eastern Bay to the Flinders Lakes, Brierley Mefell lay with her witch-daughter, Megan, in their campside bed, the dark forest all around them. The campfire had burned low, and now cast a dim, shifting light on the trees, flaring briefly, dying soon to embers. Nearby, the river splashed over its bed of stones, tumbling down the long, rocky gorge toward the distant bay. On the other side of the fire, Brierley's liegeman, Stefan Quinby, had made up his own rough camp bed of a brushy mattress and blankets, and had tried to sleep, with little help from Megan.

"Why are the trees whispering, Mother?" Megan asked, long after she should have been asleep. "What are they saying to each other?"

"I don't know, child." Brierley kissed her child's forehead. To Megan, scarcely six years old and a sheltered kitchen's child until just a few months before, all the world was a wonder, prompting constant questions that challenged Brierley to answer. In her own childhood Brierley had plagued her own mother with similar questions, and had found as little satisfaction with her mother's answers. Brierley considered, thinking carefully. "The wind blows and makes the leaves rustle, so it sounds like whispering. Maybe they are talking, but we don't know their language."

"Why does the water laugh to itself?" Megan asked then, and comfortably rubbed her cheek against Brierley's shoulder. "Is it laughing at us?"

"Why would it laugh at us?"

"I don't know," Megan said, and thought for a moment,

then shrugged and moved on. "Why do the stars shine, Mother?"

"They are great lights in the sky, far away from us."

"Are they alive?"

"What? Stars?" Brierley remembered her odd dream of a star-child and a gossamer ship sailing the stars, when the stars had throbbed with song, vividly alive—perhaps a dream of the baby daughter sleeping within her, perhaps only a fancy of her dreaming mind. Both Megan and Basoul had told Brierley she carried a daughter: indeed, Megan had known Brierley was pregnant before Brierley knew herself, and a dragon had means to know that could hardly be challenged. "Maybe they're alive," Brierley said judiciously. "I don't know, child, but I'd like to think so." Megan craned her head to look up at the dark sky dusted with stars in every direction.

"So would I," Megan decided, then suddenly pointed off to the left. "Look!"

Brierley looked obediently, but saw nothing but darkness and the gently moving trees. "Aren't you sleepy yet, Megan?"

"No. Why does it rain, Mother?"

"I don't know, child." She pulled Megan closer to her and tucked around the blanket. "I wish I had answers for you, my Megan."

Megan looked up into her face, and then patted Brierley's cheek with her small hand, and, her mood changing mercurially, added a smacking kiss. "It's all right," she said cheerfully, and laid her head on Brierley's shoulder again with a sigh. "Just conversation."

Brierley stifled a laugh, and heard an answering chuckle from across the fire. Stefan lounged on his own rough bed, his head propped wearily on one hand. He blinked sleepily, then yawned and rolled onto his back. Nearby, their horses stood comfortably, heads low to the ground, as they dozed.

"Doesn't she ever run down?" Stefan asked. "It's nearly midnight. All wells should run dry eventually, even hers."

"A well?" Megan asked, confused. She looked up at Brierley. "When did I become water, Mother?"

"Never mind, child." Brierley shook her head at Stefan. "Go to sleep."

"Go to sleep, Megan," Stefan urged desperately. "Please."

Megan closed her eyes. "Go to sleep, Megan," the child agreed.

Brierley sensed Megan's thoughts slowly scatter as the child drifted into sleep at last. She looked down at the small, shadowed face, and thought nothing could be more lovely, more cherished. Once she had hoped for such a child, a witch-child to be her daughter and apprentice, not really believing she would ever meet her; and now Megan was here, safe in the circle of Brierley's arms. There was still much danger in the world, especially for shari'a witch-kind. For three centuries Allemanii law had decreed that the shari'a be hunted and, whenever found, put to death merely because they dared to live; but in this moment, in this camp by this road in Mionn, Megan was safe. In the east the thunder growled as a storm moved closer, stirring the leaves overhead.

"It wouldn't be so bad," Stefan said, "if I didn't wonder those things, too. My little boy wanted to know why rocks are hard, why I get a beard each morning, and why his mother likes to kiss me so much. I had something of an answer on the last one, at least a theory, but why *do* I get a beard each morning? It bothers me that I don't know." He laughed softly, then yawned wide enough to crack his jawbones.

Brierley pressed her face into Megan's hair and sighed. "The eyes of a child, Stefan."

"Are precious, I agree. Is she asleep?"

"Yes."

"Good." Stefan yawned a third time, turned over in his bed, and found his own sleep. Brierley tucked their blanket more firmly around Megan, breathed in the sweet scent of the child's hair, then looked up at the starry sky.

Go upward in Mionn to the Flinders Lakes, Basoul had

bid her four days before, when the sea dragon had met her on the bayside beach at dawn. *There look for a girl named Ashdla Toldane: she is daughter to the witch Megan called "the girl in green." She will show you what Thora Jodann left here in Mionn as her last great work.*

What great work? Brierley wondered. And a girl named Ashdla? Would Brierley truly find another shari'a witch like herself? Could it be true? Aside from her mother and now Megan, Brierley had known no other shari'a witch, and had wondered sadly if she might be the last of her people, the last of everyone.

Nearly twenty years before, Brierley's mother, Jocater Mefell, had traveled south with her infant daughter to the earldom of Yarvannet, and had never told Brierley of the life she left behind, nor why she had left it. By the time Brierley was aware of herself, her mother had deliberately forgotten her past, as she had tried desperately to forget the witch-sense that colored both their lives. Above all other things, Jocater had wished for a normal life, and had sought it in an unwise marriage to a local Amelin carpenter, a dour and unpleasant man who had resented his wife's strangeness and her failure to give him sons. All Alarson wished of life was a steady piling up of coins, to be gloated over as they grew in number, and so he came to dislike his wife's shyness, and berated her for the hard burden she and her stepdaughter imposed on him, and had turned his back on her in anger. In despair Jocater had suicided when Brierley was twelve, and so left her daughter utterly alone.

But not wholly alone, in truth: in an isolated sea cave on Yarvannet's coastline, Brierley had found the comfort of the journals written by her predecessors in Yarvannet, and the company of the Everlight, an ancient Witchmere device that had life but never spoke to her, and sometimes in her dreams she met Thora Jodann, the first of the Yarvannet sea witches, a survivor of the Disasters three centuries before that had nearly destroyed the shari'a race. For eight years Brierley had lived her narrow life, finding purpose in the practice of her healing gift, hiding it behind her trade as Amelin's young midwife, hiding herself from the discovery she knew would mean her death, were she ever known as a witch to her Allemanii neighbors. In time, as perhaps inevitably, she had been discovered, but had found a different fate than the hunt and pyre the cave journals had forewarned.

A northern ship captain had accused her as witch, and Earl Melfallan had sent his soldiers to arrest her, intending mercy but bound by his politics to uphold the shari'a laws that proscribed her kind. Melfallan had not believed in the shari'a witches, thinking them an overblown legend from long ago, and Brierley might have escaped on his parole had not Lord Landreth, the son of Count Sadon of Farlost, pushed Lady Saray on the stairs. Heavily pregnant with Melfallan's child, Saray had fallen hard, cracking her skull on the stone floor. Both Saray and her baby would have died that night had Brierley not intervened. Like a fool Brierley had rushed forward to help, not thinking of her own exposure as a witch, not thinking at all: she had thought only of helping Saray, as a healer must do, but it had been a foolish thing, a mistake that should have condemned her. The resultant healing had been quite spectacular, not that Brierley had meant it to be, and had been performed in front of all the watching Yarvannet gentry, including Captain Bartol. The captain had scooted back to his ship, hasty to bear the news of a witch in Melfallan's Yarvannet to the duke; and two weeks later Duke Tejar's summons had duly come, ordering Melfallan to bring Brierley to the duke's capital for trial. Against his wishes but having no other choice, Melfallan had taken her to Darhel; and there Brierley had discovered Megan in the palace kitchens, and had fled with her into the eastern hills to escape the duke's harsh justice. Later Melfallan had found them near Witchmere's mountain valley, and had left them in the safety of a mountain cabin, bidding her to hide in Mionn when winter weather permitted the travel, to stay there in safety until he could find a way to bring her home to Yarvannet.

She sighed deeply, not knowing how he could find such a way, although she yearned that he might. They had found

love in that upland valley, an unwise love that threatened
them both but which both had chosen despite the dangers.
Were he not an Allemanii High Lord and married to a Mionn
lady, were she not a shari'a witch, all might be easy, all
might be safe. If only— She sighed again, and did not know
a way out of their dilemma. By all prudence she should give
up Melfallan and raise their baby by herself, giving to her
daughters what part of her shari'a heritage she could. It
would be a narrow and lonely life again, one of secrecy in
some hamlet in Mionn, a life of fear, a life of hiding, and far
away from Melfallan, far away.

Oh, how could I live, she thought, if I never see him
again? How? She sighed a third time, as if sighs solved anything. She frowned unhappily.

It was not wise, her love for Melfallan—it was not fair to
his wife. It was not right by the rules of good society. Although girls sometimes conceived a child outside of marriage, and the Allemanii community cared mainly that the
child was tended and raised well despite the lack of a husband, it was not considered respectable. A by-blow child,
despite all the kindness of his mother's relatives, grew up
with a taint, mild and no blame of his, but still labeled a fa-
therless child. The Allemanii rite of Blessing, when the father acknowledged his child and gave him or her legal rights
as heir, often corrected that initial fault, as she thought
Melfallan would do. But what then? What new political trouble did she create for him when she added her daughter to
his heirs, a lady child of the earl, a rival—even if female—to
his legitimate son by Saray?

For Melfallan's politics were dangerous, and his intent to
defend a witch proscribed by the shari'a laws only added to
his danger. Already Duke Tejar had tried to use Brierley
against Melfallan, and would surely try again if given the
opportunity. Duke Tejar Kobus ruled uneasily over the Allemanii lands, disliked by his High Lords, and, like every
Allemanii duke, highly resentful of the power of the earls of
Yarvannet and Mionn. As Melfallan had explained to her,
Allemanii political power was balanced between the duke

and earls, a necessary constraint against oppression by too powerful a duke. Three times in Allemanii history the earls had unmade a duke, and Tejar likely feared that Earl Giles and Melfallan contemplated a similar unmaking of him. That Melfallan and likely Earl Giles had no such intention made little difference to Duke Tejar: the threat was enough, a risk he felt intolerable, not to be borne. And so Tejar saw plots where none existed, and reacted to suspected treachery not yet in being, and so in time would provoke the very treachery he feared. Tejar had struck at Melfallan by trying to murder Brierley in secret before her trial, and then had attempted the murder of Melfallan's aunt, Countess Rowena of Airlie. Only the previous spring, Melfallan's grandfather, Earl Audric, had died suddenly of poisoning: had Tejar provoked that murder as well? Murder and betrayal, injustice and greed: nothing seemed beyond Duke Tejar in his lust for ultimate power. Or was the duke's true motive only the arrogance of his duke's rank, a weakness built into Allemanii politics by the Founders when Duke Aidan had elevated himself above the others? Or was Tejar's motive, at its foundation, a desperate fear of the very politics he had set in motion? Such politics could strip a High Lord, even a duke, of his lands and his life, ending him forever. Who could tell what truly moved the duke? Like all the Allemanii High Lords forced to deal with the tumult of their politics, the duke was a complicated man.

As was her Melfallan. She thought about him for a time, lazily warm beneath her blankets, and wondered what he was doing and thinking at this moment. Well, she amended, likely nothing at all at this hour: it was well past everyone's bedtime across all the lands, so perhaps he slept comfortably and dreamed pleasant dreams. She wished so.

Go to sleep, Brierley, too, she told herself, good counsel she chose to ignore.

She watched the movement of the firelight on the trees, then counted stars for a time, trying to remember the names of the pictures they drew on the dark sky. The Plow, the Sails, the Dolphin, the Warrior: all Allemanii names, the only names she knew. Had the ancient shari'a, too, seen patterns in the stars? Of what? Would she ever know? A mock owl hooted softly in the distance, answered by another soft voice farther still. The trees whispered, telling each other secrets that only they knew, and the river laughed to itself, tumbling and chuckling in its river bed, rushing down to the bay.

> *Water, rain, flowing, splashing,*
> *Water, rain, renewing the earth,*
> *Water, rain, the heart's own knowing,*
> *Water rain, in endless moving.*

It was Thora's poem from a book Brierley had found in Witchmere, in which Thora marshaled poetry to make an argument about religion, as Thora adapted many things to express her thought. In Yarvannet Thora Jodann had often visited her dreams, a dream-friend Brierley thought the creation of her own wishing, but perhaps those dreams had been more than wishes. Thora's book she had found in Witchmere was quite different from the much recopied journal in Brierley's Yarvannet cave. In her journal Thora had written of her present days, and had often deliberately chosen to forget the past. Her writing encouraged the future, speaking to the future daughters she would never know, with no guarantee that any would even find her book hidden in the sea rock by the shore: *believe!* she had urged. *Believe in the future!* Brierley had found her journal a constant comfort, and perhaps that connection had encouraged the frequent dreams of Thora as Brierley imagined her. A dream-friend, Brierley had thought that young woman now three hundred years gone into death.

In the Witchmere book, Brierley had met another Thora, a young adept vigorously involved in Witchmere's politics of that time, a scholar who speculated on the nature of the Four, the reasons for the shari'a gifts, the purpose of living. Thora's battles with her scholarly foes had been vigorous, often intensely passionate, and focused on a war of ideas about the Change Thora believed had already begun. The leaders of Witchmere, most of them air witches, scoffed at the Reformers' beliefs, wanting to keep the intellectual security of past centuries, with the shari'a gift arranged in orderly categories and all things thought known. A few details to discover, a few extensions of knowledge: no more was needed, they asserted, and scholarly books had devolved into list making and endless quoting from older books, a pastime the Reformers rejected with scorn. *You waste your time,* they insisted. *The future is not set, and all things must now change.* What howls of outrage! What sputtering and threats! The Reformers had ignored it all and set about their experiments, arguing among themselves as vigorously as they argued with the traditionalists, upsetting all ideas and accepting no truths until reproven. From their intellectual debate came new devices, new knowledge, and perhaps the first proofs of the Change, only to be cut short by Duke Rahorsum and his destruction of Witchmere. The shari'a had been scattered, the renewal aborted, and the Change has dissipated. Brierley had tried to translate Thora's new book, using the dictionary she and Melfallan had found in the Witchmere library, but many of the words eluded her, scholarly words beyond a simple dictionary intended for Allemanii use. Easier to understand was the poetry, an intriguing form of argument for a book on shari'a theology, but oddly fitting in the ways Thora used it.

> *Water, rain, flowing, splashing,*
> *Water, rain, renewing the earth . . .*

Now how could rain relate to what Thora was arguing? she wondered. The topic, as far as Brierley could puzzle it, was the interrelationship between the four shari'a gifts of sea, forest, air, and fire, with particular emphasis on fire, the rarest of the gifts. How did water, of all things, better explain fire? Brierley lacked the meaning for several important words in that section of the text, likely the exact clues she needed to understand it, but she liked the poetry, whatever the mystery of its relevance. She had tried to read the poems

aloud in their original shari'a, wondering how they sounded
and if the speaking might somehow lend its clue, but the dictionary either had several errors about pronunciation or,
worse, assumed the reader had a convenient witch nearby to
correct one's mistakes. Her dictionary didn't explain three
of the shari'a consonants, at least not to Brierley's confidence, and those three happened to be the most popular consonants, appearing constantly, to perplex the sound of the
words. She could gain the meanings from the dictionary, and
so generally follow Thora's line of thought, but to hear the
words aloud still eluded her.

Water, rain, flowing, splashing, she murmured. "Ashi'sa,
mashar, be'inta—" Brierley stopped and frowned in perplexity, then sighed softly. The pronunciation wasn't right,
and she hadn't a clue about why she thought so.

She put her hand behind her head and looked at the stars
glimmering in their patterns, bright points against the darkness. She listened to her baby sleep within her, scarcely begun and still dreaming of the starry void from which perhaps
all souls came, more potential than person, more wish than
witch. She smiled at her whimsy, and sent her love to her
baby, wishing her happiness and greatness and purpose and
truth, as she wished for Megan.

How long until her baby would be born? She tapped her
fingers, one by one, counting the weeks since those few
nights with Melfallan in the wayfarer cabin, before Stefan
and Sir Niall had found them there. It had been near the
first day of Yule, the first month of winter, with the snows
piled high in the valley near Witchmere, when they had
bedded. She and Sir Niall had then spent a secluded month
in the cabin, safe from both whistling winds and those frequent odd days of silently falling snow in curtains of
white. Stefan's arrival with supplies had brought the news
of Countess Rowena's injury, dealt by her traitor marcher
lord, and Brierley had traveled quickly to Carandon for the
healing, in secret as always, and as secretly away again.
During her absence, Sir Niall had died in a fall of snow—

perhaps by the malice of the Witchmere guardians, perhaps by simple accident—and then the month of Ice Lily had begun, bringing new storms and a new liegeman in Stefan, another of Rowena's trusted men. With the new month had come a new danger in the fire ghost that had seized on Megan, another witchly fancy, another odd thing to believe. The collective rage of the fire witches who had died in Duke Rahorsum's assault on Witchmere three centuries before had lingered in the empty caverns of Witchmere, only to take hold of Megan when Brierley had unwisely brought the child too close to that ancient fortress. Brierley had not intended that danger: indeed, she had only vaguely known Witchmere was nearby, sensing a change in the air, a lingering sadness in the valley. What other perils would she bring to Megan, or to her unborn baby, in her ignorance? She bit her lip, worrying.

So much knowledge had been lost of a shadowy shari'a world about which Brierley could now only guess. All she knew about the shari'a had been taught to her by the books in her cave or by her own sea gift learned by trial and error—of which the greatest learning was that its rules were not constant. She quirked her mouth. She could listen to minds, but that seemed a common shari'a gift. She could heal by exerting her will and by facing the vision of a Beast who came for her afterward, to punish and kill if it could. That, too, seemed common to the sea witches, for her predecessors had written of such a Beast following each healing— a great worm, a huge bird with sharp talons, or some monster from the sea. The cave journals wrote of healings and the common events of the witch's time, sometimes of politics, sometimes of despair, but forgot much of what the witches who lived in the Everlight's cave might have once known. The sea witches of Yarvannet had quite forgotten the other gifts given to the shari'a adepts of forest and fire and air; indeed, they had nearly forgotten the Four, the ancient dragon-spirits who had counseled and had protected the shari'a adepts from the beginnings.

Today was the eleventh of Swords. She tapped her fingers again: ten weeks now. Her baby would be born in early Hounds, the first month of autumn. She would be an autumn child, as Brierley had been, and born near a festival day. I need to think of a name, she mused. Perhaps I should name her after Clara Jacoby, my friend. If Clara has a baby girl this summer, I think she'll likely give her baby my name. It could be a trade, a mutual compliment, and a special gift to a shy friend. Another Brierley in the world: what an amazing thought! Should I make it three and so confuse all? Some mothers named their daughters after themselves: so could I. She frowned slightly, considering. Thora? But it isn't an Allemanii name—will I care that her name is a regular name and not odd? If we stay in Flinders, she will need an Allemanii name to be safe. What a problem, to name a child! Will I be able to ask Melfallan his wish, or will I name our baby alone? It was a lonely thought.

A year ago Brierley had expected a commoner's life like Clara's, at least in its outer guise. She had lived in her cave by the beach and had walked among the Yarvannet folk as a simple midwife, and found her comfort in the similarity of her days. It would have been a good life, although not with a husband—that she could not dare, not for a secret witch. Nor with children, either, another useless hope. Brierley laid her hand on her abdomen, sensing the life within—her pregnancy had truly surprised her, when it should not have been a surprise; but then neither she nor Melfallan had thought prudently when time gave them opportunity. Who had done the seducing? she thought and smiled impishly. Was it he, with his insistence on his kisses and his wooing, despite the dangers around them in Witchmere? At times a single-purposed man, her Melfallan. Or was it she, acting for foolish hope against prudence, responding boldly when he expected meekness and a shy no-no-please-well-maybe? In Amelin she had watched such courting in the byways of the town, and had heard other courting through her sensing of other minds: it was a dance, man and woman, at times a contest, a willingly yielding at others, at times a slow and fer-

vent interplay, a rush at times later, as both were tumbled
into love.

> Seeds in deep-hidden stillness,
> Gates, doorways,
> Built of living green,
> The forest yields up its life, Pass to Pass.

It was another of Thora's poems, this one related to the
forest gift and its cycle of life. The Allemanii understood
that cycle as an interplay between Mother Ocean, who gave
life to all those She loved, and Daughter Sea, who in time
took life that it might begin again, seeing both deities in the
ever-present sea near their homes whose bounty guaranteed
their living. According to Allemanii belief, those who died
lived a time in Daughter Sea's underwater realm, happily
blessed, oblivious to the life they had lived and the life to
come. It was a belief her mother had taught her, a belief she
had accepted as true since her earliest memories. According
to Thora's book, the shari'a had looked instead to the forest
for that same understanding, there finding the same cycle of
living and rebirth: that care they gave to Amina, the forest
dragon, and the forest witches were her care keepers, tending the forest and perhaps all life. And love as well as life?
Did the forest witches understand that particular facet of the
heart, when man was drawn to woman, perhaps unwisely?
Perhaps.

What lies ahead for us, myself and my daughters? she
asked herself soberly and did not have a certain answer, only
hopes, unlikely hopes, perhaps foolish hopes. Fancies,
things no reasonable person should believe. A vision of a
blue-scaled dragon on a beach, dusty words in an old book
that hinted at questions beyond questions, an entire shari'a
reality beyond anything Brierley had ever imagined. What
will I find? The worry troubled her, but still she had her
hopes, her promises.

She breathed in the sweet scent of Megan's tumbled curls,
and wished earnestly for safety for her daughters, one safe

within her arms, another safe within her womb, but a future safety perhaps to be gained only by inconsolable loss for herself. How do I choose for you, my Megan? How do I choose for your sister, my lovely star-child who dreams of sea larks and sunlight and star song?

How do I choose for me?

Go upward to the Flinders Lakes, Basoul had told her. *Now is the time of the Finding, a promise long awaited, a hope too long concealed.*

Now is the time—for what? Finding of what? The beginning of what? And would that beginning be an ending? This pleasant future she had dreamed of her return to Yarvannet, of love with Melfallan, the raising of a family in the open suns' shine, not in hiding, not in fear, a life like the cool, fresh breeze off the ocean: did she enter another destiny, one harder and more alone? Did Brierley Mefell, this Brierley as she knew herself, become irrelevant to whatever purpose the Four now put into motion?

She sighed, but the dark night had no answers for her. No answers for Megan, no answers for Brierley—at least not yet. She shook her head slightly, then closed her eyes and tried to sleep.

⌒

Two hours before dawn, the wind began a rising howl and lashed at the forest with growing fury as the storm descended on Mionn's upland valleys. The boles of sturdy everpine groaned as if in agony, and the wind shrieked as it whistled through their needled branches. The violence of Mionn's spring storms were legendary across the Allemanii lands, and even here in the uplands, in a campside glade partly shielded by the coastal mountains, the storm still descended with an almost animal rage. Brierley awoke with a start as something crashed nearby in the forest, and felt Megan clutching at her in terror. *It's all right, Megan,* she soothed, sending as much comfort as she could with her thought, for all her own heart was pounding hard in her chest. *It's only a storm.*

Only? Megan demanded in outrage, and wriggled indignantly. *It's more than an 'only,' Mother.*

True, child. But it's still only noise. Right?

They both flinched as lightning shattered the sky, followed by the rolling booming of thunder, and Megan tried to bury herself deeper into the shelter of Brierley's arms. Brierley pulled the edge of their blanket over their heads, and tried to comfort Megan with a murmur of her voice, the touch of her mind, but then the lightning crashed again, startlingly close. Megan shrieked, and the noise of the answering thunder shattered the night, a concussion of sound that blotted the mind. Brierley heard their horses neighing in terror, and she rolled quickly to her feet, pulling Megan up with her. Stefan had jumped up from his bed, too, his blankets scattering on the wet ground. He caught his mare's reins as she pulled them free from the branch, ready to bolt, and then struggled with her as she tried to rear. "Destin! Calm down!"

With Megan clinging to her skirts, Brierley hurried to the other horses. Gallant, Brierley's gelding, neighed in angry challenge at the storm, but he was more angry than frightened, ready to battle the weather with strong teeth and striking hooves. Megan's black mare, Friend, stood nearby, trembling violently, and Brierley put an arm around her neck, hugging her close. Gallant neighed another angry challenge and bobbed his head violently: in a moment he might bolt, drumming out his fear with an answering thunder of his hooves. Brierley hastily grabbed for his lead rein, then pulled the gelding's head against her chest; he calmed quickly under her touch. Megan was still clinging frantically to her skirts, and trembled just as violently.

"See, Megan?" Brierley crooned, bending down to her. "Gallant's fine. So is Friend—and so are you." Megan tightened her grasp, pressing close, but managed a brave nod despite the incoherent fear in her mind. *Megan,* Brierley soothed with both mind and touch, pulling her closer. *My dearest child, my darling.* The thunder cracked again, making all flinch, but it was farther away now. When it boomed again, it was farther still. Gallant nudged Brierley's shoulder with his nose and snorted, and Megan eased her grip slightly.

"I agree," Brierley told them both fervently. Stefan now had Destin under control, although the mare's voice rang out in challenge as she sidled away from him. Brierley heard Stefan swear vividly as her hoof stamped down solidly on his foot, then a crackling of underbrush, a shifting of the shadows, and she saw Stefan walking toward her, Destin on a lead in his hand, checking that they were all right. "That lightning was close!" he exclaimed.

"Sleeping under trees is not a good idea, Stefan."

"Where else do we sleep in a forest?" he asked irritably as he tied Destin's lead next to Gallant's on the branch. Brierley had to admit his point. Along this stretch of the river, the forest descended nearly to the riverbanks, allowing little open ground for better safety. Brierley shrugged at him, what else to say. Gallant snorted his opinion of the entire event at Destin, and Destin snorted her agreement back, and Friend sighed a few steps away, then twitched her ears briskly. The horses' mutual relief came slightly too soon.

Lightning crashed once again, and then the rain began, sluicing down through the forest canopy from the dark sky. Within moments everyone was drenched. With a weary sigh Brierley sank down by Gallant's forefeet and wrapped her arms around Megan and let the rain fall. The water dripped down her face and ran off her clothes and slid inside to chill her skin, and soaked her clothes to make her wet everywhere and, not content with that, continued to pour down more water from the sky.

Stefan sat down beside her with a soft grunt, then pulled up his legs and wrapped his arms around his knees. "There are easier ways to swim," he grumped. Destin stamped behind him and Stefan threw a warning look at the mare, nearly invisible in the downpour. Destin felt his look and snorted back, then stamped a second time to prove she could.

Brierley wrinkled her nose. "I have a good idea. I'll complain at you, Stefan, and you can complain at me, and then we'll feel better. We can copy the horses." He chuckled and shifted his seat closer, then sighed as the rain ran down his face.

"Wet," Megan said with disgust.

"That it is, sweetling," Stefan said, then got himself up to get the blankets from their beds and brought them back. Together they huddled under a tent of blankets as the skies continued to rain. Gallant snorted another comment at Destin, got a ruder comment back, but both horses quieted as the thunder moved away, ascending the inland mountains. In the distance the thunder growled again, a muted booming behind the sound of the rain drumming on the forest.

"Winter cold, cold, cold rain," Stefan murmured beside her.

"What?"

"I'm trying to remember the poem. I heard a saga once about the Mionn earls battling the Pass weather. Maybe only heroic earls get poetry written about them, but let's see: 'Stefan and Brierley, cold and wet, sat under their blankets, fret, fret, fret.' What do you think?"

Brierley muffled a laugh. "We should do something more heroic than just sit, Stefan. After all, it's a saga."

"Or we need a better poet." He shivered and pulled the blankets closer around them. "I used to like rain. This may affect me for life, I fear. You have a hard service, Brierley."

"A wet one, I admit, at least right now."

"Wet!" Megan exclaimed indignantly.

"Yes, child," Brierley said, and hugged Megan close. The rain fell harder, drumming on their blankets, bobbing the leaves of the trees, splashing high off the ground.

Brierley stirred restlessly as the rain drummed onward, then peered out from beneath the blanket, hoping vainly for some easing of the downpour. The storm was now but a flickering over the western mountains, the thunder a distant murmur, but she knew from the past few days of Mionn's weather that the rain could drum on for hours.

She laid her head on Stefan's shoulder and sighed. "Wet, wet, wet," she murmured. "There's the next line for your poem, Stefan."

"It rhymes," he allowed.

They listened to the rain for a time, and Brierley sensed that Megan had drifted back to sleep. She shifted Megan's limp body slightly to a more comfortable position for them both, and felt Stefen brace his arm on the ground to allow her to lean more heavily against him. She felt the brush of his lips on her hair and smiled. During their weeks together, as Stefan gallantly guarded her as best she allowed him to do, they had become friends, and she had found in him what Melfallan had also found in a similar friendship: loyalty, staunchness, a cheerful spirit that little could quench—and recklessness, as Melfallan could be reckless. They were peas in a pod: Melfallan and Stefan had been close friends as boys, a friendship they had carried into manhood.

"I never thought in all my life," Stefan murmured next to her ear, "that I'd do anything like this—in all aspects. I expected my comfortable courtier's life, safe in a castle with my Christina, charging off gallantly to whatever my countess bid me, solid in the world. Rain like this was something falling outside the castle window, to be watched from the comfort of my chair."

"You don't say," she said indulgently.

"I do say, and I just did," he pointed out. "Here I am, mistress witch, sitting under a blanket getting drenched in a forest, with a witch and witchling under my care—although I have a sad suspicion I'm under *their* care, whatever my manly pretensions—journeying to Ocean knows where to find Ocean knows what; every once in a while, to add spice to the dish, a dragon pops in and—"

Jain poked his muzzle under the edge of the blanket, not three inches from Stefan's face, and twitched his nostrils busily. *Yes?* the salamander inquired, then chortled as Stefan flinched in surprise.

Stefan's jerk set the blanket to swaying, and Jain dug in his small talons to keep his hold. He flicked his tail airily, colored flames sifting along his scaly sides. *Pop is a good word, I like it.* Jain vanished, then reappeared an instant later, clinging again to the blanket. *Pop.*

The next few moments were occupied by Jain's wiggling rudely between Brierley and Stefan, demanding in. The salamander settled himself between their hips, nested neatly against the night. He laid his chin companionably on Brierley's knee, his tongue flicking, nuzzled Megan's hand a moment, and then settled back with a teakettle sigh of contentment.

Brierley and Stefan exchanged a rueful glance. "He's back," Brierley noted.

"So I see," Stefan agreed.

Jain was Megan's treasured delight, companion and confidant—and whatever else, anything else, he chose to be to others. They had witnessed a range of possibilities in the last two weeks since Jain had chosen to show himself to Stefan. That Stefan had witch-blood that made the seeing even possible, Brierley had not known until that night, and Jain had bid Brierley keep the fact of Stefan's witch-blood a secret from her liegeman. She had consented, although she felt uncertain of the salamander's reasons. The shari'a gifts manifested only in women, never in men: perhaps Jain's stated reason, that the knowledge of his unrealizable fire gift would only torment him, was the true one.

Stefan poked at Jain's side with a finger. "Where have you been the last three days?" he demanded. "Megan's been wanting you."

Stop that, Jain protested, then batted hard at Stefan with his taloned forefoot as Stefan contrarily poked at him again. It was a draw, Brierley decided, and wondered how she might ease herself away from the coming fight without getting wetter than she had to. She peered out at the sheeting rain. No hope. *Just because I'm invisible,* Jain said indignantly, *doesn't mean I'm not here.*

"That really makes sense," Stefan retorted.

Of course it does. I am the fire dragon. I always make sense. Jain yawned widely, showing his needle-sharp teeth. *And the next finger that pokes me gets severed.*

Stefan wisely desisted, at least in poking fingers. "If you're a fire dragon," he asked wryly, "why doesn't the rain put you out? The campfire's out, quite decidedly—why aren't you, Jain?" Jain closed his eyes, sighed gustily, and disdained a reply.

Brierley snickered. "I don't think you'll ever win, Stefan, not with him. Ocean knows I've tried, too."

"That doesn't mean I have to give in to cowardly resignation," Stefan avowed, and she saw the flash of his smile. "A man is meant for more than collapsing into a puddle, useless and inert."

No puddles, please, Jain insisted. *It's wet enough.*

"I agree," Brierley said, and pulled the edge of the blanket lower in front of their faces, then watched the water drip its drops off the blanket edge, a dozen drops at a time, dripping to the ground, there to splash high and then join their fellows in spreading outward to dampen the earth. "All the world is water," she suggested, nudging Jain with her elbow. "A hard time for fire." Jain loftily ignored her, too, and joined Megan in a nap, decorated by soft, whistling snores.

Ah, well, Brierley thought, and heard Stefan's echoing sigh.

You'll never win, came the faintest of whispers tickling through her mind, then the soft hissing of the snicker. *Either of you.*

Brierley looked down at him and saw one eye open, a warm red flicker within the pupil, one of laughter, of love, and remembered another poem from Thora's book. " 'Let me sing the song of Fire:' " she recited softly, " 'As light, clarity, intelligence / As dependence, attachment, devotion / As weapons, lances, coats of mail, / As conscious form, as eye of memory.' Is that you, Jain? All of that?"

Sometimes, Jain replied indulgently and yawned, showing small, white fangs. A heartbeat's pause, then: *Other times not at all.*

Stefan groaned. "As he said," he said, "we're not going to win. Go to sleep, Jain."

Go to sleep, Jain, the dragon agreed, and did.

The rain fell hard for another hour but then, to Brierley's surprised relief, began to lift. By dawn the rain clouds had moved on, bringing bright sunlight into the upper canopy, golden light against the green. Water drops sparkled on every branch, filling the trees with a dazzling, dancing light, like sun sparkles on the ocean, she thought. Brierley sat contentedly next to Stefan, watching the dawn light strengthen, filling the world with warmth.

What will I find in Flinders? she wondered, and felt her heart rise joyfully again. What, indeed?

"I wonder what we'll find in Flinders," Stefan murmured, echoing her thought. He shifted his seat comfortably beside her, then squinted out at the wet morning. "I always thought I wanted adventures in my life, being the dashing young courtier that I think myself. This isn't exactly what I expected, but it'll suit. My little boy will listen, agog, when I tell him the tale. The thunder boomed, I'll say, and the water sluiced down from the sky, and I was very wet, my boy, and Brierley wet beside me, her hair dripping in strings."

"Is it in strings?" she asked indulgently.

"Not really. You've dried out a little. And then, my boy, I'll say, we caught colds, and sneezed and shivered for three whole days." He considered a moment. "Hmm. Maybe five days: it's more dramatic. Or I can drop the colds and add a sword fight here and there to spice it up. After all, this is a saga. Did you ever hear about any knight in a saga catching a cold?"

"Not that I remember."

"Me neither. They're always staunch types, oblivious to any weather." He craned his neck to check the horses, and unwisely shifted the blanket over their heads as he looked. Water gushed down like a torrent, drenching Stefan's trousers and splashing onto Jain, who promptly hissed and popped out. For several moments Stefan regarded his sodden trousers gloomily, then sighed. "I wish I was staunch," he said. "In fact, I really wish I could pop out like Jain does. Then I wouldn't need staunch."

"Am I going to hear this all the way to Flinders?"

"Probably." He grinned. "So what will we find in Flinders, Brierley?"

"A girl in green," Brierley said with satisfaction.

"And who's she, your girl in green?"

"We'll find out, you and I."

"She'll be another shari'a witch?"

"Basoul said so."

"And you and Megan won't be as lonely, nor will your girl in green." He nodded. "That will be good, and well worth the adventure." He brushed his lips against her forehead, and she sensed again Stefan's wish for all good things for her and Megan, and his fierce intent to protect them against all harm. She leaned closer to him and sighed.

They watched the suns' light strengthen into a golden glow that filled the forest, touching every branch, every blade. Nearby, the river tumbled in its stone bed, making its endless music, and birds called in the distance, greeting the dawn. A wind sighed softly through the trees, beginning far down the mountains and rising swiftly, and all the world shimmered with life and movement. Soon, Brierley thought, her heart lifting. Soon the Promise begins, and a dawn will come to end the darkness, a new dawn like this one, filling all the world with light.

Oh, let it be so, she wished earnestly. Let it be so.

3

*B*rierley turned in her saddle and looked behind them at the eastern sky, uneasy about more dark clouds roiling up from the Bay. Clouds by noon promised another night storm with its terrifying noise of lightning and drumming rain. Yesterday they had met a traveler on the road, a Flinders fishmonger traveling to Arlenn to visit his sister, and he had said that the true Pass storms still impended, the suns being still a hand-span apart at the dawning. *Oh, that was nothing, good mistress,* he had said with a flip of his hand. *'Tis still three weeks until Pass: then we'll see some real storms.* The man had seemed to take a fiendish delight in his news, had smiled and touched his broad hat, and then had ridden on his way downward toward the bay shore.

But today the Daystar had again dawned brilliantly, soon followed by its smaller bluish Companion, lifting above the trees of Mionn's highland forests. Both suns had risen steadily into a clear morning sky, warming the mountains until all the forest steamed with clouds of rising vapor. In the deep gorge cut by the river through mountain rock, the sound of the river echoed against the cliffsides, a soft roar quite different from the surf of Yarvannet's shores; here sound contained within rock, echo upon echo. It was a music that had accompanied them their entire ascent, never ceasing. Ahead, lining the western horizon, the tall, snow-covered peaks of the Mionn Range lifted into the sky, misted by hurtling gray clouds, an occasional flicker of lightning. Brierley looked behind them again at the building storm clouds and frowned. Well, no help for it, she thought.

"I refuse to look where you're looking," Stefan muttered, his shoulders hunched under his cloak. Destin had her head down, too, as she plodded step-by-step over the stony mud of the river road, and the other two horses seemed as dispirited. Megan had quite closed herself up inside Brierley's cloak, completely refusing the day. "At some point," Stefan suggested, "we should get wet enough to melt, and then we won't have any problems. We can just *ooze* along the road."

" 'Tis still three weeks until Pass, good master," Brierley reminded him, imitating Master Grayson's booming heartiness.

"I should have strangled him, I agree. Do you think all the Flinders folk are like that?" Stefan's tone was not flattering.

"Probably. Here, Megan, cheer up. The suns are shining."

Megan made a little snort and eased aside the edges of Brierley's cloak. Despite the bright suns' light, all was still damp, and Megan would not forgive the weather until all was cured of that fault.

"Wet!" she complained, and shut up her tent again.

Brierley chuckled. Once trust was lost, it seemed, Megan was slow to give it again, and she had lost trust in Mionn's weather with the first night storm. Megan had enjoyed her first snowfall at the cabin near Witchmere with its great novelty of flouncing through the drifts, to laugh when she slipped and sat down. And the hard snows on their journey to Lowyn, Mionn's southernmost fishing town on the bayside, had not troubled Megan, being yet another adventure. But this icy rain— Rain was quite another matter. Within the curve of her arms, Brierley felt Megan give a great and mournful sigh. Rain— To Megan, rain was dull, boring, and bad.

"She won't be cheered, Stefan," Brierley said.

"I don't blame her. I've never seen such storms—and it gets worse?"

"So Master Grayson said."

"A pox on Master Grayson, truly."

"One more day's ride to the Flinders Plateau, maybe two, or so the good master said, and then maybe we'll have a warm house by the lakes."

Peas in a pod with Megan, Stefan grumbled something to himself and pulled his hood lower over his face. The horses plodded on.

Brierley gave Megan a little shake. "Cheer up, Megan. The suns are out." Megan stubbornly ignored her, content with her pocket of warmth. Ah, well, she thought.

All around them the light sparkled on the wet forest, filling every branch, every bush, with a glitter. The horses plodded through the mud on the road, their hooves making a slight sucking sound with every step, but their ears flicked with interest in the scenery, with occasional snorts to each other as some new marvel came into view. Gallant, Brierley's gelding, made a pretend bite at Destin, and then pranced a playful step as the mare glared at him in outrage. Stefan absently edged Destin away from Gallant, and then moved ahead to take the lead on the road, solving that particular problem, a problem wholly created by Gallant to bless the day. Gallant did a little triumphant sidestep, then settled back to mere walking, hardly exciting, but what else to do? Brierley patted his neck and laughed softly. Gallant was Countess Rowena's gift, a very expensive horse, Stefan had said, and a gift in other ways that perhaps even the countess had not intended. In Yarvannet Brierley had had little contact with horses, her own travels being almost wholly by foot, and she enjoyed her gelding's flippant attitudes.

Can you hear me thinking, Gallant? she sent wistfully. Gallant twitched his ears but would rather watch the day, and so gave no answer. The horses apparently talked to Megan, by whatever means that was accomplished, but never replied to Brierley's thought-sending, not in words, at least. She sighed and patted his neck again. Ah, well.

He thinks Destin is full of herself, Megan supplied from her tent. *He thinks he's in charge.*

Oh, he does?

Megan yawned. *He made the thunderstorm go away again by shouting at it. He didn't like its noise; neither did I.* She sniffed.

"Oh, look, Megan!" Brierley said, suddenly pointing ahead. "It's another boat!" Another riverboat had rounded the turn in the river and now hurtled toward them.

Megan pushed aside Brierley's cloak edges to watch. Although well kept by the Arlenn count, the Flinders road had seemed little-traveled during the ride upward, for the Flinders folk apparently preferred their wide-bottomed, sturdy riverboats to horse and cart when traveling down the river. It was a swift and rushing descent, the boatmen apparently content with its price of a slow labor of poles and oars when they re-ascended the river to their upland towns on the plateau. Whenever the occasional boat had passed them, the river men had waved cheerfully, then swept onward, balancing on the flood.

"Fun!" Megan declared in open wonder, for a moment jarred from the weather's misery to exclaim.

The boatman waved from his stance by the rudder, and Brierley waved back happily. The boat hurtled past, swooping over the river current, and vanished, still hurtling, around the river bend behind them. Brierley watched it go, marveling at the rushing speed. "Maybe someday, Megan," she said, "we'll ride one of those boats."

"Promise?" Megan turned eagerly to look up into her face.

"Well—" Brierley hedged, and realized she had just been boxed. "We'll see," she said firmly, but Megan knew a promise when she got one. Her witch-daughter sighed contentedly and snuggled closer beneath Brierley's cloak, trying to find some patch of warmth not yet discovered. Brierley kissed her hair, and then returned to watching the forest and river.

Each Allemanii land has its own weather, Brierley mused, looking at the bright morning with its edge of storm clouds to the east. Yarvannet's southern seaside basked in the suns' light during summer and suffered scarcely a rime frost in winter, with only an occasional snowfall, a novelty much enjoyed by its folk. Airlie's inland meadows and hills were often hip deep with snow in winter, but rich with grass in other seasons, vast meadowlands that stretched as far as the eye could see. Mionn's bayside weather was harsher, more to the extremes, but its hardy folk coped with the harsh seasons, content with their fisheries and busy lumber towns. A secret witch might make a good life here, she told herself, even a sea-shine lass from warm Yarvannet, and pushed away a sudden sharp longing for her home. Yes, perhaps here in Mionn, she told herself even more firmly—and especially when it is warmer, in the spring.

In truth she had no significant choice otherwise. If she returned to Yarvannet, she risked too much for both herself and Melfallan. Duke Tejar had chosen to make Melfallan his enemy, and would seek any excuse to humiliate him. A proscribed shari'a witch suited deftly that purpose, as Tejar had already tried when Melfallan had been forced to bring Brierley to Darhel for trial. To save her own life, Brierley had killed the duke's torturer, and then had escaped with a Darhel kitchen's child, young Megan, a shari'a witch like herself. That escape had led her into the mountains east of Darhel, and eventually to the shelter of a cabin near the ancient shari'a fortress of Witchmere, and now into Mionn. What would she find next at the Flinders Lakes? Would she find other shari'a, as Basoul had promised?

Were there other shari'a in Flinders? Basoul had said so, and Brierley clung to that hope fiercely. Oh, let it be true, Brierley wished earnestly. Let it be true. She nudged Gallant to walk a little faster, wanting that finding to be soon, very soon.

~

The next day near noon the river road bent itself around a last towering bluff and finally ran onto the upland plateau of the Flinders Lakes, a wide expanse of meadowland and lake water several miles in breadth. Brierley reined in Gallant and marveled at the huge valley in front of them. Beyond the grassy valley the tall peaks of the central Mionn Range rose to dizzying heights, great piles of stone capped with brilliant white snow and drifting cloud. Their distant slopes were furred with trees, making an encircling forest that embraced the valley and stretched dark fingers of everpine into the meadowlands surrounding the lakes.

The lakes sparkled in the bright suns' light. Several small towns clung to the lake shores, pleasant towns of white-planked houses and busy traffic. On the lakes she could see boats, far out on the water, fishing, and the piers and river wharves at the edge of the towns.

It was a typical Allemanii scene, with the lakes replacing the seaside she had known since childhood in Yarvannet, but with a prickling of her witch-sense she felt the subtle power in the valley, a different power than her own intricate perception of other minds, other souls. This power looked to the forest and the wild things who lived there, to the turning of the seasons, the fruitfulness of the earth. Brierley closed her eyes and listened to the joy singing within the land and forest, then took a deep, shuddering breath.

"Mother, it's her," Megan whispered, for she heard it, too. She turned her head to look up at Brierley and smiled happily. "The girl in green."

"Yes, Megan. It is she." But where in this miles-wide valley with its several towns would she find her? And how? Her books in the cave gave no advice about witch finding, for its occupants had rarely numbered more than one—one solitary witch longing for the touch of another of her kind, as Brierley had longed for that touch. She looked down at Megan's bright smile, then kissed the child's hair. "Yes, it is," she whispered.

Perhaps I will be rich in witches, Brierley thought with yearning. I will have a treasure-house of witches, all kinds, all types, now that the Finding will gather all of us together, begin all things anew. Basoul had said so, had spoken that promise. Brierley looked up at the bright sky with its twin suns now westering toward the mountains, then looked at Stefan. Her liegeman had leaned an elbow on his saddle horn, looking, too, at the fertile valley before them, lush with grasses and shining water.

Stefan turned his head. "What?" he asked, lifting an eyebrow.

"The girl in green." Brierley laughed and spread her hands. "She's here! I can hear her song, Stefan. I've never heard the like, but I know what it is. It is life treasured and adored; life protected beneath shadow and branch. Oh, yes. She is here!"

"Song?" Stefan grimaced, then shook his head humorously. "Well, never mind about that. Asking you questions can test a man's daring."

Brierley tsked. "Why do I think I've heard this complaint before?"

Stefan grinned. "Because you have, and not only from me, I do suspect." He gestured grandly at the wide valley. "So where do we start?" he asked.

Brierley promptly pointed at the northernmost lake, the largest of the five, the one near the northern forest. "That one," she said, and then laughed because she knew no reason to choose that lake—and every reason she should.

"That one!" Megan agreed enthusiastically.

⁓

It was near noon when Michael counted out five copper pennies into Ashdla's hand, then raised an eyebrow when Ashdla wrinkled her nose.

"This won't buy bluestripe," she complained.

"I'm not wanting bluestripe, daughter, only flour from the market to make bread for tomorrow. We can't have fish every night, and cheese will do for any plainday's meal." He dropped the remaining coins into their earthen jar on the kitchen shelf. "After all, we're not—"

"—rich," she finished for him. "I know. And I'm not *that* greedy, Da. Don't you pretend that I am. Sigrid Witt's daughter is far worse, always wanting new dresses and anything else, and Sigrid buys them for her."

"Since when are Mistress Witt and her daughter a model?" her father rumbled. "Especially for you?"

"Just a mention, Da, nothing toward. But who can tell?" She waved her hand airily. "Plant an idea and maybe it will grow." She snickered at his expression and put the coins into her tunic pocket. "I thought I'd gather some pine nuts and tubers in the forest after I come back. Is that all right?"

"Just be back by suppertime, dear girl, so I don't worry." Michael patted her cheek, then waved her toward the door.

As she stepped off the porch, Will emerged from behind the smithy and waited, then fell into step with her. *Market?*

Yes. You're coming?

Sure.

The marketplace was busy on this plainday afternoon, with a new catch in from the lake after yesterday's break in the weather. The night's rain had blustered, spattering hard against the windows of the house, but the morning had dawned clear again, with the suns bright in the sky, however unlikely the good weather would last another day. Already new storm clouds, black and angry, built in the eastern sky, climbing the mountains from the bayside. Ashdla squinted at them, knowing the storms would roll fairly regularly now that Pass was imminent, and thus spoil any hope of wandering the forest without getting drenched to the skin. She sighed, rueing the theft of her days by the weather, a dreariness of every spring. But for today the sunlight sparkled on the water and the townsfolk moved briskly, happy to enjoy a sunny day. Ashdla stopped at the fishmonger's stand and eyed the bluestripe hungrily.

Greed doesn't suit you, Will suggested, nudging her elbow. *Da said no.*

Stow it, Ashdla advised. *I'm just looking. I don't have enough coins anyway, not at Master Grayson's prices. Every time he goes down to Arlenn to visit his daughter, his prices go up. Have you noticed?* Ashdla smiled sweetly at Grayson's tall, gangling son who minded the stand today, and got only a scowl for her trouble. Ashdla lingered another moment, then sighed and moved on. *When are you going fishing, Will?* she asked without subtlety.

Bluestripe are deep-lake fish caught on a trolling line: you know that. You can't catch them from a cockleboat. Maybe I could catch some carp tomorrow.

Carp. Ashdla sighed in dismay.

It's better than cheese again, right?

Anything's better than cheese again, so do catch some carp tomorrow, Will.

That's a promise.

"Why, Ashdla!" a voice exclaimed behind them. Ashdla turned and saw Emilie Witt, dressed in all her magnificence, goggling at her, Ocean knew why. "It's so rare to see you in the marketplace! What a delight!" Emilie walked swayingly toward them, tipping her skirt hem to and fro as she minced around the mud puddles in the market street. Ashdla sensed Will's sudden wish to run when he saw her coming. Her brother often liked the fervent attention of the town girls that sadly seemed his due, but Emilie's look right now matched Ashdla's hungry look at the bluestripe, and for the same reason. Emilie's chief purpose in life was a large catch, as many as she could get, and Will knew it. Two months ago Emilie had decided, as Will also knew, that Will Toldane was only a matter of time. During the weeks of Emilie's relentless pursuit, her brother's poise had steadily disintegrated.

Emilie's perfect lips turned upward in a lovely smile, and the long eyelashes batted. "Good morning, Will," she cooed, and laid her hand delicately on Will's arm. "You're especially handsome today." The perfect smile broadened; the blue eyes glowed. Even her ringleted hair stirred fetchingly in the breeze. Ashdla eyed her with disgust.

"Uh, good morning, Emilie," Will bumbled, blushing furiously. "You're looking pretty, too." He shuffled his feet and glanced quickly around at the market street and its crowd, hoping for rescue.

It's only because you're male, Ashdla informed her

brother dryly. *She's got some kind of female dazzle I'll never understand.* By now Emilie had, as usual, quite forgotten Ashdla standing by Will's side. Some people might call it focus, but predators like Emilie knew it better as the pause before the strike.

Emilie leaned closer, her fingers tightening possessively on Will's arm, and her perfume sifted like a cloud. "Very handsome," she crooned, smiling up at Will.

Ocean save me! Will thought in panic.

All you have to do, Will, is give in once and she'll move on.

No thanks, Will sent decisively. Ashdla snickered.

The perfect eyes shifted to Ashdla, followed by a delicate frown. "Is something amusing, Ashdla?" Emilie asked.

"You are, Emilie," Ashdla said.

Ash! Will sent, appalled. *She's the factor's daughter!*

And full of herself about it, too. Shut up: I'm rescuing you.

"How so, pray tell?" Emilie turned to face Ashdla, her frown now quite real.

Ashdla bared her teeth. "Figure it out. You have a brain to think with, or so I'm assuming. I could be wrong, of course. Come on, Will." Ashdla took her brother's elbow and pulled at him sharply, then got him into motion. After several steps Will glanced back.

"She's following us," he muttered in alarm.

"Let her. If you'd just bed one of the others and get it over with, Will, Emilie wouldn't be such a fright."

"You don't want me to bed anybody," Will reminded her. "You've made that rather clear, Ash."

"I didn't mean to," she answered, and glanced at him in embarrassed apology. "I get jealous, that's all. You know I do, but you shouldn't listen to it. You should do what you want, Will, when it's the right time and the right person. I mean it."

"Even if it's Emilie?" Will teased.

"Anybody but Emilie," Ashdla retorted. "Quick, let's go through here." She pulled Will's arm and they ducked between two market stalls, emerging into the next street. They strolled through the crowd, arm in arm.

"So do you want approval rights before I do?" he asked lightly.

"Why? Do you have somebody in mind?" she demanded. "Who?"

"Is that jealousy I hear?" Will smiled at her wryly, then gave her arm a little shake. "I love you, Ash. Always will."

"I know, but—"

A gap cleared in the crowd, and Ashdla stopped short as she saw the young woman mounted on a bay horse, a young girl seated in the saddle in front of her. The blond man with her had dismounted from his own horse and now spoke with one of the shop women at the nearby stall. She heard Will gasp softly beside her. Then the young woman turned her head and looked at them. A moment later the child looked, too.

"Hello!" the little girl caroled, and spread her small hands in delight. She turned to look up into the woman's face. *It's the girl in green, Mother!* Ashdla heard the girl's thought as clearly as if she had spoken aloud.

Yes, Megan.

The woman's mental voice was a melody in her mind, and Ashdla closed her eyes as its sound shivered through her body. All her life Ashdla had known only two other shari'a, her mother and Will, all three of them of the forest gift, but now the mental touch of the Blood was different, as if it were a low murmur of surf on a distant shore, or the coolness of brook water.

Sea gift, Will thought in awe. *It has to be.* Neither of them could move.

The young woman swung down from her horse, lifted down the little girl and spoke briefly to the man, then began walking toward them. Ashdla watched her, amazed, as she approached. *I am Brierley Mefell,* she said as she reached them, holding out her hands, and her smile was dazzling.

Ashdla lifted her hands automatically and felt slender fingers grasp hers, then caught her breath at the feeling. "Who is the girl in green?" Ashdla whispered hoarsely, staring into the woman's face. Since her mother's death she had heard only Will's mental voice, only that one voice. Amina had told them Brierley would come to Flinders: why had she not truly believed? Why was she now unable to do anything but stare like a silly loon?

You are the girl in green, Brierley answered, then laughed softly. Her head turned to Will. *And so are you,* she added in surprise. She released one of Ashdla's hands and offered her other hand to Will.

We are twinned— Ashdla began, and then felt her knees begin to give beneath her. A great roaring filled her ears, as if the Pass storm had already struck, bringing blinding wind, merciless rain.

"Ashdla!" Will cried as she stumbled, and he caught her firmly around the waist before she could fall. She clung to him, dazed, then felt Brierley supporting her from the other side. She looked into Brierley's face, and felt amazed all over again.

"Well, this is cute," a singsong voice said behind them. "Fainting heaves? Is Ashdla not as innocent as we thought? Has she bedded and mistimed the month?" Ashdla sensed Brierley bridle at the lilting malice in the voice, as if Brierley now cast a web of protection around Ashdla, ready for any battle, however fierce the defense.

"Here, come and sit down," Brierley murmured, and eased her onto a crate by a nearby market stand. The man and little girl now joined them, and the little girl ran to Ashdla, her face anxious in her distress.

"Are you all right?" she cried. "Are you sick?" She patted Ashdla's hand, and then looked up at Brierley. "Is she sick, Mother?"

"No, Megan. Never you mind." Brierley turned to face Emilie, who now had the attention of the nearby crowd, and who rattled on loudly to enjoy it.

"I do wonder," Emilie said, her voice carrying in every direction for all ears to hear, "I hadn't thought she had the beauty to win a man, small and dark-haired and puny as she is. My mother was saying just the other day—"

Brierley looked the girl up and down, a slow, raking look that made Emilie stop abruptly. She looked back at Brierley warily. "It sounds to me," Brierley drawled, "as if you have the experience to know, girl." Emilie flushed uncertainly, then found the spirit to glare.

"And who are you to say that to *me?*" Emilie asked, tossing her head.

"Ashdla's cousin," Brierley answered mildly. "My name is Clara Jacoby, just now arrived from the south—to find an ill-mannered girl with little brains insulting my cousin in the town's own market." She made a show of looking around at the crowd of a dozen persons, with a few more stopping to listen as she looked, then turned to look at the stallman standing uncomfortably behind them. "Obviously they are used to such displays by you." Brierley's head turned back to Emilie.

"I'm the factor's daughter!"

"You poor thing," Brierley sighed with pity, and shook her head. "To be so blighted at your age. But there's always hope. We aren't bound by the sad circumstances of our birth, not really." Brierley nodded earnestly. "I'm sure it's true. Find the right man and move away: yes, that will suit."

Will turned his laugh into a cough and had to turn away, and Ashdla felt her jaw slowly drop. Nobody said such things to Emilie Witt, ever. She looked up at Brierley, then looked at Emilie, then caught Brierley's hand. "It's only Emilie," Ashdla blurted. "She's chasing after Will." Ashdla looked straight at Emilie and lifted her chin. "Hasn't caught him, and she won't either," she declared bravely. A few chuckles answered her as all looked at Emilie for the next lob of the ball. The town knew Emilie's reputation, however Emilie wished otherwise.

"Well!" Emilie declared. "Well!" she declared again, but apparently she had only that one word left. With a flip of her skirts, Emilie turned and stamped off through the puddles, followed by the soft laughter of the crowd, not all of it particularly kind. As the crowd then moved on to its business, some of the townsfolk shook their heads, as amazed as Ashdla at Brierley's daring, but two winked at Ashdla as they turned away. In a few moments all had moved on, with only the grinning stallman standing nearby.

"That maybe wasn't the wisest thing to do, either you or me," Ashdla said ruefully. "She *is* the factor's daughter."

"We all have our barnacles in life," Brierley said, then smiled at the stallman as he bowed to her. A customer stepped up and distracted him, but Brierley half-turned away from him and lowered her voice still further, a caution Ashdla instantly recognized. Like Ashdla and Will, like their mother, Brierley had lived in hiding. Well, of course, Ashdla thought dazedly. Of course. "I've seen such petty tyrants before," Brierley murmured. "Every town has them. Here, can you stand?" She put a hand under Ashdla's elbow and lifted her to her feet.

"Fainting isn't what I expected to do," Ashdla murmured. "Not when we met you." She felt her face heat with its embarrassment, then sensed Will's amused sympathy. She glanced at her brother in despair.

"Never you mind," Brierley murmured, and Ashdla felt her chuckle resonate through her mind, a lilting tumbling of water, as if trees shivered above a stream. When Ashdla stood up, her face was only inches from Brierley's own, and Ashdla almost had her height, for Brierley was not tall. She had large, gray eyes, and brown hair framed by her cloak's hood, and was dressed in simple homespun, now splashed with the mud of the road. The man with her was dressed as simply, but he had a proud air, as if he was used to much finer clothing, and a very handsome face that surely gained him many friends—and—and something more, something that made the corners of Ashdla's mouth turn up quite on their own.

This is Stefan Quinby, Brierley explained silently. *He is liegeman to Countess Rowena of Airlie. He has the fire gift, but he doesn't know it, and Jain thinks it best not to tell him. That's what you hear, Ashdla, the warmth of the hearth-fire—or so Jain says.* She turned and smiled fondly at Stefan.

"So we've found her," Stefan said in a low voice, glancing at the stallman, but the man was quite busy with his customer. He bowed neatly to Ashdla and Will. "I'm, uh, Robert, uh, Carlisle."

"Jacoby," Brierley corrected wryly.

"Robert Jacoby," Stefan amended, then paused and laughed at himself, his eyes crinkling. "Truly I am." He looked down at Megan, who goggled up at him in surprise. "Aren't I, Megan?"

"If it's what you want," Megan said uncertainly. She scowled. "I suppose." Stefan stooped and lifted her, balanced her on his hip.

"I'm sure." And he smiled broadly.

"Come," Will said, his voice exultant. "Da will want to meet you."

~~~

Michael straightened painfully and reached to rub his sore back. Sometimes the pain vanished with a good night's sleep, but other times it worsened until he could scarcely move. He winced as his back sent a sharp twinge, a flash of fire down one leg to his heel, and stood still a minute, blinking at tears. His two horses, the yearling and the mare, the latter now heavy with a new foal, lifted their noses from the feed bucket and flicked their ears inquiringly.

"Nothing toward," he said through gritted teeth, and wondered if he should move or stay right where he was. After a few more moments, the fire subsided, leaving him breathing heavily, a clammy coolness of sweat on his forehead. The gray mare nudged his chest affectionately, then snuffled noisily along his tunic. Her teeth caught the edge of one of the laces and she nibbled. "Will you undress me then?" he asked her, rescuing the lace. "Hardly polite." He caressed her ears, and the yearling stepped forward, wanting his share of attention, too, which he got. But a mere man soon gave way to the interest of the feed bucket, and both went back to their noon meal. Michael took a step cautiously, then another, and stopped by the mare's shoulder, patting her, as she happily whuffled in the bucket. "That's a fine girl," he murmured.

A breath of air feathered his hair, and he looked toward the lake. The breeze was scented with the heavy smell of water, with a tang of fish, a touch of weed. The suns shone in the sky, only partly obscured by the nearing clouds. Michael sniffed at the wind, smelling rain in the air as well as the lake water, then watched the sparkles on the lake for a time, thinking of Dani.

"Da?" He heard his daughter's call near the front of the stable, and left the horses to their meal. It was a short walk across the hard-packed earth to the path alongside the stable, then a turn around the corner. When he made that turn, he stopped short.

He noticed her eyes first, large, gray eyes, like the shifting shade that went with the blues of seawater. She wasn't tall, but slender like Dani had been, and not shy like Dani, but assured, as a healer would learn to be. A small, dark-haired girl stood beside her, her hand held firmly. Behind them a young, blond man was tying the reins of three horses, a mare and a gelding, who had an issue working with each other, and a placid black mare, to the post stand in the yard. Ashdla grinned wide and spread her hands, as if only she could produce such a miracle. "Look who's here!" she exclaimed. "Where were you, Da? We've been calling for you."

And when the woman smiled, it was Dani's smile—almost, not quite, but enough to tip his heart. Michael swallowed hard and made himself step forward, then another step, until he had reached them and offered his hand to the man, then taken the woman's into his, a small, slender hand into his great paw, as it had once been with Dani. "I was in the paddock, daughter," he said distractedly, "feeding the horses."

"Will's looking for you in the house. I'll go get him."

Michael tore his attention from the gray-eyed woman and stopped Ashdla with a cluck of his tongue. "No, let's all go in. Time for the noontime meal, I believe." He nodded awkwardly, for it was so, then belatedly realized he was still holding the woman's hand and released it hastily. She tipped her head to the side, and the corners of her mouth turned up. In a moment she would be laughing at him, as Dani had laughed. "Yes, I'm sure it is," he fumbled, looking down at her. He nodded again.

"When did you hurt your back?" the woman asked softly. "You do too much, Michael." She shook her head. "It's not wise, nor fair to you."

Ashdla had turned away toward the house, following the blond man and the little girl toward the porch, but now turned quickly back, a look of alarm on her loving face. "You're hurting again? Da! Why didn't you say so?"

She was ready to chide him for not saying, for not letting Will and even herself do the work, a chiding he richly deserved, no doubt, when the woman turned her head and smiled at his daughter. Ashdla's returning smile was glorious, lighting her small face, and Michael suddenly knew in its full measure what Dani had wished for earnestly, had wanted all those years, waiting for the Finding she would never see.

"Not to worry, Ashdla," Brierley Mefell said. "It is my craft." Her voice was rich with satisfaction, as if only its sound could begin the healing, easing care, bringing peace. He looked down at her with wonder. Dani's voice had been like that when she was chanting to the forest, lost in her communion with whatever she heard of its patterns, whatever she heard that he never heard, not once. "Yes," Brierley murmured, looking up at him, and nodded gravely, as if she understood him perfectly, as likely she did, as Dani had. His eyes filled with tears and numbly he bowed his head.

"Da!" Ashdla exclaimed and seized his arm. "Why are you crying? Da?" Her sudden grip sent a lancing pain into his back, and he grunted with the impact of it. "What's wrong, Da?" Ashdla asked frantically, then released him as Brierley touched her hand.

"He's had an injury in the stable, and it's getting worse," she said calmly. "Let's help him into the house." Ashdla nodded jerkily, her eyes wide with alarm, and then softly took her father's sleeve, a down feather's touch in its carefulness, and tugged him into motion, the barest of tugs to which he yielded gratefully. Then there was the matter of the long number of steps toward the house, the lifting of the leg onto the porch, a few moments of grayness, and then the painful lowering into his wide chair at their table. When Brierley touched him, the fire in his back flickered, eased, diminished still further, and then died, and suddenly he could breathe easily again. He took in a deep breath, another, then turned and looked up at Brierley in awe.

"It is my craft," she said, almost irritably, and shook her head at him.

Michael flexed his back cautiously, then with more confidence. "It's gone!" he exclaimed, then laughed quietly at his own surprise. "Well, of course, I suppose. Thank you."

"You're welcome." She sat down in a nearby chair, then took his large hand in her own again. His smile widened, and he felt her fingers press on his.

"You are a gentle lass, suiting a healer," he said, marveling that Brierley sat at his table in his house, that she looked at him with Dani's very smile. "So was my Dani, although for different reasons, I think. For her it was gentleness with birds and beasts, each of them a joy and treasure to her, sometimes to the ignoring of me—not that I minded that much. It was a pleasure to watch her, talking as she would to the beasts, and I could easily believe they talked back to her, although I could never hear it. Sometimes I wished I could, to know what she knew." The slender fingers pressed on his hand again, encouraging him, for all he was babbling now. "I long for her still, you see, even after these five empty years." He looked past Brierley at the window and the broad lake beyond. "And I worry for our children. They haven't your healer's insight into people's hearts, and so won't hear the warning—all they think about are their animals and that cabin in the ravine, just like she did." He shook his head in worry.

He was vaguely aware of the young man standing in the other corner of the room, of the little girl next to him clinging to the young man's hand, of his two children sinking into chairs at the table, their mouths slightly agape. Was he talking such nonsense to earn such looks? he wondered, and frowned at them distractedly. Was he?

Brierley sighed. "I bring danger with me, Michael, coming here. I'm sorry."

Michael shrugged. "It's a necessary thing to do, to make the Finding. And I'm glad you did, truly. I'm just wondering how many more shari'a might show up: it might be a crowd." He frowned mildly. "Not that I'd mind a crowd, meaning what it does for the shari'a, having more left than a tiny few, but—"

"You worry for your children."

"Aye, I do." He smiled ruefully. "I'm a blessed man, having the shari'a in my life, first my wife who was my heart itself, then my twins." He nodded at her. "And now you and your daughter, if you're willing to stay for a while." He looked then around at the young man, wondering.

"Not me," the other protested, raising one hand. "I'm her liegeman, secretly Stefan Quinby from Airlie, but here I'm Robert, uh—" He frowned.

"Jacoby," Brierley supplied.

"Right. And this is Megan," He looked down at the little girl. "Megan Jacoby, I suppose. Somehow I married your mother, Megan, unless we're brother and sister now, she and I—but if we're that, who are you, Megan?"

"I'm me!" the little girl exclaimed. And with that, the tiny child ran across the wooden floor and quite contentedly climbed into Michael's lap. Michael made room for her and held her carefully, then looked back as she studied his face for a long minute. "I'm a fire witch," she confided softly. Michael nodded gravely. "But that's a secret," she added, more softly still.

"I'll remember that it is." And Megan climbed down from his lap and then greeted the table—it could be nothing but that—and moved toward the cupboards across the room and did the same. A little dazed, Michael watched her, and decided not to ask, not yet.

Instead he looked at Brierley and cleared his throat. "We haven't been unnoticed here, although it's never come to active peril, not yet," he said, and his voice still sounded strange in his own ears. "I've my cache of supplies out in the woods, a plan in mind should we have to leave suddenly, but so far we've been safe. There've always been rumors about Dani's family, passing down mother to daughter each generation, nothing particular, nothing to accuse, but just—notice, and sly words, and sharp looks. Enough for prudent worry."

Brierley nodded. "I'm your cousin," she suggested, "come to visit from Lowyn."

"Ah!" He blinked at her in surprise. "Are you indeed?"

He saw the twins exchange a look, aghast, and it suddenly made him laugh, and then laugh even more heartily, at himself for not expecting the joy of it all.

"Ashdla fainted when she saw her," Will offered.

"Will!" his sister exclaimed in outrage.

"You did! I had to hold you up."

And then everything was right again, the way it should be. The twins were tussling, dinner would be coming, and the Finding had finally come, arriving with this fair lass who reminded him so much of his Dani. Like the sparkles in the water, he thought, and the missing her did not strike like a pain. Like the wind on the lake, he thought then, nodding to himself: she is still in the world, if only in a memory caught in a sea witch's gray eyes. Michael got up from his chair, cautiously at first, but the fiery pain was truly gone. Well, of course, he thought again, and smiled large enough to make Brierley's gray eyes twinkle at him anew.

"But you're hungry, I'm sure," he told her earnestly. "Let me make a meal for you."

After the noon meal, Michael went out to the stable, taking Will with him, and Ashdla took Stefan and Megan to look at the lake, leaving Brierley alone at the large, wooden table in Michael Toldane's house. She sat comfortably in the chair and slowly examined the room, having time now to look at everything carefully. A comfortable room, she decided—it reminded her of Clara Jacoby's house in Natheby, large and square, neatly arranged, built for the sound of children's laughter, a family's closeness. Can a house take on the character of the people who lived there? Or did she give herself fancies, wishing it so?

She sensed the Beast far out at sea, coming slowly but coming as it did after every healing. A simple matter to ease the injury to the nerve, to loosen muscles tightened by pain: the Beast might delay until nighttime, perhaps not come at all. The other healing she had done for Michael's grief, for healing it had been, she had not intended, but so it was. Michael would always miss his Dani, but would now find her—more truly than his mere wishing—in the sparkles, in the ruffle of the wind, the sighing of the forest: he would believe it was so, without doubts, and through that believing be comforted. She shook her head slightly, knowing that she had found another of the rare souls with whom empathy came as easily as a breath, and who was treasured for it.

She folded her hands on the table in front of her and looked again around the room, a comfortable room, perhaps a room that might be safe. We have arrived at Flinders, she thought, and we have found the girl in green. It was pleasant to sit and not be moving, not find oneself in flight or suspension, but *arrived*. She quirked her mouth, then slightly tossed her chin at herself. Well, it's so. It truly is.

She heard Megan's piping voice in the distance, exclaiming at some wonder, then the murmur of Stefan's voice in response. Behind those sounds was a faint shirring of movement—lapping waves on the lake, a sibilant whisper of leaves stirred by the breeze, a great ocean of quiet sound surrounding the house. Dani's sound, filling the valley she had guarded, blessing the land with a shari'a's power, a different kind of healing than her own, a different kind of tending, but the same in the essentials. Brierley took a deep breath into her lungs, filling them to the bottom, and then smiled at the simple joy that resulted. She pressed her palms against the solid ever-oak of the table, looked again around the comfortable room. Yes, she thought. It was a moment of completion, a pause before life began to move on again, this small space of minutes alone in Michael's house. Not time yet to think of the next steps: not time yet to worry about mornings still to come, when danger might appear.

Nor was it time to think of losing Melfallan forever. Brierley looked around again at Michael's comfortable room, the wide windows that looked out on the lake, the neat array of shelves along the far wall. Will I ever see Melfallan again? she wondered in despair, then felt dazed by the sudden yearning that swept over her, as sharp and keen as a blade stabbing into her heart. She longed for his touch, his voice, and swayed with the strength of her yearning: oh, to see him again just for a moment! A few minutes, a dozen breaths of time to see him: was that too much to ask? And if it were never given, would she slowly strangle, away from him, and change into someone she didn't know, didn't want, and lose herself and him forever? Would she? Basoul had asked her to refound the craft, to seek out what Thora Jodann had left here in Mionn, and had spoken of a Change that would come, when Four might become Six or Seven, of the shari'a who had fled to the East and who might return, gathering together a scattered people. But how did that wish of the Four, that great destiny they wished upon her, allow Brierley a life elsewhere in Yarvannet? How? Brierley shook her head violently, angry at her fears. *The future is not set,* Basoul had also promised. She would cling to that hope as long as she could.

Jain popped into view and fluttered to the table, then

neatly arranged his wings on his back. He cocked his triangular head at her, ready as always for mischief. Impulsively, she reached to caress him, running her fingers along his scaled sides, feeling the flames slip over her fingers, a cool warmth. *Why aren't you out with Megan at the lake?* she asked.

Too much water to look at, he sniffed. *Water and fire don't mix well.* He wrinkled his snout, then sniffed again. *Never have, never will. There! I've admitted it. You and I can never be friends, Brierley. It is against our natures.*

Indeed. She smiled at him. Jain rubbed his head against the back of her hand in gentle caress, then paced down the table, looking at the room and its contents.

A pleasant house, he decided. *Megan will be happy here.*

"Yes," Brierley said softly. "I think she will."

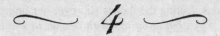

*E*arl Melfallan Courtray lifted both shield and sword to
high guard, then retreated warily as Sir Micay stalked
him across the grass of the castle quadrangle. The suns'
light shone brilliantly down on the practice field, glancing
brightly off the polished metal of sword and mail, and the
morning air rang with the loud clanging of swords and the
drumming of horse's hooves as riders leaned close over
their lances and charged a straw-stuffed target near the sea-
wall. At least once a week, Melfallan joined his castle
troops in their daily weapons practice, with Sir Micay, his
castellan, as his frequent opponent. As usual, this morning
he and Micay had dressed in full body mail, with a thigh-
length hauberk shirt, mailed leggings, sleeves, and mittens,
and a squarish iron helmet topped with feathered plumes.
Over their mail each wore a knee-length woolen surcoat in
Yarvannet's colors of blue and gray, colors repeated in the
dolphin crest painted on their shields. Today Yarvannet
fought Yarvannet in preparation for a future when Melfallan would face another High Lord's colors in combat, most
likely Duke Tejar's own crimson and gold. Allemanii politics were always tumultuous, but now the signs of impending war gathered steady strength for all the High Lords to
see. Earl Audric, Melfallan's grandfather, who had died of
poison the prior spring, had contended with Duke Tejar for
years, scorning his duke, delivering his insults, flaunting
his earl's power. Audric had married his daughter to the
count of Airlie, one of Tejar's own Ingal counties, and then
had married his grandson and heir to the daughter of the
earl of Mionn, building his webs of influence around the
duke, squeezing Tejar at every turn. The duke had re-

sponded with his own gambits, perhaps even hiring the hand that had wielded the poison into Audric's plate or glass. Now the duke's hatred for Audric flowed toward Melfallan, Yarvannet's new earl, and threatened the peace of every Allemanii land. During Melfallan's recent visit to Darhel, the duke's capital, Tejar had tried to murder Brierley Mefell, not for fear of her claimed witchery, but to destroy Melfallan, and that malicious intent had not eased in the weeks since Brierley had escaped the duke's dungeons. War was not a future Melfallan had sought, but that future now shaped itself toward near certainty. The times were not safe.

Melfallan squinted through his helmet visor, slightly dazzled by the bright light of the morning, and felt a thin trickle of sweat slide down his cheek. Fighting in a metal helmet and hauberk was part of a soldier's trade, to be learned by a High Lord as thoroughly as by the men who would fight for him. He tried to ignore the discomfort and concentrate on his opponent, but remained aware of the sweat, the weight of his mail, the fatigue in his right wrist from gripping his sword. An Allemanii broadsword, the heaviest of the Allemanii weapons, was double-edged steel three feet long, superbly balanced and lightning swift in its handling, and sharp enough to sever a hand or foot with a single strike. It was a weapon to face and wield with caution.

Micay circled to the left, trying to put the suns' light directly into Melfallan's eyes to dazzle him. Melfallan countered by circling right, then crouched low behind his shield, his sword poised, waiting. Micay feinted forward, pretending attack, but Melfallan sidestepped quickly out of range, refusing the bait, and Micay began circling again, trying to draw Melfallan into sun-dazzle. Melfallan pivoted on his right foot as the older man moved around him, then retreated in slow steps toward the castle wall.

Sir Micay stopped, lowered his sword, and glared, his eyes glinting through the eyeholes of his helmet. "This is supposed to be a sword *fight,* your grace," he reproved, "not a dance."

"Then come fight," Melfallan retorted. "Stop trying to entice me into whatever trap you're teaching today."

"Trap?" Micay demanded.

"You're the one who knows." Now Melfallan began the circle, maneuvering Micay backward across the grass. The older man slipped back into his crouch and countercircled, graciously accepting the change in their roles of stalker and prey by letting Melfallan come at him. Melfallan saw the flash of Micay's teeth beneath his visor, and bared his teeth back. The grin confirmed the trap, and Melfallan wondered what mayhem Micay had intended. Sir Micay was a canny and subtle swordsman, but, after sixteen years of weekly sword training with the grand old man, Melfallan sometimes saw it coming.

Since Melfallan's ninth year, when Micay had first put a small wooden sword into his hand, military training had been part of Melfallan's life as High Lord. In the ensuing years Melfallan had learned all of the Allemanii's weapons under Micay's tutelage—the three weights of edged swords, the lance, the long ax, the mace, the battle knife with its two-foot blade. At least once a year Micay took the castle troops into the field, pitting half the soldiers against the other in a series of raids, forest stalks, and open-field battles. Every other year they also fought at sea, the traditional war fields of the Allemanii longships in the West, blending the Allemanii crafts of seamanship and war. As High Lord, Melfallan was expected to defend his lands by leading his soldiers personally into battle. Indeed, physical ability to wield a sword was a requirement of his rank, the one indisputable test of a High Lord's right to rule. It was a tradition of noble rank that dated back to the beginning, when the Allemanii were one of a dozen tribes on a distant western shore constantly at war with each other. Of late that ancient tradition of his military duty had grown even more solemn, for war now stalked Yarvannet in the duke's malice and a rival earl's subtlety. In gentler times Melfallan might never have wielded his sword to defend his lands, might never had led his soldiers into battle, where victory meant continued living. A few High Lords in their lifetimes had enjoyed such a peace, an accident of history in the tumultuous politics of the Allemanii lands. In the times in which Melfallan lived, his military skills had become a necessity.

Watch the shoulders, not the sword, the texts said. Melfallan circled across the grass, his sword poised, focused on his opponent as Micay circled him in turn. He was conscious of his own breathing loud inside his metal helmet and controlled it, as he controlled the deliberate movements of his body, his footing, his sure grip on the sword's hilt. *Focus.* His vision tunneled, the sounds of clanging swords and hoofbeats around them faded, until all the world was confined to Micay's menace.

Sir Micay lunged at him hard. Melfallan skittered lightly backward, slashing down at the blade to parry, then quickly reversed his swing with a hard turn of his wrist and attacked. Their swords clanged on each other as Melfallan exerted all his strength, slashing at Micay; but Micay deflected the blow with his own shield, then countered deftly with a swift upstroke, as instantly parried, before dodging and circling to the left, out of range. Melfallan pursued Sir Micay aggressively, driving him back toward the castle wall.

A few of the nearby soldiers had stopped to watch, and Melfallan heard the sound of their ragged cheer. He grinned at the applause, then gave a mental shrug. Ah, well. His soldiers would hoorah anything their earl did, so long as Melfallan didn't get himself skewered before their horrified eyes. So far this morning he'd managed to avoid that, and Sir Micay was as heavily sweated as himself, definitely an accomplishment. He watched Micay circle again to the right, then began his own countercircle to the left, his sword poised in front of him.

"Good return," Micay admitted sourly. "Two passes from now I'd have had you."

"So you think, good sir. Take your guard."

Sir Micay snorted. "Boldness is good, your grace. Overconfidence is not."

"If it works, who cares?" Melfallan said carelessly, brandishing his sword in a quick flashing tracery through the air.

"Melfallan!" Micay reproved. "I expect proper attention, young earl, not stupid remarks. Show respect for a swordsman better than you."

Melfallan danced around Sir Micay, making him turn cautiously, then again swished his broadsword dramatically through the air. The effort sent a sharp twinge through his wrist, and likely he'd regret this bit of bravado tomorrow when he nursed a sore arm, but he did it anyway. "So far it's been point for point, Sir Micay," he boasted. "I don't admit betters, not this morning."

"Oh, you don't?" Sir Micay said ominously.

Melfallan laughed. "Take your guard, good sir."

Micay charged, swinging his shield forward. *The shield is also a weapon, if used correctly.* Melfallan quickly braced his feet and raised his own shield to take the blow. For a few instants, he and Micay strained against each other's strength, shield to shield, then Melfallan abruptly yielded way, pulling Micay off-balance. Micay turned his forward movement into instant attack, and struck his sword downward at Melfallan's knees. Melfallan deflected the blow with the lower edge of his shield, narrowly turned his body to avoid the next thrust, then hit down hard with his own blade, driving Micay's sword point into the grass. The rebound nearly skewered him, but Melfallan swung his shield and blocked the next strike, then attacked forward from low guard. Micay caught the strike with his shield, parried with a quick upward swing, and then slashed down at Melfallan's sword arm.

Melfallan was falling away as Micay's blade hit his upper arm, the blow partly deflected by the edge of Melfallan's shield, but the blade still drove the metal rings of his mailed sleeve hard into his flesh. He grunted softly with the impact and turned with the strike, deflecting it still farther, and then thrust his shield hard into Micay's body. Micay stumbled slightly, and Melfallan pounced again with both sword and shield, forcing the older man backward across the grass. The soldiers cheered lustily, more of them now, as Melfallan tried hard to keep his advantage. He saw the flash of Micay's grin as the wily old castellan finally sprung his trap—or so he tried. Micay threw down his shield, flipped his sword in midair, and seized the blade with both hands, then hooked low at Melfallan's ankles with the crossbar of the hilt. Melfallan made a totally ungraceful hop over the sword, staggered another step off-balance, then swung his shield with all his strength. The shield connected solidly with Micay's helmet. His head snapped back, his feet left the ground, and he fell hard; but the man instantly rolled to the side and up to his feet, as if he had planned it all, as likely he had. Micay bounced once on his toes, set his feet at guard again, and then pointedly swished his sword through the air, making it whistle. "Nice hop, your grace," he said smugly.

"You could lose your hands gripping a naked blade like that," Melfallan noted.

"Not if you grip the blade firmly, preventing its slide," Micay said equably, then grinned at Melfallan's skeptical expression. "We'll practice it next time, but today—enough. I'd not like to disable you beyond reason." His grin flashed again and then, with a sideward glance and a scowl, Micay scattered the watching soldiers back to their own practice. He watched them hurry off, still scowling, then planted his sword in the turf and leaned comfortably on the hilt. "You lost your focus when you chased me across the grass," Micay lectured, ever the teacher. "A temporary success, wrongfully used, can be mortal."

Melfallan shrugged. "Is this where I say, 'It's only sparring,' Micay? And you can scowl and remind me about getting disemboweled or my arm chopped off, or the other grisly ways I can die in battle."

"If we're at sea," Micay said, unperturbed, "there's also drowning."

Melfallan grunted. "And so you can say again, 'Focus,

young earl,' and and I still say, 'It's only sparring.' I practice the focus, Micay. I know how it feels. But never mind: when we finally face the duke in battle, I don't intend to let him and his sword get within fifty yards of me."

"Ah! And how will you accomplish that, your grace?"

"Simple. I'll charge fifty soldiers at him all at once. Or I'll run him over with a half-dozen horses. Maybe both. End of duke, whatever his *focus*."

Micay snorted. "My earl, you know that—"

Melfallan forestalled him with a lifted hand. "I know it's tradition to lead my army into battle. I know there will be one-on-one on the field, and that it will be to the death. I know all this. But keeping my focus while I'm practicing with you isn't necessary to keep me grim. I'm managing that emotion just fine without it."

"Point taken," Micay allowed. "And you still lost your focus."

"Yes, I did—but I would have killed you when I caught you at the wall."

"After I chopped off your arm first," Micay amended, nodding at Melfallan's shoulder. "You died, too. Not a desirable outcome."

"As I said," Melfallan retorted mildly, "this whole discussion is theoretical. I'll just run him over with my horses."

He signaled to a page and the boy ran up, grinning from ear to ear. The boy bowed awkwardly, and Melfallan took a swath of toweling from his hands, then repressed a sigh at the boy's expression. Well, everybody liked watching Melfallan's sword-work, especially the boys: for the men it gave some security that their earl was skillful enough to defend himself, but the boys' eyes sometimes shone with enough hero worship to make Melfallan uncomfortable. When Melfallan had been such a boy, he had watched Sir Micay and the other older men just as ardently.

It was an earl's lot to be watched every moment of his day by dozens of eyes—they all watched him: the boys, the other servants, Melfallan's soldiers, his advisors, his lords and ladies. Even now he had the attention of a good dozen soldiers again, as well as the page and Micay. He could escape the constant scrutiny by retreating to his tower study or his bath: in his tower he had privacy from watching eyes, but not always in the bath if his manservants insisted on helping, which they often did. Even when he hid in his tower, everyone knew where he was, a fact Melfallan sometimes resented. The few times he could escape his own castle always had an air of illicit freedom, of rare adventure.

He made himself smile at the page, pulled off his helmet to wipe his sweaty face, then toweled his blond hair. The boy lifted a tankard of water, offering, and Melfallan courteously gestured him toward Micay first, then finished wiping his wet hair. He shifted his arm experimentally and felt the twinge from the blow—yes, there would definitely be a bruise. Micay saw the movement and would have commented further, but Melfallan had tired of his good castellan's chiding, for all he needed it and it was part of Micay's duty and all that. Happily, the sword boy distracted Sir Micay with the tankard, and when the older man next looked, Melfallan was halfway toward the quadrangle exit. He bounded up the stairs with good speed, dodged left, past the kitchens, and emerged from another staircase onto the wide walkway over the castle gates. Perhaps escaping is a matter of degree, Melfallan thought cheerfully, and squinted a moment at the bright sky. No doubt Micay would resume his lecturing as soon as he could lay his hands on Melfallan again, but that was later.

A soldier stood at guard on the gate wall, armed with sword and lance. He half-turned to challenge when Melfallan suddenly clattered into sight, but relaxed as he recognized him, then saluted smartly. "Good morning, your grace."

Melfallan nodded. "Good morning."

Melfallan strolled over to the wall several yards from the soldier's post, then leaned on the rough, white stone of the gate battlement. He looked up at the bright sky and took in a deep breath of the brisk sea air, filling his lungs to the bottom. He shifted an elbow to find a more comfortable lounge, took another deep breath, then looked down at the bustle beneath him.

Sixty feet below his vantage, a steady traffic of carts and persons on foot passed in and out of the castle gates, traveling the road across the long bluff from the town to the castle on its headland and, in time, traveling back again. A faint sifting of dust rose above the road, quickly scattered by the brisk sea wind. Beyond the headland road, the ocean stretched to the horizon, seemingly without end, bright silver-blue today, with a tinge of green and deeper blue. A sea lark plummeted far over the sea, catching her dinner. Near the horizon two fishing boats bobbed on the waves, hunting the rich catch of late winter. Most of the fishing fleet now lay in port, not visible from this vantage, but soon would go out again to catch the last of the fishing before the Pass storms lowered in earnest. Every year in early spring, the Companion passed the Daystar in the sky, bringing its blue twilight to the early morning instead of evening, steadily advancing the length of the dawn. For reasons no one knew, Pass worsened the weather. Here in Yarvannet, known for its mildest of weathers in the Allemanii lands, the winds would blow furiously, lashing against the stone walls of the castle, whipping up the surf on the shore. In Mionn, the eastern earldom, the Pass storms were much worse, terrible gales that lifted roofs off houses and could smash a ship on the rocks in minutes.

Today, however, the weather was clear in Yarvannet, one of the bright winter mornings he loved. The sea wind blew strongly, richly scented of the sea, swirling the dust, lashing the surf, and buffeting him as he stood on the gate of his castle. Its touch quickly dried the sweat from his face, chilling his skin, and reached cool fingers into his mail, teasing under the padded clothing beneath it. He placed his helmet with its proud plumes on the battlement wall, and the wind promptly attacked the feathers, waving them wildly. He breathed deeply again, closing his eyes a moment. If one were patient in the waiting for them, some moments could give balm to the spirit.

The gate guard was watching Melfallan from the corner of his eye, no doubt wondering what the earl was doing now, but a casual glance turned the guard's attention back to his proper business of the gate watch.

The dust over the road swirled up into the sky as two wagons trundled toward the castle, carrying supplies or goods. Wheels creaked hollowly beneath the gate as another wagon passed beneath him, its driver hunched over the reins, followed by the echoing clatter of horses' hooves. He watched, quite unremarked from above, as Lord Garth Souvain and his wife, Joanna, rode out of the castle with hawks on their wrists, both gaily dressed for the occasion, and followed by four other lords and ladies, all intent on hawking. Melfallan's castle was currently filled with Yarvannet's gentry, all here for the continuing celebrations of his baby son's Blessing two days before. The lot would be here another week, perhaps ten days, busy with the nightly entertainments, the daily sports, the happy chatter with one another. More eyes to watch the earl, true, but nicely not right now. Melfallan shifted his weight comfortably, easing a small twinge in his injured arm. *Perhaps I should try gate hiding more often,* he thought lazily.

My Yarvannet, Melfallan thought wistfully, as he looked at the ocean. *Can love of a land give its lord strength for its keeping?* He would need all the strength he could find, from any source. The prior spring he had become earl suddenly, at the age of twenty-four, too young, he knew in his heart, to assume the title or the power. His grandfather, Earl Audric, had died of poisoning, by whose hand no one knew. All suspected Count Sadon Moresby of Farlost, Audric's most restless lord, but Melfallan had no proof of Sadon's guilt. Then one of the duke's toadies, Captain Bartol, had accused a Yarvannet girl of witchery, likely intending only a gambit for the duke to harass Melfallan. Hoping for her exoneration at trial, Melfallan had taken Brierley Mefell to the duke's capital, Darhel, where Duke Tejar had attempted her murder. She had escaped and now hid in a winter cabin in upper Airlie, guarded by one of his aunt's liegemen. Melfallan had bid her seek safety in Mionn in the spring, and perhaps she had already left on that journey eastward.

Out over the ocean, the sea lark plunged again, to rise triumphant with a tiny fish in her talons. He watched her soaring flight, dizzyingly upward, thinking of Brierley.

Is she safe? he worried. Where is she now? he wondered, and yearned that she might be here, standing next to him on the gate wall, so that he might ask what she was thinking. And Brierley would tilt her head to the side and smile at him, tipping the edges of his heart, and perhaps slip her hand under his elbow and lean closer to him; and he would give up his question freely and kiss her, here on the gate, in front of everyone. Melfallan sighed softly, caught as always in his dilemma. Without intending it, before he knew it had happened, he had fallen in love with Brierley Mefell, and he did not know where it would lead.

For her safety from the Allemanii laws that proscribed her life, as those shari'a laws condemned any shari'a who dared to live, he had hoped she might find sanctuary in Mionn, his father-in-law's eastern earldom, had hoped that Earl Giles might even be approached to shield her from the duke's malice. To Melfallan's dismay all those hopes had fallen into tatters, for Earl Giles had a quite different agenda. Ever since his arrival in Yarvannet for the baby's Blessing, Earl Giles had taken every opportunity to humiliate Melfallan in front of the Yarvannet gentry, perhaps to tempt the duke into believing the earls' alliance might be severed, dangling possibility, teasing the duke's greed. For what purpose? Only Giles knew, and he would admit nothing of his true plans. Two days ago at the Blessing ceremony, Giles had foolishly thrust his hand into the Blessing basin, burning his hand with poison someone had put in the water, intending the murder of Melfallan's baby son. Now his father-in-law lay nursing his injury in his comfortable upstairs suite in the castle, mildly embarrassed, no more than that, and likely undeterred in his secret intentions, whatever they were. Did he hope for the duke's own coronet? Who knew? Melfallan had tried to warn Giles, but the Mionn earls cared only about Mionn; and Giles Fauconer never listened to a lesser man's advice. Given that Giles thought all men lesser than himself, he accordingly never listened at all, as he had not listened to Melfallan. Earl Giles would pursue his plans stubbornly to the end, no matter what the cost to his daughter Saray and Melfallan, no matter what the cost to the other Allemanii lands.

Giles's plotting was only the latest of Melfallan's problems as earl, most of them not of his own making. Duke Tejar had hated Melfallan's grandfather, an emotion to which Earl Audric had been indifferent, even courted, and that hatred now extended to Melfallan. The shari'a witches had been proscribed by Allemanii law for three centuries, and those laws mandating death still existed, threatening Brierley's life. Even in Yarvannet the Courtrays' rule lay uneasy, for Audric had not attended to the divisions among Yarvannet's gentry, where unsuspected resentments, carefully tended plots, could end an earl unexpectedly, as such a plot, such a resentment—Sadon's, the duke's, some other enemy's—had ended his grandfather, leaving Melfallan bereft.

Melfallan's parents had both died young, his mother in childbed when Melfallan was nearly three, his father by Plague four years later. Melfallan remembered his mother mostly as a lovely vision bending over his nursery crib, but remembered his father better. Count Laurent was often at the hunt and diligent in the quadrangle, gifted with a natural athleticism and liking for the outdoors that Melfallan had inherited from him. Blond and tall, courteous in his manners, a noted musician, Laurent had shone at Audric's court, the glittering son, the future earl, the brilliant hope of the Courtrays. Even now Melfallan had a distinct memory of the sound of his father's voice in the Great Hall, as if Laurent sang nearby, the tones muffled only by a few intervening rooms and hallways, not by years of time.

How many years? Melfallan thought sadly, and counted them on his fingers. Nearly twenty years now, each with days and months when Laurent Courtray had not walked abroad in Yarvannet, not seen the suns dawn, not lived. Son of an earl greatly favored by Duke Selwyn, blessed by physical strength and beauty, a happy disposition, a beautiful wife sadly lost too young: how would Laurent have chosen when faced with Melfallan's choices? Would he have chosen wisely? Or did a life of ease dull a High Lord's ability to rule? Or would his father have found unsuspected strength, a strength he had perhaps passed to his son, or perhaps not? Melfallan would never know, not for certain.

I am too young to be earl, he thought wistfully.

"Well, here you are!" his aunt's voice said behind him, and he turned. Countess Rowena was superbly dressed today in lace and gray silk, her blond hair neatly styled, her head held proudly. She inspected him, making a point of it, then joined him by the wall. "The wind is cool up here," she remarked. "You could catch a chill and die young." She tsked, shaking her head.

"Yes, Aunt," he said and smiled down at her.

"Meekly said, nephew, but I see no improvement. You still stand on the battlement in your sweated mail, rushed by the wind. What are you doing up here anyway?"

"Why should you know?" he retorted, grinning at her. "But never mind that. What will satisfy you? I'm escaping Sir Micay, avoiding my gentry, watching wagons roll out and in, watching the sea, thinking about Father, admiring Earl Giles's subtlety—"

Rowena raised a gloved hand. "Enough." She slipped her hand comfortably inside his elbow and sniffed at the wind.

"Sorry you asked?" he teased.

"Not at all. I'm of an age, young man, when I don't have to regret anything, not anymore." She tossed her blond head and then showed her even, white teeth. "It's a rule: once a countess passes forty, she is excused anything. Do you believe that lie?"

"I'm glad to see you happy and enjoying yourself." He pressed her hand closer to his ribs. "I'm glad to see you alive." Only six weeks before, Rowena's marcher lord, Lord Heider, had attempted her murder, likely at the duke's prompting. Rowena had nearly died of the sword wound and its fever, but Brierley had braved discovery by traveling down to Carandon, lending her witch's gift to save Rowena's life.

"You know why I'm alive," Rowena said softly, lowering her voice so that only he would hear. "It was a great danger for her to attempt it. I had wanted to meet her, as you remember, but I promised you not to seek her out at the cabin. This was not the way I intended our meeting, but I'm blessed to have had it. Truly blessed, in more ways than the obvious. She told me much about herself, although she was still shy."

"What kind of things?" he asked promptly.

Rowena glanced at the soldier standing several yards away, although the guard stood clearly out of earshot. "Not here," she said, shaking her blond head. "We must be prudent, nephew, more prudent than ever." Rowena glanced at the guard again, shrugged slightly, then made a face. "In truth, one can be prudent beyond sensibility. That one is busy watching everything but us, as is his proper duty. Secret talk, dear nephew, is best done hidden in a corner, not on a castle wall, with our heads close together, our voices lowered, the quick glance about to see if anyone remarks our closeting, which of course all will do. That's the whole point of secret talk in corners, to intimidate by our whispered conspiracy, and thus one's rule is kept secure. I'm afraid our chat together on this gate wall hardly serves."

"You don't say," Melfallan retorted.

"I believe I did say. Perhaps Marina should check your hearing, nephew. Don't worry: I will tell you all in due time. Have you had any news from her?"

"How?" he asked in frustration. "I sent Jared Cheney to bring her home, but how he'll find her, I can't hazard."

"Cheney?" she prompted, frowning as she hunted for the name.

"The young Amelin soldier I knighted last month. Did you meet him in Darhel? He was part of Revil's company on *Star Dolphin*. No? He's Micay's nephew, a fact I hadn't known, and was a boyhood friend of Brierley's, too, someone who knew her well. Revil thought that I should knight someone our own age and suggested Jared, and so I did. And it was a good choice." He waggled his head at his aunt. "See how easily I'm led by my own cousin?" he teased. "Revil suggests and I obey: it's a fact of life. Have you ever wondered, Aunt, why you can't manage the same? With all your efforts, all your guile and wheedling and poses, you never quite—"

Rowena raised her hand. "Enough!"

"If you insist. We have our first woman soldier, by the way. Do you have any?"

Rowena tossed her blond head proudly. "No, I'm not asking 'any what' to indulge you. I will not be a party to your teasing, not in the least." Melfallan merely waited, smiling down at her, knowing she'd ask, couldn't help but ask. Despite Earl Audric's wishes otherwise, Rowena had insisted on learning the sword as a girl, and those skills had later satisfied a technical requirement to be regent for her son, and recently had saved her life when her border lord, Lord Heider, had attempted her murder. That his aunt could defend herself with the sword was a comfort to Melfallan, one that Rowena might need again, and perhaps soon. "What woman soldier?" Rowena asked reluctantly, then scowled at him fiercely.

"Her name is Evayne Ibelin, a tall woman, black-haired, and somewhat pretty. Count Parlie recommended her to us after the duke's rivermaster gave her trouble in Briding, and she settled in quite well with the castle guard. I'd have introduced her to you by now, but I sent her with Jared to Mionn, for whatever help she can lend. Micay says she's quite good with the sword, much like you are, a woman after your own heart, as it were." He paused. "I hope they can find Brierley. Ocean, how I hope that! If I sent Brierley into danger—" He stopped, then shrugged in frustration. "I need Brierley home, safe and protected. I need—" He stopped abruptly again. "I need her," he admitted. "I suspect you've guessed what's happened between us, and I worry that others might guess, as some already have. Revil knows, and likely I'm an open book to Sir James, perhaps even Sir Micay. I know our love is dangerous, Aunt. I know it's not fair to Saray. I know what I should do, but—" He broke off again, then looked away uncomfortably. "What you must think of me!"

Rowena pressed his arm affectionately. "I think you have many worries as earl, and have the strength to meet them," she answered. "I think all will be well in time, although I cannot list my good reasons for thinking so. I merely believe, because I will to believe and because I love you." She tipped her head, smiling up at him. "My guide for living, if you will."

Melfallan pressed his lips against her forehead. "You are part of my strength, Aunt."

She smiled. "And pleased to be so, dear one. And there's another person who knows: I see you have told Saray about Brierley. For all Saray's arts at pretending, she cannot hide much from me. A brave act, Melfallan, and a fair one, but I cannot tell you its solution. And, being quick-sighted in other directions, I see that Earl Giles still pursues his plots, not from my observations of that good lord's own behavior, for he hides himself away from me in his chambers, but from Robert's troubled moods. Giles inflicts his son too much; I think you should try to cheer your brother-in-law."

"Meddler," he accused. "Will you control my every action?"

"While I'm still here in Yarvannet, I will try diligently to do so, despite your foolish claim of immunity to my wiles. Once I leave you'll have to shift for yourself again, nephew." Her smile was dazzling, for all that it teased.

She looked beyond him at the headland road, her attention suddenly shifting, and Melfallan turned his head to look, too. A large party of horsemen and soldiers had emerged from the forest road onto the headland. Several horsemen rode in front at a leisurely pace, followed by the quick tramp of a full company of soldiers, lance heads winking in the sun. A bannerman rode in the lead, his lord's banner flipping briskly on the wind.

"The duke's banner, your grace," the gate guard said, approaching them. "A courier with a troop of soldiers."

"You have long sight, young man. Did the courier send word ahead of his arrival today?"

The soldier hesitated, his eyes flicking from Melfallan to Rowena. "Not that I know, your grace," he said. "It wasn't posted in this morning's orders."

"Hmm." Melfallan narrowed his eyes and watched his chief political problem ride straight toward his castle.

A full company of lancers was hardly necessary on Yarvannet's peaceful roads. Was it a comment by the duke, some intimation that Melfallan's rule faltered, making the roads unsafe? Or a reminder that the duke's army had many soldiers, surely more than Melfallan's, with more than enough to spare a full troop for a mere courier's safety?

"A full troop of lancers," Rowena murmured in displeasure, noting the same fact that he had. "What is the message there, I wonder?" she asked. "Since when does a courier travel with soldiers in his wake?" Rowena shook her head slowly. "He is dangerous, our duke. Have care, Melfallan." She pressed his arm and then left him, vanishing into the gatehouse with a swishing of her skirts. Melfallan turned back to the gate guard.

"Inform the watch captain of the courier's approach," Melfallan told him, "then go find Sir Bertrand. Tell him that I wish the courier and his party be made comfortable."

"Yes, your grace." The soldier saluted and left quickly on the errand.

Melfallan scowled at the riders now approaching his castle gate. Why is he here? he fretted. Why now? The courier's arrival during the Blessing festivities had to be deliberate timing, and Melfallan highly doubted the duke intended to send compliments for the occasion. It was another aggravation to annoy, another poking by the duke for certain fines he had demanded, privileges he claimed due, insult wrapped in a cloak of courtesy.

Melfallan studied the approaching group with narrowed eyes, considering his options. For a week now Melfallan's father-in-law had indulged himself in a pattern of disdainful behavior toward Melfallan that Earl Giles had obviously enjoyed, at least until the debacle at the Blessing. Even after that, Giles had continued his prideful ways, lying comfortably abed in his chambers, attended by his hovering wife, the powerful earl no one dared to question, not him, not Earl Giles of Mionn, never that. Earl Giles had played his arrogant act for so many years it had likely become engrained in his nature, making the man what was once a pose, if indeed Earl Giles had ever suffered from humility, even in his earliest youth.

He would borrow, he decided, from Earl Giles's ideas of intentional indifference, the studied snub. While the courier waited he would enjoy a leisurely bath, perhaps, the choosing of finer clothes, a pleasant chat with his wife, a brief huddling with his steward and justiciar on castle affairs, perhaps even a midday meal, and all the while the courier would be sitting in Melfallan's anteroom, waiting upon Melfallan's indulgence. Unannounced arrivals at Melfallan's castle, especially with excess soldiers tramping in one's dust, should have their penalty.

Melfallan lifted his helmet from the battlement wall and tucked it under his arm, took one last wistful look at the sky and ocean, then turned and left for the stair.

⁓

What do I do now? Lady Saray asked herself sadly. She was seated by the window in her chamber, the one that looked out at the sea. It was her favorite chair, where she might sit and find some comfort in the endless horizon, in the soft sounds of the sea that filtered upward to her castle window, in the changes of light during the day. She bent and undid the latch to edge the window open, for all it was still late winter and the draft was cool.

Saray knew that men often strayed from their wife's bed. Her father had engendered three children by other women, although her family carefully ignored that reality, never speaking of the other brothers and sister. Her brother, Robert, had likely also had affairs: his wife, Elena, had hinted once to Saray, but had never spoken further of it. And even her own Melfallan had strayed before, and more than once. Each time she had known within days, but had proudly said nothing and had pretended not to see what half the castlefolk knew, as she knew. It was a noble wife's lot, her mother had taught her, that proud and silent tolerance of a man's weakness in the flesh. But had her mother ever ached as Saray had ached, this pain near the heart that constricted and burned? Had her mother followed him secretly, on the lightest shoe leather, to confirm the terrible suspicion, and then keened as silently? When had her mother chosen instead to empty her heart, making it an empty room, without love, without life? When one could no longer feel, nothing could hurt.

Saray leaned her cheek upon her hand and sighed. It was something her mother would never discuss, however Saray pressed, as her mother would never discuss so many things. Lady Mionn had perfected the art of rigid silence, until all was silent and still within her breast, even for her youngest daughter. In such an empty room, with such a heart, nothing stirred. Nothing need engage the heart, not anymore. How many years ago had her mother made that choice? How many long and bitter years?

Melfallan was a different kind of man than her father, and perhaps, Saray admitted candidly, that difference was one of the reasons she loved him. At times Earl Giles was cold and abrupt, at other times passionate and hearty, a complicated man as Melfallan was complicated. Her father had married for duty, not love, and had fathered an heir and then two daughters to marry elsewhere for politics; afterward he had looked only to himself, allowing his wife to congeal into ice. Her mother now sat two floors below beside her father's bedside, doing her duty, her spine straight, her chin firm. It was useless to think of asking her, Saray told herself firmly, useless after so many years of useless asking, as many as Saray could remember.

She breathed in the sea air and looked out at the restless ocean. I could become my mother's kind of wife, she thought. I have the choosing. How easy it would be, she thought sadly, that death of the heart. So very easy. When one cannot love, one cannot be hurt. How simple. And when my son comes to me when he is older, she asked herself, will I be as rigidly cold, as unmoved by his tears when he cries, as irritated and harsh when he bothers me, wanting comfort I don't wish to give, and indeed no longer have to offer? Will I lecture him about empty rules that strip life of love, of purpose? Will I? She remembered the lonely years of her childhood, of her wistful hope for her mother's love, her mother's understanding, and never finding it, not once. No, for my son's sake, I will not. She stirred restlessly in her chair, and looked out again at the wide ocean.

I could punish Melfallan with words, she thought. I could rage at him and humiliate him in front of the court, torment him with my scorn and hatred. He is vulnerable to me, for he is ashamed—although not enough to give Brierley up, only to regret how he hurts me. Saray bit her lip, considering. Her sister, Daris, often lost her temper with her husband, with her servants, even with their father, and never regretted her passions afterward. Daris felt entitled to her bitter words, her scorn for others, her demands for the benefits of her high station. Daris never apologized, never admitted fault: all the world belonged to her use. Saray felt a mild touch of envy. Happier than me, she thought tentatively, and then wondered if it were true. She shook her head, baffled, and leaned her cheek on her hand. Yes, I could punish him with hatred—only I do not hate him. She closed her eyes wearily.

What do I do? She had known about the other women when they happened, the three affairs. Each time Melfallan had returned to Saray, but Saray now sensed, without knowing how she knew, that this time was different. The other women had not threatened Saray's position, not truly—she was Lady Yarvannet, the mother of Melfallan's heir, a high lady admired and praised by many, including her husband. Although he had bedded them, even loved them in his own way for a time, the others had not caught his heart, not truly. Brierley Mefell had. She knew it in his voice when he spoke of her, his eyes when he remembered her, in his stubborn failure to mend the matter with his wife by renouncing her. He will bring her back to Yarvannet, she knew. And then what? What will happen then?

Why can he not be content with me? Saray asked herself in anguish. He said he loved Brierley—and then said, in nearly the same breath, that he loved me, too. How can a man love two women and not just one? Was it part of their sex, that restlessness that could not find completion in one woman, one wife? Yet Saray knew of many devoted couples who found that completion in each other, and knew beyond any doubt that the husband had never looked away from his wife to others, as Saray had never looked away from Melfallan. Since she had first met Melfallan that summer evening in her father's castle in Mionn, she had never wanted any other man. She had never considered having her own affairs, when she might have, if only to hurt Melfallan as he had hurt her. Another choosing, she thought candidly: I could punish him with other men.

But he had said he loved her, and she believed him, and knew it was true. His truth had spoken from another place, quite away from their status in life as lord and lady and from the realities of their political marriage and the necessary alliances it had brought to Yarvannet, from a place existing solely between Melfallan and Saray. She looked down at the stitchery in her lap, her needle unmoving, her hands idle. He said he loved Brierley, and yet he still loves me: how could this be? Surely one must end before the other begins. Yet I believe him. How she knew that truth, she couldn't say, but she knew that fact, even if all other facts somehow eluded her. No, she would not punish him with other men.

I should, she thought sadly. Many wives would take that choice when they are betrayed. Is it another failing that I cannot? Another way I fail myself and even him? She felt tears sting her eyes, so many useless tears, tears that solved nothing.

What do I do? In a few days, perhaps a week, her family would leave Tiol to return to Mionn. For now, while they visited and the gentry continued to celebrate the baby's Blessing, she and Melfallan could pretend nothing was untoward, nothing amiss, but each day counted down one more day until that ended, and she still did not know what she would do. Her mouth quirked, then twisted into self-contempt. Poor Saray. Poor, helpless Saray.

How dare he do this to me? she thought indignantly. How dare *she* do this to me?

This Brierley, to whom Saray owed her life—

She remembered more of the night Audric was born than she had admitted to Melfallan. She remembered a beach where Brierley had defended her with a sword, her and her child, although Brierley scarcely knew Saray, and had no reason to love a noble wife and her infant child. Yet she had saved Saray, and later sang to the baby, walking him up and down the floor, guarding his life. She remembered still the sound of Brierley's voice, singing safety and peace into the night. *Oh, for such a gift!* Marina had exclaimed, when they thought she was sleeping, when they thought she slept and did not hear.

Perhaps the healing had connected them in some way, as if they were almost—friends. Were they friends? What did Brierley feel about Saray? Did she think Saray artificial and silly, a woman of vanity and pretending? Or did she think—

what? Saray shook her head again, baffled. Why can't I hate her? Why don't I grieve as I grieved the other times? Why do I simply nod to myself, thinking it right, when it's *not* right! He's mine, not hers. He belongs to me. Where is the rule that I must share him? Where is the necessity?

Oh, Brierley, you must advise me— Oh, surely not that. But Brierley might know what I should do. She thought on that for a time, almost amused by its irony, its incredible irony. She quirked her mouth, trying to feel amused, but failed. She looked out her window at the sea and sighed. Oh, my beloved, what a problem you have made for us! It would have been easier not to tell me, to hide it like you hid the other affairs, as Father hid all his affairs from Mother. Why did you tell me about Brierley? Why?

It is his nature to tell me, Saray decided, to be honest when dissembling would be easier. It was one of the reasons she loved him, had found in him truth after her parents gave her only lies. Melfallan always chose the path he thought right, even in this. She could define the qualities in him against other men, puzzle out her list of differences, but she did not need the accounting. He was worthy of trust, worthy of her love. She had made him her whole world, and would not change that now.

But if not ice nor anger nor lust, what do I do about it? Saray asked herself in frustration. Why don't I *know?*

She heard footsteps in the hall and caught her breath as she recognized them as his. Her stitchery slipped from her fingers, and she bent to retrieve it as Melfallan walked into the room. She hesitated, still stooped, and did not want to look up, not until she had her answers. She must know what to do, but she did not.

"Saray? Are you all right?"

Saray fumbled for the cloth and then reached for the bundles of threads that had fallen with it. Then Melfallan was kneeling beside her, helping her collect the scattered bundles. She smelled the dusky sweat on his body, and remembered that he had planned sword practice this morning. He will want a bath, she thought distractedly. Where is his manservant Philippe? She should find him and order the bath. She straightened, took the several bundles Melfallan gave her to add to the others, then lifted her face and made herself smile at her husband. He studied her face intently.

"Saray?" he asked quietly. "Can I help?"

Saray opened her mouth, but not one word came out, not one. She shut her mouth foolishly, then opened it again, flapping like a fish. She clamped her lips together and closed her eyes in despair, then sighed despite herself. Melfallan took the stitchery from her hands, then lifted her fingers to his mouth for a soft kiss. She opened her eyes and looked at him, kneeling in front of her chair, then gently tugged one of her hands loose and caressed the side of his face and tousled his blond hair gently. "Did you win against Sir Micay this morning?" she asked.

"Sort of. Anything short of total defeat is an accomplishment when it's Sir Micay."

He caught her hand and kissed it again, and she pressed her fingers a moment against his mouth. "Saray?" he persisted.

She sighed. "I've been thinking about my choices," she said reluctantly. "My mother chose ice, becoming cold and empty. You can't be hurt ever again when you're ice." Was that dread in his eyes? She did not wish him to fear her. She shifted her hand to lay her palm against his face, caressing it. "Or I could have affairs to get even, but I don't want anybody else, only you."

Melfallan caught his breath and closed his eyes, as if in pain, as likely it was. She leaned forward and touched her forehead to his, leaning comfortably against him. "I've been puzzling what to do," she murmured, "and all I can think is that I should ask Brierley. Isn't that odd? Daris says a shari'a witch can steal your soul, but I remember Brierley's song that night, its peace, its safety. If Brierley is like her song, I understand why you love her." She lifted her head and looked into his eyes, and saw his anguish.

"I never meant to hurt you this way, Saray," he whispered. "I never wanted to hurt you." His hands pressed hard on hers.

"I know that." She caressed his face again, and then took time to reorder his sweaty hair from her tousling, smoothing it back into place. "I know many things about you, more than you think I do. I don't understand how I can make so many mistakes when I know you this well, but so it is."

"Don't turn into ice, Saray," he said earnestly. "If not for me, then for Audric's sake."

"For you *and* Audric, I won't."

"And your own affairs, well, that would be fair, I suppose." Melfallan looked decidedly uncomfortable, the way he always looked when he had to struggle hard to do what was right, as he saw it. How funny, she thought, that he would offer. How funny, that he would think she might.

"Never," she said firmly. "As I told you, I want only you—and I don't want to share you." She sighed. "That is my dilemma, Melfallan Courtray. It seems you *are* shared." She tapped her finger against his nose. "And you are not uncomfortable enough to please me; unhappy, yes, even anguished at this moment, wishing you could have both her and me without hurt, without harm. And that is the love I can trust, the place between us that exists despite my mistakes." Saray smiled at him sadly. "If I punished you, would you give her up?"

He hesitated, then let his shoulders slump. "No," he muttered unhappily. "I can't."

"Is she that remarkable a woman?" Saray asked curiously. "Is she that different from me?"

"Saray—" Melfallan said helplessly.

"I love you, Melfallan. I always will. I just don't know what to do." Saray leaned back in her chair and sighed. "Please don't look that anguished. I'm not getting even by hurting you back. If you like we can talk about something else—such as your need for a bath. You smell quite distinctly."

Melfallan shook his head. "That's too easy, Saray."

"Pretending usually is. But we *can* talk later, can't we? Go enjoy your bath. You truly need one." With an effort she tipped her head to the side and smiled at him again.

"Why don't you join me?" Melfallan suggested, surprising her. "If we get arranged correctly, I'm sure we can both fit."

"I don't smell," Saray retorted, shaking her head. Melfallan grinned, then caught her hand and pulled her to her feet, scattering her stitchery to the floor. Saray started to bend to pick it up, but Melfallan pulled her tightly against him, then lightly kissed her nose, then bent his head to kiss her soundly on the lips.

"That wasn't what I meant," he said, and kissed her again. "Yours is the bigger bathtub. Let's go see."

"Melfallan!" she protested. "What will the servants think?"

"So?"

"It's the middle of the morning! I already bathed."

"So?" he said again. "Do you melt if you take more than one bath a day?"

Saray tossed her chin. "I don't know. I haven't tried."

"So?" he insisted.

Saray glared another moment. "It's not proper," she declared firmly. "Either for the bath or what you're intending afterward." She shook her head coyly. "I know that look, my lord. You can't fool me." Melfallan hesitated, then sighed softly and released her.

"I suppose you're right," he said, and turned away. With a pang, Saray suddenly knew she had failed him again—but how? Because I won't take a bath with him? For only that? Or because he wants to bed me—at the middle of the day? When all the servants would know and talk about it? Because of *that?* But Melfallan was already leaving the room, and it was too late.

Why do I fail him? Saray thought in frustration. Who can tell me? She bent to pick up her stitchery and sat down again in her chair. How? she asked herself vainly, and blinked through tears as she took the next stitch with her needle.

Who can I ask? she thought in frustration. Who might give her the clue, the simple answer that made all things clear? She could not ask her mother or Daris: neither would understand, neither would care. Who else did she know? Who was a friend who might know the answer?

Although she would never admit it to Melfallan, Saray did not have an easy life among Yarvannet's noble ladies. Lady Alice Tolland was a domineering and self-important woman who reminded Saray too much of her mother's bullying; and Lord Eldon's two daughters, whatever their father's noble rank as port lord, were unattractive and dumpy and still merchant's daughters oddly elevated to noble rank, never fitting in. Lord Valery's wife rarely said anything, being rather stupid, and Lord Tauler's wife, another older woman like Lady Tolland, was commoner-born and rarely at Tiol. She toyed with the idea of asking her senior lady-maid, Jenny Halliwell. Jenny was a knight's daughter, minor nobility, true, but had always seemed friendly. Better, she and Melfallan had known each other since childhoold, and still seemed friends. Perhaps Jenny would know. She considered another moment, then shook her head sadly. One could not ask a ladymaid about such a matter: it just wasn't done. Besides, Jenny wasn't yet married—how could she know what Saray needed? How could she understand a husband's failings when she had no husband?

No, of all the ladies at the court, the most beautiful and accomplished lady wife was Lady Joanna Souvain, to Saray's sincere admiration. Joanna was stylish, unafraid to speak her mind, and openly adored by her handsome husband, Lord Garth. Joanna always entered any room with grace and confidence, her blonde head held high, her dresses magnificent. And Joanna seemed to like Saray for herself, not for Saray's rank, even greater reason. She never sniped like the others, seemed always happy to see her friend Saray when she and Garth visited Tiol.

Saray's hand stilled, her needle poised, and her heart lifted slightly. Had Garth ever had affairs? she wondered. Garth was handsome enough to attract other women's attention, as Melfallan did. Saray had never heard the slightest rumor, despite how much the ladies chattered, but could it be? If he had, how had Joanna managed? Even if he hadn't,

Saray thought, perhaps Joanna would know what Saray was doing wrong as wife. Garth openly adored her, for all the court to see. Saray considered another careful moment, afraid to believe it might be the hope she needed, and then smiled in happy relief. Yes, I will ask Joanna! Of course! Joanna will know what I should do!

Saray smiled at the sea beyond her window, then leaned to close the pane against the chill. Yes, she thought happily, and nodded. Yes.

5

$\mathcal{M}$elfallan enjoyed a refreshing bath, with his manservant, Philippe, hovering to help, then escaped to his tower for the rest of the morning. After the duke's courier had waited two hours in the Great Hall, no doubt fuming as he paced, he had demanded to be shown to his compartments, and made much of seeing his companion knight and soldiers settled, their horses groomed and watered, his men fed from Melfallan's kitchens. And all the while Melfallan was sitting in his tower study, exquisitely undisturbed by everyone except by Philippe, who brought him regular reports. Disturb the earl in his study? the courier was told, hands fluttering in horror. Gasp. We never do that, my lord. It just isn't done. Gasp.

Melfallan looked up as another tap came at his study door, and saw Philippe come to attention in the doorway.

"Now he's taking a nap," Philippe reported. "He said he was fatigued from his long travel. Earl Giles is arguing with Count Robert in the earl's sickroom, and your lady wife is visiting Lady Joanna."

"And Countess Rowena?" Melfallan asked.

"Visiting the baby in the nursery."

"Thank you, Philippe."

Philippe hesitated a moment, then shook his gray-haired head, sighed, and left. Melfallan chuckled softly. Philippe Artois had tended Melfallan's since Melfallan's boyhood, always clucking over his comforts, arranging his clothes, straightening each wrinkle, but never even thought to question Melfallan's decisions, whatever they were. It just wasn't done. Gasp.

Melfallan threw down his pen on the table, then leaned back in his chair and stretched. He got up to ease his cramped back, winced as his arm hurt with the movement, then slipped up his sleeve to poke at his bruise. The mail had left perfect blue and red circles in his flesh, decorating him, and it was his own fault. He tentatively flexed his arm, twisting it through a parry, winced again.

"Ouch," he announced to the room, and sat down again.

He lounged a moment in his chair, looking at the window and the wide blue sky beyond it. *I wish Saray had tried the bath,* he thought wistfully. He had intended some playful fun, something to lift Saray's unhappy mood, to ease the pain he had caused her, but she had misread him again, thinking he wanted sex. Nudity for Saray had no other connotations, and his wife was shy about showing her body to him even after six years of marriage. Careful clothing at all times, all occasions, even in the bedroom, was one of Saray's lady rules: after six years, he knew them all. Duty ruled most of his wife's behavior, that concept carefully marshaled into the list of lady rules that her mother had taught her in girlhood. In truth, Melfallan wasn't sure if Saray even liked to bed with him, and the not knowing troubled him. If he asked her, she would say yes, of course, but from truth or because a lady rule said she must? He shook his head unhappily. *What will the servants think?* It was Saray's first reaction to any spontaneous impulse, this idea that one's outward behavior was everything, that the rules must be followed with exquisite care, as if she and Melfallan were constantly on display, watched and examined and judged every minute of the day, as he supposed they were.

What do I do? he wondered. *I know what I should do, what Saray has every right to demand that I do, but I cannot.* He closed his eyes wearily. Whenever he thought of Saray, he inevitably thought of Brierley, caught in his unfair comparisons, his longing for Brierley, his wishes Saray might be happy, the impossibility of it all. *I won't give up Brierley,* he told himself stubbornly, but in the deepest corner of his heart, he feared he might have to, that some inexorable choice of rule, some misfortune, would appear to force him away from her, and that he might strangle slowly afterward, emptied and useless from long, endless years of supposed living.

He couldn't bear the idea of it, and thrust it away.

Is she safe? he worried. Where is she now? A week ago he had sent Jared and Evayne to find Brierley and bring her home to Yarvannet. How Jared would find her, he couldn't hazard, but witchery often involved odd chance, unlikely outcome. What would happen then, once Brierley was home, he couldn't guess either: he cared only that Brierley was safe in Yarvannet, whatever Ocean's blessing brought them afterward. It would be weeks before Melfallan had any further word about her. He took a deep breath, then forced himself to accept that fact.

"Patience, fair lord," Brierley's voice said next to his ear. Melfallan nearly jerked off his chair in surprise, then scowled ferociously as he reseated himself.

"That's not funny, Everlight," he growled, then heard its laugh. Recently the Everlight, the ancient witchly device that guarded Brierley's sea cave beyond the headland, managed to speak to him even in daytime, not content with invading his dreams at night. Each time, its voice startled him badly, making him drop whatever he was holding or trip or gasp or otherwise violently twitch, and each time the Everlight thoroughly enjoyed the surprise. Poke, poke.

He smiled as the Everlight laughed again somewhere nearby, under the table, outside the window, in the hallway outside, everywhere and nowhere. It was Brierley's laugh, remembered from the few times he had heard her laugh; and that laugh and the Everlight's other presence in his life were the Everlight's gift and grace, a comfort to him. He supposed he should wonder at his sanity, but he fully believed in the lady who visited his dreams, unreal as she was. Through their dreams the Everlight had allowed him to explore the contents of Brierley's cave in the sea rock beyond the headland, although he had never physically set foot there, and he had read Brierley's array of journals, both those of her predecessors in the cave and Brierley's own. It was a way to understand her better, as was another shade, Thora Jodann, who also visited his dreams through the Everlight's witchery. Thora was also an expression, an essence, of what Brierley was, what all the shari'a had been and might be again, and he treasured the comfort the Everlight gave him until Brierley could come home again.

Soon, he wished yearningly. Whatever comfort the Everlight brought him in its illusions, he still wished for the real woman, with a yearning that sometimes threatened to overwhelm him almost as a physical pain. The Everlight had told him he shared a bond with Brierley, a witchly bond called a resonance, and perhaps it was true. In Witchmere, one of the guardians there had wounded him with its shooting fire; and Brierley had healed him of the wound, somehow going too far into the healing and linking their souls. The ancient shari'a had feared and avoided the sea witch's resonance, for it joined the two permanently in life and doomed them to the same fate in death. Or so the Everlight had explained.

He didn't understand the Everlight's dread, nor did he fully believe in this bond it claimed: he only wanted Brierley home with him, safe under his protection. What happened then with Brierley—well, perhaps that lay as much between himself and Saray as with Brierley. And whatever grief the resonance later brought to him, he would accept that as the price of their love.

Through Brierley he had found a purpose he had never expected, a purpose of the heart in loving her, a purpose of his rule in righting an old wrong and preserving the shari'a world the Allemanii had nearly destroyed. He had expected to rule as his grandfather had ruled all his life, outmaneuvering the duke when needed, giving justice to his folk, fathering heirs to continue the Courtray rule, and otherwise

living his lord's life with its comforts: all the efforts of a
dutiful High Lord careful in his rule. He had expected
those efforts would satisfy him eventually, if only by the
passing of more years. He had thought his restlessness a
defect in his character, a silly wish to avoid his duty as earl
by wishing for a different life than an earl's, any life that
would spare him the worries—perhaps a comfortable life
as a scholar, or a life at sea as a fisherman, perhaps even a
soldier's life, where questions of loyalty and duty were
simpler. But perhaps the restlessness was never a defect,
only a search for a better purpose than that given him by
his rank, one he had now found in Brierley and her shari'a
people. Perhaps. The proof had yet to come; at present he
had only the hope.

But what a problem I've made, he thought tiredly, when
Yarvannet has more desperate worries. Perhaps he should
worry more about the Everlight's warnings about this bond,
but he simply hadn't room to worry about shari'a beliefs he
didn't understand. Perhaps he should worry more about
Saray, and how he might manage to live onward if he did
what he should and renounced Brierley as was proper.

He shied from the thought, then stood up restlessly and
paced the short length of the room from door to window. Finally he stopped and looked out on the harbor he loved, the
sea stretching forever to the right, the rising green hills of
the coastal mountains to the left.

Will my son love Yarvannet as much? he wondered wistfully. He hoped so. Yarvannet was an anchor for Melfallan's life, a strength he had drawn upon often in his short
months as earl. He wished his son the same blessing, when
Audric came into his own as earl. An anchor for my living,
he thought. As is Brierley, his heart whispered. You know
it's so. When will she come home to me? he yearned.
When will I know that she is safe? Melfallan bowed his
head and sighed.

Another soft tap came at the door, and Melfallan turned
toward it, welcoming the distraction from thoughts he didn't
want to continue. "Yes?" he called out.

The door cracked open and Philippe stuck his head around the door-edge. "The courier asked me to tell you," he announced gravely, "that he's the son of Lord Dail, whom everybody knows is the duke's chief advisor and a very important man in Darhel, and he's not accustomed to waiting three hours on anybody. I told him that's too bad and it can't be fixed, and perhaps he might resume his nap. The gentleman knight who's with him laughed, and not very nicely either."

Melfallan snorted with amusement. "You have a gift, Philippe."

"I thought you might think so, your grace. Sir James told me to tell you that the courier is Lord Dail's third son, not the first or the second, and that napping is good for one's health, even for a son of Lord Dail. Sir James also said he'd like to come up to see you about something, but it can wait if you don't wish the intrusion."

"Tell him that's fine. I'll see him now."

"Yes, your grace." Philippe withdrew and closed the door.

A few minutes later another rap at the door brought in his justiciar, Sir James, and Melfallan waved him into one of the chairs at the table. Tall and lean, dressed in his customary midnight blue, Sir James was Melfallan's tutor, counselor, and right hand as earl, as he had similarly served Melfallan's grandfather for over thirty years. To Melfallan's recent surprise, he had learned Sir James had not always approved of Audric's choices, although Sir James had labored to create the political confusions in the duke's own lands that Audric had wanted. Together Earl Audric and Sir James had made secret friends of Parlie Lutke, the count of Briding, which lay north of Yarvannet, and had strengthened Yarvannet's ties with Airlie to the northeast through Rowena's marriage to Count Ralf. Melfallan's own marriage to the other earl's second daughter had laid another strand of the web around the duke, confining the duke's choices, undermining the duke's loyalties. In response the duke had meddled in Yarvannet, no doubt courting Count Sadon's resentments, perhaps meddling with other lords. Had Earl Audric's actions been wise? Melfallan wondered. Or had his grandfather's dislike for Selwyn's youngest son, a dislike fully shared by Duke Selwyn himself, led him into rashness? How much of Yarvannet's current danger lay rooted in his grandfather's choices? Melfallan grimaced, still uncomfortable with criticism of the old man he had loved.

All I want is the truth, he thought stubbornly, whatever it is, as he watched Sir James open a book at a marker, then lay out several legal papers on the table. Unfortunately, truth was a hard fact to find among the machinations of the Allemanii High Lords. The High Lords practiced subtlety as a great art, hiding their intentions, betraying each other for their own gain, restless, active, undaunted. They justified their treacheries as the necessity of rule, and greatly admired the text written by the first Hamelin duke, the duke who had betrayed his wife's father and taken the coronet by misdirection and murder. In his text Duke Rainalt counseled the pretense of virtue, for all lords admired for virtue enjoyed an easier rule, but also advised as easy a readiness to discard that virtue for political necessity. Lies were tools of rule, he solemnly advised, and great promises of loyalty only the means to weaken one's rivals through their foolish believing, the most solemn of alliances mere whimsy if the needs of one's rule bid elsewhere. Rainalt had advised the preemptive murder of rivals, as Rainalt himself had murdered the Lutke heirs in Briding, and so had begun the tradition of murdering all the house of a defeated lord, as Earl Audric had murdered when he conquered Yarvannet. All that mattered to Rainalt, it seemed, was the keeping of one's rule, however that might be accomplished. Melfallan had studied Rainalt's text during his schooling with Sir James, a requirement of any High Lord's political education, and still returned to it often, although in truth he did not know what he thought of it. He shook his head slightly and looked away at the window again.

"Your grace," Sir James said, and cleared his throat, then handed him one of the papers. They conferred about the minor legal matter Sir James had chosen for Melfallan's attention, agreed on the solution, and Sir James then left, not once having mentioned the third son of Lord Dail. Earl Giles wasn't alone in subtlety, Melfallan thought wryly. By a simple trivial errand and a determined silence about any courier who might be waiting downstairs, Sir James had made clear his support without admitting anything of the kind, a bit of game playing he knew would amuse Melfallan, to that useful cheering of his earl. Melfallan shook his head fondly.

Melfallan got up to pace again, walking up and down the short length of his tower room, his clasped hands working behind his back. Both he and Sir James knew what the courier brought—more demands for the exorbitant amercements the duke had chosen to levy, more nagging about Lord Landreth, the disgraced son of Count Sadon whom Melfallan had sent to Darhel for trial, a trial the duke delayed beyond reason and without excuse. A few months ago Melfallan had sought to prosecute Landreth for several rapes, but the duke had intervened by taking Landreth's appeal and then doing nothing whatsoever about it. No doubt Lord Landreth currently lived a life of leisure in the duke's palace, pampered with fine clothes and women when he wanted them, strutting his assumed importance in front of all the duke's court. Melfallan narrowed his eyes, sensing danger to Yarvannet in the rift between himself and Farlost's count, but at the moment he hadn't a clue what to do about it. His grandfather had mistreated Count Sadon for thirty years, and Sadon's son was a fool, believing anything Tejar said. What had Duke Tejar promised him now? Melfallan asked himself grimly. My earl's circlet? Earl Landreth of Yarvannet? Landreth might be fool enough to believe it, and perhaps his father did, too.

Who had poisoned Earl Audric last spring? he fretted. Sir James still had not found that answer, despite long investigations and the constant suspicion directed at Farlost. Who had made an attempt on the baby's life two days ago by poisoning the Blessing basin? Sir James had arrested Norris Mallory, one of the baby's manservants, but Melfallan seriously doubted the young man's guilt, despite Norris's quick saddling of a horse in an attempt to flee. If Norris were indeed guilty, it challenged Melfallan's judgment of people, for Norris had seemed reliable, cheerful, and totally devoted to his son's care. Sir Bertrand, the castle's chief steward, had recommended Norris to the nursery post, having the same opinion of Norris's good character. How could they both be so wrong? Melfallan shook his head, baffled, then grimly contemplated another problem he might soon face. His grandfather had hanged several men for capital crimes within Melfallan's memory, and decades ago had killed most of Yarvannet's nobility when he crushed Earl Pullen's rebellion. As Yarvannet's current earl, Melfallan had not ordered a death, not yet. *Can I hang Norris?* he wondered sadly. *Am I capable of hanging someone I knew and trusted? Must I? But if I don't, do I embolden other traitors to act?*

He stopped in front of the window again and watched one of Tiol's fishing ships sail out of the harbor, its white sails spread before the wind. It was nearly noon, rather late to be leaving for the fishing grounds, but the fishing season had been exceptionally good this winter, with rich catches and moderate weather: that fine prosperity allowed leisure to be lazy on a suitable day, sailing out more for the sport and the brisk wind in the sails than worry for one's living.

I want to go fishing, Melfallan decided, as he watched the ship's sails catch the wind. *Who's to say I can't? I'm the earl. All I have to do is march down to the dock and climb aboard* Southwind, *now tied up right over there, and tell Master Cronin to put to sea. We'd sail out to the horizon, the wind booming in the sails, the ship's motion lively, and all would be fresh and new, untroubled by problems I can't solve. Only for an afternoon,* he wished earnestly. *Half a day at most, no more. Is that so much to ask?*

And likely half the castle would follow him down to the

docks if he tried, wondering what the earl was doing now. They'd stand on the wharf, pointing at him and chattering to each other, shaking their heads, amazed. Melfallan sighed, then promised himself that someday he'd do it, not minding that they pointed and gawked, not in the slightest, but sadly not today. He watched the ship turn gracefully past the rocks at the mouth of the harbor and pass out of his view, then with another sigh turned and left his tower to rejoin the day.

⤙⤚

That night as he slept Melfallan and the Everlight watched the ocean from atop Brierley's island home. A winding stair led several man-heights upward from the central chamber of Brierley's cave, its treads deeply worn by three centuries of ascent by the cave's occupants, and emerged between two tall door stones on top of the island. Water splashed eighty feet below the ledge, surging powerfully against the hard stone of the sea rock. On the far horizon, the Companion had nearly set, its flattened orb spreading dim blues and silvers across the water. The air was cool, scented by the smell of salt. Tonight, as it usually did when it sent him dreams, the Everlight made itself an illusion of Brierley, giving to Melfallan the form, the face, the voice, and the smile, comforting him with Brierley's presence. He treasured that presence, and believed it made life possible until he held the real woman again. Whimsical, often prim, and easily distracted by the patterns it loved, the Everlight sometimes slipped in its pretending as Brierley or Thora and became someone else entirely, a very special self Melfallan had also come to cherish. He lightly kissed the top of her ear.

"She often watches the sea from here," the Everlight murmured. "She likes to watch the ocean moving." She gestured at the water. "Immensity lends its own perspective, fair lord. During my three centuries in Yarvannet, I've found a similar purpose in watching the sea. Here life can be heard in the movement of the water, the cry of the sea larks, the wind through the trees beyond the beach. It is harder to hear life when entombed."

"Entombed?" he asked.

She shrugged, a delicate lift of the shoulders. "I was made in Witchmere, as you know, and I spent my first forty years there. Dripping water, cold drafts, an occasional witch passing by on some errand to the storerooms, with no time to stop and talk to me. They put me in a distant corridor, you see, as one of the wardens of the northern gate, a gate little used by Witchmere's folk and almost forgotten. I was lonely there."

Melfallan pressed his face into her hair. "We passed an Everlight when we went down to find Megan. Its face was cold and dark."

The Everlight sighed. "Most of them must be dead now. I am old and losing my faculties, one by one, but I am still living. Perhaps I still live because I could listen to the sea, like now. Perhaps." She lifted her chin and sniffed the wind. "But perhaps, too, not much longer. All things close in time, even me."

"You're wistful tonight," he said. "And sad. Why?"

"Not sad, I think—just old. I feel my years weigh upon me tonight. How many sunsets have I watched on this shore, the thousands of sunsets, too often alone? At times many years lay between the witches I tended, while I waited and listened for my next witch-daughter, fearful there might not be another, that the Blood might fail, even here in Yarvannet. I am a dayi's Everlight, fair lord: the dayi, the healer witches of the shari'a, live for other persons as much as themselves. Their being is focused on what they perceive in others, and on what they can lend through their gift, binding persons, lending life. As with them, loneliness is hard for me. I have spent many lonely days on this small island, too many." She pressed his hands at her waist, then turned in his arms to smile up at him.

"There: you can stop worrying that our dreams burden me, that comfort flows in only one direction."

He smiled. "I'm pleased you say so. But I still wonder if you're real, and what you are, Everlight." He regarded her a moment, pursing his lips. "What exactly *are* you anyway?" It was his frequent question that always prompted an answer, but never what he expected and never the same twice.

"What am I?" she asked, amused. "Ah, shall we discuss descriptives and their limitations? If I asked what *you* are, Melfallan Courtray, what would you say? Earl of Yarvannet, Saray's husband, father to Audric, grandson of Earl Audric, Duke Tejar's foil? Or, simplest of all, a man, the easiest answer applicable to your sex. Yes, that will do."

"And, simplest of all, you're a woman?"

"In a sense, I suppose I am." She turned back to the sea, wriggling comfortably within his arms to settle herself again. "But then, too," she continued, "each descriptive requires a contrary, and by that contrast we are further defined. You are not a count but an earl, and a man and not a woman." She gestured airily. "And I am not a gentleman knight nor a carpenter nor a sailor nor a tree. Yet I might fish, and if I like, I might build a chair, odd as that task might be for a dream-friend. And so might you, if you chose. We can learn many things about ourselves by naming what we are and what we aren't, and then applying the contraries to our further elaboration."

Melfallan sighed in mild irritation, which amused the lady in his arms all the more. It had definitely been a snicker, somewhere in front of his chest and above his arms. "All I asked was—"

"You assume that I know what I am; perhaps I don't." She nodded to herself. "Yes, perhaps that is true."

"Somewhere in there," Melfallan pointed out, "I notice you still didn't answer my question. What *are* you, Everlight?"

"I noticed that, too. Qualities, too, can define: 'I am observant,' you could claim, and then proceed through your other qualities, each implying a contrary of its own, and from that we can act."

"Enough!" he protested, then laughed softly. "I *observe* that you've decided to be yourself tonight, Everlight."

"Ah, and what is that?"

"An Everlight likes word puzzles, usually beyond reason." He tightened his arms around her again. "You build patterns out of thoughts, like piling up stones or weaving a net. Does Brierley do this, too?"

"Not as much as I, in fact not often at all, for I am an Everlight and she is a sea witch. Not a contrary there." She frowned. "We take from the same essence, but in different ways, another way to define. Is not alikeness better than difference when we seek truth?"

"I suppose," he said indulgently.

The first stars appeared in the sky as the Companion's blue twilight slowly faded. The wind lifted over the ledge, scented with the salt of the sea, and tugged at their clothes, teased with invisible fingers light and cool. Melfallan breathed in the sea air, then closed his eyes a moment, content beyond words to be standing here on this ledge with Brierley's Everlight, for all it was a dream, for all it might be fancy and never real. The Everlight had begun these dreams with him, responding to his longing for Brierley, and had brought him comfort beyond his expectations. However he might fret while awake, here was peace without struggle; here was love, a different love than Brierley's, but love all the same. *How can I not love someone she herself loves?* the Everlight had asked, thinking the love she gave him only part of the illusion that she created for him, but the love, too, was distinct, the whimsical and gentle love of an Everlight, a love Brierley had also known. What other wonders had the ancient shari'a made, perhaps not knowing the whole of what they crafted? What else had they built into their hidden world, a world of thought and magic only they knew? He looked up at the darkening sky with its panoply of stars. Beneath it the Companion's azures and violets colored the moving sea in broad bands of color to the far horizon, defining the waves into ever-moving light. Suddenly he wished to live always in this lovely dream world, a wish unwise and impossible, but a wish nonetheless. He pressed his face against her hair and sighed.

She laughed softly. "You're being remarkably patient with my prattling, fair lord, man of action that you are. Yet in another life, you might have been a scholar, Melfallan, in love with thought and words as I am. Have you not thought so?"

"Perhaps," he said. "But in another life, surely: in this one I am an earl."

"Even in this life, you could have been things other than earl, as you have in other turnings of Mother Ocean's willing. A castellan, a soldier of Airlie, a fisherman's son—there was truth in the vision sent to you by the Four. The essence remains from life to life, something more than mere earl or Allemanii or man. All souls are unique, and all are blessed by the Four in one way or another." She tipped her head to the side and considered. "Perhaps even mine. Am I not also one of Mother Ocean's creatures? And with all the souls I have met, each becoming in their way part of me, could I not acquire a soul of my own?" She paused. "Perhaps enough to be reborn," she whispered to the sea and sky, and he heard the yearning in her voice, as if she spoke of a wish long cherished and long concealed.

"Is that what you want?" he asked softly. "To be reborn as a mortal woman?"

She sighed and leaned her head on his shoulder, and together they looked out at the fading twilight, the first pinpoint stars. "What I wish, you ask? An Everlight is not defined by wishing. That belongs to mortal souls, not a thing crafted by witchery. But I sometimes wonder if I, too, could truly live, with my own descriptives of shari'a and woman, mother and teacher. I wonder if someday I, too, will walk on the roads as my daughters have walked, perhaps heal as they have healed, not be bound within a porcelain box. I wonder if three centuries of service, of tending my beloveds, for surely they are my beloveds, my daughters as surely as if I, too, were flesh—I wonder if that will be enough to win me rebirth. Do you think so?"

Although she spoke lightly, Melfallan again heard the longing in her voice, the wistfulness, the shade of grief that it might not be true.

"The future is not set," he whispered in her ear, and saw the curve of her smile on her half-averted face.

"You tease me now," she said comfortably.

"No." He gently turned her around to face him squarely. "I believe in your soul, Everlight. I am certain of it." He looked down into her gray eyes, Brierley's eyes, and lifted his hand to caress her face. "Certain," he repeated, for her eyes were still shadowed with doubt. "You've appeared to me as Brierley and sometimes as Thora: if you could be yourself, whoever that is, since you obviously won't answer my question about what and whom and by what nature, what would you look like?" He touched her hair. "Would your hair be brown like hers? Would you be thin or plump, tall or short? How would you choose your descriptives?

"Umph," he said next, for suddenly a different woman stood within his embrace. She was slim like Brierley but not as tall, with delicate features, her deep auburn hair bound up in braids, her chin pointed, her mouth a shade too large for prettiness, and her eyes a vivid blue. "Umph," he said again, and blinked down at her.

The girl smiled impishly, the blue eyes dancing with mischief. "You forget this is a dream," she teased. "You forget it is all my illusion, to change as I will."

"A useful way to remind me," he retorted mildly. "I suppose I invited it."

"As you did."

He smiled and took a moment to brush back a vagrant strand of hair from her face, making it a caress as his hand lingered, then studied her face another moment and nodded. "I like it," he decided. "You look like you, if you can understand that odd thought. Will you do me a favor, Everlight?"

"What favor?"

"Sometimes be yourself with me, this image of what you'd like to be someday. After all you've given me these past weeks, I'd like to help you feel less alone, for you are lonely, dear one, even when I'm here with you. You worry you might be foolish and mislead me, and from this great grief may happen, but I have no such fear." He touched the tip of her nose with his finger. "You are the essence of the dayi and, like Brierley, any misstep is excused for the grace of what you are. Perhaps when you were made in Witchmere you were only a device, but you are more now, far more. And another favor—when Brierley comes home, be more than just Thora with her." He caressed her cheek, her chin, the softness of her hair. "Be this person, not Thora. Be part of us."

The girl's eyes filled with sudden tears, and she looked away. "But I am only an Everlight," she murmured.

"I think you are far more than that. Maybe Witchmere made more than they knew."

"I have liked making dreams with you," she said softly, her face still averted. "You are very kind."

"Another descriptive, but one I'm pleased to allow you."

She turned her face back to him and lifted her chin. "Descriptives are useful," she said briskly, "especially in their patterns. Patterns are always useful, for they reveal the Real—if one is deft."

"As I must be deft in my politics," he agreed, "but where is my pattern?" He frowned slightly, perplexed. "That courier from the duke is still waiting to see me, and I'm inclined to make him wait forever. I wish I could, but I can't." He grimaced. "Let's define 'mistake,' Everlight, especially big compared to small."

"You'll decide what's best to do," she reassured him. "Let the courier sit: it won't hurt him. It's what a courier does most of the time anyway—part of his definition, as it were."

"But I worry about missteps, especially the big ones. I know you nag me about worrying too much—I know it's a fault of mine—but if I worry hard enough, maybe I'll find the answers I need. Do you think so?"

She leaned comfortably against him and sniffed at the sea wind. "It's one method," she primly allowed. "There are better ones, fair lord." He laughed softly, and tightened his arms around her.

They stood comfortably together between the door stones, watching the sea as the Companion merged into the horizon, blue on darkening blue. The wind was cold, but not unpleasantly. As the world's suns neared each other at the zenith, they brought the barest of new green to the ice-frosted fields and new leaf buds to the trees. Soon tall towers of clouds would build each night in the evening sky, dark and turbulent shadows against the dimming twilight, erasing the stars, but in the Everlight's dream world, storms only threatened, never descended—not yet. As the Companion fully set, the wind rose more briskly, flapping at their sleeves and tousling their hair.

"Yes, perhaps," the Everlight murmured elliptically, and smiled at the sea.

~⁀⊃

His dream shifted and he stood beside a river road, muddy with the rains and shadowed by a forest of everpine. Thunder rolled in the distance, and heavy rain clouds hurtled overhead, driven by a brisk wind. Beyond the narrow road, a wide river plunged and splashed, swollen with rains, its music echoing off the high cliffs of the gorge. He saw a riverboat turn the bend upriver and hurtle toward him, the man at the rudder standing easily, balancing the flood; his family of wife and two little girls waved cheerily at Melfallan as they swept past, then all disappeared downriver, boat and man and family, as the riverboat swung around the next bend, holding true to the central channel between the rocks.

The future is not set, a deep voice said, a voice he did not know. The voice seemed to have no direction, no focus: it spoke next to his ear, or within his head, or outside him and inside him. Startled, he turned and looked behind him, but saw no one among the tree boles, then looked up into the canopy.

The dragon was a drifting green shadow coiled around a huge branch, nearly hidden within the darkness it had gathered around itself. Golden eyes regarded him, almost indifferently, and golden claws flexed into the wood. The gaze sharpened, and he sensed its amusement as he gaped. *I am Amina of the forest wood.*

"You—" Melfallan cleared his throat. "You certainly are."

The dragon chuckled—was it sound or only inside Melfallan's head?—then stretched comfortably along the branch. Melfallan frankly gawked, and realized until this moment he had not believed in dragons, not really. The eyes were strange, he decided, as if centuries flickered within their depths, centuries of quiet thinking and love for all that lived.

A hidden world, he thought, swallowing hard. Hidden beauty—

Were it not for the resonance, Melfallan, you could not see me at all, Amina said smoothly. *No Allemanii can, for I am an essence of the shari'a, existing only for them. But now is the time of the Finding, of which you will have a part. For three centuries we Four have sought the two who might make a new beginning, the healing of an old wound, both yours and theirs. Much is at stake, perhaps even a final hope.* The golden eyes flickered. *Be faithful, young lord.* He heard the pleading undertone in her voice, a wistful hope that he might, a wistful belief he might not. *Be true.*

"I will try," he answered and sank to one knee at his promise, then lifted his head. "Is she safe, Amina?" he asked softly. "Please tell me that she is safe."

Amina nodded downriver with her chin. *See now, young lord. See through the dream I send you this night.* Melfallan turned his head to look.

Three horses had turned the far bend in the river road and now walked toward him. In the front, Stefan rode his spirited mare, and Brierley rode a tall gelding behind him, Megan seated in front of her, a black packhorse trailing behind on a lead. The horses plodded wearily, their hooves sucking in the mud with each step, and Brierley looked as tired, her face pale and drawn. He watched as they approached him and, as they drew abreast of where he stood by the road, he reached out his hand toward her. But she didn't see him, didn't sense him, only looked wearily up at the rocks of the bluffsides, then squinted at the turbulent sky. And then they had passed where he stood, ascending the road upward. He watched until all three disappeared around the upward bend. The river tumbled hard in its bed, its liquid roar echoing hollowly off the rocks.

She is safe, Amina assured him, *as safe as any shari'a can be in these times*.

"Thank you," he murmured, but when he turned back to the everpine, the dragon was gone.

Melfallan opened his eyes and found himself in the familiar darkness of his bedroom. He heard Saray's soft breathing beside him, sensed the slack weight of her body as she lay next to him in the bed. Outside the window across the bedroom, the sky was darkness spangled with the stars of the True Night, and a winter chill seeped through the panes, stealing into the room. He heard the distant murmur of the constant surf, little more than a whisper on the night air, more felt through the body than heard through the ears, the sea's voice that had been part of him as long as he could remember.

Had he actually stood on that road in Mionn, somewhat transferred there by an Everlight's magic and his own yearning? Or had truly one of the Four taken him there? By what means? For what purpose? Or was it all fancy, a silliness crafted by his gift for worrying and his wanting relief from his own lacks? Who could tell? Melfallan smiled and decided to believe in that road, that river. He listened to his wife's soft breathing for a time, closed his eyes, and then drifted again into sleep.

6

 $\mathcal{B}$ rierley awoke near dawn, and lay comfortably in the large bed beside Stefan, Megan curled on her other side, and listened for a time to the rain drum on the roof. A faint, gray light stole through the bedroom window, strengthening steadily. She blinked sleepily, puzzled by her dreams again. First had come a series of sweeping visions of a great bay, a white pavilion atop a cliff gleaming in the dawn's light, and then a shadowed black dragon surrounded by dark mists, its eyes an impenetrable void. In a desert wasteland, several black-shrouded figures toiled to climb a cliffside, hating the Daystar's light as they climbed, and a clever-footed girl ran ahead of them across the stones of the cliff top, eluding their pursuit. There had been her swift descent into a small canyon to a cavern within the reddish rock, and within the cavern a still pool of water, a black mirror within the darkness. The girl had knelt briefly beside the pool, looked behind her for several moments and listened, and then vanished into the tunnels beyond the pool. Who was she? Brierley wondered, if this girl were anyone at all, of course, beyond the silly fancies of a dream. The dream had then shifted to Yarvannet, and Brierley stood by the door stones of her cave home, Melfallan beside her, a dream that made as little sense as the other, for Melfallan had never visited her sea cave. What did it mean, if anything? Brierley wrinkled her nose with mild irritation at herself. I have problems enough with the questions I have, she thought: I hardly need more. She listened to the pleasant sound of the rain, happily outside on a roof, then listened as comfortably to Stefan's soft snores beside her—he was dreaming of his wife again, happy dreams, as Stefan was happy so easily—

and then listened a time to Megan's dreams. Her child chose to play by Brierley's seashore this night, splashing in the water. Brierley began to drift asleep again.

Almost. She sensed the twins' approach to the bedroom door, and a few moments later Ashdla and Will came softly into the room, both in their nightclothes, and carefully closed the door quietly behind them. Brierley watched as they settled cross-legged on the floor next to the bed, a sly-eyed ferret in Will's arms, a mock owl perched on Ashdla's shoulder. They grinned at her in the dim light of the bedroom.

We heard that you were awake, Will sent. *Do you mind?*

Not at all.

Ashdla smiled shyly. *There wasn't time to talk yesterday with all the excitement.*

Your excitement, Will corrected her.

And yours, too, his sister retorted. She folded her hands in her lap and grinned as wide as a barn door. *You're really here, Brierley. You can't imagine how long we've waited, how long all the forest witches have waited for the Finding. We've been promised it every generation, but you never came—until now. And now you're here.* She stopped and tossed her head impatiently as Will made a soft noise, then glared at her brother. *Go ahead and snicker, both of you: it's still true.*

I wasn't snickering, Brierley said cautiously. *I would never laugh at you, Ashdla, not in the way you're thinking. Nor would Will, if you'd think enough about it.*

Ashdla pressed her hands together earnestly. *I didn't mean—Oh dear, here we've spent all this time thinking about the Finding when it came, and now that's it here, we didn't spend any time thinking about what we'd do when it was here and . . .* Her thought trailed off, and Brierley sensed the heat rising to the girl's cheeks in her embarrassment.

Brierley reached over Megan to hold out her hand. *You are lovely,* she said gently. She felt Ashdla's shy touch, as elusive as a fluttering bird, and as quickly gone. *We will be sisters.*

Will we?

Why not?

Maybe you won't like us, Ashdla said uncertainly, then looked at her brother. *Do you think it's so?*

Will rolled his eyes dramatically. *She's been lying in bed for the last hour, stewing about that,* he explained. *Will she, won't she, and all that twig-fuzz. I hope you'll put up with our foolishness, Brierley, hers and mine.* He smiled broadly and spread his hands. *You are welcome, perhaps more than you know. Forest gift has held the Promise in its keeping, waiting for the gathering of the shari'a, waiting for the new beginning. It has been difficult to hope, difficult to keep believing; however the Four encourage us, however we chant the rites. We see the shades at the Well, watch the light change with the seasons, and tell ourselves it's true.*

Shades? Brierley asked with interest. *What Well?*

The Star Well that was left here, Ashdla answered, puzzled that she didn't know. *We'll take you there today, if it doesn't rain too hard. Soon, for sure. It's part of the Finding.* She nodded at Megan, who was still fast asleep, undisturbed by their silent conversation. *With Megan as fire witch, it's three of the four we need, or so the books said before they were ruined by the rains. We need an air witch, too.* Ashdla and Will looked at each other.

There will be another witch, Will said gleefully, nodding at his sister. *At least one more.*

A wealth of witches, Brierley suggested, and both twins laughed softly in response.

The ferret in Will's lap squeaked for attention, and Will tickled her, then lifted the animal up onto the bed. *Say hello to Brierley, you silly thing.* The ferret minced along the coverlet until she came nose to nose with Brierley. They stared at each other for a long moment, and Brierley held her breath: never in her life had she been this close to a living ferret. They were shy and elusive animals, rare in the Yarvannet forests even when they ventured near to the towns, and were often hunted by the boys as sport. Slinkfoot squeaked softly, and reached out a paw and tapped her nose, then blithely climbed up onto Brierley's face, turning once to lie down comfortably, one hindpaw poking into Brierley's ear. "Oof!" Brierley said, as the ferret settled firmly on her face.

"Hey!" Will said softly. "Stop that, Slinkfoot!" He jumped to his feet and rescued Brierley from the ferret, then draped the animal around his shoulders. Slinkfoot hung blissfully, her black eyes gleaming in the dim light. "I think that means she likes you," Will suggested with a grin. "Or at least we can say so. Are you going to get up soon?" he added unsubtly. Ashdla nudged his ankle. "What?" Will asked, looking down at her.

You're talking out loud, Will, Ashdla warned. *You'll wake Stefan.*

Oh. He winked at Brierley. *Get up soon—please? We're both going crazy wanting to show you everything. Come on, Ash: let's leave before I get as silly as you are.* Ashdla gasped and surged to her feet, setting the mock owl to a wild flapping of its wings. Will escaped neatly through the door, Ashdla in quick pursuit. She turned at the doorway. *It's called tussling. It doesn't mean anything. Don't worry.*

I won't.

Ashdla smiled and then vanished through the bedroom door, pulling it shut behind her. Their ferret might have moved as neatly, as quickly.

"Did I hear a conversation?" Stefan murmured beside her. He stretched lazily, then opened his eyes. "I don't think I did, but definitely there was one."

"More witchery, Stefan. I hope you're prepared."

Stefan slipped his arms around her and pulled her closer, then chuckled into Brierley's hair. "It's too bad we're not lovers," he said sleepily. "This could be a lovely wakening, once we dumped Megan outside the door." He heard himself then and came fully awake, abruptly embarrassed. "I'm sorry, Brierley," he said, appalled. "I can't believe I said that."

"Not to worry. It's only because I'm not Christina." She

clicked her tongue, then turned her head around to look at him. "Don't be silly, Stefan. If you move away, I'll be offended, I warn you. Shall we talk about what else I know about you right now?" she teased. "I hadn't known men often woke up that way. It's a new thing to know."

Stefan sighed. "I haven't had sex for four weeks, and, yes, men often wake up this way, a problem soon corrected, one way or the other." He winked at her. "Is that part of being a healer witch, accepting embarrassments with grace, as if all things are natural and untoward?"

"So what isn't natural when you've been dreaming about Christina? I would expect a little confusion, and might even appreciate the compliment. Don't you think it's so?"

"You can hear my dreams?" he asked, bemused.

"Yes."

"What a marvelous gift," he murmured, then yawned comfortably, taking his time with it. He turned his head to squint at the window. "Is that really dawn?" he asked with dismay. "It's too early to be awake, Brierley."

"So go back to sleep. Here, let me get out of bed first." She eased herself over Megan and slipped out of bed. Megan promptly turned over and draped her arms around Stefan's neck, and Stefan pulled her close to him. He drowsily arranged the child in his embrace, yawned, then closed his eyes. Megan slept onward, a rooted stone in her sleeping.

Brierley stood by the bed and watched them sleep, finding yet another of those brief instances when time itself slowed and one knew this moment would be remembered later for its perfection, and be cherished for it. The rain drummed steadily on the roof and dripped watery curtains across the window, the strengthening daylight sparkling on the water drops as they fell. As she listened, the rain fell harder and the wind began to rise, moaning through the trees in the nearby forest, as another of the Pass rainstorms moved into the valley.

Water, rain, flowing, splashing,
Water, rain, renewing the earth—

She had thought Thora wrote of their own sea gift, that poem about water, but here in Dani's house she heard differently. Perhaps through Megan's gift of memory, perhaps through some other part of Brierley's own heritage, she heard Dani's voice in the rain. A happy voice, part of the endless cycle of life as the forest gift understood it. A wistful voice, that had wished for more years in one life but had now accepted another. A quiet voice, the girl in green. Brierley smiled and spread her hands in welcome, listening.

Brierley's own gift focused on other persons, giving her insight into souls; Dani's gift had looked out into the world, of which persons were only one part, and saw more. The forest, the animals who lived within it, the shimmering lakes, the clouds hurtling across the sky: all were unity, all part of the Patterns of Life, ever moving, ever changing, but ever constant. Her own gift depended upon touch, and through touch to heal; Dani's gift was to hear, and to answer with voice and heart, weaving the Patterns through the chant. Alike, yet not the same. Another entire world behind the facade of what seemed to be, but which had made of itself only a part of the possible. Brierley closed her eyes and shuddered slightly with her own gestalt.

It is sea gift to understand the others, a deep voice whispered in her mind. *Welcome, daughter.*

Brierley gasped softly, but saw no one in the room, nor beyond the window. She clasped her hands at her breast and then, not knowing why she did, bowed with quiet solemnity, returning the greeting. It was not Basoul, and Jain appeared only as the salamander, and Soren she had never met—but she had heard that voice before, weeks earlier in a forest glade high above Darhel, when she and Megan had fled into the mountains. "Amina," she whispered happily, and bowed again.

You are the keystone, the voice continued, its melody flowing like the lazy day's light on moving leaves. *You are the awaited, the Beginning of the New. Time resumes its flow, and the dawn now comes.*

Brierley smiled. "Such great titles," she murmured. "I'm only a commoner midwife, Amina, little more."

Nothing more is needed, my daughter, the forest dragon replied. *You will see.*

Brierley took a deep breath and looked around her vaguely, then looked down at her nightdress and found what next to do. She rummaged in their saddle packs along the wall, seeking another skirt and tunic, but her spares were badly wrinkled. She tried to smooth the fabric with her hands, and found great use in never traveling so that clothes could hang on pins, neatly arranged. She did the best she could and dressed quickly, then found her brush and comb. Then she quietly left the bedroom.

The twins were sitting patiently at the table, both dressed for the day. Slinkfoot squeaked a greeting as Brierley appeared, and the mock owl blinked sleepily on its perch on the chairback, then tucked its head under its wing.

"Owree's a night bird," Ashdla explained. "Don't mind him. He's happy to see you, too."

Brierley pulled out a chair and sat down across from them. "You hear what he thinks? Does he talk to you?"

Ashdla shrugged. "Not in words. I just know." She twisted around and reached into her pocket and brought out three tiny mice, furred and whiskered—no, not mice, Brierley realized. "Pocket shrews," Ashdla said. Another quick grin. "Uh, rather obviously, the way I carry them around. Most of the time they sleep in a nest, but they like to ride in my pocket, too. This is Nit and Bit and one of their daughters." The shrews huddled together on the table and eyed Brierley warily, whiskers twitching. "And the other two children." Slinkfoot craned her head around Will's arm and snuffled busily, and Ashdla promptly swept up the shrews and dropped them back into her pocket. "Stop that, Slinkfoot," she said severely, shaking her head at the ferret. "We don't eat friends." Slinkfoot twitched her whiskers, her black eyes gleaming.

Brierley impulsively reached out her hand to Will's ferret.

She watched in delight as Slinkfoot curled both forefeet around her hand and happily chewed on her fingers, not enough to hurt at all. "I've never had a pet animal," she said, and smiled when the ferret's whiskers tickled. "They're so tame."

"No pets?" Ashdla asked, amazed, and Will nudged her hard, enough nearly to push her right off her chair.

"This is going to get old real fast," Will commented, "the goggling and all. As if there's only one pattern for living, and all others are an amazement, drop the jaw, glaze the eyes, gasp."

"Oh, stuff it, Will. I don't think she minds." Ashdla ducked her head shyly and giggled. "I can't help it. It's such a marvel to meet somebody else like us."

Brierley smiled. "I can hear your mother in the rain," she said softly. "I can hear the power in the valley." Both twins sobered and nodded solemnly.

"Forest gift," Will said. "It's our nature to give to the land, and it remembers us because we have—but I'm a little surprised you can hear it. Well, maybe I shouldn't be surprised. We can hear you, too, you know—it's all water and its music." He flushed slightly. "Words aren't enough," he muttered, then looked at Ashdla in frustration. His sister sighed as heavily. "Now that we've got you—" Will said drolly, spreading his hands.

"—you don't know what to do with me." Brierley finished, and laughed with them. "Well, let's see, what can I tell you about myself? My mother's name was Jocater Mefell. I think she was born in Ingal, but she moved to Yarvannet when I was a baby. I grew up in Amelin, a seatown south of Tiol, the earl's capital. Mother married a carpenter named Alarson, but the marriage wasn't happy. Alarson didn't like that she and I were strange, and in the end Mother couldn't bear how he felt. She suicided when I was twelve."

"I'm sorry," Ashdla said quietly.

Brierley shook her head. "It was long ago. Mother was the only shari'a I knew, but I had found the cave with its journals by then. Shortly after she died, I began trying to heal. I had heard the Voice on the beach, you see, a call to a new kind of living. I could have lived a narrow life, denying the gift as my mother did, but I decided to be true to—" She looked away at the window and the lake beyond it. The rain sheeted downward, lifted into broad curtains by the wind, pattering on the water. "Do you really think we can refound the craft?" she asked softly. "After so long? The Four say I am the re-newer, the witch who's supposed to make it happen, but I don't find any such greatness in myself. I only worry for Megan. I found her in Darhel's kitchens, the witch-apprentice I had yearned for. She's a fire witch, and I don't really understand her. I worry that I don't." She smiled wryly. "So you see, I'm not the wonder-worker you might think I am."

"We have been lonely," Will said. "Now we are less lonely—and so are you, Brierley. All we can do is try." Brierley nodded.

"How did you get into trouble with the duke?" Ashdla asked, and leaned her cheek on her hand. "All we've got is Sigrid's gossip."

"Sigrid?"

"Sigrid Witt, the factor's wife," Ashdla said with a snort. "Emilie's her daughter—you met her yesterday, and, acorns sure to fall, Sigrid will show her nose here today to snoop you out. Be careful with her, Brierley. She's a horrible gos-sip who thinks she owns the place, and makes all kinds of mischief, getting people not to like each other, saying nasty things behind their back—and not always behind their back either. Emilie's only grace is that she's not as bad as her mother. Maybe, though, that's just a matter of time." She made a face, and again looked at Will.

Peas in a pod, Brierley mused, with the twins so deeply entwined that neither was quite aware of the whole of it. If her own twin, Lana, had lived, would Brierley have had this second self, this extension into another person? Maybe.

"Emilie wants me," Will agreed tiredly. "She's got a tro-phy wall."

"So that's what that was about," Brierley said.

Ashdla shrugged. "I called Emilie names, and probably I shouldn't have. It's *not* allowed." Ashdla grinned, then nudged her brother in the ribs. "Poor Will, all that pursuit and flight, although I suppose there are worse fates."

"So you say," Will retorted, poking her back. "Stop interrupting her, Ash. I want to hear. Go on, Brierley. How did you get taken to Darhel?"

So Brierley told them about Captain Bartol and how he had raised a hue and cry about witches loose in the town. Brierley had wisely hidden in her sea cave for the next week, but then the Calling had taken her to Tiol, a Calling to the earl's own lady, who was then heavily pregnant. "Lord Landreth had pushed her down the stairs, making her fall. She cracked her skull on the stone floor and began to go into labor. Both Saray and her baby would have died if I hadn't helped her."

"But why did Lord Landreth push Lady Saray?" Ashdla demanded, her eyes wide.

"Why do the High Lords do anything to each other?" Brierley asked tiredly. "Likely it all traces back to Duke Tejar, that evil man—Bartol coming to Yarvannet to make trouble and then leaguing himself with Lord Landreth, and Landreth having ambitions he shouldn't have and thinking an injury to Melfallan's lady would help his own hopes. Landreth had some role in Earl Audric's poisoning last spring, I'm not sure what, but something." She sighed. "The High Lords' politics create such dangers for Melfallan—and now dangers for me, too. If I had been a prudent witch, I'd have done nothing to help Saray, but I didn't even think, just plowed ahead, and so I saved her life and her baby's life and won the earl's gratitude, despite all the new problems I created for him." She fluted her hand. "Off went Bartol to Darhel to tell the duke about me, and back came the duke's order that Melfallan bring me to Darhel for trial. You know what happens when that starts against us. I expected to be condemned and burned like all the other shari'a the Allemanii have burned since the Disasters. I thought it was the end of me, despite Melfallan's wishing otherwise."

"The rumors said you had died," Will said, "but not anything about a trial in Darhel."

Brierley shook her head. "I never had a trial. Duke Tejar decided I shouldn't have one." The twins' eyes widened as Brierley told them about how the duke had thought that Melfallan had played some gambit against him, and had bid his torturer, Gammel Hagan, to kill Brierley in secret. She had made her narrow escape from Hagan's dungeon, then rescued Megan from the kitchens and fled into the mountains, where Melfallan had found her. Their eyes widened still further as she told them about Witchmere and its dangerous guardians, how one of the guardians had desperately wounded Melfallan with its shooting fire, and how they had finally found some safety in the wayfarer cabin at the end of Witchmere's narrow valley.

"Megan and I spent nearly two months at the cabin, until the guardians drove us away," Brierley said. "In Lowyn we were nearly caught by one of the duke's spies, but we escaped, and now have journeyed here to Flinders to meet you." She grinned at their expressions. "If your mouths stay open longer," she suggested, "flies can get in."

Ashdla closed her mouth with a snap and then giggled, glancing at her brother.

"What a marvelous tale," Will said, making a face, "but not so much fun, I'd hazard, to live through it."

"True." Brierley gave him a smile. "Megan remembered your mother in the cabin stable," she told them. "It's her gift to remember places and persons, some from very long ago. More often I share what Megan dreams, but sometimes I see what she remembers, and I saw your mother. She was dark-haired like you, and dressed in green leather. She had a ferret with her, and a horse named Star." The twins looked at each other in amazement.

"Star died just last winter," Will said, "and Bright Eyes was Slinkfoot's grandmother. But that was years ago, Brierley! Mother went to Witchmere when we were only four."

He shook his head sadly. "She couldn't get into the fortress because of the guardians. She thought she might find answers, the answers we lost when the Well books were destroyed. The cabin witches kept the important texts in the cavern with the Well, you see, the ones about the Finding and how the Well would bring it about, all the important answers about the Promise and the Reformers' new ideas about the gifts that would make it possible, but the Pass rains got into the Well one winter about a century ago and destroyed the books."

Ashdla nodded. "All we have left," she said, "are whatever the cabin witches had copied into their journals, which is a lot but not everything—and we have the rites for the Finding itself, of course. The early witches of our line made sure we had more than one copy of those, but a lot of the other knowledge was lost." She grimaced. " 'Patience,' Amina tells us." She grinned then, her face lighting. "Well, obviously she was right. You're here now. Maybe the rest will be given, too."

"Do you see Amina often?" Brierley asked curiously.

Ashdla shrugged. "Always at chant, of course, but she doesn't come much during winter—until lately, that is. All of the Four have been popping in because of you. It's usually Amina and Soren, less the other two. Flinders was a sacred valley for the old shari'a, you see, one of the three heartlands in Mionn, and I think it's a kind of home for the Four, if the Four have a home, that is. There are shari'a ruins everywhere in the forest, although the Flinders folk have broken most of them up for building stone. A century ago they found one of the shrines, and its Everlight attacked them, so they smashed it and tore everything apart and then burned the forest all around. Nothing grows there, even now, and they stay away from it. So do we. It was a hard time for the forest witch then, with the folk all stirred up again about the shari'a, but they arrested somebody else." Ashdla sighed. "Marren always blamed herself, but how could she tell them they were burning an innocent? They'd only have burned her instead." She spread her hands helplessly.

Brierley shifted uncomfortably on her chair. "So the legends are much more alive here."

"How can they help it?" Will said heavily. "Even after three centuries, this valley is still more shari'a than Allemanii, and even the Allemanii can sense it. They tear down the ruins whenever they find new ones and avoid certain parts of the forest, but they know. Da worries about us, and worries still more because we seem careless to him, and I suppose we are. Ashdla doesn't always watch behind her when she goes up to the cabin." He shrugged, then absently lifted Slinkfoot to his shoulder when she softly squeaked at him, wanting up. "Neither do I sometimes, and it worries him. He's afraid someone will follow us."

"Amina would warn us if they did," Ashdla said impatiently.

"Even so, that's no reason to be stupid, and I'm not saying it's just you. Mother was always careful, and you know that we aren't as careful as we should be."

Ashdla nodded her reluctant agreement, then shrugged ruefully. "I don't like to think about it."

"That's part of the problem, Ash," Will said irritably, "as Brierley will surely tell you."

Brierley raised her hands quickly. "Oh no, I'm not getting in the middle. Don't you even start that, Will." The twins looked startled, then grinned before they nodded together, peas in a pod.

"Sorry," Will said.

"I had a twin, too," Brierley offered. "But she died when I was a baby, and I didn't even know about her until a few months ago. I've wondered since what it's like."

"Will is my second self," Ashdla said simply, and looked at her brother. "Several of the cabin witches have been twinned with a brother. Sometimes I think Will's gift might be greater than mine, although I really can't say why I think so."

"You think that?" Will demanded with obvious surprise, and rounded on his sister. "When did you reach *that* conclusion?"

"Stuff it, Will," Ashdla advised.

"Now, Ashdla," a deep voice rumbled behind them, "be kind to your brother." Michael emerged from his bedroom, dressed in pants and a heavy tunic, his feet bare. "Good morning, Brierley," he said with a smile, then yawned behind his hand. "Good morning, children."

"I was complimenting him, Da," Ashdla said indignantly. "Truly I was."

"Didn't sound like it to me," Michael grumbled, "but then who am I to say? Only the sad father who listens to it all day long." He gave his daughter a stern look, got only a giggle in response. Michael sighed deeply, walked to the stove and shifted a pot onto the hot, black surface, then bent to inspect the low fire burning inside. "We need more wood, son."

"All right." Will gave Brierley a quick smile, got up and handed Slinkfoot to his sister, then plucked a cloak off the peg near the door and went outside.

"We've been talking," Ashdla informed her father with great satisfaction.

"A good thing to do," he agreed, not turning around. He looked inside one jar on the shelf by the stove, then another. "Why is that owl on the chair, I'm asking?"

Ashdla sighed and shoved Slinkfoot across the table to Brierley. "Your turn to watch the beast," she said. "Don't let her bite you too much." She winked. "Just think of it as tasting and you'll find the right measure. Come on, Owree, time for the barn." She woke up the owl without too much of a flapping, and carried the bird outside.

Brierley looked down into Slinkfoot's bright eyes, then pulled her into the cradle of her arms, arranging her on her back to cuddle her. The ferret yawned hugely, showing white teeth, then sniggered softly and companionably began to chew. "Hello, Slinkfoot," she said softly, then turned her head to Michael. "I have never in my life held a ferret."

"Around forest witches," he said, turning with a smile, "there's a lot with animals you've never done before."

"Do you need any help with breakfast, Michael?"

"No, you're a guest, my dear. Sit there and let Slinkfoot

indulge herself, and when Will comes back, he can hide her, too. We'll have visitors today." Michael crossed to the front window and looked out at the rain, then peered to look up the lane to the side. "The Flinders folk are a nosy bunch, and I expect all of my neighbors will drop by today to give you a looking over. Best we get our story straight before they do. You're my cousin, you said."

"Have you a sister or brother?"

"No, and that's the problem. Neither did Dani, but you didn't know that, of course."

"Second cousin?" Brierley ruffled Slinkfoot's silken ears, then dangled the ferret's tail-tip over her snout to see if she would bite it. She did, and chewed as comfortably on herself as she did on Brierley's fingers.

Michael frowned thoughtfully. "Well, there was an aunt once. Moved away somewhere when I was a boy, and died young. Her name was Freda, would be your grandmother. What were the names you were using yesterday? I've forgotten."

"Clara and Robert."

"Jacoby. Ah, I remember." He gave her a bow. "Pleased much to meet you, cousin."

"Likewise, I'm sure." Brierley batted her eyelashes at him, and heard his chuckle. "I don't want to bring danger to you, Michael," she added more seriously.

"Then we'll be deft in our pretending, lass. And truly the danger isn't that much more than before, so long as your young one doesn't give real names to the neighbor children."

"I think she understands."

Michael nodded, then returned to the stove. By the time the meal was ready, Megan was up, and Stefan soon followed the good smells of food cooking.

By noon a dozen of Michael's neighbors had poked their heads in, shaking their cloaks free of water on the porch and leaving their wet boots outside. All were affable, pleased to meet the pretty young visitor and her child and husband, and wanting their life story from the start to the present. Stefan proved greatly inventive, and so Robert Jacoby became a farmer with a small farm on Lowyn's outskirts, with the rains too hard in the south to make planting worthwhile as yet, and his wife had wanted to visit Michael, whom they hadn't seen in years, and so here they were. Megan sat on Stefan's lap and listened to him, frankly agog, as Stefan rolled happily on, inventing two more horses left behind on their farm, a cow, some chickens, an adventure with a snow leopard that had taken a calf some years back, a barn with a paddock, the small house his father had built, a timber stand nearby for firewood, and a rather more accurate description of Lowyn, including Bart's inn near the harbor. Brierley only hoped she could remember all of the tale—or that Stefan would remember to tell her later after two of the neighbor women sat down firmly to chat with Brierley, too, talking of cooking and making do with too little money and wondering if folk were happy in the south at Lowyn. Finally Michael invited the whole lot to dinner, but only half stayed, the cooper and his wife and daughter, a fisherman's wife and her boys, and, of course, Sigrid Witt.

The factor's wife arrived shortly before noon, quite damp, her sullen daughter in tow. Emilie had glared at Ashdla, and Ashdla had glared back, but Sigrid had better matters in mind. Not a word was said of Ashdla's slurs against her daughter the previous day. Rather, Sigrid wanted every detail of this cousin relationship she had not suspected, and Stefan smoothly supplied them, point for point, then flattered the woman outrageously, so broadly that the others hid smiles behind their sleeves. Sigrid simpered in response, and Stefan waxed even more outrageous in his compliments, until Brierley firmly kicked his leg under the table.

Brierley watched cautiously as Sigrid played her cherished role of great lady among the unworthies. Perhaps she even convinced herself, but Sigrid's dress, although rich in its fabric, could not hide the unattractive bulges, nor the stylish arrangement of her hair ease the sagging flesh beneath her chin. Behind Sigrid's posing, Brierley sensed the un-happy marriage with the factor, a taciturn man too easily in-different to Sigrid's wishes, as well as the other frustrations in Sigrid's life, the drifting sense that her pretense had no re-ality, that Sigrid was truly an unimportant and disliked silly old woman, with only worse years to come. Were it not for Sigrid's great liking to hurt with her gossip, especially the vulnerable and shy, Brierley might have pitied her. Gossip can kill a witch, she remembered suddenly, and shivered.

"A most pleasant young man," Sigrid finally said to Michael at the door as she was leaving, the last of the neigh-bors to go. "Yes, it's a pleasure to have them visiting Ellestown."

"I'm happy you approve, Sigrid," Michael said dryly, but Sigrid entirely missed his irony. "Good afternoon." Sigrid batted her thin eyelashes fetchingly, took her daughter in tow, and left to splash home through the puddles. Michael firmly shut the front door behind her, then turned around to consider Stefan. "It's a gift you have, Stefan," he decided at last, "not that I'm sure it's a blessing."

Stefan grinned. "She liked me," he protested cheerfully. "What's wrong with that?"

"Well, it amused the others, that I'll give you—only they'll tell her about it in time, you see. It's too good a chance to give up. Mistress Witt is not liked, for good rea-son. A factor's wife has influence in a small town like ours, more than she deserves, and her brother can be even worse, helping Sigrid with her rumors. Most of the folk here are afraid of their poking." Michael sat down at the table and sighed. "As am I, I'll admit. When Dani was alive, Sigrid took a dislike to her for some reason and spread rumors all over the town, and some of the Ellestown folk still believe that Sigrid and I were lovers at the time, for that was the tale. Sigrid had some beauty in her younger days like her daugh-ter does now, and had many of the same ways in the flirting. Why she did it, I don't know—just to hurt Dani, I suspect. That type always likes to hurt the shy ones."

"Sigrid said *that?*" Will sputtered indignantly. "And let Mother hear about it?"

Michael shook his head firmly. "Never mind, son. It's years past now and your mother didn't believe it, not for a minute. It was the looks the other women gave her that hurt. No one respects a wife who can't keep her man."

Brierley looked down uncomfortably at her clasped hands. Nor the woman, she thought, who takes that husband away from her. How could she explain herself to Michael, this decent man who knew the right for what it was, and struggled with its exceptions? In two more months, perhaps three, her pregnancy would be quite apparent for all to see, and she would need those explanations for Michael, and knew she would not lie to him. Ah me, she thought in dismay. This wasn't what I expected.

"Brierley?" Michael rumbled. "What's wrong?"

Brierley looked at Stefan and saw his wry sympathy, then sighed. "A secret I'll tell you later, if you will, Michael."

"Of course," Michael said, if mildly baffled. "Not to worry, lass." He smiled, then looked more sternly at Stefan. "In a few weeks we'll need a newer tale of why you're staying on and on, Stefan, once your planting season is here. That farm in Lowyn will need managing."

"I have other cousins in Lowyn," Stefan said, with an easy shrug. "Especially one who's lusted after my farm for years, and indeed thought he should have had the inheriting and not me, and this valley is so pleasant that my wife thought—"

Michael raised his hands in protest. "Enough!" he said dryly. "Like I said, it's a gift." He looked up as the rain drummed harder on the roof. Lightning flashed against the growing darkness outside the house as another storm moved into the valley.

"Do the storms get worse, Michael?" Megan asked fearfully.

"Only a little," Michael assured her. "But we're safe inside this house while they do, and once Pass comes and goes, Megan, it's the suns shining every day, and the suns' light sparkling on the lake. I know as a fact that two of the houses down the lane have children in them, two girls almost your age and a boy not much older. And beyond their houses are other children in other houses. When the rains are over, they'll all come out of their houses like mice sniffing their noses out of their burrows, ready to run and play."

"Play what?" Megan demanded.

"That's for you children to decide, don't you think? But I think, as I remember, there's hide-and-seeking, dragon hunts, water splash, and running races. If you've an older boy or girl along, perhaps even boating along the edge of the lake."

Megan craned her head around to look at Brierley. "Really? A boat?"

"Michael says so," Brierley said. "It must be true."

Megan considered a few moments more, not entirely certain about boats.

"A small boat," Brierley said. "Not like the big ones on the river. That's for later, Megan." She winked at Michael.

Megan brightened. "Good!"

Toward evening, when Stefan and Michael went out to the stables to settle the horses, taking Megan with them, Brierley brought out the shari'a books she had found in Witchmere to show them to the twins. "It's probably not safe to keep them here at your house," she suggested reluctantly.

Ashdla nodded. "We keep everything at the cabin. It's not really necessary, I suppose, but Mother thought it best. My, these are old!" She carefully opened the air witch book and scanned the first few pages. "Oh, look, Will! It's an air witch text with all the wind spells." She handed the book to Will, who thumbed through the pages with interest.

"What do the diagrams mean?" Brierley asked curiously.

"The air gift is based on the sense of sight," Will replied. "When an air witch rides the storms with Soren, she can see faraway people and places, as if she were flying with him. I think these diagrams focus the air gift, but I'll admit I don't really know." He turned a few more pages. "The gifts seem to divide up the senses, touch for you, hearing for us, and anything they want for fire witches." He grinned. "I think you've already guessed the trend about the fire gift. Except for shifting worlds to see the past, fire witches never did settle down into a definition. It used to drive the Witchmere air witches crazy."

"Megan can talk to horses," Brierley said.

"Can't you?" Ashdla asked, sounding surprised, then looked at Will. Will made a face at her, then picked up another of the shari'a books. "Oh, it's *Propositions*. We have this one up at the cabin."

"Is it philosophy? I couldn't understand most of the words," Brierley admitted, "even using my dictionary."

Ashdla looked startled again. "A dictionary? What do you need a dictionary for? Can't you read shari'a?"

Brierley shook her head. "Until I found the books in Witchmere, I didn't even know the shari'a had a different language." She shrugged humorously. "Well, 'of course,' you think later, but all the books in my cave, at least those I could handle without breaking them, were written in Allemanii. I've been trying to translate these books, but I'm not good at the study, and a lot of the words aren't in the dictionary." She picked up Thora's book from the short pile on the table and turned its cover toward Ashdla to show the title. "Especially this one. It's a book by the first sea witch in Yarvannet. Can you help me read it?"

Ashdla gave her a quick smile. "Of course. Mother began teaching us shari'a when we were five, because of the chants, you see. All the chants are in shari'a, and most of the books at the cabin, too. Mother always insisted that we use the old words whenever we were at the cabin, even just talking to each other, but that's slipped since she died. Sometimes now I use Allemanii even during the chants, and I wonder if I shouldn't."

"I don't think it makes any difference, Ash," Will said reassuringly. "What counts is hearing the patterns, however they come."

Ashdla shrugged. "That's what he thinks, and probably he's right. Some of the books say that the rites work only if you use the old words, but it doesn't seem to be true, at least not all the time, or at least not with us." She opened Thora's book and looked at the title page, then flipped through the first chapter. "Oh, she's one of the Reformers," she murmured, in mild surprise. "Oh, look, Will! She's got the Change poems, and—" She turned several more pages, then stopped to stare at another page. "Oh, my gosh. Here's the rest of the *Lists of the Change,* Will!"

"What?" Will asked, startled.

"Look! Look!" Ashdla said excitedly. "She has the fifteenth stanza!" Will got up quickly from his chair and bent over the book. He ran his fingers down the page, turned to the next.

"The sixth and eighth are different," he muttered. "Arlina *did* misquote them, just like Laran argued she must have. And look, Ash, there're more after the fifteenth! Sixteen, seventeen—" He turned to the next page. "To twenty-four! He was right about that, too." He looked down at his sister in awe, and Ashdla seemed as stunned.

Will glanced at Brierley, and suddenly laughed. "Oh, look at her face, Ash," he said. "We're sorry, Brierley. You must think we're mad. These are part of the lost texts from the Well, called the *Lists of the Change.* Two hundred years ago the forest witch of that time, Arlina, happened to copy the *Lists of the Change* into her journal. After the rains later destroyed the Well books, it was the only text we had left of the Lists. Our great-grandfather felt convinced that Arlina must have miscopied the chant, citing all kinds of scholarly reasons that never persuaded Great-Grandmama. They argued about it most of their lives." He caressed the page with his fingers. "The Lists were a prophecy supposedly made by blending the air and fire gifts. The Witchmere Reformers believed that, once the Change began, the gifts could be blended, yielding new abilities and patterns, maybe even form entirely new gifts. The Lists were one of the few blendings that the Reformers thought might be genuine, not just another wishful fancy. And—" He stopped and closed the book to look at its cover. "Jodann. Her last name was Jodann." He and Ashdla looked at each other. "Do you think—" Will swiveled his head back to Brierley. "What more do you know about this Thora?" he asked eagerly.

"Basoul told me she left the Well here," Brierley said uncertainly, looking from one to the other. "Why?"

Will abruptly sat down and stared at her.

Ashdla laughed in delight, then waggled her finger at her brother. "Patience, Will," she teased. "Amina always says that, enough to drive us crazy. The name of the fire witch at the Well is Kaare Jodann," she explained. "The sea witch looks much like her, enough to be sisters. And it was the sea witch who led the making of the Well." She looked down at the book and marveled anew. "Thora Jodann was her name," she said with great satisfaction. "Oh, Brierley! How Mother worried about the lost books! We forest witches are the keepers of the texts, you see, the texts necessary for the Finding, but they were destroyed by the rains decades ago. It tormented her that they were lost, because the Finding itself might be lost, too, that we had failed the trust. That's why she went to Witchmere." She caressed the book's cover with her hand. "If only the Witchmere guardians had permitted, she might have found this book there. She might have known the Finding could still be true." She looked at Will.

"I wonder if it's all there in that book," Will said huskily. "I wonder if— I'm almost afraid to look, but of course we will."

"But what is the Well supposed to do, Will?" Brierley asked, perplexed. "What is this Finding supposed to be? *What* do we find?"

"The Exiles," Will said happily. "The other shari'a who survived when they fled into the East. It is the time of the Summoning, when we will regather the shari'a in Mionn and renew the world, when the gifts will Change again, becoming six, perhaps seven. The Four have promised for three hundred years that it would happen, that it would become true. And now it will."

Brierley stared at him. *You are the keystone,* Amina had

told her. *You are the awaited, the Beginning of the New*. But I'm not a prophet, Brierley thought in panic. I'm only a simple midwife! I'm not that great of a person to— But she saw the trust shining in the twins' eyes, and felt in their minds their unshakeable confidence. She shuddered, dismayed.

Where are my hopes against such dreams? she thought in despair. A life with Melfallan, my home in Yarvannet? Such cherished dreams! To walk the road by the coast again; to see the faces of the folk I love? And Melfallan! Must I give up all my own hopes for the sake of this Finding? Oh, why must I?

"Brierley?" Ashdla asked with concern. "What's wrong?"

"I'm not that great person you think me," Brierley said wearily, and looked down at her hands. "I'm not." The twins looked at each other, perplexed.

"But—" Ashdla began, then stopped after her brother gave her a firm nudge. "What?" she demanded, rounding on him.

"Hush," Will said, insisting. "She doesn't have to explain everything to you. Where's that rule?"

"But I don't understand! Why is Brierley unhappy?"

"I don't know, but shut up anyway. Surely you can do that at least once." Will picked up Thora's book and tucked it possessively under his arm, then gave Brierley a quick smile. "We're going out on the porch to look at your book, Brierley—aren't we, Ash? You can sit here and feel easy, Brierley, and not at all plagued by you-know-who. Come on, Ashdla."

"I'm not totally dense," Ashdla protested, and shook off his hand.

"Oh?"

"So I'm coming with you: stop pulling at me. I'm sorry, Brierley, if I hurt your feelings. I don't know how I did, but—"

"Ashdla!"

"All right, all right, I'm coming. Let's just collapse in a puddle and call it a day. Let's not fix it at all—" The door shut quietly behind them.

Brierley leaned her face on her hand and smiled as she listened to the murmur of their voices out on the porch, the twins arguing onward, 'tussling,' as they called it. How easy it will be to love them, she thought, how very easy. I have found other shari'a, she reminded herself, just as I found Megan against all accounting after so many years of lonely wishing. *A wealth of witches,* she had said, and it was true.

The future is not set. She clung to the hope that she might have all she wished, not merely part, but all. Perhaps. Oh yes, perhaps.

7

Count Robert Fauconer stopped outside his father's chamber door and took a deep breath, bracing himself, then knocked. He heard a murmur of voices within, then footsteps approaching the door. His mother opened the heavy wooden door, hesitated as she saw him, then nodded coolly. She was dressed in a gray morning robe, her jewels winking on her throat and wrists, her hair swept up into an elegant style. Once a beautiful woman, his mother still clung to the fragments of her beauty in dress and grooming, unaware that true beauty lay in animation and spontaneity, qualities she had given up decades ago. Others might note her jewels and fine clothing, but saw mainly her lack of emotion, her ice. Even if she knew how she failed, Robert believed, she would not care, as she chose not to care about everything.

"Good morning, son," Lady Mionn said.

"Good morning, Mother." Robert bent to kiss her cheek, but she averted her face, turning away from him, then calmly walked back toward his father's bedside. Robert stepped into the bedchamber and closed the door. The Daystar's light streamed into the room, filling it with a golden glow. His father, comfortably arranged in the huge bed by the window, glared at him.

"Good morning, Father," Robert said tightly.

"What are you dressed up for?" Earl Giles demanded.

Robert paused, trying to keep his temper, then borrowed a few more moments by strolling across the floor to the bedside. It was always like this: the rude shouts, the scowls of contempt, the constant goading to make Robert lose his temper. When he did, as he usually did eventually, his father sneered and called him weak.

"There's a hunt this morning," Robert replied evenly. "Another of the baby's celebrations, and so, Father, I am dressed for the hunt. Before the gentry rides out, I thought to stop by and see how you are doing, as my son's duty."

"Done only because it's duty," Earl Giles grumped, and irritably rearranged the delicate counterpane on his bedcovers, crumpling the fine lace. His right hand was still bound up in its poultice, and Robert could see he moved that hand carefully. Sea-puffer toxin had a solid bite, and Giles would be uncomfortable for another week at least, according to Marina, Melfallan's healer. Suits him right, Robert thought angrily. His father had behaved abominably at the Blessing, not that you could tell a whit from his attitude since.

"Father, you know that's not so," Robert said. Lady Mionn had drifted to the window on the opposite side of the room and looked out at the ocean, indifferent to their quarrel. Robert glanced at her, then focused again on his irascible father. "How are you feeling?" he persisted.

"Why do you care?"

"If you want to quarrel, I'm not helping you." Robert fetched a chair from the several along the wall, set it by his father's bedside, and sat down. "You seem improved," he said firmly.

Earl Giles grunted. "So I'm improved. I hear Melfallan has had a courier from the duke." His father smirked, Ocean knew why, and Robert earnestly wished he knew that why, if only for Melfallan's sake. Earl Giles never confided his plans to his son, and now held some gambit close to his breast, some ploy against Melfallan involving a Lim bride and the duke—or perhaps not. Perhaps Earl Giles merely entertained himself: he enjoyed shouting and bullying, liked the cringing and fear he caused, and so why not? "Has he seen him yet?" Earl Giles demanded.

Robert glanced at his mother, but she coldly ignored them still. It was her solution to marriage with his father, however it ended all other things with her children. She would not help him; she never helped him. "Not yet, or so I've heard," Robert temporized. "He's busy."

"Hmph." His father smiled, a gloating smile, and Robert tightened his hands on his knees, struggling for control. He would not ask what that smile meant; he would not help his father hurt Melfallan. Of late, Robert's loyalties had become a tightening noose, to his father, to Melfallan, to his wife, Elena, and he knew a choice would be coming, a choice he did not want to face—not for fear of choosing the right, but because his father would win and he would lose. It was the pattern of his life as his father's heir to be belittled and out-maneuvered and scorned. *I wonder if I hate him by now?* Robert thought it might be true. *He's given me cause enough.*

"Have you reconsidered your bid for the Lim heiress?" Robert asked coolly. "I've told you I won't divorce Elena. I've told you I won't change my mind."

"We'll see, boy," Earl Giles said, idly waving his left hand, then smirked again. "Hand me that glass of water," he commanded.

Robert got up obediently to get the glass and brought it to the bedside. A month ago Count Toral's son had died in a riding accident, putting the county in play for a new count when Toral died, whomever the duke chose. Earl Giles had bid Robert for husband to their heiress, an absurd idea. They had quarreled about it for a month now, but his father would not relent. Only two nights ago Earl Giles had told Melfallan he would give up the Lim marriage for the sake of their alliance, but it had been a lie, as always. Giles's pressure on Robert had not relented, to be renewed every morning, reminded every night. Robert handed his father the glass and watched him swallow. His mother looked out her window, her face without expression. "As I said," Earl Giles growled, "we'll see."

"Father—" Robert stopped, then tightened his lips and stared down at his father, his temper rising. It was always the same, always the contempt, the pride, the mule-headed stubbornness.

"Don't glare at me," Earl Giles warned him. "Don't dare to advise me, Robert. You're an ignorant weakling, just like Melfallan. You two are peas in a pod, thinking you know so much, thinking you understand High Lord politics. You're both idiots."

"Maybe I'm an idiot," Robert said calmly, "but he's not. Don't underestimate him, I warn you. He'll be everything Earl Audric was and more. The duke doesn't know that and will suffer for it. Don't make the same mistake for Mionn, Father. Don't throw away our alliance with Yarvannet."

"Hmph."

No use, Robert thought. He returned the chair to stand by the wall. "I'm glad to hear you're feeling better, Father." He bowed and then headed for the door.

"And you *will* divorce her," Earl Giles said smugly. "I'll see you as Count of Lim, Robert. I'm determined on it."

Robert turned. "No, you won't."

"I'll disenfeoff you!"

"Do that," Robert retorted. "If the choice is the earldom or my wife, I choose my wife." His father's eyes bulged in surprise, the heavy jaw sagged. Such foolishness! Such idiocy to choose a mere woman over a land! Robert smiled coldly, and knew his father would never understand how a son's choice could be made not for the woman, however he loved Elena, but to win, just once to win, whatever the cost. "Daris has a husband," he challenged. "Make him your heir. And I am late for the hunt. Good morning, Father—and to you, Mother." Robert swung open the bedroom door and stalked out.

"Robert! Come back here!"

Robert did not obey.

～⌒

Saray watched Lady Joanna settle the elegant hat on her curls, then waited for the lady-maid to scurry out of the room. All the gentry were gathering for a hunt that morning, and Joanna had spent twenty minutes selecting the perfect costume. Saray had watched her, dressed in her own hunting skirts and leather boots, a feathered hat fastened securely to her hair. Saray did not particularly enjoy riding and usually avoided the hunts, but today was another of the celebrations for the baby, and so she had no choice. Ah, well, she thought. "What did you mean yesterday by 'sexual arts,' Joanna?" she asked.

Joanna turned around, her hands still poised, and smiled in surprise. "Oh, Saray, surely you don't have to ask! He does bed you often, doesn't he? So you must be doing something right."

"But—"

Joanna took Saray's elbow and drew her to a nearby chair, then sat down beside her. "You must show passion, even take the lead. If you dazzle him, if you make him want you, he won't think about Brierley. He'll think only about you. Trust me: it's the way men are. You win them by making them want you—so long as you deliver what they want—and then give them more, more than they ever expected." She pressed Saray's arm. "Garth can't wait to get me into bed, even after all these years we've been married. He likes it when I'm bold. He likes me asking for it, especially when it's something different."

Saray blinked at her. "Different?"

"Do you ever do anything besides him on top of you? Do you ever let him spend his seed into your mouth? Or let him couple from behind?"

Saray gasped and blushed hotly, averting her eyes. Joanna sighed and patted Saray's arm.

"Obviously not. Oh, dear one, I wish there was a book on this, although I've never seen one. Then you could study everything in secret, without having to blush and gasp and look anywhere except at me." She waited until Saray glanced at her. "You asked for my help," Joanna reminded her.

"I know, but— I've never talked about this with *anyone*."

Joanna shook her blond head vigorously. "Well, it's time you did. You do everything else right, Saray. We've agreed on that. You're beautiful and gracious, you pay attention to his wishes, you flatter and compliment him."

"Not always. We do quarrel—too much."

"That is something *you* can control. You must never quarrel with him, Saray. You always do what he wants, or so he thinks. You shine as his lady. Other men envy how you adore him because they want you, too, and that increases his power as lord. He sees how they envy him and that makes him think more about sex. And that's where you control it, by giving him more than he expects. It's how men are: trust me." Joanna spoke with confidence, and truly she had a right to confidence. Garth's eyes followed her constantly; Saray had seen it herself.

She sighed, and heard Joanna chuckle softly. "I hope you're right," Saray said. "I don't know if I can do that. Be bold, I mean."

"Well, think of another advantage. If he beds you often, you'll get pregnant again, and that, too, flatters him in front of other men. A lusty lord who makes many children is admired—and envied. The envy of other men is what you give him and that makes him happy. They'll see it in how he walks and how he looks at you: they always see it, the other men, when a wife is bedding her husband well. But aren't you worrying about nothing, Saray? Surely Brierley Mefell died in Darhel. Everyone says so."

"No, Melfallan said she is alive. I told you that. It's her for certain, and it's different this time than the other times. She—" Saray looked away unhappily. "I can't say how, but it's different."

"Well, if she's alive, where is she?" Joanna asked. "In Airlie? I can't believe Countess Rowena would risk hiding her, the way the duke feels about Rowena."

Saray shook her head. "I don't think she's in Airlie."

"Briding?" Joanna persisted. "Garth says that Count Parlie is Yarvannet's friend."

Saray shook her head. "I don't know, Joanna. He didn't tell me *where* she is, just that she's not dead. Does it matter where she is? He's going to bring her home eventually, and what do I do then?"

Joanna patted Saray's arm. "You make sure that he's besotted with you by then. If you can manage that, he'll forget her, maybe just leave her where she is, and that's the best outcome. Trust me. I know this. Keep on doing everything else you've been doing right—you have a fine opportunity now with all the celebrations. There's the hunt this morning and then luncheon and the entertainment tonight. Be Lady Yarvannet, a triumph for him as his lady wife, and when you take him to bed tonight, show him what he gets because he married you."

"Show him what?" Saray asked stubbornly. "Don't shake your head at me, Joanna. I honestly don't know. No one has ever told me these things."

Joanna folded her hands in her lap and sighed. She thought a moment. "Let's assume the ball is over and Melfallan comes into the bedroom. What do you do?" Saray opened her mouth and then shut it foolishly. Joanna winked at her, then stood up. She retreated several steps across the room and then walked toward Saray, swaying her hips. "My lord," Joanna said, lifting her arms lazily, almost as if they were too heavy to lift. "I've been waiting for you," Joanna crooned, then wiggled from side to side. Saray watched her in amazement. "Kiss, kiss. And then I take him by the hand and lead him to the bed, and I say, 'I want you badly.' You'll see an immediate effect as you take off his clothes, and that's when you use your mouth on his organ to excite him further."

"I take off his clothes?" Saray goggled. "And—"

"Why not? He'll like it!"

"He will?"

"Yes." Joanna tsked. "Oh, Saray, wake up. At least *try* it. It can't hurt."

Saray rolled her eyes. "I can't believe this," she muttered, and hid her face with her hands.

"If you want to keep him," Joanna advised sternly, "you must do this."

Saray nodded, knowing it was so. "I just don't know if I'll have the nerve, especially for—" She fluttered her hands helplessly.

"So plan it out ahead of time, and include what you feel you can do. Save that other for another time. So: you've just strolled to him in your clinging gown and kissed him, then undressed him and pulled him to the bed. What do you think should come next?"

"Next?" Saray asked blankly.

Joanna chuckled. "Oh, Saray. Where was your mother when you were being readied as a bride? Or your lady friends? But never mind that. I'll tell you some ideas. We'll plan it all out together and then you'll practice it in your mind, and tonight you'll do it."

"Or maybe tomorrow night," Saray amended.

"Whatever—but soon. You can't delay anymore, Saray. You have to win him back so thoroughly that no woman will ever again be a threat. I've managed that in my marriage. Garth has never strayed on me because I give him everything he wants in our bed. You have to do it, too."

"All right." Saray firmed her chin. "Tell me some ideas," she said bravely, although her faced heated again.

"Blushing is all right," Joanna said kindly, then bent and gave Saray a quick hug. "This is Melfallan's fault, not yours, Saray. He should have stayed true to you, but he didn't. It's too bad that his lacks as lord extend to lacks as a husband." Her mouth tightened severely.

"Lacks as a lord?"

"Never mind that," Joanna said quickly, then smiled prettily. "What counts is that men are weak in matters of the flesh, and the wife has to be their strength—and this is how you do it. If he gets what he wants from you, he won't look anywhere else. It's simple. He'll forget her and will look only to you, like Garth does with me. That's what you want, right?"

Saray nodded slowly. "Yes. It's what I want."

"Then I'll help you, as I said I would. Truly I will."

~⌇

The belling of the hounds sounded clearly on the morning air. Melfallan rose slightly in his saddle as his stallion glided over a log on the forest trail, then fought to bring Glaeve back to a slow canter. His horse champed furiously at the bit, wanting to race, but Melfallan kept a firm hold on the reins. With a touch of his spurs on the stallion's sides, Melfallan rewon control over his stubborn-minded mount. Trained as a battle stallion, Glaeve's temperament did not really suit hunting, but Melfallan liked to ride him whenever he could. This morning's hunt, another of the continuing Blessing celebrations, offered another opportunity, one Glaeve didn't wholly appreciate, not as Melfallan did. The horse wanted to run, not this silly cantering through the forest. Melfallan could almost hear the horse thinking, and grinned. Glaeve tossed his head and snorted his disdain, then simmered along beneath him.

Their prey this morning was a boar, and Melfallan occasionally caught a glimpse of the animal when it turned at bay to menace the hounds that followed him. Whenever the fierce boar turned, the hound master held back the scent-hound, the lymer, who was tracking the boar, but the other dogs usually had the animal in sight now and the lymer's role had lessened. Other huntsmen on foot had the small beagles on leashes, and the entire pack belled their sweet, clear tones of excitement, signaling to the noble folk who followed that the prey was near.

Most of the principal Yarvannet lords and their ladies had joined the hunting party this morning, as they had joined every event of the past two days: nearby rode his cousin Revil, his marcher lords Garth and Tauler, Sir Justin the armorer, Tiol's minor lords like Lord Jarvis, young Valery Tolland from Yarvannet's southern holdings, and Keldon Grosmont, heir to the port lord, Lord Eldon.

Keldon looked stout and uncomfortable on his horse, awkward in his hunt clothes. He had come to the Blessing as his father's representative, for Lord Eldon was crippled with Plague and usually in bad health during the winter. The other lords, even the kind ones like Garth and Revil, always found Keldon awkward, a bit too dull-minded to keep up with the bright society around him, a bit too earnest to fit in. Those less kind disdained Keldon as a mere "merchant's son," a label that fit, true, but not suitably said to a fellow lord, and those others were not always careful to keep that opinion out of Keldon's hearing—but Keldon still stubbornly tried, for his father's sake if not his own. But, in truth, Keldon did better at counting coins than acting the nobleman. Lord Eldon still searched uselessly for husbands for Keldon's ugly sisters, but Keldon himself had acquired a wife three years ago, likely to Keldon's great surprise. The girl was not a beauty and quite stout, but Keldon had applied himself as earnestly to his duties of marriage as he did to everything else, and by all accounts both he and his wife were happy, and now parents of a two-year-old son.

Behind Keldon, Lord Valery Tolland had fallen off the pace, not really interested in the hunt, as he was so little interested in anything but his own ease. As he glanced back, Melfallan saw Valery take another swig from his flask, already well launched into his daily routine of an alcoholic haze. What if I gave Keldon Valery's southern lands? Melfallan mused. I'm the earl: I can arrange feofs as I choose, and Valery has proven his unfitness to rule, not just because of the drinking, but for his utter self-indulgence, the indifference to his debts, to gossip about his frequent affairs with his lady mother's avid covering of every misdeed. Valery had a wife, but she never came to court in Tiol, for reasons Melfallan found vague. What a flurry of feathers it would be, like a ferret in a coop! Melfallan smiled grimly and bent his attention again on his reins. I just might, he thought.

Whatever the other events associated with the Blessing, whatever his various lords' motives for attending, that acknowledgment of Audric's rank was now completed. Somehow the legal conclusion of such an event brought its own satisfaction. The Allemanii ordinarily waited four months to ensure a child would live, although that good health had never really been in doubt for Audric. His son was now a wiggly, happy little creature, delighted to see his father each morning, comfortable in the arms of his nurse, happy with his nursery companion of the wet nurse's little daughter, and carefully guarded in his bright, sun-drenched nursery on the western side of the castle by half a dozen soldiers keeping the watch in the hallways.

I will keep him safe, Melfallan vowed.

Melfallan guided Glaeve over another log, the other lords' horses thundering behind them, and they entered a broad woodland glade. Across the glade, the boar had turned at bay in front of the trees, and it seemed this would be the final challenge to the hounds. Melfallan hung back as Lord Garth surged past him with his lance in hand, followed by Count Robert and Sir Justin Halliwell. The three thundered forward, scattering the hounds and dog handlers before them, and charged the boar, who stood at bay against the large bole of an ever-oak tree. The boar gnashed its tusks and squealed a high, ringing challenge, but could not dodge the ascending lances that pierced deep into bowel and heart. The beast leapt convulsively into the air, jerking the killing lance out of Robert's hand, then fell to the earth, twitching.

Robert shook his fist in the air in exaltation, and then grinned broadly back at the other lords. "Mine was the first thrust!" he exclaimed. "I claim the kill! My lance was first!" He trotted back toward the other gentry, most of whom now gathered in a circle in the clearing, all happily talking in their excitement.

Melfallan leaned an elbow on the pommel of Glaeve's saddle and watched the boar die on the grass. As it shuddered convulsively, a great flow of blood issued from its champing mouth; then it lay still. In the ancient West, such hunts fed the families in winter when storms held the fishing boats in port; like those other dead beasts centuries ago, this boar would be taken back to Tiol and duly cooked for the banquet tonight, although one boar would hardly feed the multitude of folk gathered for the Blessing and its festivities. Hunting was now more a noble sport than a need, even if nothing was wasted afterward. Melfallan shrugged mentally, the purpose served. He turned his attention to Lord Tauler as the marcher lord eased his horse beside his own.

"A good hunt, your grace," Tauler said, his craggy face flushed with the cold wind of their ride that morning.

"Yes, a good hunt," Melfallan replied, nodding. Tauler might have said more, he sensed, but the ladies' party had now entered the clearing, Countess Rowena at the fore. Tauler nodded again and moved on, still the cautious lord, still the lord Melfallan wanted most to win to his side. Melfallan repressed a sigh, sensing another chance missed, as his aunt rode toward him, Saray and Joanna and the other ladies chattering behind her. Saray smiled brilliantly at Melfallan and twiddled her fingers playfully, a gesture he had seen Joanna use over and over again at Garth, and it puzzled him that Saray used it now. He almost twiddled back, but thankfully caught himself in time.

Today Saray was the picture of happiness with her husband, praising him before the other ladies, flirting with him, exclaiming her admiration whenever he did anything at all, however trivial. It flattered him, true, and Saray had glittered this way many times before, but— What *is* she up to? he fretted, but made himself smile at his wife. On one side of the clearing, the servants were erecting the broad canvas pavilions for their luncheon in the woods, the next item on Saray's long agenda for the baby's entertainments, and other servants from the castle now tramped into view, laden with bundles and pots for the feast.

"Nephew!" Rowena exclaimed, as if that role had sprung upon Melfallan only this instant, then chuckled as he frowned at her. She shook her blonde head, tsking. "My congratulations! Why didn't you tell me earlier?"

"Tell you what?" Melfallan asked stupidly.

"The pregnancy, of course! A second son for Yarvannet! What joyous news! Or better yet, let it be a girl this time. I approve of girls." Rowena smiled sunnily at Saray, who ducked her head and blushed prettily.

"Now, Aunt," Saray reproved sweetly, "I'm not sure yet. You shouldn't have told him." She smiled broadly at Melfallan. "Although I admit Melfallan's constant attentions to our bed make it likely. He is a lusty lord indeed." Saray looked around at her ladies proudly. "Not that I intend to have him stop," she added, nodding her head, then winked archly at Melfallan. "He pleases me greatly in our bed with his vigor," she declared loudly, "as he does in all other things." Rowena gave Saray a sharp look of dismay. Lady Joanna beamed, nodding her head in high approval, but the other ladies, Solange and Tauler's wife in particular, looked at each other uncomfortably.

"Uh—" Melfallan managed. "That's good news, Saray," he managed further, still bumbling. "Uh— I hope it's true."

"I'm sure it is, my lord husband." She waggled a finger. "Now, don't you stop those attentions! I won't have it. I want it long and lusty tonight!" Her smile was enchanting, and Melfallan felt himself blush furiously. Glaeve shifted uneasily beneath him, sensitive as always to Melfallan's mood.

"I see the tents are almost ready," Rowena announced briskly. "Come, Saray, let's see that all is done rightly." Rowena heeled her horse and led Saray and the other ladies away. When she glanced back at Melfallan, he sent her a look of gratitude.

"Melfallan?" Revil had obviously heard everything, as had several other noble folk nearby. Saray's voice had carried well; likely all had heard, even the servants now bustling to and fro across the grass. Melfallan tried not to slump his shoulders, tried not to raise his hand to his eyes, tried desperately to control his expression before his lords. Instead, he sat straightly, proudly, on his horse, the lusty lord who so satisfied his wife that she loudly exclaimed the fact to everyone—not just once, but twice, to make it true. Revil maneuvered his horse around Glaeve and blocked him from easy view of the other lords. "What in the Hells is going on?" he muttered angrily. "That kind of comment in front of everyone! Is she really pregnant again?"

"I hadn't heard," Melfallan said tautly, "at least until now, along with everybody else." He heard anger trembling in his voice but, oddly, hardly felt the anger behind his shock.

"Well, don't faint," Revil said drolly, then shrugged. "Yes, that wasn't amusing. Glare at me as you will: that's my purpose in life."

"Not you, too, Revil!"

"What?" Revil demanded. "What did I say?" Revil looked honestly dismayed, then shook his head vigorously. "Let's start over: what in the Hells is going on, Melfallan?"

"I don't know," Melfallan muttered in despair. Sex was a part of everyone's life, of course, but even men usually kept their boasting discreet in polite company. By Saray's lady rules, it was ignored completely, as if children happened by their own accord. "Why would she—" Melfallan stopped and this time he did rub his eyes, then saw Revil gesture angrily at Robert as his brother-in-law walked toward them. Robert promptly obeyed, but looked back at them, his face full of questions, then changed direction toward his sister, striding forcefully.

"Tauler will stop him," Revil said reassuringly, and indeed the Penafeld lord smoothly intercepted Robert's angry advance, drawing him instead toward a nearby group of lords.

Melfallan watched the other ripples spread among his lords and ladies at Saray's brazen announcement, the heads put closely together to snigger, the gestures of dismay at such open sexual talk by a proper lady wife, the buzz about another child as heir to Yarvannet. The servants bustled about, unconcerned about such high matters, more eager to lay out the fine meal for the noble folk they served. "Ocean save me," Melfallan muttered.

"I sincerely hope She does," Revil said. "Listen, I'll ask Solange and bring you word. Maybe she can find out a fact that makes it explainable. Until then, I still love and serve you, my earl, however lusty you are in bed, pleasuring your wife beyond compare. Cheer up: at least it's a compliment she said so." Melfallan stared at him in disbelief, and Revil laughed outright. "The world's still here, Melfallan. It hasn't fallen into ruins."

Melfallan snorted. "You're a comfort to me, cousin."

"I hope that, too. Is your composure back? It seems so."

Melfallan nodded, and swung heavily off his horse. Together, he and Revil walked toward the tents and joined Saray's luncheon party. Saray smiled happily at him and patted the cushion beside her, waited until he sat down, then continued her chatter with Rowena and the other ladies, as if nothing were untoward, as if all were right. Saray was exquisitely skilled at pretending, and Melfallan tried to join her in the art, at least for the rest of the afternoon. He nodded affably as all bent to compliment him on the new pregnancy, as all nodded sagely about that good for Yarvannet, that their earl could sire more than a single child—and lustily, too, to his wife's good pleasure. What more could a land and its noble folk want? Then the talk graciously turned to other things, as his lords and ladies chattered gaily to each other, happy with the day.

As they ate the fine meal set before them, the boar's carcass was duly spitted on a branch and the castle huntsmen began the long tramp with it back to Tiol, taking the hounds with them. In time the gentry rose from their meal and followed, riding easily through the forest, talking lightly, graciously to each other, amused by each other's jokes, with some flirting, some posing, all perhaps imagining themselves part of a romantic tale, a nobleman's lot larger than life.

This was his noble world as an earl, Melfallan reminded himself as he rode in their midst, these lords and ladies. Each was different from the other, some bent to frivolity and cheer and having the means to ensure it, some rising above that noble affliction of too much comfort to greater purpose, like Revil, like Sir James, like Lord Tauler. He looked over at Tauler and watched the marcher lord chatting pleasantly with Sir Justin, and again measured Tauler's value to Yarvannet: it might be very great, more than Melfallan appreciated. Penafeld's cautious lord made himself a genial part of the celebrations, but Melfallan remembered quite clearly, when Giles had insulted Melfallan at the Blessing, that Tauler had surged to his feet in outrage only a scant second after Revil. Have I won that able lord? Melfallan wished. Could he win the others before it might be too late? Would that he had only strong and capable lords, a fierce fence of such lords around Yarvannet and all he loved here, to keep out any menace, any threat.

Three days ago someone had tried to murder his son, yet today few of his gentry appeared disturbed, fluting their hands and turning to their own pleasure. He had seen the same noble habit again and again in Saray, trained to it by her mother's lady rules: the world was not as it was, only what one preferred, filling with light and graciousness, clever talk, beautiful gowns, and a never-ending soiree as the lords and ladies swirled around each other, waxing more brightly as the suns set, glittering in the torchlight—all was perfect. Saray's gaffe was just as easily transformed, it seemed, as all nodded to him pleasantly, then turned to flatter his wife. A land can be ended by such fancies, he thought grimly: did any of them realize that? Or did he resent their easy minds, wishing he could escape into their glittering daydream?

Yet the Yarvannet nobility seemed content with his rule. They did not huddle in corners and cast him unhappy looks, nor show other signs of treachery, when signs were there to be seen—and such signs weren't always overt. Someone had struck at Melfallan's grandfather, ending his life, then struck at Melfallan's son, but likely only one person, not several. He thought about Norris, now locked up in a dungeon cell, a pleasant young man, tall and lean and well-spoken, who had seemed devoted to the baby, confident in his charge. What had impelled a young man to attempt murder? What hatred might compel such an act? For the duke to inspire treachery, or the duke's tool if Norris's master were Count Sadon, there must be fertile ground for the seed to take root and grow into its malignant plant of jealousy and hatred and murder. He shook his head slightly, grieved. He had liked Norris. Is this pleasant enjoyment with his gentry today another still water where monsters stirred beneath? How can I know? He shook his head again, realized that Norris's treachery had shaken him more than a nobleman's would. He expected treachery from lords, but in the commoners, the folk like Brierley and Marina and Jared, he placed more trust. Must I distrust everyone? he wondered sadly. Must I become sour and hating like Count Sadon, disappointed in all hopes?

I wish I knew the future, he thought, just a small portion of it to give hope, to know the shape of the outcome. I wish I had a future self who could advise back through the times, an older brother of sorts, someone a little wiser than me, one who could reassure—or warn. I would take either comfort or warning rather than this uncertainty. Uncertain, I may misstep. I may already have misstepped and now only wait the unraveling of everything. He raised his hand to his eyes and rubbed them slowly, his horse plodding easily along the road.

"Does your head hurt, my lord?" Saray asked promptly, bending toward him in concern.

"Not at all," he said. "The suns' light is a little bright."

"It *is* a beautiful day, isn't it?" Saray smiled graciously, beaming with love at her husband, then turned to exclaim to Lady Alice riding on her other side. "I'm so happy when we have such fine days in winter. Don't you agree?" Melfellan felt his stomach begin to roil.

Only twenty minutes more, he promised himself, the rest of this short ride up that stretch of road, down that hill, across the castle road into the castle courtyard. Surely he had some important brief in his tower study—or perhaps he could inspect the soldiers in the barracks, or closet himself with Sir James about—about what? The courier! Yes, that would suit. He would be forced to leave Saray's side for his earl's business, with much regret, but she would smile sweetly, as always, and forgive him.

And he could escape her simpering and bowing and all the rest, at least until the evening. He ground his teeth silently as Saray continued to exclaim beside him, her smile entrancing, her beauty stunning as she flattered him—and none of the posing was real, he knew, only more of her pretending. Was the pregnancy as much a lie? he wondered, and felt ashamed that he doubted her. But was it? he persisted, and doubted her still.

The suns had long passed the zenith by the time Count Sadon Moresby and his party reached the coast road ten miles south of Tiol, three days late for the earl's ceremony. Sadon reined up his horse and glared angrily at the Daystar, as if the world's principal sun lay at fault. He gritted his teeth, and might have torn his hair from his head in his frustration, but so it was, that next day's nooning, and there was nothing he could do about it.

He had left Farlost early enough for a pleasant four days' ride across the marshes to the earl's capital on the coast, early enough to arrive in Tiol for the Blessing of Earl Melfallan's new son and heir. He had determined to make peace with Melfallan, at whatever the cost to his pride. The first step in that plan was a timely arrival at the earl's great event, followed by pleasantness and good cheer at the entertainments to follow, even the practice of rusty social skills learned in his youth. He had not forgotten those skills, after all, merely neglected to use them for the past few decades. And, perhaps, if his pleasant behavior made an impression—which it almost certainly would, he admitted—he might win a private meeting with the new earl himself.

In that private meeting, he had hoped to plead for his son, Landreth, whom Melfallan had sent to the duke's capital in chains, charged with the rape of four Tiol servant girls. He had hoped to speak solemnly with his young earl, acknowledging his son's defects, abjectly admitting his own fault to whatever degree Melfallan demanded, speaking as one father to another. He would give up his anger at the Courtrays, he had vowed, would set aside thirty years of contempt inflicted by Earl Audric, accept anything from Melfallan's hands, if only Melfallan would spare his son.

But on the first day of their journey to Tiol, a bridge weakened by winter rains had collapsed beneath half the folk riding with him, a groaning and cracking rumble of twisting struts and ripping wood and sudden screams of terror. Had Daughter Sea timed the fall but a minute earlier, Sadon himself might have tumbled into the deep gorge, to lie broken and injured on the rocks with the others of his folk. Three of his soldiers had died in the fall, and five others had been badly injured, and all of the horses who had fallen had died or needed a quick, merciful killing to end their agony. Sadon had delayed to see that the injured were tended and then carried back to Farlost, as was his duty to his folk whatever the cost elsewhere, before setting out again by a different road, knowing he would be late, and wondering these past four days why he even tried. Sadon stared at the Daystar and might have groaned had he not clamped his jaw hard to keep back the sound. No use now. No use for anything.

Beneath the tall, sandy bluff the ocean murmured in Her many voices as waves sighed easily onto the sand, one upon the other in never-ending succession, in the restless rhythm of the sea. How little I see the ocean, Sadon thought, bound as he was to his inland holding, its marshes and forests, its winding streams and flat plains, and wondered how that might change a man beyond redemption. It was a thought that had preoccupied him lately as he sought answers he could not find. The Allemanii were a sea folk, their souls bound to the ocean and its waters: perhaps his unnatural life away from the sea had brought down on him the long defeat, the wreckage of his life and his boyhood hopes, a ruin now nearly completed. Perhaps. What use to keep asking a question no one would answer?

Sir Kaene Cassiere, a principal knight of his household and Sadon's lifelong friend, nudged his horse forward to join him at the bluffside. "My lord?" he asked solicitously.

"We're turning back," Sadon decided.

Kaene's jaw sagged in surprise. "But we're only ten miles from Tiol!" he protested. "Another two hours' ride at most! Why turn back now?"

Sadon looked wearily at his loyal knight. Kaene was solid and patient, never minding Sadon's temper, never minding the abuse he had often suffered at Sadon's hands, being Sadon's sworn man for over forty years and never failing in that trust. His friend had aged more gracefully than his count, free of the chronic headaches that had afflicted Sadon for decades, free of Earl Audric's contempt, free of frustration with a wayward and stupid son. Sir Kaene was still tall and hale, gray-haired but unbent by the years, with his daughter Joanna well married to Melfallan's northern marcher lord, Garth Souvain, and his son well settled as captain of Farlost's northern guard. I envy him, Sadon thought candidly, and knew that his faithful Kaene would never understand why.

"It's no use, Kaene," Sadon said heavily. "The earl won't listen to my reasons about the bridge: he'll still think I deliberately delayed on the road, intending insult to his son, because it will please him to think so, as it pleased his grandfather whenever he had similar excuses. I could protest my innocence, as always, rant in my indignation, scorch all with my rage, as always—and it will change nothing." Sadon lifted his gloved hand to his forehead to knead the flesh a moment as the headache seized anew on his skull, then resettled his hand on the pommel of his saddle, gripping hard. "I feel old, Kaene, tired and old. We're going home."

"I don't believe Melfallan would do any such thing!" Kaene argued, his honest face filled with his indignation. "A lord tends his people when they have need! You couldn't leave the wounded there in the gorge to make their way back to Farlost however they might. Surely the earl will understand that!"

Sadon squinted at his knight, wishing an honest heart's protest might make all things right. "You think so?" he asked ironically. "I sometimes wonder, my good Kaene, if my holding the inland marshlands is unnatural, and from that flows all the troubles of my house. An Allemanii is meant to

live upon the sea and her coastlands. We are a sea people,
and the sea is in our blood. Take us too far from it, and we
begin to strangle, to waver and fail. Perhaps that is Duke Tejar's flaw also, we inland lords." He grimaced, then glanced
back at the rest of their party, the half-troop of soldiers, the
several servants and housemen, who waited patiently on
Sadon's pleasure, as they always waited, no doubt as puzzled
as Kaene was puzzled by this odd stopping by the bluffside;
but Farlost folk were well used to their count's willful behavior after all these many years and were patient with it.

How did they find such patience? Sadon wondered. Why
do they still stand with me after all the years of Farlost's disgrace, all the failing fortunes of my house? Did his folk even
think in such terms, as Kaene never did, instead content with
the simple fact of Sadon as their lord and needing nothing
else? When he glanced around at them, several smiled in response, and Sadon wondered anew how he earned those
smiles, as they always gave their smiles to him whenever he
looked, despite how often he had shouted at them. With a
baffled sigh, he turned back to Kaene.

"Did you know, Kaene," he asked, and his voice sounded
strange even to himself, "that my son Landreth is now the
duke's great favorite? No longer in disgrace, quite cleared of
the accusations Earl Melfallan brought against him—
although there was no trial, of course, no finding of the truth,
only the duke's decree that it is so. My son is now full of triumph, full of joy." Sadon touched his tunic pocket, and
heard the soft crackle of the paper next to his heart. "I know
that because Landreth has sent me a letter. His words reek
with contempt for my warnings about this duke, for the years
I have counseled against ever trusting any Kobus duke again,
reek even with contempt for me."

"A letter, my lord?" Kaene asked, obviously wanting to
offer sympathy, but what more could be added than what already had been said between them, and that said more than
once? What more, in truth, could Kaene say about Landreth,
Sadon's stupid son who had doomed them all, and thought
himself brilliant in doing it? Sadon listened another few mo-

ments to the sound of the waves below, a comforting sound he always missed. Now the sound seemed to strike at him like a knife, and he might tear at his hair like a madman, keening shrilly until his throat was raw with it, mourning his son, his house, all the ardent hopes of his youth. It is over, he thought. It is time to surrender the hopes, to give up the trying. It is time to die, perhaps. With a sigh, Count Sadon extracted the letter and gave it to Kaene, then waited as his friend read the pages.

The duke has given me Melfallan's own apartments in Darhel, Landreth had exulted. *He shows me attentive favor at every court gathering. Indeed, Father, he consults with me daily, and hints I might be Yarvannet's earl in time, if all goes well.*

If all goes well, Sadon thought contemptuously. In his son's need to boast, in his need to flaunt his father's error about this faithless duke, Landreth had put such a duke's promise in a letter, a letter that might be intercepted and read by the very earl Landreth hoped to replace. And, error compounded, he had blithely sent that letter to his father, implicating Sadon himself in the duke's plot. For twenty years Sadon had resisted Duke Tejar's wheedling, his wishes for treachery, his vague promises of reward, only to be undone by his idiot son.

"He writes here that—" Kaene said, astounded.

"Yes, I know."

"And sent *you* the letter, as if you shared the ambition?"

"Keep reading," Sadon said heavily.

In the spring, Landreth had written, *there may be new opportunities for our reward, Father. Even now Duke Tejar lays able plans.*

Had Tejar prompted Landreth to that boast? Count Sadon wondered. Write to your father, my favored young man, and tell him of our hopes. Write to your father, my good young man, and destroy him if the message goes astray. Had Tejar hoped for that destruction? Write to your father—

What had Tejar plotted with that prompting? Or had he cared at all about the outcome? Affable, with many nods and smiles, a genial man when he chose to be, Duke Tejar had shown Sadon that same genial face in the series of letters over the years, the wheedling, the pressure, the subtle threat. And now, in his son's frailty, more pressure, more threat, with the son as the father's betrayer. A subtle man, their duke, and comfortable with patient waiting until the snare could be snapped, the strangling begun.

Kaene raised his head, his eyes widened. "Reward?" he croaked.

"Yes, reward for what? Yarvannet's former earl is recently poisoned: the connection is obvious, my stupid, stupid son." Sadon raised his hand to his head again as the throbbing lanced its pains in his temples, then slowly rubbed his eyebrows. Since he had read the letter, brought to him by a courier as he pulled his dying soldiers from the wreckage of the bridge, Sadon had lived in an odd daze, as if thought could not connect to the day, as if breathing were irrelevant to the next moment. So profound was his shock that his headache had disappeared for hours at a time, not just the first day, but the second and the third as well. For once he could think clearly without pain—for a while at least. He sighed at the irony, and then regretted that his sigh led only to a next breath, a next breath he believed he did not want.

He shook his head slowly, then met Kaene's worried eyes. "My son had told the duke, Kaene, that Farlost murdered Earl Audric. I hadn't known Landreth had a hand in that. Now I do—or maybe I don't. He lies so easily, lies for no reason, lies to amuse himself and for no other purpose: who can tell? For years I've ignored Tejar's insinuations, his flatteries, his prompting, his fake promises. I trusted a Kobus duke once and paid the price of it for thirty years—never again. Instead I kept my loyalty to my earl, despite how thoroughly Earl Audric despised me, however much I hated him in return. All that trying. All that useless trying. How does that saga line go, Kaene? 'The wave mounts the beach, higher and higher, and even now descends.' And when it does, it will crush Landreth—and me." Sadon stared unseeingly at the horizon. "Earl Melfallan might accept my excuse about the bridge, perhaps you're right about that, but he will never believe my claim of ignorance about Earl Audric's death. He knows too well how much I hated his grandfather. I've spent thirty years showing it."

Kaene frowned down at the pages of the letter, turned to the third page and read again. "What does he mean about the spring?" he asked slowly, although surely he had guessed the answer. "Is he talking about invasion? Of *Yarvannet?*"

Sadon chuckled bitterly. "Yes, how else to put the earl's circlet on Landreth's head? What greater excuse for invasion than a High Lord wrongly accused by his liege? You see how the duke is using my son, and Landreth is allowing him to do it. Tejar will have the high moral ground, the defender of Landreth's right. And Landreth will have a part in the attack on Yarvannet, of course, thinking himself the returning hero, the new earl to be welcomed with a great shout of joy." He twisted his mouth. "I wonder if the duke will kill him before or after the invasion—afterward, most likely. One mustn't murder the excuse too soon." He drew in a sudden breath and closed his eyes.

"You could warn Earl Melfallan, my lord. You could prove your loyalty—"

"—by betraying my son." Sadon grimaced. "I've been called a traitor for thirty years, Kaene. At least I'd be consistent." He shook his head. "No, Melfallan already knows war is coming. Anyone can see it, like a storm written on the clouds. There's no need for me tell him what he already knows. And he won't believe in my innocence of the plot, both against his grandfather and now against him. The whispers against me have filled Yarvannet since Audric died; everyone knows I wielded the poison. No, best to go home, my loyal friend. It's over now. The duke has trapped Landreth—no, not trapped. All Tejar had to do was open the snare and let Landreth walk willingly in. Now Tejar can spring the latch, then watch the fear and convulsions, the brief spate of blood from the mouth, the dying, the death, the first faint stench of decay."

"My lord—" Kaene began, but had nothing more to offer, and fell silent.

Sadon regarded his friend with sad affection. "You've been faithful to me all our lives, my dear Kaene. You put up with my anger and shouting, and you've never complained. I'm sorry this will destroy you, too. You are too much known as my sworn man, and my treachery taints you. These Courtrays murder those who cling to a treacherous lord—Audric did it, and, no doubt, so will his grandson. You don't deserve such a reward, my dear old friend. I'm sorry, more than you can guess. I'm sorry your loyalty brought you to this." Sadon reined up his horse and turned its head around. "We return to Farlost."

"No," Kaene said quietly, reaching for the reins of Sadon's horse.

"What did you say?" Sadon asked, shocked, and would have pulled his horse out of Kaene's grasp.

"Listen to me," Kaene said firmly, and would not relent his hold on Sadon's horse. "Is it not right that a knight give his lord counsel? Wasn't that the oath I swore to you forty years ago? And wasn't it your oath to me to *seek* my counsel, and to be faithful and true as my liege, and to defend my right? The years have weathered us both, Sadon, but I still believe in my feof oath and so do you, not only your oath to me all those years ago, but your oath to Melfallan, just as you believed in your oath to Earl Audric. Without those oaths, it would be right to despair—but we have those oaths." He held out Landreth's letter. Numbly, Sadon took it and refolded it, then placed it inside his tunic. "And so I am offering my counsel, my count, and I am asking you to defend my right and to defend Farlost by giving that letter to Melfallan—tonight, after we arrive in Tiol."

"But—"

Kaene twisted his mouth, as if in pain. "How do you know Melfallan is like Audric? Please, my lord. Don't give up! You're a fine count, my lord, despite your tempers and outrages, and I will speak plainly on that whatever it costs me. When your people had need of you at the bridge, you stayed and saw that they were tended. That's what a lord does for his folk. Why assume Melfallan is less than you are?"

"But what if you're wrong?"

"Then you've lost nothing, because nothing is all you choose right now." Kaene glared at him, as an old friend had every right to glare, had every liberty to do.

Sadon thought about forty years of Kaene's loyalty, then turned his head to look at the sea and thought of other loyalties, not all of them as kind. He considered, weighing hopes against fears, but could not find the strength Kaene asked of him, not anymore.

"I'm sorry, my Kaene," he said heavily, "but it's too late. I'm sorry to disappoint you, old friend. I'm sorry to fail you." He took a deep breath, grimaced violently at the sea, then heeled his horse around. "We return to Farlost."

*N*ear midnight, the night wind rose strongly from the sea far below, swirling against the white stone walls of Yarvannet Castle. Melfallan stood on the chapel balcony high on the castle's western wall. Behind him, through the chapel and the hallway that led to the Great Hall, he heard the murmur of happy conversation as Yarvannet's noble folk again celebrated the Blessing with another ball, the third of several nightly entertainments in his son's honor. The object of that honor now slept soundly in his nursery, safe from any further attempts on his life.

Did Norris belong to Tejar? Melfallan wondered, probing at the question as one might probe at an aching tooth. Had the duke truly ordered Earl Audric's earlier death, and now struck at Melfallan's child? Or did Norris belong to Yarvannet's discontent count, Sadon of Farlost? If the master was known, the truth of the danger would be known—and from there he could take steps, make his own plans, guard what was precious to him. Or was Norris innocent, and the traitor now hiding in plain sight among the castle servants or even Melfallan's lords? *I will have answers,* Melfallan thought coldly. *This time I will know.*

The sounds of the surf echoed quietly in the air, patterning with the murmur of waves on the harbor piers. Melfallan took a deep breath, breathing in the chill air of the night. Far out at sea, waves flickered dimly, catching the starlight, and night and sea merged at the horizon, without division. Near him seawater murmured in the series of stone pools on the chapel balcony, where tiny damio fish darted, starlight gleams within the darkness of the water. The Allemanii had always been a sea folk; here in Yarvannet, the southernmost of the Allemanii lands, the sea ordered all life, mild in its tempers, moderate in its winds, unlike the dangerous storms of Mionn far to the east. Melfallan had been born in Yarvannet and loved his land with a fullness of the heart that was sometimes lost in the bustle of the day and his earl's duties but was easily found in the short stretches of peace like this, here on this balcony, surrounded by the night and the sounds of the sea.

He bowed his head. Thank you for saving my son, he thought in gratitude to Mother Ocean. Help me to protect him, and all that I love.

He heard a step behind him and turned, then saw Lord Tauler silhouetted in the chapel doorway. "Do I disturb your solitude, your grace?" Tauler asked softly.

"Yes, but I'm not offended." Melfallan sat down on the low stone wall of the damio pool and regarded his marcher lord. Lord Tauler held the river headlands that bordered his aunt's county of Airlie, one of the two doorways into Yarvannet for an invader. Enfeoffed to Count Sadon, the older lord had tread a careful path between his fractious count and powerful earl. He watched as Tauler walked forward and stopped near him, then saw Tauler look out at the sea. Tauler was dressed simply, as always, although the fabric of his tunic was subtly rich, and he wore a short sword at his side, a gleaming chain on his breast. The real worth of the man lay in the proud carriage of his head, the compact muscles of his soldier's body, gifts Tauler also did not flaunt.

"I miss the sea," Tauler said quietly. "My lands are pleasant enough, but I've always thought they lack an essential connection for an Allemanii." He looked at Melfallan, shrugged slightly. "I was your age when I inherited my river lands. My father survived your grandfather's conquest of Yarvannet—by chance alone, for my father was beholden to Count Sadon and Sadon chose Audric's side, and thus my father was spared—and me."

"Much wrong was done then."

"You admit that?" Tauler asked with mild surprise.

Melfallan shrugged in turn. "My grandfather made mistakes, and I know that many of my problems would not be mine if he had chosen otherwise. But I loved him, and he was a strong earl for Yarvannet."

"In some ways you are stronger, my earl."

"Then I am your earl now, Lord Tauler? We discussed that before."

Tauler shook his head, and did not answer the question, not directly. "This was a foul thing, the attempt on your son," he said.

"Sir James will question Norris again in the morning. He may not say much. The soldiers beat him badly when he was caught, and perhaps he fears to say anything at all, thinking I will let them beat him again. Even if not, kept spies, if Norris is a spy, often have an inner resolve, if only from fear of their master."

Tauler rested one foot comfortably on the wall, then folded his arms on his knee. "Sadon or Tejar: is that your choice for master?"

"The apparent choice. Sometimes the answer isn't the obvious." Melfallan sighed. "But at least I have time again, Tauler, time to prepare Yarvannet. Earl Giles made a fool of himself at the Blessing, enough to damage his reputation among the High Lords—and I don't think he realizes it, not yet. Whatever he had planned with this Lim marriage is lost now, whether as a way to build his wealth, or to restrain the duke at my expense, or even greater ambition."

"The coronet? I warned you, you'll remember. Sadon always thought that Earl Giles encouraged Pullen's rebellion."

"And I heard you, and it's not polite to say, 'I told you so.' Sometimes, my good lord, I wish life was simpler, for my son's sake, if nothing else. Do you often think of your own son, when you're caught on your anvil as your earl and your count hold our hammers high?"

Tauler smiled. "I think of my son constantly. He is a good lad, and will be a fine man—more his mother's doing than mine. She has raised him to be faithful and true, to give loyalty that is unquestioned, a true gentleman knight." He shrugged. "Better than I've managed to be. My son will be better than I, and that's a comfort to any father, and Gwinon's gift to me. Some lords forget that lordship began in the knight's tradition, and prospers best within it." He paused. "You made a good choice in knighting Jared Cheney. He will serve you well."

"Actually, it wasn't my idea; Revil suggested it. I just agreed it was a good idea—another truth of lordship, perhaps."

"Where is Sir Jared, by the way?"

"Ah! The real reason you came out here?"

Tauler shrugged affably, then grinned. "Not really. Keep your secrets, your grace, if you will. Why am I here? I've decided it is time I gave better assurances to my liege lord than my dodging and talk of my anvil. I would not have done that for Earl Audric, not after he butchered Yarvannet." He paused. "Shall I be candid?"

"You have a gift for it, Lord Tauler."

"So do you—and we both feel uneasy with it, after all our upbringing that truth is dangerous when let out into the world." He hesitated, then quirked his mouth wryly. "So how shall I say it? I admit I've practiced, this way and that. Which is best?" He thought another moment, then shrugged as wryly. "Ah, well, I can do only what I can. You know as well as I do that the time of crisis is coming. I can see your worry, and I share it. Our High Lord politics can bear only so much strain before we erupt again into conflict: despite your grandfather's conquest, despite all the reasons I could withhold my trust, I stand with the Courtrays and our Yarvannet." Tauler straightened. "I swore fealty to you some months ago, but all lords do that for their liege at accession. There is a deeper fealty that comes in time, one of the heart, shown by conduct and action, not mere words—but sometimes by words, too, as I do now. In some ways you are the young lord I might have been, had Mother Ocean given me higher rank and a less troubled history—or so I flatter myself. And so the time has come to choose." He offered his hand, and Melfallan gripped it.

"Thank you," Melfallan said softly. "I had been hoping for more than my one certain lord in Revil."

"You'll earn them, one by one. I have that confidence. Can I make a suggestion?"

"Of course." Melfallan looked at the older man and suspected they'd come to Tauler's real reason for this quiet conference on the balcony, not an invitation Melfallan had actually intended when he escaped the party, but one Tauler had promptly accepted. Tauler's next words confirmed it.

"Look at Count Sadon with different eyes than your grandfather."

"I intended to, but Sadon chose otherwise," Melfallan said sourly. "Was it a game? To send word that he would attend the Blessing, and then not come?" He shook his head. "How can I make peace with him when he hides in his marshlands?"

Tauler sighed. "I truly thought he'd come, and perhaps there are other reasons than spite that he didn't."

"Perhaps," Melfallan said dubiously, and wished it were so, however little he believed it.

"Yes, perhaps," Tauler agreed. "It's always 'perhaps' with Count Sadon, especially in recent years. He fights the world by being contrary, for his problems truly have no solution and he knows it. You at least still hope for a solution to each of your problems of rule; Sadon has long since lost that hope. I've known him all my life, Melfallan, and I remember him before Pullen rebelled. He's now soured with disappointment and all the years your grandfather disdained him, but traces of the younger count still remain, stubbornly at the core. The largest part of his disappointment lies in his son— we were talking about sons." He nodded toward the chapel through the balcony doors, where the Blessing had been held three days before. "Don't assume that attempt on the baby was caused by him, I beg you. Don't assume, as your grandfather assumed, that all treachery in Yarvannet lies in Farlost." He grimaced, made a vague gesture with his hand, then let it fall. "My count has been surly and insulting to me, hasn't given my proper due as his vassal in respect and courtesy, but he's never betrayed me. Lectured, shouted, sulked, called me names, as he did my father, too, but there's another essence to the man beneath all that, one he formed in his youth and has never lost. Otherwise, good earl, my anvil would have been less perplexing. On the one hand, I swore fealty to the earl, but on the other, I swore fealty to Sadon; and I consider both lords worthy of my trust, not just one—but I didn't always find fully what I hoped in either liege. I'm hoping you'll be different." He looked out again at the sea. "I wonder if lordship was easier in the West, before we came to these lands and created a duke to make our politics dangerous. I wonder if a sworn man was enough to anchor one's life, needing nothing more. It was a simpler life, truly. I think Count Sadon thinks so, too."

"Compassion for Sadon?" Melfallan asked soberly. "You surprise me."

"Why? Do I truly surprise you?" Tauler asked ruefully. "He's a difficult man to love when he shouts, but Norris could belong to Tejar just as well—or to Lord Garth."

"Garth?" Melfallan blurted.

"Not to Garth himself—he's largely as he appears, bluff and hearty like his prized horses—but to his lady. There's a rumor out, Melfallan, one that has passed from lady-maid to river wife to my own servants in Penafeld, a rumor of a letter gone off to Duke Tejar, maybe more than one. Joanna doesn't like you, whatever she hides behind her pretty smiles—and she fools herself when she thinks she understands you. She's not as clever as she thinks she is, not in the hiding or in whatever games she's begun."

"And you don't like her."

Tauler grinned. "True, but I mostly follow my wife's opinion there. That comment today by your lady wife is something Joanna might do, and has done from time to time, thinking Garth likes it. Maybe he does, but my wife doesn't, not because she disapproves of sex, to my great relief and pleasure that she doesn't," he added with a grin, "but because Gwinon disapproves of boasting of any kind, especially when it embarrasses another."

"You think Joanna—" Melfallan frowned. "But why?"

"I haven't a clue, but the suggestion is Gwinon's, not

mine, and I have now duly delivered it, as instructed." He cocked his blond head. "Have you noticed a trend of how thoroughly ruled by my wife I am, poor pitiful soul? Gwinon caught my heart years ago, and I've never regretted the capture. She has clearer sight than I do, understands hearts better. I am incomparably rich that she loves me. And so when I note that my wife, who earnestly tries to love all persons, forms a pointed dislike for Lady Joanna, I pay attention. To Joanna's excuse, she likely fears for her father, Sir Kaene. She thinks you'll attack Count Sadon and ruin her father as your grandfather ruined other knights thirty years ago. A wife sometimes forgets that her house changes when she marries a lord, and so attends more carefully to the father than to the husband. It's too bad. Garth deserved better."

"You're a mine of information, Lord Tauler, and you certainly don't like her at all."

Tauler shrugged. "Measure it as you will. I told you I am my wife's pawn. You asked my reasons for coming out here, away from your excellent party, and those are two of them."

"Are there others?"

Tauler's face sobered, although a smile teased at his lips. "One more. To wish your son good health, my liege. In time my son will look to yours, if Yarvannet is preserved against the dangers that now threaten us. May we begin something new, you and I, something to be continued by our sons, to Yarvannet's safety."

"Indeed." Melfallan paused, then offered his hand again. "Thank you, Tauler. Thank you for your reasons."

Tauler gripped Melfallan's hand, then nodded. "Ocean's Blessing, your grace."

"I worry for Yarvannet," Melfallan said quietly. "I wonder if I'm earl enough, and I look for strength in my lords. I can't say how much I value your loyalty, Tauler, and I choose to believe in it, for all that folly."

Tauler's eyes crinkled in amusement. "It *is* hard to ignore all those sober warnings in the texts."

"Indeed. Garth offered me his loyalty, too, and I believe in it, too, but it didn't bring the same assurance as yours. Words are easy to offer when they flatter, and Garth likes to flatter."

"I still think him honest."

"So do I. And perhaps Count Sadon is more than my grandfather believed, as you wish me to think. I want to know why he didn't come to the Blessing."

"I'm willing to ride to Farlost to find out," Tauler said, a bit too quickly, and Melfallan tsked at him, shaking his head.

"I thought you might," he said dryly, "but you had the grace to be subtle in your poking. Perhaps I might think of it myself, after all, given a subtle nudge or two by you tonight, and if not, there's always tomorrow night—"

Tauler chuckled. "Wheedling one's liege is an art, I agree. Gwinon says so." He shrugged. "It must be true."

"Hmph. Wheedle as you will, my lord Tauler, but it saves time just to say it out loud."

"Also true," Tauler admitted, and they grinned at each other.

"So go find out for me," Melfallan said. "Find me the truth about Farlost, that I might do justice my grandfather denied and so mend Yarvannet."

"You mean that?" Tauler asked, startled. "Even if Sadon *did* poison Earl Audric?"

Melfallan sighed. "I don't know if I can yield that far. I honestly don't know. I'm hoping you're right about him, and that all the rumors are wrong. I'm hoping Norris is innocent and not the traitor he seems. I hope many things—perhaps some of those hopes are foolish. If they are, I'll deal with them as best I can, however I can." He grimaced. "Find the truth for me, Tauler, if you will. Give me that first step."

"I will, your grace." Tauler bowed low, then withdrew gracefully through the chapel doorway. Melfallan listened to his retreating footsteps, bemused, then wondered exactly how he had won Tauler's loyalty, enough that this cautious lord would speak plainly, against all of Duke Rainalt's advising, against all prudence to wait and see.

When had it happened? How had he prompted this gracious offer of Tauler's counsel, plainly stated as a loyal man would speak, prompting Melfallan to speak in kind, more wisely than Melfallan might otherwise have managed? The Allemanii lords in the West had greatly valued the sworn man, finding in that bond a strength rarely found elsewhere. Melfallan narrowed his eyes, wondering if that particular strength was found only in such a bond, a truth Duke Rainalt had chosen to ignore, a truth Duke Tejar overlooked as easily, thinking instead men were always bought and never won, and that selfish interest outruled all other cares.

When had it happened? he wondered, almost light-headed in his relief. What did I do to prompt Tauler to abandon his caution and take such risks with me? Will I ever know? He looked out at the dark sea, and felt the chill air sigh against his skin, then heard the breeze stir the leaves of the plants that hung above his head. The damios flickered in the balcony pools, flashing silver. Melfallan took a deep breath, then shook his head. *One is a fool to trust, when one is a High Lord.* Well, Melfallan would test that rule when he could.

Melfallan lingered awhile longer on the balcony, liking its cool peace, then returned to the Great Hall, where the torches burned brightly and the Yarvannet nobility still danced and smiled and flattered each other. He sat down beside Revil and Solange at one of the high tables, and smiled as Solange bent toward him to tease, as she always teased. He watched Saray dance with Sir Justin, then be whirled away by Garth, smiling and laughing. She caught him watching her and smiled brilliantly, to all eyes without a care, beautiful and laughing, the exquisite loveliness of Lady Yarvannet that Saray created effortlessly. Saray teased her brother, Robert, and was teased in turn, and Melfallan listened as she came breathlessly up to him to excuse herself, as if she must now gain his permission for any absence, then watched her guide her frigid mother away from the ball, wanting to say good night to her father lying abed upstairs, a good daughter to her parents, a good wife to her husband, a perfection in the art of the lady wife. He felt happy to see her happy, he told himself, but still felt uneasy as Saray sparkled and laughed. Yesterday he had found her deeply unhappy, as he knew she truly was, but all this day Saray had shown no trace of it, playing her perfection of the the gracious hostess, the perfect lady, even the bold-spoken wife pleased with her husband and the new child he had placed inside her, telling all proudly of her joys in her husband, every one. Will I ever understand her? he thought in despair. And I must.

"Melfallan, you are too sober for this ball," Solange announced. "Dance with me." She rose from her chair and imperiously held out her hand.

"I'm always sober," Melfallan said, and leaned back lazily. "It's also called dull."

"You won't escape me," Solange insisted. "I am relentless."

He sniffed at her, making it a dare, and Solange pounced on him, dragging him to his feet and off onto the floor. They danced together for the next set, and then Revil firmly claimed his wife again, and Melfallan found himself dancing with Lady Gwinon. Tauler's lady smiled up at him, her blue eyes twinkling.

"I hear that you are the strength of Penafeld," he said gallantly, as he squired her around the floor.

"Don't listen to his nonsense," she said, shaking her head. "All his life my husband has yearned for a lord to love, one worthy of his talents and devotion. I merely pointed out a few facts, nothing more. It was no great gift of mine, your grace."

"I wish you and Tauler would visit Tiol more often. Your presence has been missed, my lady."

"We will now," she said simply. "That I can promise."

By the time they had finished their dance, many of the noble folk had begun to drift off to bed, pleased with the glittering entertainment that evening. The musicians finally put up their instruments, and Melfallan followed the last few noble folk up the stairs. On the way to his own bedchamber, he stopped by the baby's nursery, late as it was, and so disturbed the baby's servants when likely he should not have. He told Audric's nurse not to get up, but she did, clutching her blanket around her. Audric slept peacefully in his crib by the window, fierce in his determined sleeping and quite unaware that his father stood there by the cradle, watching him sleep. In the next crib slept Leila's little girl just as soundly.

"I really shouldn't have woken you," Melfallan said, turning his head to smile. "You have a busy enough day as it is, Leila."

"And how am I afflicted by that?" Leila teased, easy with him. "He is well, your grace."

"Yes, I know." Melfallan bid her go back to sleep, then left the nursery.

He found Saray still awake in their bedroom, and stopped short in surprise when he saw what she was wearing. All of Saray's nightdresses suited her ideas of a modest lady wife, opaque and comfortable, but this gown plunged low and clung silkily to Saray's body, revealing every line, every curve of breast and waist and the long line of her legs. Saray turned around in place, letting him see it all, swaying seductively as she moved.

"Do you like it?" she asked coyly.

Melfallan cleared his throat, then stared another moment. "Is that new?"

"Oh, a present from Lady Joanna." Saray flipped her hand negligently, and then walked toward him, her hips swaying. With a graceful pull of her hands, she brought the gown upward over her head and finished her advance in the nude. Melfallan's jaw dropped full open, and he hadn't a word to say, not that Saray needed it. She wound her arms around his neck and pressed closely to him. "You wear too many clothes," she whispered and slowly rubbed her body against his. "Take them off." Then she pulled his head down to kiss him.

He belatedly responded, trying to overcome his surprise. Saray had never behaved like this in the bedroom, but now took the lead throughout, stripping him out of his clothes, pulling him to the bed, guiding his hands, moving and crying out as she had never done. And then, after they lay sweated together in the dark bedroom, limbs tangled, she insisted on a second time and boldly straddled him when he was ready, taking the lead again and prolonging the lovemaking for another half hour. Then, making pleased noises in her throat, she snuggled next to him, yawned, and went to sleep.

And throughout it all, he knew, none of her passion was real. He knew her too well, knew how she felt about sex. She was playacting, perhaps at Joanna's careful instruction of how to seduce a husband. All had been more of her pretending, all of it: the bold nudity, the eager cries, the tossing of the head as she coupled with him, all of it. Her perfume, her loveliness, the stimulation of her body against his brought the inevitable result, as it usually did, and so Saray forced him to pretend as she pretended, violating this most intimate part of their lives. Why had she done it? Why?

He lay on his back in the bed, Saray's naked body entwined against him, and stared at the bedroom ceiling, a painful heaviness in his throat. He felt—used, even raped, he decided, an emotion he had not known a man could feel, had not known at all. He stared unseeingly at the ceiling, one minute after the other. His chest rose and fell as he breathed, pacing the minutes as they passed, in subtle rhythm with Saray's deeper breaths beside him.

What do I do? Saray had sadly asked him only yesterday, and had thought of coldness, fury, other men. Saray's final choice dismayed him. She was not quite the actress she believed herself, not quite easy enough with sex to make it seem true. And, ironically, his proof lay in the other women he had bedded, the other women who had given honestly of themselves, not for design, shy when they should be shy, bold when they chose to be bold, as Brierley had been when she bedded with him. He sighed and closed his eyes wearily. He could not think of a better revenge, if revenge she intended.

But why do you feel this way? he argued at himself angrily. You always wanted Saray to enjoy the bedding, not merely do her duty in the submitting. Of course he should be pleased that she now sought to excite him, to pleasure him, to please him in every way. But why did it have to come with the pretending? He felt so weary of Saray's pretending, wanting honesty, wanting what she simply could not give him. Yet, he knew, the kindest act he could do was to make her believe she'd succeeded, flattering her as she flattered him, and so enter into her pretense, the perfect world Saray desperately wanted. Can I manage that? he asked himself candidly. Do I owe Saray that? Is loving Brierley such a crime to demand such a price?

When he was sure she was deeply asleep, he eased away from her and slipped out of bed. Pulling on hose and a robe, he left their bedchamber, escaping her again, as he must. He wandered restlessly through the cold hallways, surprising the occasional soldier on guard, and then wearily climbed the stairs to his tower study. How he would explain sleeping on the cot again, he couldn't hazard, not after Saray had arranged her night of passionate love, or so she would think it. It would hurt Saray when she found him gone again in the morning, and he did not want to hurt her, desperately did not want to hurt her.

I'll get up early, he thought vaguely. I'll be there again in the morning when she wakes. She'll never know. Wearily, he threw himself on the cot by the tower window and covered his eyes with his arm. Beyond the window, the sea murmured and cried in Her many voices, an unending sound that followed him into sleep.

His dreams shifted uneasily from place to place, first to a white pavilion on a cliff, then to a wide meadowland near a glittering expanse of a lake, to places he knew, places he did not, seeking desperately something he could not name and did not find. He awoke finally in his tower study, stiff from sleeping on the cot, and little rested. He sat up, yawning, then saw a slender woman, dressed in homespun, bending over his books on the table. Well, not awake, he amended wryly.

He watched her turn a page. "Where am I sleeping now?" he asked ironically. "In my own bed where I hoped to return before Saray missed me, or up here?"

"Does it matter?" Thora murmured, and turned another page. "What is dreaming, and what is awake? Let us define."

"Hmph."

"Grunting does not flatter an earl," she chided him. "You should give it up, fair lord, and be improved."

"Hmph," he repeated.

She lifted her head and wrinkled her nose, amused, then tsked at him, shaking her head. "Do not worry: I will wake you and send you back to your bed before Saray knows you are gone. You will not have that further grief in the new day when it comes." She set her chin firmly.

"Why did she do it?" Melfallan asked in anguish, and wished the Everlight would answer, just once, despite its cautions about advising too much.

"I don't know," Thora admitted bleakly. "I honestly don't know. Your wife isn't witch-born, not in the slightest, and so I have no clue. I would tell you if I could, truly, but she baffles me as much as she baffles you." She shook her head. "I do not understand pretending used to avoid truth. Is not truth better?" She shook her head again. "Is that not obvious, a truth in itself that no one can deny? But enough of this new bafflement, my dear one: accept the dream I send you now, and be comforted."

He nodded numbly. She waited until he looked up to meet her eyes, and he saw the worry for him. "I'm all right," he assured her.

"No, you're not, but we'll pretend." She quirked her mouth at the irony.

Melfallan lay back on the cot and sighed. "I never get

away from the pretending, not with her, not with my lords—except perhaps my good Tauler, my loving Revil."

"And with Brierley?" she suggested.

"Yes, especially with her. It's a comparison I always make when I'm wanting her, and it's not fair to Saray and I know it, but I do it anyway. This new plan of Saray's won't help us. It should, I agree, but I know it won't."

"Patience, fair lord."

"Yes," he agreed heavily, "patience. So where do I find patience, Everlight? In a shop or on the beach, perhaps on a shelf somewhere inside a box? Where?"

"Speaking of patience," she countered briskly, "that duke's courier is still waiting to see you. For a second day he has fumed in his pleasant apartments, having only one excuse after another for the delay. Philippe will wear out his feet, going up and down all those stairs."

Melfallan put his hands behind his head and smiled at the ceiling. "He brought too many soldiers with him. I'm affronted."

"You're afflicted," the Everlight corrected, "and visiting that unhappy emotion on a helpless courier. But why not? Every day an earl must attend matters of rule when he'd rather go fishing, be watched by every eye when he'd rather not, and wheedle at his lords whenever they misbehave. What can that courier do to you, after all, being the third son of Lord Dail and not the first or second? And you already know what he brings to harass you."

"All true. Tejar deliberately sent him to disrupt the baby's celebrations. I'm retorting." He paused, then turned his head to look at her. "Do you think it's a mistake? It's something Grandfather would do. Does that mean I shouldn't?"

"Not at all. When pushed, a vigorous lord pushes back—within reason. It's in every text."

"Hmph." He sat up again and swung his feet to the floor. "I thought I'd make him wait one more day—to keep within reason, as you advise. Three days is enough to make a point, but four a bit too much. Do you agree?"

"I agree." She smiled and nodded, then bent over the book

again. "Why are you reading poetry?" she asked curiously. "And ancient sagas at that?"

He got to his feet and walked around the table to her side. Her clear, gray eyes regarded him solemnly, a twinkle of affection in their depths. Whenever the Everlight appeared in his dreams as Thora Jodann, always in his tower study and never at the cave, the Everlight completely changed personality, drawing from its memories of that first witch in Yarvannet, a witch who had seen the Disasters and who had later made herself Brierley's dream-friend, mother, comforter, and guide. *As Megan is my child,* Brierley had told him, *so I am hers.* Perhaps in some way the Everlight truly became Thora as she had once been centuries before, by whatever process it remembered her. Perhaps, in a way, he truly spoke to the woman who had once lived, more than to a memory. Who could say? Certainly she seemed a real woman, as real as Brierley when the Everlight brought those other dreams. Those other dreams of Brierley made life possible, he believed, until he could bring her home to Yarvannet. Thora came to his dreams for a different purpose, to lend the Everlight's political counsel and to help him think.

"Poetry catches the temper of an age," he said, "or so I was taught. I thought those older times in the West, when matters were clearer, might lend some better direction. Tauler said much the same thing tonight, a coincidence I like."

"I like him," she said, nodding with approval. "He will be true."

"Does Tauler have witch-blood?" Melfallan asked.

"No, fair lord. And we're not going through the roster of everyone in Yarvannet, is he, isn't she, at least not tonight." Thora shook her red head. "Why poetry?" she prompted again.

Melfallan covered another yawn with his hand, and then scowled, wondering why he yawned at all, being still asleep. "I'm tired of Duke Rainalt and his cold counsels. 'If a High Lord is to keep his folk loyal and united,' Rainalt says, 'he must be indifferent to the charge of cruelty. Having set an example once or twice, he can then act more mercifully and yet avoid disorder.' " Melfallan shook his head. "As if mercy is an indulgence of some kind, a gloss on the reality of rule. Grandfather told Sir James to make me memorize most of Rainalt's book, and then he'd test me, making me recite." He sighed. "A boy has better things to do at twelve."

"Duke Rainalt's ethics need hardly be your model, Melfallan."

Melfallan grimaced. "But what he describes, Everlight, fits exactly how the High Lords behave. It's a fact. First comes the pretense of virtue to conceal hidden intentions, then the ease of lies, the treachery behind every glad hand of friendship, the use of power to keep advantage by whatever means. All is justified by the end of keeping one's power." He scowled more fiercely. "Earl Giles would toss Yarvannet into the sea if he thought it brought him even a mild advantage, and think himself canny to do so. I saw him this afternoon in his bedchamber, another of my duties of rule, to visit afflicted relatives, and he was the same as always, thinking himself so very clever, thinking himself better than everybody. He won't admit anything about his plots, even now, even when I tried to talk reason with him again. He tempts the duke with his games, and Yarvannet isn't the only land in peril because he does." Melfallan frowned, frustrated with his contrary father-in-law. "I can't make him see his mistake."

"Perhaps not," Thora agreed. "But whatever Earl Giles's bluster and pride, not all lords fit Rainalt's perfect example of the deft High Lord. Some are better men than others, and fail quite completely in Rainalt's evil, to the betterment of the world. I worry more about Tejar measuring himself to Rainalt's model, as do you. The good man accepts restrictions on his behavior; the evil does not, and so gains advantage over the good. It is the moral dilemma of all politics, yours and mine." She sighed. "I, too, argued to those who would not hear, dear one. I argued, then pleaded, and they merely shut up their ears all the more. Despite all my warnings, the shari'a loosed the Great Plague on the Allemanii, murdering hundreds of your people in revenge for Witchmere's destruction, and some of the survivors called it just." Her jaw tightened. "I called it evil, and still do. But evil cannot be ignored, fair lord. It is the dilemma of the good to remember our restrictions lest we become like them, wrecking the world. However Duke Rainalt justified his treacheries and murdering, virtue is not a disposable goal, nor a mere self-indulgence allowable once a lord feels easy in his rule. Don't doubt your different choices."

"Oh, I don't. I only worry that virtue might be exploited as a weakness. Rainalt was a cruel man, cold and unprincipled. Unfortunately, such lords often win, exactly because they lack virtue—your indifference to restrictions. Tejar would have murdered Brierley, whom he knew only as a commoner girl and nothing more, and not cared that she had no trial, that his own laws were violated. All he cared about was some secret gambit he thought I played, and so made his countermove." He scowled uneasily. "And I'm sure he prompted Lord Heider to murder my aunt, although I don't know the means he used—nor do I have proof he did it."

"Virtue is easily pretended: one merely hides inconvenient facts. Your duke is deft at ignoring what he does not wish to exist. It will pinch him in the end. The good does have some advantage: truth exists, however the evil may wish otherwise."

"True." He smiled down at her. "Why do I sense texts being quoted at me?"

She sniffed. "Merely because the shari'a did not mount armies does not mean our political warfare was any less bloody—figuratively speaking, of course. Scholars wield words, not weapons, but the murderous intent can be the same."

He grinned, then nodded his chin at the two volumes of poetry on the table. "Have you read these books before?" he asked.

"Only when you do, if I'm listening." She tsked at him, shaking her head. "Now how am I supposed to read books in your castle? I hardly have a means of transport from my cave, where I have been affixed to a wall for three hundred years."

"I didn't know," he said comfortably. "Maybe you can lurk through minds?"

She sniffed. "Unless the lurked has witch-blood—or a resonance, as you do—I cannot lurk at all. Besides," she added, "until recently I had little interest in your castle and its folk. Why should I?"

"Why do you now?" he countered with a smile.

She touched his sleeve, the lightest of touches, then let her hand fall. "For love of you, of course, and through you the love of your folk, as Brierley loves." She winked at him, then leaned forward to look at the book again, where it lay open to Lucian's tribute to an ancient Western hero named Artillius. " 'Thinking nothing done when much was left to do,' " Thora read aloud, " 'Lord Artillius knew / No rest—his only shame was to lose a fight. / Keen and untamed, he turned his hand to war, / and never quailed to stain his sword: / To make a path by havoc was his joy.' A path by havoc was his joy," she repeated thoughtfully, then looked up at him. "This is inspiring?"

"The West honored its warriors," Melfallan said with a shrug, and perched one hip on the table. "Most of our early sagas celebrated war as a form of artistic expression." He grinned as she made a face. "Well, it's true. War brings out the best—and the worst—in men, or so goes the theory, and the theory has some truth, I think. A lord defends his lands and his folk: it's the cornerstone of Allemanii rule. If defense requires violence, you use violence. Don't scowl like that. I've trained for war since I was nine years old—sword skills, horseback drills, battle theory, tactics, battle history. It's a necessary part of my rule, and I accept it. I've never gone to war. I've never actually killed. I think I could, if I had to—I mean, if it's a choice between him and me." He shrugged again. "And they say the 'heat of battle' allows even a good man to do things he usually can't contemplate—the nightmares come later."

"I do not understand war," Thora said flatly.

"You're an Everlight to a sea witch: your wars are a different sort, a battle against a Beast to save life and defeat Death. Your purpose is to preserve: so in part is mine. True, some men enjoy the slaughter, the danger, the imagined glory in hacking the enemy." He paused. "I don't think I will. But it doesn't mean I can pretend war out of my life. If I tried, I would fail as lord, fail in my duty."

Thora sighed feelingly. "Sir James has taught you well."

"Of course he has." He bent and turned the page to the next marker. "To save your good opinion of me, dear one, I do like Jovenal better. Listen: 'I celebrate a day that will banish dark cares, / When the world is bound by peaceful laws; / I need not apprehend / War nor a violent end. / While Martenius stands guard, peace is come, / The peace no power can break.' I want that 'peace no power can break.' I want Yarvannet protected, and if I can, I want to make it a land where the shari'a can live in peace, too, to live without fear, and thus create what should have existed between our peoples, not the destructions Duke Rahorsum inflicted. It's a second chance for us, Thora, part of Brierley's 'refounding of the craft.' I want to refound something that eluded the Allemanii in the Disasters and shouldn't have. Why did we lose that chance for peace between our peoples? Was it a lust for war, as Artillius lusted? Was it Duke Rainalt's cold calculation of the value of treachery? The High Lords draw from both traditions, and each gives us strength, truly they do, but perhaps there is another possible order, perhaps a better way to rule." He set his jaw stubbornly. "Perhaps one can trust a sworn man and not be destroyed. I'll take that chance with Tauler and any other lord who will offer it. Perhaps one *can* choose virtue, and not make of it a pretending. I want to find that other way, if I can—but first I have to understand Artillius and Rainalt. First I may have to wield my war and build my betrayals—perhaps. I'd be a fool to ignore the realities of High Lord politics, and I can't gain anything just by wishing them otherwise—in fact, I'd lose everything if I tried. Duke Tejar would see to that."

He sighed. "One could say war is honest—at least that. It has no pretensions about what it is—violence, death, strength, valor or cowardice, fortune or misfortune. A battle can be turned by a chance of weather, or a slip in the mud at the crux. Signals can go astray and bring the flank into motion too late—or too soon. War is an art, with lives at stake, lands at stake. Like I said, war does not pretend. My politics are different—there pretense rules. Everyone admires Duke Rainalt for his practical mind, unencumbered by the good. Everyone studies his text to learn matters of rule, as I did, as my grandfather did, as do all the sons of prudent High Lords." He tipped up Rainalt's text to show her the name on the spine, then dropped it again with a thud on the table. "As shall my son, when it's time. Duke Rainalt simply cannot be ignored."

Thora leaned against the table and raised a skeptical eyebrow. "It's true," Melfallan insisted. "After Rainalt betrayed his duke and murdered all the Briding house, he ruled well, untroubled by rebellions—he had ruthlessly cowed everyone and so could be merciful, I suppose, as he advises in his book. His text is considered one of the masterpieces of our political literature." Thora's eyes narrowed but she listened, as she always listened. Melfallan shook his head at her expression. "He advises the murder of whole families to keep the later stability of rule. He argues for the appearance of virtue, but that virtue is instantly abandoned when there is need, however one pretends the other just misunderstands. 'Betray you? How can you claim such a thing?' Earnest hand on earnest breast, the hurt look, the denial of everything. Just deny it, and it must be so, whatever you will. How often have I seen that among the High Lords?"

"Your duke?"

"Him, and others. Count Parlie of Briding is Yarvannet's friend, but his tactics borrow much from Duke Rainalt—even my allies follow his lessons. I'm sure Duke Tejar studied Rainalt's book as diligently in his boyhood, but his temperament suits it better. He's a strong duke, Thora: that's the irony. Why does evil so often lend strength, not weakness? Are honest men disadvantaged by the relentlessly practical?" He regarded her for a long moment as she squinted at him. "So what does that smile mean? That your maxim about the good and the evil is proved by my experience? Or do you disapprove that I admire relentless men? Do I sound bitter?"

"Wary, yes. Entirely unconvinced, given the man you are, but intrigued."

"Why intrigued?" he asked curiously.

"Because you wonder if your own answers are wrong, dear one. You wonder if you could secure your rule by becoming utterly selfish, ready to use anyone like the duke will. Power is all. Power is purpose. Many High Lords have ruled by that precept, but you—you don't agree." She fluted her pale hand. "Rainalt's practicality in politics is a familiar mind-set: several of the Witchmere leaders I knew would have nodded sagely at his precepts. Is not preservation of self the most important good? But by choosing that manner of rule we lost, I believe, what we hoped to keep." She was silent for a few moments. "I may not understand war, but that doesn't mean I don't know it. Near the end, you see, we shari'a tried to fight back. The road to the ships on the bay was drenched with blood, both Allemanii and shari'a alike. One of the Allemanii counts chased the Exiles when they tried to reach the ships they had hidden in the cove, and there was a great battle at the river ford near Arlenn. My sister—and my Peladius, the Allemanii lord I dared to love—died on that day, but four of the five ships escaped—to safety, I hope."

"Escaped?" Melfallan asked, startled. "To where?"

Thora smiled slightly. "The other side of the bay, to the

catling lands. You are not the only sailors in the world, fair lord. We shari'a had some skills in the art as well—and no other choice that day but to use them."

"Catlings?" Melfallan protested. "I thought the catlings were only a legend, an old tale."

"Like the shari'a are legends?" Thora's smile was wry. "Oh, they exist, Melfallan. Legends are sometimes oddly true in certain facts, sometimes the oddest of facts one would never imagine could be true. Our tales, based on contact centuries before your Landing and never renewed, said that the catlings had pointed ears and even tails, a wolflike people beneath their black shrouds, a night people who love the darkness and hate the Daystar's bright glare. Perhaps they are such." She shrugged. "You received the legend from us, but even we did not know for certain: we had little contact with them and, to be admitted, little interest. When one is met with unrelenting hostility at every chance encounter, one finds better tasks elsewhere. Did the Exiles survive their meeting across the bay? Do they wander now in the East? Or did the Promise I gave them fail? I never knew while I was alive." She sighed. "Perhaps it was folly to send them into the East. We were not great travelers, Melfallan, not like you. We liked our settled lives, our hills and forests, our quiet villages where we could sit and think and speculate about ourselves. Our journeys were those of the mind, not the lands and seas, and we found them just as interesting as your voyaging. But perhaps the Exiles survived the Landing and whatever life that came beyond it." Thora smiled. "Perhaps you are not the only folk who have made a great Voyage." She ran her fingers slowly over the pages of Jovenal's book. "I do find it interesting that you seek answers in poetry."

"It's a book, poetry or not. Books are useful."

"Oh, I'm not faulting you. I approve of poetry. Your Western sagas catch the essence of the seafarers that you still are, of what you thought important, how you governed yourselves, how you bound yourselves together as a folk. In one sense, you fled your own Disasters in the West, although that cause was not of men's making, not in the beginning: that came later when the other tribes attacked you, driven to their senseless slaughter by starvation and fear. All the world seemed to be ending when the seas failed you and the Red Blight struck your coastlands, emptying the ocean of its life. The Allemanii might have died as a folk on that night of the assault, had you chosen that fate. You might have surrendered to the terror come suddenly down upon you, yielded up your wives and children to their swords, your very lives to their terrible fear. But your noble brothers, Aidan and Farrar, led you instead to a new destiny, away from the blight and war, and you journeyed over a thousand miles of icy sea, never giving up hope of finding a new green land—and so found what you sought. Perhaps the Exiles found what they sought, too: I hope so. Perhaps destiny is only a matter of willing the future, to believe with all your strength and heart and mind in a single hope." She nodded slowly. "Yes, perhaps it is so."

"Perhaps that's an answer to my own dilemma of practical politics—not giving up." He looked down into her clear, gray eyes. "You never gave up, Thora, and look at what you preserved for your people."

To his surprise Thora's face twisted; she sighed and looked away. "You're mistaken about me," she said. "At the end I despaired, when the earl's men hunted me throughout Yarvannet and would not relent. I had no great struggle in my death, fair lord: no brave sword fight in battle, no desperate struggle against a wound or mortal illness. One morning I lay down in my bed and I listened to the sea and the wind for a time, and then I died. I was only twenty-six, your age. You have possible years of living ahead of you, perhaps even the pleasures of old age that many of my own people enjoyed in their own time, but I did not. A shari'a gift is powered by the mind, you see, and a healer's gift can turn inward, stopping the breath, quieting the heart, if one becomes too weary of living. To heal, a dayi tampers with the links between mind and body, especially her own, and I grew too weary of living, fair lord, of striving, of hoping against hope, and finally I despaired." She looked down at her slim hands. "For five long years I lived after Peladius had died, and every day I thought of him, every day I longed for him, and that longing was a knife in my heart that never eased. It was not a resonance that destroyed me—I was wiser than that—only love, dear one, only love. For five years I struggled to find meaning beyond his loss, mourning my Peladius gone into the ground, lost to me. Believe! I told myself and wrote to my daughters-to-come: believe! Do not give up the believing, for there lies the heart and all that truly matters, there is the purpose for living. I dreamed of the Promise, and told myself it would come true: the Promise must be believed or all is darkness, and I struggled to hope. In the end my hope failed, and I failed." She sighed, her shoulders slumping. "I am not proud of my ending. It was a coward's death."

"Nonsense," he said softly, and took her hands into his. "Do you know how many times I have read your journal and felt thrilled by your words?"

"Of course I know how often you read it," she said irritably. "I'm there, after all. I make it possible."

"And do you know how many times Brierley read your words, finding the same hope?"

"Yes." Her eyes remained troubled. "But still I failed."

"No." He smiled and pressed her fingers. "No, you didn't fail. Your Everlight remembers you, and you left your words for Brierley—and me—in your book, and for all the other daughters your words have comforted." He laid his palm on the book in front of them. "It is my lack, as you have often reminded me, to doubt myself and my decisions: Am I earl enough? I ask myself, and I worry I am not. But meeting Brierley and coming to understand her better through you, and, in truth, by knowing you, brave Thora, I've found a purpose I cannot doubt, a shari'a world that must be saved, a refounding that must be made. It is a purpose I would never have had except for her and now you. It is a purpose worth living for, a guide for the future, a purpose that might save me from Duke Rainalt's pattern for the world. You gave me that through your words, and you gave it to Brierley, too, and we are enriched."

The corners of her mouth tipped up. "You comfort me."

He smiled at her. "That, too, is part of my purpose." He bent and closed up each of the books on the table, one by one, a series of small thuds. "So tell me, if we aren't teaching me politics or diverting me from Saray or reminding me of Brierley to comfort me, if we gave up all those purposes related to me, what would you like to do next with this dream?"

"I don't understand," she said slowly, and frowned, perplexed. "Do?"

Melfallan spread his hands expansively. "Should we walk on the beach? My shore lands are pretty at night, especially in the winter when the stars are out. You can tell me how things are defined into categories." He winked at her. "I've noticed you like to do that. Hard to believe, but it's a fact. Or you can choose a memory, one you treasure, of your many daughters. We can make a dream for you, not me."

"A dream for me?" she asked, astonished.

"Why not?"

"But— What foolishness! I don't make dreams for myself."

"What would you dream, Everlight," he insisted gently, "if you had the choosing?"

She hesitated another moment, then began to smile. "I—I think I should like to go to one of Marlenda's parties, and wear the silken gown she wore when she danced with all the young men who admired her. Do you remember Marlenda?"

"Yes. She was the sea witch before Brierley, the witch my grandfather's invasion drove into hiding and desperation and death."

"That was not your fault, Melfallan," the Everlight said gently. "In my memory, dear one, Marlenda is still young and carefree, the beautiful nobleman's daughter, happy and laughing as she danced with all the young men in her lovely silken gown. It's not really my dream, only one of Brierley's pretend games, but I always wondered how it felt to— Would you dance with me if we went there?"

Melfallan gave her a sweeping bow. "Of course—but only if you give me every dance," he said. "And only if you come as the redhead with the braids." He winked at her. "Let the other young men envy me, all those other admirers of yours that I already detest. Let them watch me with jealous eyes as I dance with you, the curs that they are." He held out his hand.

And there she was, the girl with the braids, dimpling as she smiled. Her green eyes sparkled. She curtseyed and gave him her slender hand. "My pleasure to be so, fair lord," she murmured coyly, batting her eyelashes. "Let us be frivolous and give up our sober talk of treachery and war, at least for a time."

"Let us be joyful," he amended, "and remember better things."

"Yes," she said. "Let us do that. And then I will wake you, as I promised, to go back to your proper bed before Saray wakes."

He nodded, then sighed, but the grief did not pull at him as it had, the hopelessness did not seem as deep, the Everlight's gift to him, yet again. "I've always assumed every problem has a solution," he said ruefully. "All you have to do is think long enough. But maybe not."

"Problems come in categories," she offered. "Let us define."

"Really?" he retorted. "Why don't you define them to me while we dance?"

"If you insist," the Everlight said, and laughed up at him.

~

Brierley awoke before dawn in the large, comfortable bed in Michael's house, Megan and Stefan beside her, both deeply asleep. Beyond the bedroom window, the trees were black shadows beneath the sparkling stars of the True Night, stars that glittered and seemed to dance gracefully, one with another as they winked in and out behind branches stirred by the wind. Was that music? She turned her head toward the bedroom door and listened. Silly, she told herself. Of course it's not. The musicians who had played the dances at the festival had long since packed up their instruments and gone home to their beds, as had all the Flinders folk who had gathered in the market square for an evening of dancing and laughter. Now the night's silence lay on the town and drifted slowly over the lake, broken only by the soft sighing of the wind and an occasional tapping of a branch end on the bedroom window.

Restless, Brierley eased away from Megan, who tonight slept safely nestled within Stefan's arms, and slipped out of their bed, then stood a moment on the braided rug. Where are you going, Brierley? she asked herself crossly. She thought a moment and then shrugged. I don't know, to admit the truth. Whom do I ask?

To find the dancers? For surely there were dancers— She shook her head slightly, then scowled more fiercely and put her hands on her hips. You silly woman, she scolded herself. Why are you out of bed? What dancers?

In her cave, she had sometimes dressed in Marlenda's lovely silken gown and pretended herself a fine lady at a ball, dancing with an invisible swain up and down the stone floor of the cave as invisible watchers oohed and aahed— Now why had she thought of that?

Brierley—

Brierley turned her head and caught her breath to listen. She fumbled through the darkness for her robe, then slipped out of the bedroom, passing quickly on bare feet across the outer room to the porch door. Her hand reached for the knob, then good sense asserted itself and she reached for Michael's heavy cloak on its peg on the wall. It was, after all, still winter: best to add boots. She tried Michael's boots first, then giggled at their enormity on her feet, and found a smaller pair nearby, probably Will's. Then she went outside.

The night air was cold, crisp with the lingering winter.

Starlight sparkled on the lake, a thousand tiny stars in end-less movement, air and fire within the water. She stopped on the porch, breathing in the moist air from the lake, then closed her eyes.

Brierley— The Voice called to her again, the Voice that years before had called her to the cave and her shari'a life of healing, the Voice that had called her again only a week ago on the beach of the bay, the Voice that was Basoul.

I am here, she answered eagerly. *Where are you?*

Far out on the lake the sparkles gathered with fresh energy, swirling forward toward her. A gomphrey, a great sea snake from the bay, lifted its massive head from the lake water, its eyes gleaming with an inner light. It swam toward her, lash-ing its tail against the water, and the starlight flowed with it, a brilliant river of sparkles against the dark, heaving surface of the lake. Brierley skipped down the porch steps and ran across the sand toward the water. Several yards from shore the gomphrey heaved up its great body and metamorphed into a blue-scaled dragon, her fins flashing silver, her eyes a vivid aquamarine blue. Basoul spread her wings wide, water drops sparkling down in a brilliant cascade, and displayed a moment more for the dramatic effect, then folded her wings to her back and calmly waddled ashore. *How was that?* she asked smugly.

Brierley put her hands on her hips and considered. "Well, *I* was impressed."

Good. Brierley looked cautiously toward the town, wor-ried that others might be about in the near-dawn. Fishermen rose early to catch their fish, she knew, and others of the townsfolk might be up, too. *No one can see us,* Basoul reas-sured her, *not when I will otherwise. As I am invisible to them, so now are you.*

Brierley laughed in relief and ran forward, then threw her arms as far as she could around Basoul's curving neck. She felt herself gathered close and gently seated on the dragon's tail; then she leaned against Basoul's broad shoulder and sighed. She looked up into the brilliance of the dragon's eyes, to find herself dazzled again by the dragon's smile. "I have missed you, Basoul."

It's only been a week or so.

"That's too long."

Yes, it is. Basoul lowered her chin to the sand and regarded her with one eye. *Why are you troubled, Brierley? Why do you worry?*

"I'm not this great person you want me to be, Basoul. You know I'm not."

You can be, my daughter. For three hundred years the Four have waited for the sea witch and her Allemanii lord who could mend what was long ago broken. Time and time again we have watched, waiting, as first one was reborn, then the other, born into the same time when destiny might allow them to meet. Twice you did meet, first as a Briding soldier and his beloved, then as a Mionn castellan and his fair wife: but both times, first the lord, then the witch, died untimely. You have lived several times since you were Thora and loved your Peladius, my daughter: several times Thora's spirit has risen again to new life, new hope.

"Thora?" Brierley asked, bewildered. "What are you talking about?"

Don't the Allemanii teach that new life arises from the old, that after Daughter Sea takes you into death you will be reborn?

"Well, yes, but—"

It is a truth both the Allemanii and the shari'a know. The soul survives death and rises to new life, an endless cycle of new possibility, of new life and love and yearning. Just as the day cycles from dawn to dusk, as the seasons change from Pass to deep winter, as all the natural world dies and is reborn. Thora's spirit is your spirit, subtly changed by the transitions but still true in its essence. And so Melfallan was also once Earl Farrar's sturdy pilot who saw first the green shores of Briding, then later lived as young Peladius and Dram the soldier and Mionn's brave castellan. Time and again since the Disasters you two have nearly found each other, and twice succeeded and loved for a time, even if the full promise of what you could be was cut short. It is destiny there, my daughter: we Four have seen the pattern too often to doubt its truth.

Brierley stared up at Basoul, struggling to understand. "But I'm not this great person you want for your Finding! Maybe Melfallan is, but—"

Basoul smiled. *Aren't you? Haven't you thought that we never know when we are heroes? Yes, perhaps that is true.*

"You tease me now."

A little, Basoul admitted. *I told you on the beach to stop thinking of yourself as a blight. You are not your mother, that poor unhappy woman who denied all that she was. You are not responsible for her death: that was Jocater's own choosing. And you are not right in thinking you should choose for both yourself and Mefallan, as if he had no voice for himself. He will not now let you go, however you try to hide from him—and you should not think of yourself as wrong for him. He does not agree, and neither do I.* Basoul looked at her sternly. *Whatever moves the cycle of living, and I myself do not know all of the reasons, you have been chosen for each other. Of that I am certain. Do I finally persuade you?*

Brierley frowned stubbornly, then crossed her arms across her breasts. "But—"

No buts. Dear child, we don't intend to seize you and rob you of what you are. We don't intend to drive you into a destiny you don't want. We love you, both you and your Allemanii earl, and love does not empty: it fills. If all that we hope does not happen, as it has not happened twice before, then that will be accepted. We will hope again.

"I believe that," Brierley said soberly. "But I also know that you think time is running out, Basoul. I heard your fear on the beach: you are afraid of a storm in the east, a storm that is coming and might destroy your hopes forever, and the shari'a with them, and perhaps the Allemanii, too. You are afraid that it has been too long, with too many cycles, too many lost chances." Basoul sighed deeply, but did not answer. "I know it's so."

The future is not set, Basoul said stubbornly.

Brierley stretched her arms around the dragon's neck and clung to her, then slowly caressed the warm, scaly hide. "I love you, Basoul," she whispered. "You are the Voice who called me to living. I wish I could be this great person you want me to be," she added shyly, "for your sake, not mine."

Thora never thought herself great either. It seems that has not changed. Basoul blew out a breath, scattering sand in every direction. *But perhaps you will not worry as deeply?*

Brierley chuckled. "You worry that I worry?"

Of course I do. I will tell you a secret now: Melfallan has met your Everlight.

"What?" Brierley asked, startled. "What do you mean?"

Perhaps you can think about that instead of all the reasons why you should give him up. Yes, it would be a definite improvement.

The next instant the dragon was gone. "Oof!" Brierley grunted, as she fell out of the open air and dropped hard onto the lakeshore sand. She sprawled badly, then sat up, rubbed her hip, and scowled.

"You're as bad as Jain," she complained. "Pop in, pop out." Then all around her she heard the lilting answer of the sea dragon's laughter, like a rushing fall of rain, like the sweet sound of the unending surf, and then Basoul was truly gone.

Brierley drew up her legs and hugged them, then leaned her chin on her knees. Melfallan has met the Everlight? What in Ocean's mercy had Basoul meant by *that?*

And then she laughed softly, knowing that Basoul had quite deftly accomplished what she wanted, as likely the dragons usually managed to do. It was something new to think about, something quite startling. Well, she admitted ruefully, I've certainly worn a rut in my mind on the other. She gestured her surrender to the lake. "All right, I'm not a blight," she said. "And all right, I should hope for the future, and let it come when it will. I'll try." She rubbed her sore hip again and winced. "And next time I want some warning before you do that. I mean it, Basoul." The lake did not answer.

A light moved in the town as a fisherman carried a lantern to his boat, and a low murmur of voices elsewhere drifted lazily on the early morning air. Brierley got to her feet, listened a few more moments to the air and the lake, and then went into the house.

⤳

Melfallan returned to Saray's bed as the first gray glimmerings of the Daystar's rising sifted through the bedroom window. Saray stirred sleepily as he eased into the bed beside her, then murmured indistinctly to herself before she slept again. Melfallan rested his head on one hand and watched her sleep, admiring her beauty, wishing useless things. He knew Saray loved him deeply—he had the proofs every day. He knew how hard she tried to please him—and that he often made her fail by wishing useless things. What would it cost him to accept what she offered? Why did he insist on honesty when she found honesty too hard to bear? He could guess at the pains of her upbringing in Earl Giles's court, the ignored younger daughter, the unpleasant parents, the sniping sister who resented her beauty. Why not escape into a perfect world? Why not seek escape from the pain? Melfallan bent close and kissed her brow, then moved his mouth to her lips, awakening her. When he raised his head, she blinked at him in drowsy surprise.

"Oh, it's early," she murmured.

"I liked last night," he whispered, then moved his face against her hair, his hands moving to her breasts. "Did you like it, too?"

"Oh, yes," she said promptly, and it was a lie, but he forgave her the lie. He kissed her, and Saray's arms came around him, a little too late, but he forgave her that, too.

"What else have you in mind for me?" he asked suggestively, and moved his mouth to her breast. She recoiled slightly, as she always did, but did not move away.

"I thought we might share a bath," she said hesitantly. "Like you wanted to do." Melfallan felt the grief rise hard in his throat, that she would offer, that she would try valiantly for him. He kissed her deeply, and held her, and when Saray let the passion slide away, not really wanting sex, not now, but still thinking of him, he allowed it. They lay quietly together for the next hour, their bodies pressed closely, as the dawn's light slowly strengthened from grays to gold.

"I love you, Melfallan," she whispered.

"Yes, I know, dear heart," Melfallan said. "I know you do."

∽ 9 ∽

$\mathcal{M}$elfallan sat down in his chair in the Great Hall, then signaled to the guard to summon the courier. Sir James stood at his right elbow, and Sir Micay had decided to stand along the wall with a dozen soldiers in helmets and mail, each armed with sword, dagger, and lance. The display probably wouldn't impress the courier, but it couldn't hurt. Melfallan adjusted his silver circlet on his head, straightened a wrinkle in his tunic sleeve, and waited. Keep your temper, he reminded himself.

A few minutes later Lord Royce Dail stalked angrily into the hall. He was a stocky young man, richly dressed in the duke's colors of red and gold, Ingal's dragon crest emblazoned on his tunic. A gray-haired knight and four soldiers in similar dress followed in his wake, swords clanking, and Melfallan tightened his mouth into a thin line. Soldiers had no place at a courier's mere delivery of a message, and likely this Lord Royce meant to remind Melfallan, perhaps by Duke Tejar's express order, of the many other soldiers Tejar had at his command. When it came to flaunting his power as duke, Tejar rarely bothered with subtlety. He glanced at his soldiers along the wall. Well, I suppose I'm not particularly subtle today either.

He sighed softly, sensing a disaster now marching toward him across the Great Hall. I could have made him wait a month, he told himself. Why didn't I?

Lord Royce paraded grandly across the Great Hall, then stopped in front of Melfallan's chair on the dais. He gestured imperiously to the knight beside him. "Sir Galbert!" he exclaimed. "The message!" Melfallan raised an eyebrow at the dramatics, then schooled his expression back to cool waiting. The knight, an older man dressed in full body mail beneath the brilliant colors of his surcoat, stepped forward and knelt to present a rolled paper. Without expression, Melfallan accepted the paper, then took a few moments to slip the ribbon and unroll it.

"That document requests—" Lord Royce began.

"A moment of courtesy so I can read," Melfallan interrupted calmly. Royce flushed, hearing a reproof whether Melfallan meant one or not, and so now both had set the tone for the interview. Melfallan told himself he didn't care, and then told himself he probably should care, then skimmed through Landreth's petition. For such it was, demanding a full pardon for the rapes and the later attack on Brierley in her cell. At the end the duke's clark had pompously noted that the duke had approved Landreth's request and so expected Melfallan's compliance.

Compliance? Melfallan's eyes widened at the choice of word. As duke, Tejar might be liege to all the High Lords, but Melfallan's legal jurisdiction within his own lands was a matter of unchallengeable right, enshrined in the Lutke Charter that still governed Allemanii rule. He raised his eyes and stared at Lord Royce.

"Do you know the contents of this letter?" he asked.

"I do." Royce pulled back his shoulders and stuck out his chin, posing in his self-importance. "I am the duke's confidante," he added pompously, as if Melfallan should gape and drop to his knees at the news. "My father—"

"—is Lord Dail. Yes, I know."

"My father is the duke's principal counselor!" The chin rose even more proudly.

"Lucky you," Melfallan retorted, although he shouldn't have, he knew.

The young lord gawked, then a boiling fury entered his weak, pale eyes, with that edge of dangerousness Melfallan had sensed in Captain Bartol, a common trait among the duke's toadies. Yes, this Royce and the captain would be friends, if this young fop truly had Bartol's confidence as well as the duke's. He sensed Sir James stir warningly by his side, and likely Sir James was right, but Melfallan could already guess that this audience was a ship headed for the rocks. "Does Duke Tejar honestly expect me to revoke the charges against Lord Landreth?"

"These charges are false!" Royce exclaimed.

"No, they're not," Melfallan retorted coldly. "As a trial will show, once it is held in Darhel. Why does the duke delay the proceedings?"

"The duke," Royce said loftily, his nose high in the air, "is not answerable to you."

"Really?" Melfallan retorted. "Read the Charter, young lord, before you ever enter into the rule of a land. Be educated more than you are." Melfallan handed the petition to Sir James, then studied the courier for a few moments, considering. Tejar was not stupid about men, and would see Royce in an instant for what he was, a posturer, a young man puffed up with his father's rank and little sense to go with it. What had possessed the duke to send this young fool on such an errand? Did he intend only an insult to the baby's Blessing? Or did he prompt Melfallan's refusal by sending a fool? Even had the messenger been otherwise, Melfallan would still refuse such a demand, as any High Lord would refuse, and so Duke Tejar did not expect Melfallan to comply. It was insult, nothing more.

"A court should decide Lord Landreth's guilt," he said evenly. "It would have been *my* court, but Landreth's father filed an appeal to the duke. Count Sadon wanted his son tried by his peers in the duke's court rather than here, as is Landreth's right, and I consented. I expect that trial to take place."

"The charges should never have been filed!" Royce declared. Sir Galbert, standing beside him, frowned, then stirred warningly, but the young fop ignored him.

"I had complaints made," Melfallan said tightly. "As the duke well knows, it is my duty as earl—"

"The word of some stupid girls?" Royce snorted. Now even the knight opened his mouth, ready to protest, but subsided again. He and Melfallan traded a glance.

"Lord Royce," Melfallan said coldly, "my laws protect commoner women from rape. Four girls, one of them only thirteen, claimed rape by Lord Landreth. All are credible witnesses, with no reason to lie—"

"The word of a commoner!" Royce said contemptuously, interrupting again. How could a canny lord have birthed such an idiot? Melfallan wondered angrily.

"—and I consider their claims to be serious charges," he continued, even more coldly. "As earl of Yarvannet I will do my duty. I refuse to look the other way merely because Landreth is nobly born and a count's son. Pray tell the duke I cannot dismiss the case. Let him try Landreth in Darhel, for that is Landreth's right of appeal, but there must be a trial."

"The duke will not be pleased!"

"So be it," Melfallan said, his tone final. Lord Royce smirked, as if Melfallan had just made a great error. He loftily gestured to the knight at his side.

"As you will, your grace. I have other messages. Sir Galbert!" The gray-haired knight hesitated, then advanced with the second letter. "You owe tallages and amercements you have not paid," Lord Royce announced. "The duke has sent me to collect them." Melfallan accepted the new letter with a nod to the knight, then handed it to Sir James.

"Not in this lifetime, Lord Royce," Melfallan said. He gestured airily with his hand. "Be welcome to the courtesy of Castle Yarvannet during your remaining short stay. I'm sure you wish to ride out tomorrow. Before then my justiciar will provide you my letter to carry to the duke. I would not want my words misspoken." Melfallan stood, nodded, then walked out of the Great Hall, leaving the courier to stand there, gaping.

Sir James caught up with him in the hallway. " 'Not in this lifetime'?" he asked, lifting an eyebrow.

"I liked 'lucky you' even better. It was pithy. Is this Royce important?"

"Probably not," Sir James rumbled. "So why not indulge?" He courteously gestured toward his office near the library. Melfallan nodded and followed him down the next hallway and into the small room, its shelves and tables cluttered with paper and books. He sat down heavily in one of the chairs, then scowled, took off his silver circlet, and laid it on the table. He eyed it gloomily. Sir James sat down in another chair.

"Make sure our letter clearly cites the Charter," Melfallan said, "and have the copy witnessed. Not that it'll do any good." Through the window came the faint sounds of the soldiers at practice, underlain by the endless murmur of the sea. Melfallan blew out a breath. "Well, that's that."

"It bothers you that it was only an insult," Sir James observed. "It was too easy."

Melfallan nodded. "What did we accomplish, after all? He insults me, I insult him, and the courier goes home. Tejar wouldn't waste a courier for such a stupid purpose. Count Toral might, maybe even Earl Giles just for the insulting, but not the duke."

"Your grandfather wouldn't have seen the gap." Sir James smiled. "Nor listen when I warned him."

"Would Grandfather have said 'lucky you'?" Melfallan retorted. "You know he would, and I'm not entirely comfortable in adopting his tactics. I loved him, Sir James, and so did you, but Grandfather wasn't always wise. But I don't still see any error today, not with this Lord Royce. He's a fool, and Tejar knew he was a fool but sent him anyway. Why?" He scowled. "To stall? To lay the ground for his *next* courier?"

Sir James's eyes widened in dismay as the same thought occurred to him. "He wouldn't!"

"Oh yes, he would. If I can think of it, he can. Lord Landreth is my vassal lord, the son of my most restless count. If I arrest Landreth, I assault another High Lord's courier and so violate the Charter. A minor provision, true, and not enough for the other High Lords to support my disenfeoffment. After all, the High Lords insult each other's couriers all the time and nobody loses their land because of it. Tejar has the same problem with the amercements he wants: he needs something more, something that imperils the legal rights of the other lords. And he'll find it by sending Landreth to Yarvannet. When I arrest Landreth, I also arrest Count Sadon's son, a High Lord who has already appealed to the duke for justice. Sadon makes his demands on me, and I, believing Farlost murdered my grandfather and tried to poison my son, retaliate by hanging Lord Landreth—after a trial, of course. We must observe the legalities, however false their truth. Farlost rebels, and Duke Tejar invades to protect Farlost's right." He gestured angrily. "When the duke sends Landreth to Yarvannet, as he most surely will, Sir James, the war begins." Melfallan stood up and walked to the window, then looked out at the ocean.

There was a long silence, then Sir James stirred uncomfortably in his chair. "I can't see any fault in your suspicions. It's like him, our duke."

"And it's like what he thinks I am. He thinks me a fool like Royce, someone who hasn't a clue how to rule. After all, look what I've done so far: arresting Sadon's son for mere rape, then defending a commoner girl in Darhel on witchery charges. A prudent lord overlooks his vassal's excesses when the vassal is important—after all, what was charged? A little play with unimportant servant girls—and for that I *arrest* him? And defending a commoner girl on a losing issue like shari'a witchcraft? Better to let the girl be burned: she's just a commoner girl, one of hundreds in Yarvannet. Duke Rainalt would have gawked in disbelief at my stupid decisions, and then would have smiled, as Tejar has certainly smiled, about the hawk soon to be plucked." He turned and looked bitterly at his justiciar. "I've no doubt that Tejar expects me to hang Landreth, that I would be that kind of rash fool. And that means I can't hang him, Sir James, even if Landreth murdered Earl Audric. I can't do anything to him at all." He shrugged helplessly. "And so Count Sadon gets his dearest wish, a pardon for his traitorous son." He sighed. "I admit that I wanted a better reason."

"If Count Sadon still asks. He might not. Where is Lord Tauler, by the way?"

"Don't nag me, Sir James. I'm not in the mood."

Sir James chuckled. "At least you saw it coming. To predict correctly allows time to form the needed response."

"Yes. There's that, not that it does me much good." Melfallan crossed his arms across his chest and scowled. "I should have made him wait a month." He scowled even more fiercely, then scowled at Sir James because he smiled. "So what do we do now?" he asked pointedly.

"Set up Earl Giles," Sir James offered. "Point the duke at him instead of you. It could be done."

Melfallan blinked. "What?"

"Earl Giles is still raging at Robert about the divorce, despite his promise to you that he'd abandon the Lim marriage." Sir James shrugged. "I have a servant listening."

"You mean a spy."

"All High Lords need spies," Sir James said imperturbably. "Duke Tejar has them; so do you." He smiled thinly. "As I've arranged, here and there."

"Just because Giles tries to manipulate me doesn't mean I should manipulate him."

Sir James shrugged, not pushing it. "You lose an advantage that might be useful," he said.

"I lose Yarvannet," Melfallan replied harshly. "To keep my land by treachery and deceit, to keep my land as Duke Rainalt advised, isn't worth the keeping, Sir James. I won't do it."

Sir James nodded slowly. "As you will, your grace. It is my role as your justiciar—"

"—to suggest all the possibilities. I know." He shrugged and deliberately changed the subject. "Saray may be pregnant."

"Excellent," Sir James said, a smile lighting his face. "I hope she is. And I hope this phase of seeking Lady Joanna's counsel is extremely short-lived. Did she really say—"

"Yes, she did. And brace yourself, Sir James: she'll likely do it again, as publicly as possible. It's now part of praising me in front of the gentry."

"So ask her to stop, Melfallan."

Melfallan grimaced. "I thought about that, but she wouldn't understand why I ask. It would only make her fail again, as she sees it, and I don't want to hurt her any more than I already have." He sighed. "And, as Revil told me, the world won't fall into ruins because my wife loudly announces my prowess in bed to everyone who can hear. I suppose all I can do is bask in it."

"Well," Sir James opined solemnly, "it *is* the fundamental praise for any man." His eyes twinkled.

"It's in every text, I'm sure," Melfallan retorted. "And, by the way, Lord Tauler thinks Joanna has been writing to the duke."

"He does?" Sir James asked, startled. "Really? Hmm." He thought a moment. "I'll look into it."

"But subtly, Sir James," Melfallan cautioned. "I don't think Garth is involved, and, besides, what could Joanna tell the duke about me that he doesn't already know?"

"True," Sir James agreed. "A silly woman, who is making Saray look silly, too."

Melfallan smiled wryly. "Not that silly. After all, as you said, it *is* the fundamental praise. Joanna is Saray's only real friend among the noble ladies. You've seen how the others treat her. If she's happy asking Joanna's advice, even about *that*, I don't see the harm. In the meantime, it certainly makes our bedroom interesting." Sir James raised an eyebrow, but Melfallan only shook his head at him. "Don't ask. I want Lord Royce and his soldiers out of my castle by tomorrow morning."

"I'll see to it, your grace."

"Good."

~

A short time later Melfallan leaned against the wall outside Norris's cell and listened to the low murmur of Sir James's voice, insistent, patient, relentless. Norris said nothing in response, as he had said nothing the past three days. Several feet away a dungeon guard stood with his lance, his eyes glittering through the eyeholes of his helmet. The soldiers who had caught Norris in the stable had beaten him badly:

only Melfallan's sternest of orders had prevented the dungeon guards from adding their own punishments as Norris lay helpless in his cell. He eyed the soldier and saw resentment in the man's eyes.

"The first man who lays a hand on him again," he said coldly, raising his voice enough that the guard could hear him clearly, "will be sorry he did."

"He's a traitor, your grace."

"That's not proven. Did you hear my warning?"

The guard shifted his weight uncomfortably, then lowered his eyes. "Yes, your grace."

"Did you believe it?"

The young man looked up at him, and Melfallan saw the hurt. "I'll obey you, your grace," he protested. "I'm no traitor!" He gestured angrily with his chin at the cell door. "Not like him." He grimaced, then looked down at the floor again. "Not like him," he repeated in a mutter. Melfallan tightened his lips, but knew he would get no more out of this young, angry soldier, not today.

Melfallan pushed himself off the wall and opened the cell door. Norris lay huddled on the narrow cot, his legs drawn up, his bandaged face pressed close to the wall. At first it had been a stubborn silence, with Norris simply refusing to say anything at all, however Sir James pressed him, but yesterday Norris had drifted into a daze. Marina now worried about a head injury, and thought that Norris might be bleeding inside his skull. Sir James turned.

"Enough for today, Sir James," Melfallan said. "Let him rest."

"He won't speak."

"I'm not sure he can, given what the soldiers did to him. Has Marina seen him today?" Sir James nodded. Melfallan stepped into the cell and stood over Norris, who determinedly blotted out the world. Melfallan bent forward to look at him more closely, wondering if Norris was even conscious. He pressed the young man's shoulder gently, but Norris did not respond to the touch, did not move. "Send the guard for Marina," he ordered. "He's too still."

"I'll bring her myself," Sir James said, and left the cell.

Melfallan shifted Norris's legs and sat down beside him on the cot, then rested his hand on Norris's shoulder. "I don't believe you did it, Norris. They'll tell me I'm a fool to think that, but I don't believe it. Can you hear me?" Norris's chest rose and fell slowly beneath Melfallan's hand. "Don't die, lad," Melfallan said softly, pleading with him. "Don't end like this." Norris did not answer, did not move. "Can you hear me, Norris?"

Was there an answer? Melfallan bent forward, straining to hear. Had that breathed word been more than a simple breath, one of many as Norris struggled to keep his life? Where was Marina? He looked anxiously at the cell door.

"I hear you," Norris mumbled, though likely he was caught half in a dream, barely conscious as perhaps he bled inside his head, a slow, steady hemorrhage stealing his life. Still, Melfallan breathed a sigh of relief, and pressed his shoulder again.

"Good," he said. "That is good. Hold on, Norris. Marina's coming."

He heard the approaching footsteps a few minutes later, the solid tread of Sir James's boots, Marina's lighter footsteps. He looked up as the healer bustled into the cell. "He spoke to me."

"He did?" she asked, and he saw relief wash across her careworn face.

"Only a few words," he added cautiously.

"A few words is a start," she said, and gave him a quick smile. Melfallan made way for her, and watched as the midwife carefully turned Norris on his back, her hands gentle.

"No more questions, Sir James," Melfallan said. "Not until he's well."

"He must be examined—"

Melfallan looked at him. "No."

Sir James bowed. Sometimes his good justiciar forgot mercy, too determined as he was to find justice. Sometimes even Sir James had to be reminded of the right, and he saw the wry understanding in the older man's eyes, the acknowledgment of his fault here, rare as those faults were. "As you will, your grace."

Melfallan nodded, then left the cell. As he passed the guard outside the door, he eyed him warningly, saw the uneasy shuffle.

"I'll remind the others, your grace," the soldier said. "I'll make sure he's left alone."

Melfallan stopped. "If it were you in that cell, Kay, you'd appreciate that promise."

Kay looked abashed, not that it dented his stubbornness. "But he was on his horse, ready to flee!"

"A fact to consider, but there are other facts, and beyond that more than one choice."

The sober blue eyes regarded him, troubled. "Yes, your grace," he said doubtfully. Melfallan smiled at him.

"A soldier's life is simpler than an earl's, Kay, and if it were you in that cell, the guard standing here would get the same warning—and for the same reasons. Nothing is proven yet, despite your single fact, and, even when proven, nothing is set. Leave the decision to me, as is your duty."

Kay smiled. "I hear you, your grace."

"Good." Melfallan took in a deep breath, and went on his way.

⁓

Lord Royce stormed into his assigned chamber and stopped in the center of the room, ready for something to smash and rend. Sir Galbert smoothly entered the room in his wake and watched the young man for a few moments, then grimaced. He knew the duke's purpose in sending Royce, a purpose of which Royce himself was quite unaware, but that knowing didn't help much in dealing with the young fool. Puffed up by his mission to Yarvannet and his recent close connection to Captain Bartol, the duchess's bastard nephew, Royce had quite worn away Galbert's patience in the fortnight of their travel to Yarvannet. During Galbert's thirty years of service to the duchess, he had trained many young courtiers to better manners, to the subtlety and cunning necessary for a lord's trusted man. Royce hadn't the capacity for such training, but, then, he wasn't meant to have it. Diversions never did.

Galbert crossed the room to the sideboard and poured himself a glass of wine. "Anger at a High Lord," he said coolly, "usually accomplishes nothing. What did you expect Melfallan to do?"

Royce stopped abruptly in his pacing and glared at the knight. "Obey the duke, of course!"

"Not this earl." Galbert sipped at the excellent wine, then turned. "Calm down, my lord. The duke didn't expect a different outcome. You haven't failed. I assume that's the reason for this stalking up and down the room." Galbert saluted the young man with his glass. "Subtlety is an art, Royce, not a charge across the field. But you have served your purpose. The duke will be pleased."

"Purpose?" Royce asked, confused. Yes, not the sort even to begin the training, Galbert thought tiredly. "What do you mean?" Royce insisted.

Galbert smiled tightly. "Never mind. Perhaps the duke will explain it to you himself when we return to Darhel. As Earl Melfallan suggested, we should leave tomorrow." Galbert lifted his glass and savored the sweet bite of the wine. "As for me, I think I'll walk around the castle awhile. You will stay here."

"You're giving me an order?" Royce asked incredulously.

Galbert eyed him without favor. "Add 'sir' to that question, Royce, and give respect to a knight older than you. Yes, stay here. Get drunk: this is an excellent wine. I doubt we'll be invited to the earl's dinner tonight, so have a good meal here in your room. Spend the evening however you like." Galbert splashed more wine into his glass. "Just stay put. I'll be back in an hour or so."

"I remind you that I am Lord Dail's—"

"—third son," Galbert finished for him. "Yes, I know. I also know that Lord Dail is the duke's principal advisor. That is a fact. It is a further fact that you are indeed Lord Dail's son known as 'the fool.' You certainly proved it just now." He pointed at Royce with his glass. "Did you bother at all to consider your approach? These earls think themselves the equal of the duke, Lord Royce. They rule their lands as if they *were* duke, and the Charter lets them do it. 'The earls restrain the duke.' Duke Lutke built that principle into our politics, and every duke has faced its dangers. Yet here you come, prancing into his Great Hall, the buffoon, the fop, to insult Earl Melfallan to his face." Royce had paled, and now leaned weakly against a chair. "But not to worry, young lordling. The duke expected nothing else. Indeed, his father told him whom to choose—you. Even your father thinks you're a fool."

"How dare you," Royce breathed, his face now blotched with anger. "It's not true. My father has confidence in me!"

"Confidence that you'll act the fool. Perhaps Lord Dail's acumen skipped a generation in your case, and, should you have a son, he might breed more to the line. Who can say? The duke didn't expect Earl Melfallan to pay the amercements, you idiot. Of course not. Half his annual income for trumped-up fines? And to pardon Lord Landreth, son of the Farlost count who by all accounts poisoned his grandfather? An absurd demand. But the duke needed your sincerity in believing such absurdity, and you nicely delivered it. So your task is done, young man."

"That doesn't make sense!" Royce insisted. "Why would he send me if—"

"Come now, Royce. Didn't you even wonder when the duke included me as your aide? Do you think gentlemen knights are mere window curtains for your vanity, like the half troop of soldiers we brought with us? I've served the duchess for thirty years, and serve the duke as loyally to serve her. Your noise is a cover for my work here, so shut up. Take another nap, eat your dinner—and stay put until we leave tomorrow." He drained his glass with a long swallow. "That's an order, my lord," he added coldly, menacing him. Galbert watched as Royce numbly retreated, slinking like a chastened hound, into the adjoining bedroom. The shock was good for what ailed the young fop, Galbert thought, but he doubted Dail would ever get much better use out of his third son. Sadly, a stupid man had only limited play.

A knock came, and a moment later a servant girl peeked around the door as she opened it, hesitant as a fawn, and held out a pitcher and toweling in her hands. Galbert kindly gestured her in, and she scurried to the chest near the bed, laid the pitcher of water and towel near the bowl already resting there, and then fled. A few minutes later, after another discreet knock, another servant opened the door. He was a stocky, red-haired man, dressed in the rough smock and trousers of a cook. "Will you have food or drink, my lord?" he asked politely.

"Lord Royce is hungry. Aren't you, my lord?" Galbert called out. There was a rush of fabric rustling, two quick steps to the bedroom door, and the slam. Galbert smiled thinly, then turned back to the cook. "Come in. I need you for a task."

The cook closed the door carefully behind him, then straightened from his deferent slump. He grinned rakishly. "Hey there, Galbert, you old lizard," he said softly.

"I'm a lizard?" Galbert retorted, and crossed the floor to grasp the cook's hand, then pointedly looked him up and down. "You've put on weight, Hugh."

"Fits the role." The cook shrugged. "Sorry I didn't come to you last night. I had errands and couldn't get free."

"Best not to push it," Galbert agreed. "What news?" Galbert gestured him into a chair, and then sat down in another.

"Well, the big news here was an attempt on the earl's baby at the Blessing."

"Yes, I heard."

"Earl Giles got the worst of it, acting up as he's done his entire visit. Burned his hand with the poison." He shrugged. "Had I known he'd do that, I would have put more sea-puffer toxin in the water, but the duke's orders were clear: the baby dead but not Melfallan."

"Who got the blame?" Galbert asked.

"One of the baby's manservants, Norris. Seems he's the son of one of Earl Pullen's knights, although few know that.

Sadon raised him after the parents were killed—he and the knight were old friends, it seems, if you can imagine Sadon Moresby having friends—and made him one of Landreth's body servants. After Landreth got dragged off in chains to Darhel, Norris was promoted to the baby's chambers. I cultivated him soon afterward. He thinks of me as a benevolent uncle." Hugh smiled.

"And then?"

"And so I rubbed the toxin around the edge of the basin, and Norris put it into its place in the chapel, unknowing. He's a bright young man—he knew his peril immediately after the drama with Earl Giles." Hugh shrugged again and crossed one ankle over his knee. "All it needed was a little nudge, given that Norris trusts me. I've been an uncle to him, after all, him the orphaned son of one of Pullen's knights killed by Earl Audric. He looked to me for guidance. In my role as uncle, I advised him to flee. With him taking horse, he pinned the guilt on himself very nicely."

Galbert nodded approvingly. "And away from yourself."

The cook shrugged. "Oh, no one suspects *me*. I'm just a fat cook, a little stupid, tending a bit too much to excessive drink. No one pays attention to me: I'm harmless." He smiled blandly. "Isn't blending in the essence of a good spy? To make sure, I gave the bowl to another servant, who then gave it to Norris, and Norris had the bowl to himself, unobserved, for a good half hour, long enough to rub the dry poison around the bowl. The earl won't bother to trace that bowl's handling before Norris had it. His guilt is obvious: after all, he was saddling his horse when they caught him."

"Even so," Galbert reluctantly told his old friend, "you still failed in carrying out the duke's order. The duke wants Earl Melfallan to be heirless again. It's necessary."

"All in due time. The plan should have worked. I don't know why it didn't, but fate is fate."

"Duke Tejar doesn't believe in your 'fate.' "

"Don't you threaten me, Sir Galbert. I serve the duke well, as I served the duchess. There'll be another opportunity: that baby isn't going anywhere and not even Earl

Melfallan can watch him all the time. The duke will get his wish. I'll see to it."

"Sooner rather than later."

The cook scowled. "No threats. I won't have it. I'm not intimidated by you, you old lizard. We shared too many drunken nights in our wasted youth. I'm as trusty to the duke as you are to his duchess, and I've served him just as long as I served her. So tell the duke it went astray, but I won't take the fault."

Galbert grunted, then let it go. As he claimed, the cook had been an able spy, and no plan ever had a guarantee. "What about Count Sadon? Did he come to the Blessing?"

"Ah, no, but no one expected him to. He sits in his marshes, unpleasant as ever. I'm hoping Norris will be as foolish with the earl as he was with me and tell Melfallan about his birthright. It won't take much after that to trace him back to Sadon—and the guilt with him. After all, he placed a young man in the earl's own castle, and this man later tries to murder the earl's baby son? Yes, I think the count will listen to reason now when the duke writes to him." The cook showed white teeth. "Especially when everybody already knew Sadon poisoned Earl Audric, too. Or so the rumors go."

"When you and I both know it was by your hand, Hugh," Galbert amended. "However did you start the rumors in his direction?"

"I didn't have to. Count Sadon's hatred for the old earl was too well-known. Even Landreth believed his father did it." He shrugged. "Besides, I'm just one of a dozen cooks in the kitchen, and that an old fat fool who drinks too much ale. Why should they look at me?" His smile broadened.

"Why indeed?" Galbert nodded in approval. "I think you like being fat."

"If you mention fat once more, Galbert, I'll push your face in, believe me. I do what I must. You can be the elegant one, all decorated up in fine fabrics and a sword: you don't have to hide in plain sight. But I was always deft, thin or fat or in between, even when I was only captain of Lady Charlotte's household guard. How does she fare now, our sweet lady?"

"She's dying," Galbert said, and shook his head in regret. "There is no hope."

The cook nodded mutely, then let out a breath. "A hard death she has," he said, shaking his head.

"Most deaths are hard," Galbert said harshly, "but I agree Duchess Charlotte doesn't deserve what she now suffers, especially after twenty years of marriage to our good duke. A hard life she's had with him, and now a hard death." He sighed. "I serve the duke because I have always served her, and I will see the duke's purposes performed for Charlotte's sake, and for the sake of the two sons, who are hers as much as his. I serve the Kobus house because it is her house." He blew out a breath. "I admit it was easier, that service, in her father's house in Sennet, when she was still unmarried and the apple of Lord Waldemar's eye—and of mine and yours and all her folk. Do you remember her then, Hugh? Do you remember how she gathered the garden flowers and put them in every corner of the house, delighting in their colors and grace? Do you remember how she danced in the Great Hall among all the gentry? Every eye followed her when she danced, although other ladies were more beautiful. Every eye." He fell silent, remembering.

"Too bad the duke killed that witch," Hugh rumbled. "There's rumor here that she had a true gift of healing. Maybe she could have saved Lady Charlotte."

"There's no such healing," Galbert retorted angrily, "especially not for the wasting sickness. It always kills. We've known that from the beginning."

"I'm sorry," Hugh murmured. "I know how much you love her, Galbert, as do I. We dream foolish things, hope against hope, and I'm not immune to it. Thought I might be sensible by now, but it seems I'm not." He shook his head sadly.

Galbert nodded, and they traded a bleak look.

"So why are you here, Galbert?" Hugh asked. "I assume there's a reason."

"Who's the duke's spy in Carbrooke?" Galbert asked. "Is it still that lady-maid?"

"Yes."

Galbert rose and found a scrap of paper on the sideboard, hunted for a pen, then scribbled a brief note. "Take this message to her, and have her give it to Lady Joanna. She's to be vague about who gave it to her, saying she got it from a castle servant she didn't know."

"As you wish." Hugh pocketed the note in his apron. "Should I come back to you again?"

Galbert frowned for a moment. "No, best not," he decided. "We're leaving tomorrow, and you can send messages by the usual route if you get more news."

"As you will." The cook nodded and rose from his chair. The two men embraced, then Hugh let himself out. A few minutes later, Galbert followed, strolling casually toward the kitchens.

In a hallway, he stopped a maidservant for directions to the stable courtyards. He emerged into the open air and found his way easily to the mews, where Melfallan's hawks were guarded by a grizzled older man, his eyes bright and suspicious. Galbert made small talk about the hawks to lull the man's suspicions, expressing interest and using his expertise to divert him. This Talbot talked easily, once he had warmed to his enthusiasm, and Galbert listened politely as he waited for the lady's appearance. She could not dare refuse the meeting, not with the letters she had written to the duke, not while he owned that secret. Duke Tejar had decided to use the tool she had offered, although Lady Joanna would not like the manner of the using.

After ten minutes she appeared in the courtyard, glancing nervously around her. She was a beautiful woman, blond and tall, and by all repute a faithful wife to her marcher lord, but women had an art for foolishness, especially ambitious women. She had some connection to Count Sadon, Galbert remembered, and perhaps that alone explained her rashness. Two of her recent letters to the duke could win death for both her and her lord, were Melfallan true to his Courtray blood in how he punished treachery. He hoped the lady appreciated that fact: if not, he would remind her.

Lady Joanna endured Talbot's respectful greeting as he went to meet her, then glanced beyond him at Galbert. She waved Talbot away and advanced toward Galbert, stepping lightly across the cobblestones. Galbert bowed.

"My lady," he murmured.

"And you are?" she asked pleasantly. "I don't believe I've met you before, good knight."

"Sir Galbert Lydell, of the duchess's service." He bowed again. "I'm interested in hawks, and so found my way here to Master Talbot's lair."

"Hawking is indeed a fair art. No, I don't need you now, Master Talbot. I just wanted to visit my merlin, and I'll come see her in a moment. If you could uncage her? I think she'd like a bit of open air."

Talbot bowed and went into the mews on her errand. Joanna's face hardened as she turned back to Galbert. "I did not like the tone of your summons, Sir Galbert," she hissed.

"Your letters set the tone, my lady, not I. The duke has instructions for you."

"What?" Joanna paled.

"Instructions, as I said. I've heard you're a confidante of Lady Saray. The duke wishes you to cultivate that friendship, find out Earl Melfallan's true intentions."

"He doesn't tell her anything," Joanna said, with a toss of her chin. Galbert's attention immediately sharpened, for he sensed a lie.

"Then cultivate someone who does know," he drawled, provoking her. "If a man, use your charms. A man talks more easily in bed, isn't it so?"

"I have never betrayed my husband," she flared.

"Now you will," Galbert said inexorably. "So there *is* someone who occurs to you. A trusted courtier, high in his councils? Good." He studied her a moment, then smiled thinly. "Ideally, you realize, your new lover should be the earl himself. How better to learn truths than from the source?"

"He never would," she said desperately. Another lie. Galbert smiled, knowing the lady would miss the meaning of the smile, and not see it for the leopard's pounce it portended. She was not as intelligent as she thought herself, not as deft and cool—and that would ultimately be her ruin, although not yet. She still had value to the duke, and Galbert meant to get that value.

He shrugged. "I've heard differently."

"Those were servant girls. Garth is his marcher lord; he wouldn't dare alienate him by pursuing me."

"But he won't be doing the pursuing, my lady, will he?" He nodded, as if to himself, pleased by the fear in her eyes. "You are trapped, my lady, and have enough intelligence to know it. The duke asks only that you improve your letters with better information." Lady Joanna stared at him in shock. "You can guess the penalty if you don't. The duke will not hesitate to expose you. After all, Melfallan's son was nearly poisoned only three days ago."

"We had nothing to do with that!"

"Keep your voice under control, lady. We are having a pleasant talk, remember, something about hawks and the beauty of your marcher lands. A second question from the duke: does Earl Melfallan speak openly of his intended treason? The duke wants all possible remarks. And finally: when does Melfallan plan to march north? In the spring? Or will he wait until summer?"

"March north?" Joanna asked blankly.

"Surely you know that war is coming, and perhaps sooner than you'd imagine."

"But there can't be a war!"

"Indeed? Then what was the purpose of your seditious letters? May I quote you? 'Earl Melfallan is frivolous and vain, much talked about by his gentry for his odd behavior.' What did you expect the duke to do with such news?" Joanna tightened her lips. "And there was more: 'And there are rumors of another affair, and the Lady Saray is quite angry about it. She thinks she hides it, but her face can be read like an open book.' And I thought you were her friend, my lady." He tsked.

"I *am* her friend."

"An odd way to show it."

Joanna's eyes narrowed. "I won't be judged by you, Sir Galbert," she said with spirit.

"Ah, but yes, you will, for I am the true courier on this visit, you see, not our foolish young man who dares to joust with an earl. And my messages are not for the earl, but for you, Lady Joanna. You know something I want to know. What is it?"

"I don't know anything."

"The study of lies is a useful art. And you're lying. What is it? I warn you, lady. I warn you most seriously. You have value to the duke, but value can shift. To expose you would be a deft blow to Earl Melfallan, depriving him of his marcher lord to the north and all that chaos to his rule: yes, I think that is the better value. What can you give the duke? Ladies' rumors? A little spleen, a little jealousy, a woman's prattling about court affairs she doesn't understand? Really?" His eyes bored into hers. "I suggest you consider your value, Lady Joanna—or the easy lack of it."

Her mouth flapped uselessly, and he saw the stark terror in her eyes at last. He took her elbow and guided her into a walk, a pleasant walk up and down the courtyard as a gentleman knight solemnly flattering a beautiful lady. He smiled pleasantly as they strolled. A stableboy passed quickly through the courtyard, carrying a saddle, and a kitchen girl passed as quickly in the other direction, busy on her errand. He saw Talbot emerge with Joanna's merlin, watch them cautiously, and then retreat back into the mews.

Galbert pressed Joanna's arm closer to his side. "This isn't a romantic tale we live in, my lady," he said softly. "In real life, ladies fair may be pleasing in form, as you definitely are, but lack that same beauty in their character as you do. You chose to write to the duke. You disliked your new earl, for whatever unimportant reasons you had, and your sour opinions prompted you to betray him. The duke didn't approach you: you approached the duke and now you're trapped by it. Step away from the line and you'll destroy your husband—and yourself and your children and your other family. Earl Audric removed all of Earl Pullen's lords from living for similar treachery. Do you expect the duke to surrender his own easy advantage? Why? Because the tales hold that a knight owes pleasant courtesy to a lady? That a lady's faults are kindly ignored in tribute to her beauty?" He snorted his derision. "Don't be naïve, Lady Joanna." They paced a few yards more. "What do you know?" he asked again, for the last time, and she heard the menace in his voice.

"I know something else," she stammered, and would not look at him. His grip tightened harder on her elbow.

"Tell me," he ordered.

"Brierley Mefell is still alive."

"What?" Galbert blurted, startled despite himself.

"She's alive. Lady Saray told me so. She's Melfallan's new lover, and she's in hiding someplace. Saray is worried about her and asked my advice." Joanna choked back a low moan of anguish, then bit her lip. "Why do you make me do this? I hate you!"

"*Where* is she?"

"I don't know—and I don't know if Saray knows either." Joanna cringed from him. "Don't tell me to go press her. She'd be suspicious."

"Never mind then." Galbert thought for a moment. "If you find out, be sure to send the news." He paused, considering. "I think that will be enough for today. You've been useful again, Lady Joanna. As long as you continue to be useful, you may count on some security." He pressed her arm, hard enough to make her wince. "Write what you've told me in a letter, and bid your lady-maid bring it to me within an hour."

"A letter?" Her eyes widened, now in genuine fear. "I can't—"

"Shall we continue to discuss your ruin, my lady?" He gripped still harder, knowing he would bruise her soft flesh. Let her explain that to her husband, however she could. She resisted a few moments longer—truly a lady with spirit—then nodded her defeat. And with that, Galbert relented. He released her elbow, and gave her an exquisite bow of courtesy. He would not push her too much, lest she do some fool-ishness like confessing to her husband or even to Saray. Women liked to confess: they always believed honesty set all things right, erasing the wrong as if it had never been. A prudent man knew otherwise.

By happy timing, Talbot again emerged from the mews—likely he had been watching them for the right time—and brought forward her hawk. Galbert admired Joanna's merlin, gave it extravagant praise, added still more praise for the lady, and then bowed and took his leave. He smiled, his mind turning over the new possibilities for the duke. Yes, Tejar would be pleased. It set the witch gambit in motion again, another knife to aim at Melfallan's throat. He nodded to him-self as he passed into the hallways, nodded in satisfaction.

"My lady?" Talbot prompted. Lady Joanna tore her gaze from Galbert's retreating back and looked blankly at the fal-coner. "Are you all right?" Talbot persisted.

"Yes! Um—" She smiled automatically. "You can take Bellwing back. She seems to be doing very well in your care, Master Talbot."

The older man smiled his thanks politely and took the hawk, then disappeared back into the mews. Had he heard any part of the conversation? Joanna wondered fearfully, and looked around at the empty courtyard. Had anyone else seen her talking to Galbert? Would it appear as anything but innocent? Oh, let it be so! Joanna closed her eyes and let out a deep breath, struggling for control.

You fool! You fool! she keened. What have I done? she asked herself, and could have shrieked and beat her hands against the mews wall, crying against herself. Instead, Lady Joanna forced herself to put up her chin and stroll toward the doorway into the castle, gracefully, beautifully, her particu-lar art as a woman. At the moment it was her only strength.

Somehow she managed to reach the rooms she shared with Garth. Her husband was lying on the bed with a book, his hair still damp from his bath. "Where have you been?" he asked pleasantly.

"Down to see my hawk," she murmured.

"You worry too much about that hawk, my love. She's only a bird."

"So you say," Joanna said, tossing her chin and posing a little. "And if I said, 'she's only a horse,' would I see those eyes widen in outrage?" Garth rumbled to himself, amused, and looked back down at his book. As Joanna watched him read, her love for him washed through her like a rushing wind, sweeping away her breath: she loved the way he moved, the sound of his voice, the very clothes he wore. She was part of him and he part of her, and she could not imagine him harmed in any way. For all she had told Saray about a woman's arts in the bedroom, for all she hinted that such boldness kept a man's heart securely held, for all she sometimes told herself that such things were true, Joanna adored Garth as much as he adored her, and that was the real truth of it. Don't be naïve, the duke's spy had said. The duke would destroy Garth without a qualm. What have I done to us? she thought in panic.

To hide her discomposure, Joanna walked over to the bureau and rearranged the glass flasks there, aware that her husband was now watching her. She glanced around and saw his smile. His smile for her always lit his face, in a way subtly different from how he smiled at others, although Garth was charming to all folk, popular among the gentry, graced in his manners, altogether pleasant. He was tall and handsome, with an accomplished horseman's strong body and a lilting grace in moving. Heads sometimes turned when he walked into the room; certainly hers did. She smiled back, knowing that her smile might not be perfect, but, Ocean be thanked, he didn't seem to notice.

He loves me too much to suspect, she thought bleakly. "Saray is planning another dance tonight," she said, clinking the glass containers on the bureau, moving the tall one to the back and shifting two others. "You should wear your blue velvet. You look wonderful in that."

"Then wear your silver gown and we'll dazzle the gentry." Garth smiled at her lazily, probably thinking lustful thoughts, but then regretfully gave them up as the lady-maid bustled in again and out. "I went to visit Earl Giles in his sickbed," Garth said, turning his eyes back to his book. "He was as gruff as ever."

"It's best to flatter him," Joanna said. "He's Melfallan's father-in-law and an earl in his own right."

"But hard to endure. I'm glad our lands lie in Yarvannet, and this infliction by Earl Giles happens years apart when he comes to visit."

"Now, Garth. You shouldn't speak so of the earl."

"Why not? I'm just saying it to you. I flatter him because it will please Melfallan, but it doesn't mean I enjoy it. I can't believe his behavior at the Blessing: he deserved that poison burn."

"Garth!" she protested.

"Well?" he challenged.

"Well, maybe he did, but—"

"No buts. I don't like his insults to Melfallan, and I don't understand them either. Not just that scene at the Blessing, but what went on before, ever since he got off his ship. But we have to flatter him because he's Melfallan's father-in-law." Garth snorted, then determinedly read his book.

Joanna almost said that Melfallan deserved the insults, but knew that Garth didn't want to hear it. He never did. He liked Melfallan, even though Joanna did not, and little budged Garth in his likings once he had made them, not even her. She sighed and turned back to the flasks on the bureau, moving one, then another, into a different arrangement. I was angry at Melfallan because he betrayed Saray, my friend. I was angry because I was jealous, she admitted further, more honestly, because Garth is not the earl. She bit her lip. What if Garth finds out what I have done? What will he do? A chasm opened beneath her feet, the loss of everything, everything that was Garth. Will he hate me, when he knows? The thought was agony to her.

Maybe I should ask Father, she thought distractedly, but

Sir Kaene was far away in Farlost, serving Count Sadon, and Sadon had not come to the Blessing. She could hardly travel to Farlost to visit, not now, not without questions, and she dared not send a letter lest it be intercepted. Perhaps Father will know what to do, she hoped earnestly, but Joanna suspected there was nothing to do, not now, not after what she had already done. She bit her lip harder, punishing herself, relished the short stab of pain, and wondered what she could do, but had no answer, no answer at all.

Paper, she thought dully. I must find paper and a pen.

10

*H*eavy rains fell continuously for four days on the Flinders Plateau as the suns moved steadily toward Pass, with thunderstorms every night. The heavy rainfall overfilled the lakes, with some flooding into the town, but the Flinders folk were used to this annual inundation and cheerfully set about building low earth dams to contain the worst of the overflow. Michael and Will joined the efforts, taking Stefan with them when he offered to help, and worked with a group of other men in the rain, and came home each night muddy and exhausted. The suns were now very close in the sky, and the Flinders folk readied for another of the Pass festivals, should the rain relent. "Usually doesn't," Michael said, "but we've tents to keep off the rain and we're long used to the spring mud getting into everything."

Despite Michael's prediction, a week before Pass the rains lifted, bringing another rare day of brilliant sunshine. The suns' light sparkled on the lake and began to dry the mud, and the count's factor, Hinton Witt, announced that a festival dance would be held that evening, a celebration of the new season at which all were welcome. While Brierley helped Megan into her dress and combed her hair, the twins had a low-voiced, intense conversation about Ashdla's wish to take Brierley to the cabin that day. The rains had delayed the visit, to Ashdla's frustration.

"No, Ash," Will said. "It'll be noticed. Tonight's the festival dance: they'll expect us to attend, and they'll notice if we're not there. Ask Da; he'll agree with me."

"But the dance isn't until tonight," Ashdla argued. "We have time. The mud work is done—you can come, too."

"I want to come, of course," Will said, shaking his head,

"but we can't both disappear when the townsfolk are watching. And you know they are—and talking about us, too. And it's a long walk for Megan if we take her. She'll slow us down."

Brierley ran a last pass of her comb through Megan's dark curls, then bent to kiss her daughter. "I'd like to see the cabin today," she said, "if we can go safely. Perhaps we could leave Megan here."

"No!" Megan declared. "I want to go, too!"

Brierley tugged Megan around to face her. "Maybe Stefan can take you on a ride on Friend," she suggested. "Or let you ride in a boat along the shore."

Megan was not appeased by the bribes, and put out her lower lip in a pout, then looked toward the shelves over the stove and scowled even more fiercely. Brierley turned to look, but saw nothing there. "It's not fair!" Megan told the shelves, listened, then gave a gusty sigh. "All right," she said reluctantly. "If you say so."

"Who are you talking to, Megan?" Brierley asked, although she could guess.

"Jain. He agrees with you." Megan glared again at the shelves. "I think you should be on *my* side, not theirs. This isn't right." She tipped her head, then brightened. "Jain says I get *two* rides on Friend, Mother, *and* the boat."

"Oh, he does?"

"If Jain says so, it must be true," Megan said firmly, and dared Brierley with a fierce look to say otherwise. Brierley chuckled.

"Then it's settled," she said.

To Brierley's regret, Michael insisted that they carry the books from Witchmere. Each evening, when no townsfolk were expected to visit, she and Ashdla had studied the shari'a texts in Brierley's books, with Ashdla explaining the words and some of the grammar. To Brierley's surprise, most of the chants had an older grammar, even different fundamental words, a discrepancy easily explained. "Some of the chants are centuries old," Will said with a smile. "Time enough for even our speech to change. When you think the words are important, you don't change them, right?"

"I suppose." Brierley had wrinkled her nose.

But this morning Michael had made his prudent suggestion, and Brierley had reluctantly agreed that the books should be moved. Michael didn't expect a search by the factor's men, nor any real danger from the books hidden away in her saddlebags, but she shared his unease about the books, for reasons she couldn't say, only that she did.

"Well, your company is bringing me more business, I'll give you that." Michael had sighed as he shut the door on the first morning visitor. Even after a week, visitors found cause to drop in, each one pleasant enough, even after they'd already seen Brierley before. "After all, they need some excuse to visit, and why not a harness that needs mending? I think you should wait, Ashdla."

"But, Da!" Ashdla exclaimed.

Michael raised his hand, forestalling her protest. "But not enough to say no, my girl, not when Brierley is eager to see the Well. Just be sure to come back early. Don't dawdle too much."

"We won't, Da," Ashdla said, relieved. "Come on, Brierley. Have fun with your boat, Megan." Ashdla tugged at Brierley's sleeve, impatient to be going.

The forest path to the cabin wound steadily upward into the northern hills, winding around the boles of trees, crossing an occasionally grassy clearing, often disappearing altogether. The suns' light sparkled on every leaf, and birds called cheerfully to each other. As they walked, Ashdla pointed out one sight after another, exclaiming much as Megan had exclaimed at everything she found a wonder. First a squirrel, who berated Ashdla briskly, then a tall everpine, centuries old and deeply rooted in the earth, then stepstones across the stream, heavy with moss. In truth, Brierley enjoyed watching Ashdla exclaim more than she admired the marvels Ashdla shared. Here was the true girl, alive to the forest, and herself a living part of the land, shared and sharing, each taking from the same essence.

Three miles north of Ellestown they reached the mouth of

a ravine and the small stream that issued from it. Here the path became clearer, winding up and down one side of the ravine and twice crossing the stream. Brierley's skirt and shoes were soon wet from the damp, but she didn't mind. After several days of confinement in the house, she liked the long walk, especially when the forest seemed so very alive all around her. Perhaps it was her company of a forest witch, perhaps only a lifting of the spirits brought by the bright sunshine. Whatever the cause, she accepted it gratefully. Today was a day when all seemed possible.

They walked for nearly two hours through the forest north of the lakes, steadily ascending into the northern hills, and finally came upon the cabin beneath the eaves of the forest canopy. Built of forest wood and stone, it was nearly invisible in the shadows of the trees, and might be easily passed by, unseen. Ashdla led the way, skipping nimbly across several stones in the stream, and Brierley followed. They climbed the short path to the base of the porch, then up the ladder on one side. As they emerged onto the flat boards of the porch, Ashdla spread her hands expansively.

"Welcome to the forest's homely home," she said.

Ashdla opened the door and gestured her inside. As Brierley stepped into the room, Ashdla quickly followed, then spread her hands and turned a full circle. "What do you think?" she asked with pride.

The cabin was small, little more than a single room and an attached storage shed, obviously very old and carefully mended many times over. Brierley saw plank walls of solid everpine with cleverly fitted shelves and cabinets, a table, a bed with a brightly colored quilt, a small fireplace and stone chimney to keep out bitter cold, a long row of bound journals, dusty with age, on a high shelf—and everywhere bits of twigs, stones, large feathers, clumps of grass, dried flowers, some organized neatly in sectioned boxes, some still lying at random on any available flat surface. She turned, following the shelves and their collections with her eyes, until she faced the front door—and saw the Everlight mounted on the wall beside it.

Stunned, she stepped forward and impulsively laid her palm on the cool, porcelain face. *Welcome, daughter,* said a gentle voice into her mind, a voice that seemed to resonate with a sway of branches in the breeze, the dappling of light on stream and leaf, the endless shades of green.

"Y-you can speak?" she blurted in surprise, and nearly jerked her hand away.

To those who can hear me, the Everlight replied hesitantly, as if confused by her question. *Why is this a surprise?*

Brierley caressed the smooth face with her fingers a moment longer. "Mine cannot," she said wistfully. "It is too old."

I also am old, the Everlight said contentedly. Brierley let her hand fall away.

"You have an Everlight, too?" Ashdla asked eagerly.

"Yes, in my cave by the beach. It guards me, and I think it sends me dreams." She looked at Ashdla. "Do you keep a journal?" she asked curiously.

Ashdla shook her head. "Not yet. I'm not old enough."

"Excuse me?"

"A forest witch must learn her craft and be certain of her wisdom before— Why? Do you?" Ashdla looked Brierley up and down. "But you can't be more than a few years older than us!"

"I'm nineteen."

"And you've started writing? That's very odd."

Brierley shook her head mildly. "Let's not start the divisions again, odd this and odd that."

"All right. Sorry." Ashdla shrugged, then watched as Brierley scanned the room again.

"You have many collections of things," Brierley commented.

"Why? Is that odd?"

Brierley looked back at her, ready to reprove—although mildly, because they hardly knew each other and were indeed nearly of an age—and saw Ashdla's wide grin, her dark eyes dancing with the tease. "Hmph," Brierley said.

Ashdla giggled. "Sea witches get stuffy, the journals say,

with all their 'now, dear' comments. They're always trying to make everybody *like* each other."

"Do we?" Brierley asked, amused.

"And forest witches try to show them what's in front of their eyes, all the patterns of life, but the sea witches sniff, thinking they know everything already."

"You're making that up," Brierley accused mildly, sensing a tease that had to stretch.

"Well, actually, it's air witches who think they know everything."

"And what do fire witches do?" Brierley asked.

"Anything they want," Ashdla replied with a smile. "Like Will said, it used to drive the air witches crazy. All that uncontrolled behavior that just comes out of nowhere, no rules. The air witches wanted everything *explained,* you see. Come on, Brierley. I'll show you the Well."

Brierley hesitated. "The Well? It's near here?"

"Of course." Ashdla looked at her blankly.

"Oh." Brierley laughed softly. "Somehow I thought we still had to find it, perhaps as a kind of quest. You know, go off into the raging storm, struggle up a mountain, ford a river, struggle down a mountain, panting and heaving all the way." Ashdla was staring at her now. Brierley said, "You know, an adventure."

Ashdla frowned uncertainly, then sighed. "Will would call me a stick-in-the-mud, I'm sure."

"And other comments, I think."

"Oh, I don't mind the tussling, Brierley. Neither does he, not really." She put one hand on her breast. "Inside here, it's all that matters. He knows that I love him and I know that he loves me, that we are one, not two. He pretends that I'm a sludge and too conservative, and I goggle at his wild ideas, and it's fun. Sometimes I go too far, but he always forgives me. Lately my problem has been the wife he's eventually going to marry." She sighed, then looked mildly embarrassed. "I'm jealous already, and I shouldn't be." She tugged at Brierley's sleeve. "Come on."

They left the house and Ashdla led the way along a narrow path that clung to the side of the ravine. The soft loam and underbrush changed to hard-veined stone, then a cliffside half buried in dirt and the few shrubs that could find a crevice to send down roots. When they came to an opening in the rock, Brierley followed Ashdla into the cool darkness within: a faint glow lay ahead. The soft sound of their footfalls echoed hollowly in the enclosed space. Except for the lack of sea sounds, it reminded Brierley of her cave. She trailed her hand briefly over the rough, stone wall. Witchmere, her cave, now this cavern: did witches often wall themselves inside stone? Why? She stepped into a circular room hollowed from stone and lit from above through an opening in the roof. In the center stood a low stone well, its mortar-work walls scarcely knee-high, but enclosing a space across taller than a man. Brierley drew in a sudden breath.

Four shadowy figures stood facing the well, near-transparent against the gloom, one at each compass point. They stood unmoving, their eyes bent upon the stone well, each dressed in cloak and hood, each frozen in silent gesture. Yet the one to the west—Brierley took a step forward, and her eyes suddenly blurred with tears. "Thora," she breathed, and raised her hands: but this Thora did not move and smile, did not speak, unlike the Thora in her dreams. This Thora waited, as she had waited for centuries.

"So she *is* Thora," Ashdla said.

"Yes," Brierley said softly. "Yes, she is."

Brierley slowly paced the circle of the chamber, looking closely at each of the shades. She noticed at once the facial resemblance between Thora and the young fire witch, but Kaare's eyes were curiously empty, bereft and withdrawn. Her young face—her very young face, for she was scarcely more than twelve—was lined with pain. The tall and willowy air witch, dressed in golden draperies and standing motionless across the Well from Thora, held a small glass globe within which light seemed to move, flaring as Brierley stopped beside her. She heard Ashdla's soft intake of breath and turned.

"It doesn't usually do that?" she asked.

"Not that much. Look! The light turns on itself, round and round." Ashdla joined her and they both craned their heads to watch the shifting light within the globe until it faded a few moments later. Anxious watching did not prompt the globe further, and finally they sighed together, then grinned that they had.

"This Well does the most amazing things from time to time," Ashdla said, "but only subtly—and only when you're not looking very hard. You have to watch for it and when you notice, it usually stops doing whatever it was doing." She pointed at the hawk on the forest shade's shoulder. "Sometimes the hawk turns its head and looks at you, but when you look back, it's not looking anymore. Sometimes the shades seem to smile, or even move slightly, or maybe they don't. No sounds, nothing you can touch, only sight. And never a sense of anything really alive here, not that you can be sure of. It's easy to imagine things, and then wonder if you sensed something real or just made it up."

Ashdla pointed at the engraved lines spread across each of the walls of the chamber. "The suns' light moves across those lines as the seasons change, but not always like they should when the suns' light comes in at an angle." She pointed at the hole in the ceiling shadowed by branches of trees above. "See? The light is nearly straight down now, so why do those lines over there seem to glow? And why are those lines in shadow when they should be lit? The light doesn't match up. The cabin witches have watched the light on the walls for hours and hours, making charts and drawings, but never quite found the pattern, if there even is a pattern."

"A calendar?" Brierley asked dubiously.

"If it is, I surely can't tell the time. Personally, I think it's just artwork. See? If you connect that line with those, you can see a dragon." She pointed to another part of the wall. "And that group is a horse and rider, and those over there a kind of house—or a boat or a box." She grinned. "The eye makes connections, like with stars in the True Night, but I sincerely believe *that* is a house."

Brierley nodded and looked around at the dimly lit walls. "And what does Will think?" she asked impishly, sensing yet another tussle.

"A boat, naturally." Ashdla's sigh was heavily dramatic. "And I have this horrible feeling he might be right. It's hardly fair, but I suppose twins have to deal with half and half most of the time." She shrugged.

"You're very blessed to have him as a brother, your second self, as you are to him. I thought men could never be adepts because the gift is repressed by their sex. At least that's what my books in the cave told me, and Jain had said much the same about Stefan's fire gift. And a book I found in Witchmere said it, too, that men can't be witches."

Ashdla nodded. "That's supposed to be the rule, but the Flinders line has had several male twins, all of them clearly gifted—a little different in the gift, but the truth of it is undeniable. Will can invoke the forest, can weave the patterns: all the male twins could. And all of them think differently, to every sister's complaint, but how much was tussling and how much was real? Sometimes Will calls himself a dawn witch, and I swear I don't know what he means."

"A what?" Brierley blinked.

"That's what I say each time. I can't always tell if he's serious or just saying things to provoke me, but I think he believes it. 'Dawn is my best time of the day,' he says, and truly, Brierley, when he leads the dawn chant, it's always different, always . . . " She trailed off, thinking hard. "It's always special, better than mine in ways I can't define. It's like crystals chiming deep in the earth, or bird calls changed into moving air, like a musical wind—" She clucked her tongue in frustration. "I can never find the right words. But I sense potential deep inside him, just as he does, but we don't know potential for *what*. In truth, I think he's a greater witch than I. I'm your ordinary, run-of-the-mill forest witch, maybe a little more gifted than most, but I'm fairly now what I'll always be; but Will is still *becoming,* if you can catch my meaning. He's 'becoming' all the time." She shook her head slightly. "Becoming what, I can't hazard, but there's no fear in it, no danger, only—great joy, like any dawn bringing a new day." She sighed. "So that's probably a boat on the wall, not a house, and there's nothing to do about it, I guess. Here, come look at these, too."

Behind Thora's shade was a small alcove, framed on each side by a tall bookcase filled with water-ruined books. Brierley craned to look at each of the objects on the ledge, then looked inquiringly at Ashdla. The girl spread her hands and shrugged. "More subtlety?" Brierley asked ruefully.

"Well, at least those things don't move around, at least not that I've seen. Maybe the Well books said their purpose, but the books are lost, as you can see. A winter storm got into the Well and ruined them, and so we lost all their answers. I hope we didn't lose too much."

Brierley looked around the Well, feeling baffled by its strangeness. "Ashdla, I don't know anything about this place. It's entirely new to me. I don't know how to invoke this Well."

"You're supposed to. You're the keystone."

"Dear one, I—" Brierley shook her head.

Ashdla smiled. "Not to worry, Brierley. The Four have promised us the Finding, and I believe them, as Mother believed them, as every Flinders witch has believed since the Disasters when these four witches, whoever they were, made the Well. If you get down to the essence, I believe in that dawn because I believe in Will. That's all I need to believe, firmly as a rock solid in the earth. What, were you worrying that we think you're some kind of miracle worker? That, poof, you'd make the Well work with a sweep of the hand, a firmly stamped foot? Don't be silly. The answers will come. The air witch isn't here yet, but she will be here soon. The pattern is forming, but it is not completed, not yet." Ashdla spoke with total confidence.

"But you look at me and—" Brierley shook her head. "Well, all right, if you say so."

"I do firmly say so." Ashdla grinned at her. "Personally, I think you're perfect."

"I'm *not* perfect, Ashdla."

"That's an argument you won't win, trust me. Ask Will if you must, and you'll get the same answer. Forest and sea were always friends, closer than the other gifts. After all, Thora gave the Well into our keeping, and so we have kept it safe as best we could, waiting for you. I'm not particularly gifted in understanding people. I like animals better and always will. But if my confidence in you helps ease your worries," Ashdla said earnestly, "for I know you worry, even if I don't know all the reasons, and especially if it helps you hope when hope is difficult, then where's the fault that I'm silly? I don't mind. I don't mind being a fool for you." Ashdla held out her hand, and Brierley clasped her fingers tightly. "You haven't told us everything," Ashdla said softly. "That much I know, limited as I am. You saw something in Sigrid Witt that worried you, Will says, and then you wanted to tell Da something but couldn't. Whatever they are, those two things, you'll still be perfect, I warn you. It's your fate, Brierley."

"I'm in love with Earl Melfallan, and I'm carrying his baby." Ashdla's eyes widened. Brierley sighed at her stunned expression, and probably shouldn't have told, she knew. "I worry I can't have both, your Finding and a life with him. Basoul lectures me, but I can't help it, however I try. I worry that I will murder your hope and yet not realize mine, and Sigrid is somehow at the heart of it." She frowned. "I don't know why. She's dangerous, Ashdla, more than you realize, and I can't say why." She looked around at the Well again. "I used to be a sensible midwife, not given to fancies and understandings that appear from nowhere. And what will your father think when he knows? Melfallan is married, and I have no right. And—" She broke off and looked miserably down at her shoes.

Ashdla slipped her arm around Brierley's waist, then laid her head gently on Brierley's shoulder. "I believe in you," she murmured. "That's all that counts." Brierley felt tears come into her eyes at the gentleness of the girl's acceptance, the ease of it, and sensed again the chime of Dani's laughter on the wind, the sparkle of light on the lake, the love for all that lived and moved that was forest gift. "I have missed you," Ashdla whispered. "I have missed you all my life, Brierley, but you are here now."

"Yes, I am here." She kissed Ashdla's forehead.

Brierley saw a flicker along the lines engraved on the wall, as if the ship suddenly filled its sails, or the horse broke into a run, but when she looked she saw only engraven lines, as enigmatic as before. Then she and Ashdla gasped aloud as the suns' light suddenly flashed into the Well chamber from above, flaring dizzily around the walls, and leapt from pattern to pattern. A dragon arched its neck and roared, a horse flowed across the grass, a ship filled its sails valiantly against the wind. Brierley's vision blurred, and she saw a great vista beneath her, a wild rushing of the wind over the sea. She and Ashdla were two sea larks hurtling on the wind, one a bright, vivid green, the other shimmering blue. Their wings swept patterns on the sky, tumbling, darting, entwining, as they passed over an Eastern beach and climbed the coastland mountains. The greens of the bay-shore forest gave way to stark brown and palest white of sand and bitter cliffs, baking in the harsh suns' light, with dry plains beyond, cut deeply by shadowed canyons.

A girl crouched on the top of a cliff and looked downward at the arroyo below. She was dressed in a loose tunic and trousers colored as the sand, and her reddish hair was knotted in an intricate pattern at her nape, and she wore a crystal star on her brow. She glanced behind her, then returned her gaze to the streambed below. Several figures robed in black toiled there, struggling over the rocks, and she smiled. It was a feral smile, with a glint of defiance in her eyes. As the hunters below saw her on the cliff top, a growling shout echoed up from the canyon. The girl stood, standing lazily against the sky, and then slipped away.

The vision held for a moment longer, then faded. The Well's light shifted into grays, roared suddenly into hot flame, then was abruptly itself again. Brierley took a gasping breath, and then stepped backward dizzily.

"Brierley?" Ashdla gripped her sleeve.

"Did you see?" Brierley whispered.

"Yes." Ashdla shook her head, as dazed as Brierley. "How did you do that?" she demanded.

"I didn't *do* anything, but I've dreamed of that girl several times since I came here. Who do you think she is?"

"Don't ask me," Ashdla said, and frowned perplexedly. "If she's one of the Exiles, how can we see her over such a distance? It must be three hundred leagues to the Eastern deserts. Oh, I wish Will was here! He guesses better than I do."

They waited several more minutes, but the Well did nothing more. The shades did not move, nor did light move around the walls, nor the girl reappear.

"I guess that's it," Ashdla decided, disappointed.

Brierley laughed. "Oh, what marvels," she said.

"But there're supposed to be *four* of us, not two," Ashdla insisted. "How can the Well work with only two? I don't understand this at *all*."

"Does it matter?"

"Of *course* it matters. Don't be dense." She shook her head vigorously. "Listen, since the Well is obviously through with its antics today, we've got to get back. Will wasn't kidding about the neighbors—they watch all the time, and, besides, the festival's on for tonight, a real festival, not just the party you saw before. You'll like it: the Flinders folk are great at celebrating. And Will wants to dance with you—uh, if you can dance right now," she added uncertainly.

"Expectant women dance all the time, Ashdla."

"Well, I wouldn't know." Ashdla grinned, brashly enough, and tugged hard at Brierley's hand. "Come on. Move your feet."

Michael welcomed them back with great relief, having reconsidered his permission several times during the day and worried about it. "Ah, there you are," he greeted them when they returned to the house.

Brierley took off her wet cloak and hung it by the door. "Where's Megan?" she asked, looking around the room.

"A bundle of busy she is, that one, but even she runs down eventually it seems. Stefan is helping her take a nap in your bedroom."

Brierley smiled, and indeed found Megan sleeping in the other room, and Stefan, too. Brierley bent over the bed and caressed her daughter's dark curls, then stopped when she saw the grayish blemish on Megan's forehead. She brushed away the soot.

Ashes.

When the fire ghost had attacked Megan near Witchmere, it had left a similar trace. But she's supposed to be safe here! Brierley thought in sudden panic. The fire ghost drew its strength from the collective grief that still lingered in Witchmere, now leagues and leagues away. She's supposed to be safe! What has happened? Why is Megan in danger again?

Brierley sat down on the bed, and Stefan stirred sleepily, then opened his eyes. Brierley shook Megan lightly, trying to wake her.

"What's wrong?" Stefan asked.

"She has ashes on her forehead, Stefan."

"What?" Stefan sat up abruptly, drawing up Megan in his arms. "Megan?" he called, but Megan slept onward and would not respond. "But—"

"I know. Taking her away from Witchmere was supposed to help. That's what the books said, and Basoul said so, too. So why—" Brierley shook her head. Did my visit to the Well today have some connection? Could the fire ghost draw on whatever power lay within the Well? And where was Jain? "Have you seen Jain this afternoon?" she asked.

"No. Megan was complaining about it before we lay down." Stefan shook Megan gently. "Megan?" Megan muttered indistinctly and hid her face against Stefan's chest, clinging to him, but would not wake. Stefan looked up and met Brierley's worried eyes.

"Can we help?" Brierley turned and saw the twins standing in the doorway of the bedroom. "What's wrong with her?" Will insisted. "I—I smell smoke in here."

And indeed a scent of smoke now drifted on the air. Megan writhed in Stefan's arms and made a little cry of anguish, then fell limp again, her head lolling against Stefan's arm. Brierley tightened her lips to a narrow line as ashes again appeared on Megan's face.

Not my child, she thought fiercely. Not ever.

Brierley held out her arms. "Give her to me, Stefan."

Brierley stood on the steps of Megan's dream castle, and saw new marks of fire on the white facade, cracked stone, black char on the large, wooden front door. And Megan's dream world had changed, too. The daytime suns shone harshly overhead, and the nearby river flowed sluggishly among the reeds, coated with a sheen of oil. Beyond the river a thick spiral of smoke snaked into the sky where the fire ghost still built her own castle on the plain, invading Megan's dream world with her hatred and rage.

As fire witch it was Megan's gift to remember. In Witchmere, when the guardians had threatened them and had wounded Melfallan, Megan had drawn upon a memory of that ancient shari'a fortress, a memory of the fire witches who had battled Duke Rahorsum on that last horrible day of butchery. Their collective rage at defeat and loss had taken form within Megan as a rival witch, a fire ghost, who now sought to control Megan's mind. For what purpose? To merely exist again within a living mind? Or to use Megan's body to reenter the world and wreak their terrible vengeance against the Allemanii they hated? Brierley looked around sadly at Megan's one safe place, this lovely river land with its white castle that Megan had created to escape her harsh world in Darhel's kitchens. The fire witch's castle was a mark of her craft, a place where she guarded the memories she preserved, or so said the few books Brierley had found in Witchmere. But a memory could take dangerous life and seize the witch, as the fire ghost had already tried to seize Megan and now tried again.

When do they stop, my mistakes with her? Brierley grieved. She mounted the stairs and opened the large, wooden door, and went in.

The air inside the castle bore a faint odor of smoke and charred wood. The walls of the entryway were streaked with soot, the flagstones fire cracked. To the left, she saw more charring in the parlor, the chairs upended, the fabric of the sofa melted. From the kitchen beyond drifted a metallic scent of food burned in its pot.

I am a healer, Brierley told herself, trying to counter her doubt with that confidence. But where was Megan?

As she stepped toward the staircase that led to the upper floors, she heard a soft sound in the library to her right and stopped short, her neck prickling. Through the half-closed door, she could see the suns' light streaming through the front window, gleaming on the velvet of a comfortable chair.

"Megan?" she called uncertainly, but heard no answer. Cautiously, Brierley pushed the library door open. Had the fire ghost gained such power that she could now enter Megan's own castle? And what would happen when she did?

A young girl stood in front of the shelves on the opposite wall, her back to the door. Brierley watched as she lifted a book and settled it firmly between two others, then turned around as she heard the soft creak of the door, a second book suspended in her hand. Her face was pale as the fairest linen, delicate in its features, a stark contrast to the tumble of her red hair and the vivid blue-green of her eyes; she appeared no older than twelve, and was dressed in a simple homespun tunic and skirt. She seemed oddly familiar, although Brierley knew she had never met her before.

"Hello!" the girl said, and smiled.

"Who are you?" Brierley stepped into the room, then

looked around the library in amazement. The last Brierley had seen this room, the walls had been fire scorched, the books thrown down to the floor, the comfortable chairs overturned, their cushions slashed and torn. Now the walls were cleaned of char and soot, and every broken chair stood upright and mended, with half the books reshelved into neat order. The suns' light shone brightly through the window and glanced off the bright bindings of Megan's books, the gleam of solid wood.

"Did you do all this?" Brierley demanded.

The girl smiled at Brierley's preemptive tone, and mischief danced in her eyes, making her look even younger. "A fire witch remembers," she replied solemnly. "I am such a memory, but little more. Once I was whole, but no longer." She sighed, put the book in her hand on a shelf, then stooped to pick up two more from the tumble scattered on the floor. "I was the first to cry the danger of our arrogance, we witches of Witchmere, but none of Witchmere's leaders would listen to a mere child. Later others listened, but not soon enough to save the fortress." The girl set another book on the shelf, then shifted it to a different place between two other books. "Or maybe just enough," she said wistfully. "Four ships escaped while Peladius and I held the ford against the Allemanii. There might have been more ships, but his courage that day allowed those four." She shook her head sadly. "Sad Peladius, who died defending us at the ford. The Allemanii called him traitor for defending the shari'a, their definition for his choice. And so Thora lost her beloved, and in time lost everything else."

"Ships?" Brierley asked, bewildered. "Thora? I don't understand. Who *are* you? And what are you doing here?"

The girl smiled. "You're slow today, dear one. Don't you recognize me from the Well?"

"Kaare?" Brierley gawked at her, for so it was, only this girl was vibrantly alive, not blank-eyed and empty. The smile deepened again into mischief, the blue-green eyes dancing.

The girl nodded. "Once I was Kaare, but most of me has passed into oblivion. When Count Jadus killed me at the ford, my soul was rent and scattered, and was never reborn into a new life. Your peril as sea witch, Brierley, is the bond that links souls. A fire witch's peril is to lose that soul altogether. We anshan'ia sometimes do not consent to death, fierce as always in defense. I did not consent so that I might stay with the Well, as Megan's fire ghost has not consented in that need for vengeance. It is both our strength and weakness, as is the nature of all gifts."

She stooped for more books, then frowned delicately at a title, looked distractedly at the second book in her other hand. "Perhaps the rest of me has gone where Jadus is now," she said, "gone to the Allemanii Hells he believed in, and there we are together, to whatever revenge I take on him there." She sniffed. "I would be a good demon for his Hells. I had an inventive mind despite my youth, and little minding for rules." She grinned. "Fire witches rarely do. Yes, I hope the rest of me is tormenting him there, with great skill and unrelenting evil, but even the Four cannot say." She sighed. "Ah, well."

She put the books in her hands onto the shelf beside the others. "Sit down, Brierley, and rest your feet. A sea witch walks many miles for her craft, to the pain of tired toes and the loss of shoe leather. My sister always pretended to complain about her shoes; it was one of her jokes."

"Where is Megan, Kaare? Is she all right?" Brierley hesitated, then sat down in a nearby chair, a large and comfortable chair upholstered in gray-blue, a sea color. Odd, she thought. When last she had seen this chair, it was a strong reddish color, like most of the furniture in Megan's castle.

"Megan is all right," Kaare said reassuringly. "Do not worry." She pointed at the ceiling. "She hears us now, and is coming down, as is—"

On cue, Jain popped into sight, then fluttered to Kaare's shoulder. The girl smiled and caressed him, and Jain rubbed his small head against the girl's cheek, crooning to her. His small jewel-like eyes gleamed, and flames of blue, red, and yellow sifted along his sides, cool fire. He craned his head to look at Brierley. *Basoul said she would help,* Jain announced. *So will I.*

Kaare tsked. "You're not supposed to help, Jain," she reproved, and made him flutter as she stooped for another book. "I already told you that."

I am Fire, Jain replied archly. *I can do anything I want.*

Kaare made a rude noise, then calmly detached Jain from her shoulder and shelved him among the books. "Sit there and be quiet," she commanded.

Jain sniffed. *I am Jain,* he said proudly.

"She already knows that," Kaare retorted. "So do I. Hush." To Brierley's surprise, Jain did.

"How do you do that, make him behave?" It was a skill Brierley truly envied.

"I don't *make* him do anything: he chooses to obey, or so he contends." She shook her finger at the salamander. "And you know you're not supposed to help. Basoul has told you; so have the others. The fire ghost is also yours, and you may not help." She looked at Brierley and smiled. "We always went our own way, we fire witches, to Witchmere's irritation and reproof. Fire is ever fickle and the most mutable of the elements: the Change would naturally begin with us, and almost did in me, but I was cut short. Perhaps it has already flowered in the East."

"We saw a girl—"

Kaare nodded. "A star witch. Air and fire combined, as Thora predicted. Her name is Persa Medoni, and she is the one who will hear our Summoning when it is sent." She glanced at Jain on the shelf. "Isn't it amazing, Jain, that you don't know everything? Isn't it amazing to find that what you *thought* you believed, were convinced you believed, turns out to be utterly wrong?"

Jain sniffed sourly. *I never said it couldn't happen.*

"Yes, you did. I remember quite distinctly."

Something in Kaare's tone of voice seemed oddly familiar, but then the girl looked past Brierley, distracting her, and Brierley turned to look, too. Megan clung to the wooden lintel of the doorway, her eyes wary and frightened. Brierley held out her arms, and Megan slipped across the room to her embrace, clinging, then climbed firmly into Brierley's lap. Brierley rocked her, and felt Megan's fingers tighten on her arm.

"There's fire in my top room, Mother," Megan whispered. "The bear is all burned up, and everything smells of smoke. The hands in the walls are flame and grab at me, even up there. They never got so high in the castle before." Megan lifted her head and looked at Brierley's face in grief, tears shining in her eyes. "Why? Why is everything burning, Mother?" Megan seemed to notice Kaare for the first time, and her eyes widened. "Who are *you?*" she asked, bewildered. "Oh," she said a moment later, then looked around at the library, the mended chairs, the repaired shelves of books. "Thank you," she added shyly.

"You're welcome, my child," the girl said, smiling at her. Jain winged across the room and settled into Megan's lap, and the child bent to kiss him, then held him tightly against her chest.

Not so tight, Megan, the salamander complained and rattled his wings fiercely. *Don't strangle me.* Megan kissed him again, then arranged him more comfortably in her lap.

Kaare regarded Megan solemnly. "You must not fear, Megan. Memory is the power, and all memories must be embraced, both pleasant and terrible. We are guardians, we fire witches, and there are no limits. We commit everything to what we are."

"She wants me so hard," Megan said. "She burns me." Jain crooned and rubbed his head on Megan's arm.

"Pain is the most fearful memory of all, dear child," Kaare said gently, "but like your mother when she heals, we must rise to meet it, however afraid we are, however much the pain burns us. We might be destroyed, as I was. We might fail in all our hopes, as the fire ghost did on that horrible day in Witchmere. We are not promised that we will win, and often we do not. But still we must try. Do you understand?"

Megan nodded. "But I don't know how to stop her," she said helplessly.

"I do," Kaare said. "And though you do not believe it, so do you, child."

It's not right, Jain complained, rustling his wings. *Megan will need me there.*

"Pain is never fair," Kaare said sternly. "The collective selves who are the fire ghost are yours, Jain, as much as Megan is. You know that. You cannot harm one to save the other. Don't let the passions of your present youth betray what you are. Listen to us, brother," she said, more softly, her expression tender. "Please." Again, something in her voice shivered through Brierley's mind, something familiar, as if the surf were nearby, and from that surf had risen a vision of shimmering blue.

Jain hesitated, then drooped his head. *I will listen.* He caressed Megan's face with his forepaw for a moment, then leaned into her, humming. *I love you, child.* His mental voice was barely a whisper. Then he lifted his wings, rose into the air, and disappeared.

Brierley slid Megan to the floor and rose from her chair, her eyes fixed on Kaare. "Hmph," the girl said in chagrin. "I should have known better than to try illusions with you."

"Basoul," Brierley said happily. "Whatever is this?" She looked around Megan's library. "And why Kaare? I don't understand this." The girl made another wry face and sat down in the opposite chair with a great sigh. "Is it important that I believe you are Kaare?" Brierley asked uncertainly.

"Not essential, I suppose. I should have known you'd guess, but you might have pleased my vanity by believing my illusion awhile longer than this. What exists within Megan's dream world can take different forms, and Kaare suits best here, completing the past to fit the present." She crossed her arms and let out a great sigh, then shrugged. "Ah, well, ah, well, endlessly on. As I said, I should have known better."

"But why?" Brierley asked, and looked again around the room. "I can see that you are healing her castle, but why is Megan even afflicted again? Why is she in danger this far from Witchmere?" She looked at the girl sitting in the chair. "And why are you here in her dream world?"

"Ah, yes, why."

"What happened to 'find it out yourself'?" Brierley teased.

"Be quiet," she chided mildly. "I'm chagrined quite enough already. What you did not know, Brierley, is that Megan is the first fire witch born since the Disasters. I told you that we have waited, but each time you and Melfallan were reborn again, Kaare was not. Did Thora bind her soul into the Well? Did Kaare refuse to rise again, as the fire ghost refused? We didn't know. And then you found Megan and Jain soon appeared, too—a salamander, true, but undeniably Jain." She wrinkled her nose. "After so long a time! You see, every fire witch died in the Disasters—not only the collective of Witchmere who afflict Megan as the fire ghost, but every fire witch who stayed in her hamlet to defend her folk. Even the few fire witches among the Exiles, such as Kaare, who stayed to defend us at the ford, all died." She shook her head sadly. "They are always rare, always precious. And when they died, Jain died, too. The Witchmere scholars always speculated that we dragons are the common vision of a collective shari'a mind, and perhaps they are right." She quirked her mouth. "It's not an issue upon which I choose to think, lest I think myself out of existence."

"Can you do that?" Brierley asked, startled.

"My child, I have no intention of trying it. Megan is not currently in danger, despite this new damage." She gestured at the room and the fire-damaged hallway beyond. "This came from today, when the fire ghost tried to seize the Well's power; but Witchmere is far away, and the Star Well is warded. I didn't expect her to follow you to the Well through your link with Megan. Indeed, I didn't even think it possible." She shrugged, bemused. "Fire gift: who will ever understand it? But Ashdla was right: the Well requires four witches, not two, and the fire ghost's meddling only partly activated the Well, not quite succeeding in her attempt. If the fire ghost tried this today, she will try again when all four witches are finally present, and that we cannot allow. And there is other need, too, for I would see Jain whole again after all this time." She smiled at Megan. "Will you help us, Megan?"

Megan nodded vigorously.

"Then let us begin." Basoul stood and raised a graceful hand.

The next instant they stood upon the blackened plain in front of the fire ghost's castle. Flames flickered uneasily among the charred grasses, moved across the blackened timbers of the window casements. The castle, still unfinished, its first floor solid stone, stood with a skeleton of wood timbers extending upward. It had no roof, but had a front stair, broad risers of stone like Megan's castle, and a great, oaken door, although that door was splintered by fire. A haze drifted through the air, and heat shimmered above the open story. Megan clung hard to Brierley's hand, and Brierley could feel the child trembling.

"So much pain," Basoul said faintly. "Oh, I remember how it was." She bowed her head a moment, then stared bleakly at the castle for another moment. "Come forth," she said quietly. "Come forth and answer for yourself, and what you have done here."

The castle door slowly swung open, revealing a vast emptiness within. A woman stood there, her clothes rent and tattered, her body marked with fire. Her eyes burned. *Go away,* she commanded. *I rule here.* Her eyes shifted malevolently to Megan, and the child gasped and leaned harder into Brierley.

Basoul shook her head vigorously. "Your time is past, sister, and the world has moved beyond you. Release the flame and be healed."

No.

Brierley gasped in dismay as a blackened dragon's head lifted above the upper-story timbers, followed by a coil of a long neck, charred and bleeding. The dragon's great eyes were blinded, his snout a bleeding wound, and he moaned, a wild, keening moan of pain and loss and bewilderment. His head hunted vaguely for what it could not see, moving from side to side, as he flickered a slivered tongue. He bumped his jaw against one of the timbers that confined him, and recoiled weakly with a cry of pain. Brierley watched through a shimmer of tears, appalled.

"Jain!" Megan cried. "Oh, what happened to you? Oh, Jain!" Megan slipped from Brierley's hold and stumbled forward, her hands outstretched.

"Megan!" Brierley reached vainly to stop her.

"No," Basoul said quickly. "Let her go."

"But—"

"Let her go," Basoul repeated. "The die is cast. She will survive, or she will not."

"I don't accept that!" Brierley shouted, and ran after Megan. "Megan, stop!"

The fire ghost laughed in triumph and swept down the castle stairs, reaching for Megan with eager hands. Megan eluded her grasp and darted to the side, then stopped two paces away to glare. "No!" she cried, then looked back at Brierley. "No, Mother! Don't come closer. Not yet."

Brierley slowed, then felt Basoul's hand on her arm and obeyed them both. What do I know here? she thought in despair. The vision that had been Jain swung his neck from side to side, seeking vainly through blinded eyes, lost, bereft, in agony. Brierley choked back a sob.

Megan turned back to the fire ghost, her small face defiant. "You are old," she announced. "You are wrong."

I am not wrong. I am Vengeance.

"You are old times," Megan insisted. "You want to hurt the people my mother loves, and I do not permit! I guard! I guard! I guard!" Megan's voice rose into a scream, and the fire ghost took a step back in confusion. "I do not permit!"

Megan stabbed her finger at the injured dragon above them. "You hurt Jain by wanting what you want. You blinded him. You burned him by hating. It's not right. Let him go!" She stamped her foot angrily. "Now!"

"Let him go," Kaare echoed, raising her hands. The fire ghost's eyes shifted to the slender fire witch standing beside Brierley, then narrowed.

Stay out of this, Basoul, she said malevolently. *You are sea gift. You do not belong here.* She gestured contemptuously at Brierley. *Nor does she, your keystone, as you call her.*

"No," Basoul declared. "As Kaare I can say 'no' as loudly as you. She has said 'no' since she died, refusing the next world, choosing oblivion over life. She has waited inside a shade for the hope that died with her, and now it is reborn. Megan is the living flame, sister, as you were, as Kaare was. She is now the hope reborn, the hope in which you have despaired. For three hundred years the flame has not been rekindled, and perhaps you are partly at fault, in your denials, in your willfulness, in our choice for hate, but despite you Jain's fire has risen again in a living child. Yield to her!"

No!

Brierley stepped forward, spreading her hands. "Yield, beloved," she said in anguish. "Believe, and be healed. Let him go."

You cannot heal me, the fire ghost answered, but Brierley heard a note of uncertainty in that maddened voice.

"Believe," Brierley said, and smiled. "Listen to my child, and let Jain go as she bids."

And if I don't? she sneered.

Basoul lifted her hands. "I will kill you, beloved." Her voice was implacable. "I will raise the Beast from the sea and set him upon you, to rend and tear. I will give you to Death, to save the living."

Brierley looked at her in dismay. "No, Basoul," she protested. "We heal, not kill. You can't become the Beast, Basoul. You're the Voice." She seized Basoul's arm. "Don't be the Beast," she pleaded.

"It might be our last chance, child," Basoul said in grief. "It may be too long already, too long to find a new beginning."

"Not at the price of changing what we are." Brierley lifted her hands to Basoul's face, and forced Basoul to look at her. "What is the use of believing if we betray our own hopes? What is the use of winning if we win nothing?"

The girl's blue-green eyes shimmered with tears. "We may lose Megan if I don't."

Brierley stifled a low moan and dropped her hands. She closed her eyes and struggled against her own love, her own hopes. "Then we must." Brierley threw her hands to her face and bowed forward in agony. A small hand touched her sleeve.

"I'm not lost," Megan said. Her small chin firmed. "And I'm not going to be." She turned to face the fire ghost. "See?" she cried triumphantly. "See what I guard? What you guarded long ago but have forgotten?" She pointed her finger at the tormented woman in fire-rent clothing. "Your time is over; it ended long ago. Now is my time. It could be yours, too, if you try."

I cannot yield, the fire ghost said, her mental voice laced with agony. *I cannot give up my trust.*

Megan nodded. "I understand that." She raised her hands to the wounded dragon who swayed above the fire-blackened castle. "Come to me, Jain," she called, and her voice was a loving croon. "Come to me. Leave this place and forget that time forever, and be with me." The fire dragon lifted his head slowly, as if he listened. Smoke then billowed up around him, dark and black. A small, winged shape flew upward, and fluttered to Megan's arms, where she cuddled him closely.

You destroy me, the fire ghost wailed.

"No," Megan said. She looked down at Jain for a moment. "Can we do that? It's really not her fault." Jain rubbed his head against her neck, and Megan turned to face the fire ghost again. "You may live here," she quavered. "There is room to share in my world, for you—" Megan turned her head and smiled at the redheaded girl standing beside Brierley "—and for you, Kaare," she added shyly, "if you will honor me."

The redheaded girl shook her head. "I'm not really Kaare, Megan," she said regretfully. "You know that. I'm only Basoul's illusion. Kaare is lost to us."

It can't be, mourned the tattered figure in the doorway. *It is too late for us.*

Megan shook her head firmly. "No, she's not, because I remember her." Megan held out her hands and smiled. "It is time to remember the world, and all that might be in it. It is time to remember joy, Kaare. Didn't you say that to Thora? Didn't you tell Thora exactly that when you lay dying in her arms and Peladius had already died, there at the ford, and she could not bear the grief? I remember, and I remember what came after. Because of you and what you said, Thora went on to build the Well. Because of you she lived for a time in Yarvannet and left her books for my mother to find. Believe! she told her daughters. Believe against all hope, for the dawn that will come. Those were your words first. Thora never forgot them—nor you." Megan caressed the salamander in her arms. "Together we will make Jain strong again." She looked around at the fire ghost and nodded gravely. "And you can help us," she said softly. "Not right away, because you're still hurting, but you can live here in my river land, and maybe sometimes you can come to my castle and see me. I will teach you a different fire to live by—my fire, the fire my mother has taught me, the healing fire. And in time, my sisters, you will be healed."

I cannot, the ghost wailed. *I cannot give up my trust. Vengeance! Vengeance! Who will give us vengeance for what they did to the people? I cannot forget. Never! Never!*

"My mother is the keystone," Megan said, her voice ringing out in challenge, as again Megan drew upon some memory and transformed herself into someone more than herself: was it Kaare? Or another fire witch of Kaare's time, or perhaps even a more ancient voice, a voice Megan remembered from centuries in the past? "The Change now begins," Megan intoned gravely, "as it has already begun in the East, where fire has now melded into air to remember the stars. Here now we blend fire and water, to heal the past and make the future." She made a commanding gesture with her small hand and the air all around them crackled. Before Brierley's astonished eyes, the fire ghost's castle knit itself up, easing broken stone, mending shattered timbers, and then rebuilt itself with blue-white stones, tier upon tier of stones, first a broad step to a wide front door, a first, solid story, a second above it, and finally a third story with a wide balcony. A breeze lifted from the river and swept toward them over the grasses, mending all as it came.

The fire ghost turned and looked up at the castle, gleaming in the suns' light. *I can live here?* she asked uncertainly, struggling for hope and not quite succeeding, not yet.

"We will be sisters," Megan replied firmly. The fire ghost stared at Megan for several moments, then put her foot on the first tread of the stairs, then the other on the second, and went in through the large, wooden door.

"Good," Megan said softly, and turned to look up at Brierley. "I can't promise, but I don't think she'll attack the Well again. We could make sure by killing her, but does she really deserve to be killed, Mother? You didn't think so."

"No, child, I didn't." Brierley knelt and gathered both daughter and salamander into her arms, hugged them, then kissed Megan, and Jain, too.

Stop that, Jain complained.

"You're all right?" Brierley asked. "You're really all right?"

"I'm fine," Megan declared.

"Fire gift," Basoul whispered in awe, shaking her head. "It simply *never* follows the rules."

Megan giggled and pointed mockingly at Basoul. "You thought you'd have to solve it. You thought you'd have to do everything."

"Well, yes, child, I did," Basoul admitted with chagrin.

Jain smirked from his couch in Megan's arms. *Isn't it amazing, Basoul,* he offered, *when you find out you're utterly wrong?*

Basoul glared at him. "Be quiet."

"She didn't expect this," Megan told Brierley, peas in a pod with Jain's smugness. "She thought she'd have to kill the fire ghost, and worried that she would kill Jain when she did, and maybe even me. She loves Jain, you see, more than she's supposed to. She always has, and that's why this worked." She grinned up at the tall girl with the vivid aquamarine eyes. "I'm a surprise to you," she said triumphantly. "I'm going to be a surprise to everybody."

"That, child," Basoul agreed, "I can believe."

*E*ach morning the suns rose closer together, bringing the approaching Pass. Ashdla told Brierley the storms were milder on the plateau, more a series of driving rainstorms that quickly blew themselves out than the violent sea storms that caused great destruction on the bay shore. The winds blew down branches, whipped up the waves on the lakes, and often howled around the eaves at night, but the coastal mountains between the bay and Flinders brunted most of the force of the Pass storms. All the Flinders folk seemed to comment on the "mildness" of the weather this spring, to Brierley's wry amusement. In Yarvannet such storms would be discussed for days, with much headshaking and tsking: here the Flinders folk took their weather in stride. Brierley sensed the deep contentment of the folk on the plateau, happy with their lakes, happy with the richness of their upland valley, and largely happy with each other.

This morning Brierley sat alone on the front porch, warmly wrapped in a woolen shawl, to watch the dawn. The colors of the dawning shifted across the surface of the lake, first broad bands of gold and crimson from the Daystar, then mellowed by the twilights of the Companion. The two suns were now scarcely a hand-span apart, and today would be another of the clear, sunlit mornings before the afternoon clouds built again in the east. Now all was quiet and still, before the bustle began in the town marketplace and the boats put out on the lake for fishing before the winds blew up again. Brierley took in a deep breath of the cool air and closed her eyes, listening to the silence.

In the mountain cabin near Witchmere, Brierley had found a peace of sorts—a lonely peace, away from people, and too close to the dangers of Witchmere. Here in Flinders she found herself surrounded by people, all interested in her in a friendly way, who smiled at Megan, were affable to Stefan, thinking the three a good young family come to visit their friends, the Toldanes, whom everyone knew well. It was hiding of a different sort, hiding in plain view, and except for Sigrid Witt, Brierley found their regard comfortable, and no danger to herself or Megan. That the Toldanes approved of them and took the three into their house and showed them every favor, well, that was enough for most of the good folk of Flinders.

I might be happy here, she thought wistfully, if only I could practice my healing craft. I could give to them a part of what they offer me, as I found in Amelin among Yarvannet's folk. So far, however, she had not found the opportunity, and hesitated to take on the guise of a healer when rumors about the witch found in Darhel, thought safely dead, still fascinated the Flinders folk. How they loved their tales! In Yarvannet the shari'a were thought an old story long past any relevance, if indeed the old story had ever been true: here the folk believed busily in witches and enjoyed their delicious alarm, their wild tales of strangeness and magic, their headshaking over the perils should another witch ever be found among them. Parts of the forest were thought unsafe and carefully avoided, and some never walked abroad at night, lest a witch spring from the shadows and ensorcel them. Perhaps Ashdla was right: they sensed the shari'a power in this valley and so spun their uneasy tales—or perhaps the Flinders folk, having such comfort elsewhere in their lives, simply liked to scare each other.

And they gossiped, with everyone taking intense interest in everybody else's business—who was courting, who had built a new boat, who was expecting yet another child that summer, who had worn a new dress to market. A fisherman's broken leg was thoroughly discussed, and a consensus reached that he'd only himself to blame, being a reckless boy in his youth and no better after he'd married, for all that his young wife was a practical sort and skilled in her managements of children and home. Tsk, tsk, they wagged their heads: well, a few more years and her practical sense should cure his lacks. Yes, that will surely be the outcome. No need for worry: he was comfortable enough in their home, with his leg propped up and his brother bringing in an extra catch for the family until he was mended. When a spirited horse trampled a market stand and nearly trampled the stand man with it, hands fluttered in dismay, but none was hurt and the horse owner had promptly paid for the damage: the stand man hadn't even had to file a claim with the factor, and all complimented the horse owner for his ready acknowledgment of his fault. Yes, that was the way in Flinders, with all its good folk meaning well for each other.

It was a pleasant gossip, endlessly cycling through the town, rarely malicious in its usual intent—and persistent, even when well-intentioned. To Brierley's unease, Sigrid Witt continued her avid interest in Michael's visitors, visiting too often in order to spy them out. Brierley had spent several afternoons sitting uncomfortably with the older woman on the porch, listening to Sigrid exclaim and gossip and poke unsubtly at Brierley. Encouraged by Stefan's example, Brierley had crafted a quite interesting person for herself, drawing heavily upon her memories of the other Clara in Amelin. And so Brierley's house in Lowyn acquired blue curtains at its windows, an array of brass pots on its kitchen wall, a small garden, a white fence, and two dogs in the yard. Brierley spoke freely of neighbors she had never met, and a life she had never lived, skillfully enough not to add to Sigrid's suspicions. One afternoon Sigrid had brought her hulking brother, Jake, who largely ignored their silly women's talk and watched Brierley with narrowed eyes, waiting for the mistake. Brierley did not like him, sensing in him cold depths and a potential for cruelty that reminded her unpleasantly of Gammel Hagan, the duke's torturer. For all her gossipy faults, her easy malice, Sigrid had limits to how she might hurt others to appease her own inner wants, but Jake did not. Were he a duke's man in Darhel, Jake would fit nicely among Tejar's "graspers," as Melfallan called them:

the new upstart men who toadied to the duke and did whatever he ordered, without thought for its evil. It was a perilous game, those visits with Sigrid, but the only peril, it seemed, in Brierley's pleasant new life at the Flinders Lakes.

All of Michael's nearby neighbors had now found cause to stick their heads in Michael's door, curious about his visitors, kindly so. They smiled at Brierley, nodding their heads in welcome, and gossiped happily with Michael about the minor doings of their lakeside town. He welcomed them all with quiet courtesy, and Brierley sensed his contentment among them and the townsfolk's genuine liking for the large-bodied blacksmith. To the neighbors, Michael Toldane was a good man, sadly bereft of his young wife too soon, a good father to his active children, a patient man with their animals—a gift, some said, nodding approvingly, and then went away again, the wind teasing briskly at their clothes, enough to clap a hand to one's hat or prudent palms to flapping skirts.

Yes, I could be happy here, she thought, if only because Megan is happy. The previous afternoon Megan had run and laughed with the other children by the lakeshore, enjoying a normal childhood. Megan now enjoyed the simple joys of running, laughing, liking the children who played with her. Although Megan was often out of Brierley's sight, Brierley could hear her child with her witch-sense, and so could guess that the game involved some kind of leather ball, to be tossed and chased wildly, with shrieks and boasts and laughter. Sometimes the girls played house, with their dolls as children or neighbors or Count Charles come to visit, while the boys went fishing or rock hunting or helped their fathers. During the night, when Megan dreamed, to Brierley's amused astonishment, Megan invited the fire ghost, whom she had named Rasheen, to her castle balcony for pretend parties. Often joined by Kaare, Megan and Rasheen gravely mimicked Brierley's own daily visits with Michael's neighbors while Megan served her guests with a beverage and small cakes. One afternoon in the dream world, the three young girls were joined by a handsome young boy dressed in vivid reds, and the party became an entertainment much like the nightly dances in the town square, with Jain flattering each girl outrageously and then inviting them to dance. Brierley often watched from Megan's comfortable feather bed in the inner room, not wishing to intrude, and felt happy that Megan was happy.

Even now, she sensed, Megan sat on her sun-drenched balcony in her dream world with the fire ghost again her guest, and smiled and laughed, and earned a wan smile in response, the first of smiles. Brierley shook her head, bemused. It had been Brierley's dearest wish that Megan might have a child's normal life, a wish she had always had for herself when she was little. How she had longed to play with the other children! How she had grieved when her mother had forced her away from Jared, her only childhood friend! Her mother, carefully prudent about discovery of their secret witches' life, had forbidden friendships with the other children, fearful that Brierley would say dangerous words, or betray herself in some manner, and so bring death down upon them. She had grown up listening to her mother's fear, a fear she did not wish to give to Megan. Here in this happy town, with children who liked her, Megan lived without such fears.

I wonder where Jared is now? she thought wistfully. I wonder if he is happy? Will I ever see him again? Will I ever see any of the Yarvannet folk again? Will I ever see Melfallan? Must we stay here at Flinders? She crossed her arms across her breasts and frowned irritably at the lake. When am I going to know these things? Answer that, Basoul, if nothing else.

Melfallan had met the Everlight: whatever had Basoul meant? How could he— How could it— She frowned again, mildly annoyed by Basoul's new puzzle. If the sea dragon had thought Brierley needed a distraction, she could have chosen better, at least something Brierley had means to answer instead of sitting leagues away from Yarvannet, scowling at a lake. Actually, Brierley hadn't known there was an Everlight to meet: it had never spoken to Brierley, not even in her dreams, or at least as far as she knew. She knew its presence, sensed its love, but "meeting" implied a person, even conversation—

Whatever *was* going on in Yarvannet? She fumed a few moments more, then again gave up the puzzle, at least for now. "Hells," she muttered, and decided she liked the word—pithy and to the point, like all swearing. Perhaps I should swear more than I do, she thought. Maybe even at you, she added, glaring at the lake, then quirked her mouth.

Oh, I want to go home, and you know that I do.

Could I live here, unremarked and happy, she asked herself candidly, and give up everything else that might have been? For Megan's sake, I could choose this, but is choosing for Megan the only question? She looked down at her pale hands and latticed her fingers, shifted them idly. They were quiet hands, hands without work. She could not heal anyone here, at least not yet, and thus resume her craft. She already appreciated the difficulties if she were to try: Michael had told her that the rumors about Brierley Mefell had carried the fact of her craft of midwife, to the scoffing of the Flinders folk that any witch might have some good within her, and open speculation about what this Brierley did with the babies she delivered. She repressed a wince: the tales of witches were much more alive in Mionn than in Yarvannet, and it was a danger she must not forget.

But, more to the point, Brierley had not named herself as a healer when she arrived, too cautious perhaps, and was now finding that omission a restriction. To Ellestown, she was merely the wife of Robert Jacoby, that fine young cousin from southern Mionn, and then mother of Megan, but not a woman with any particular trade or craft. Better to be what she appeared the pleasant Flinders folk, a young wife like dozens of others, pretty enough and happy with her husband, but no different than the scores of other young wives who married and raised their children. Better for them all, especially given the danger she might bring to Ashdla and Will. To begin her healing again would require too many explanations and, if unsatisfying, cause too many questions.

Must I give up my healing? Is that the price of safety? And if I do that, what remains of me? In truth, she did not want to be a pleasant young housewife, content with her supposed husband and child, content to gossip and bake bread and perhaps attempt some lace making from time to time. And Stefan was now more restless than she, although he would not admit it yet, longing for his wife and children, missing his Airlie courtier's life, finding Flinders far too bland and—ordinary. She dimpled. Poor Stefan. He liked the Flinders folk, for their cheer reminded him of his own Airlie folk, but Stefan wished no more for a blacksmith's trade than Brierley her role as simple housewife.

And what of the Well? The constant rainstorms had forbidden another visit—as did her consciousness of the watching eyes. What was the Finding, and why was Brierley the keystone? Who was the girl with the crystal star on her forehead? The Yarvannet witches had nearly forgotten the Four, never knew about the Star Well and the Exiles in the East; in Flinders, the witches guarded an ancient shari'a place and knew many of its reasons. Dusty places, shifting sunlight, a coolness that emanated from the Well: what was the Well? What had Thora built here? And what was Brierley supposed to do with it? Will thought they still awaited the air witch, but after three weeks of patient waiting, no one else had appeared.

Maybe no one ever would, she thought bleakly—but Basoul had promised otherwise. Her doubts warred with her belief, and likely it merely came with these days of sitting and doing nothing. I wanted safety, she reminded herself: I did not expect it to be boring.

You have a wealth of witches, she told herself, a mystery to plumb, perhaps a great Summoning to make, but right now, as too frequently so far, she merely sat on Michael's porch, her hands in her lap, and wished for elsewhere.

But Megan was happy, she thought fiercely, and perhaps her unborn daughter would be as happy, growing up strong and safe in Michael Toldane's home, in this valley by these lakes. Perhaps. Why then, Brierley, do you want a different answer? She looked out at the lake, where the suns' light made the surface a shifting, blazing light, a mirror of light that constantly moved. *How do I choose?*

She heard the front door open, and sensed Will behind her. She turned and smiled.

"Good morning," he said, nodding to her. "You're up early."

"Good morning, Will. And so are you."

Will sat down cross-legged beside her chair and folded his hands in his lap. "I'm often up early. I think you're a dawn person, too."

"When the dawn looks like this, I like to be."

Will cocked his head at her, then hesitated. "We haven't shown you any of our rites," he said. "Would you like to see one?"

Brierley shifted in her chair to face him. In some ways but not all, Will was as shy as his sister: she sensed his deliberate intent in this meeting on the porch, of several days of watching to find her alone, without Ashdla as a distraction. Will loved his sister as fervently as Ashdla loved him, but he knew a Pattern when he saw one, and their tussling interfered in gaining what Will wanted to know. Ashdla was largely content with the explanations in their books, but Will felt quite differently, restless about their answers and wanting more.

"Is that allowed?" Brierley asked uncertainly.

Will shrugged. "Well, at least I can show you how it works. Ashdla thinks that the rituals have to be, well, rituals with all the formalities, but I think sometimes a rite can be a pause beneath a tree to listen to the forest, or watching the colors on the lake, like now. What do you think?"

Brierley smiled. "I'm hardly an expert, Will."

Will shrugged. "I think all the gifts are one, like the Reformers said. I think the old shari'a saw too many differences and missed the binding. Don't tell Ashdla I said so; she gets nervous about my ideas."

"So show me how you invoke the Patterns," she invited.

"All right." He smiled. "Let me get some stuff from my room." He got up and went briefly into the house.

Brierley watched Owree wing in to the porch rafters, where he perched. "Ashdla was looking for you yesterday," she said to the bird. Owree ruffled his feathers and blinked golden eyes. "Do you understand me, Owree?" Brierley asked, but sensed nothing in response. "Ah, well."

When Will returned, Slinkfoot was riding his shoulder, and Will sat down beside Brierley with a much-worn book and a leather bag, then laid out a crystal stone, a small glass flask of water, an everholly leaf, and a feather from the bag on the planking in front of him. "We really shouldn't keep one of the chant-books here at the house, I suppose, but I don't get up to the cabin as much as Ashdla does, so I fudge. I know all the chants from memory, of course, but the book is part of it somehow, I don't know why. It just feels right to have it here, and not quite right if it's not. Does that make sense?"

"I think it does."

"You're being polite, I think."

"My gift is nearly entirely intuitive, Will. It makes perfect sense to me."

"Well—"

"It truly does," she assured him.

Slinkfoot chittered at Will impatiently. "All right, all right," he said. "Don't nag at me, you silly beast." He lifted the ferret down from his shoulder, cuddled her a moment, then set her down on the planking of the porch between him. "You sit there and be quiet." Brierley reached out her fingers to the ferret, and found the next few moments filled with Slinkfoot climbing up the chair leg and into her lap—then came a toothy smile and a soft snigger, a turn in place and then another, and Slinkfoot was settled.

"Well, take that, Will," Brierley murmured, and allowed the ferret a finger for the chewing.

Will sighed feelingly. "Slinkfoot always wins—and why not? Whenever she's about to lose, she changes the rules. It's her pattern—it's also called cheating." Slinkfoot ignored him loftily.

Will spread his hands and looked up at Brierley with a smile. "Well, let's see, where do I start? Let me recite to you from a text I like. 'For those born with the forest gift, everything has a pattern. Air and forest, sea and fire, each drawing from an essence of being, and together the four elements comprise reality. The cycle of life is in the patterns, which themselves make a larger pattern and a larger pattern beyond that, until all the world is enclosed within them, and the patterns are life.' So when we make a rite, we choose a symbol to evoke that reality of life, one-in-four, four-in-one. For air, I could use a feather, or thistledown, a wind-key, a spiderweb, even a stone that has caught a star." He turned the crystal stone until the interior fractures of the stone caught the suns' light. "See how the star shines within the stone? That is my first pattern, sky on stone."

He touched the small flask of water. "For water," he said, "I could dip river water into a flask, like here, or gather dew in the early morning on a grass blade, or use the snow around me—or this." He put the flask back into the bag, and took out instead a small mirror, scarcely three inches across, and beveled to a high gloss. "Water, when still, reflects the sky. River, when running, carves rock. Sea, when surging, shifts sand. A mirror is water on stone in all these guises, but today I call it as sky on water." Will set the crystal carefully on the palm-sized mirror. "And now stone on water." He smiled.

Brierley cupped her chin in her hand. "Patterns."

"Everywhere," Will agreed. "They sing to me, Brierley. The movement of the air through the trees, the way the light moves, all greens, endless flickering: this is sky on forest. The coolness of the soil on my hand, the brush of grass stems, the dance of the wind-keys in autumn: this is forest on land, a doubling of the element in a way. On a certain day there might be a thousand wind-keys aloft on the air, spinning in a great dance, the forest's life on air, the image of new beginnings, of potential, Forest on sky. And so the forest lives its cycle, making the patterns. If you look, you can see them. If you listen, you can hear them. Isn't it this way for you?"

"I don't hear patterns in stones or leaves, but I do hear them in people. I don't know how I hear it; I *know* it more than hear." She paused, considering. "I never really thought to analyze it, like you do. It just is." She shrugged wistfully. "I can see some connections in your patterns and mine, but the gifts are still different."

"People as patterns." Will paused, fascinated by the idea.

"As I hear them."

Will nodded. "Four distinct gifts, each with things a particular gift can do and things it can't. At least that's how the scholars defined them." He shrugged. "The gifts didn't always stay put in their definitions, of course, and it drove the air witches crazy that they wouldn't. Fire gift was always unpredictable, of course, but still the fire witches were usually guardians, and their gift always involving 'shifting worlds,' whatever that is. Even forest gift, which was probably the most stable of the gifts, had its minor variations, but not many. Most of us, for instance, could hear animals thinking, but not in words like mind-speech. Neither Owree nor Slinkfoot think in words. We do, but they don't. They have language in a different way."

"Like horses," Brierley suggested. "Megan talks to our horses, but they don't talk to me, at least not in a way I'd expect for talking." She pointed to Owree overhead, where the mock owl watched everything with interest. "Just like your owl. You can hear him, but I can't."

"And I can't hear people well, if I do at all when they're not witch-born. Sometimes I think I do, but I probably don't. Da thinks Ashdla and I prefer our animals to people, and probably he's right; I think Mother was the same. He also thinks our mind-speech is blunted, probably because we like animals better, or maybe that's part of the forest gift, too, as if we can think in only one direction, not two, toward animals but not people." He shrugged humorously. "Maybe it's so. We have lots of old books, but I'm not sure if even the ancient shari'a really understood ourselves." He nodded toward his stone and mirror. "But the rites work, Brierley. Ashdla and I can *feel* them work, and Amina says they work, too. She always told Mother that, too, although Amina wasn't very clear about what 'work' means. Do the rites preserve the hope of the Finding? Or do they give strength to the land? Or both? Sea gift has a definite purpose—you can see the person healed, after all. It's the same for air gift's storm spelling and the fire witches' remembering. But what do the forest rites do out in the world? The books really aren't that clear, and most of the cabin witches didn't wonder about it." He grimaced. "We forest witches are bid to be a practical sort, in order to temper the foolishness of other adepts, we say, but there is still an ecstasy when one hears the forest." He lifted his chin and narrowed his eyes as he looked out on the lake, and took in a deep breath. The suns' light shifted in moving color, moving on the water, sparkling within the sands of the lakeshore. "Can't you hear it, Brierley? Life breathes here."

He raised his hands, and Brierley felt a strange chill fall down her spine, then looked around in wonder. The forest behind the house had seemed to pause, as if it had caught its breath for a moment when Will beckoned, stilling itself, waiting.

"Liin-adani, shari'a shaba'it," Will chanted softly. "Litiyaad soom, tahad jalid." He lowered his hands and smiled at Brierley. "That means 'I come in power for the shari'a, blessed of the Four. I call on the Four to bless me.' It's how you start every rite. Here, look at this." He opened the small book, thumbed a few pages, and then handed it to Brierley.

"The writing's different!" Brierley exclaimed with some dismay. "I recognize that letter and that one—" She bent over the book, and saw other letters she recognized, but some she did not.

"Not too much," Will assured her. "The old script just connects the letters more. See here? And there? Same letters, just written differently. Chant speech is an older version of our language, although nobody knows how old. Probably it goes back to the beginning of everything, maybe thousands of years. Nobody knows how long ago the Two changed and forest gift was born." He pointed to a line on the page. "Some of the words are different, too. See the words for 'I am?' Here it's 'liin-adani,' but later it changed to 'il-bajaarin.' Maybe the air witches knew how that happened. The old shari'a tried to figure out everything."

Brierley nodded, then handed the chant-book back to him. "What comes next?" she asked curiously.

"We greet the Four, beginning with the east." He turned to the next page. "See? I'll translate. 'I greet the east, the domain of Soren and the swift storms of the air; dragon of mist and vapor and cloud, stormmaker, the breath of life, welcome.' The others are summoned in the same way. 'I greet the south, the domain of Jain and the fire of memory; dragon of the hearth-fire and the rushing flame, the warmth and passion of life. I greet the west, the domain of Basoul and the healing sea; dragon of comfort and wisdom, page of the inner world, renewer of life. I greet the north, the domain of Amina and the patterns of living; dragon of the lands, bone, and crystal, ward of the living trees, the beasts and birds, the stability of life.' Aren't they wonderful words?"

"The page of the inner world." Brierley smiled. "Yes, that fits Basoul. I think using words is part of your gift, too."

Will nodded. "I think so, too. We speak out into the world, summoning life, weaving the patterns, and then we listen. That, too, is part of the pattern, to speak and to hear." He glanced around and hesitated. "Amina hasn't come, so I guess I won't make it a real chant. Amina doesn't appear much during winter, Ocean knows why, but she always comes to the chants when we do them, even in winter. Maybe the world is sleeping during winter, buds and trees, and she does, too. Maybe. She won't answer that question, like a lot of others. It's really frustrating."

"You see her often?"

"Yes. Not daily, but often, especially since Mother died, and maybe more now because the Finding is near. Sometimes Soren comes with the wind, especially when I'm leading the chant, another mystery about me; and occasionally we see Basoul on the lake, but the others rarely speak to us. I had seen Jain only twice until Megan brought him here, and Mother never saw him at all." He shrugged. "Why? Who can say?"

"I have the same problem about answers. Maybe it makes life interesting, Will."

He snorted. "Life is already interesting enough, as Ashdla will complain to you." Brierley chuckled.

Brierley sensed again, as Ashdla had said, the depths within Will, a potential that had not yet stirred to full awareness. Will was largely content with his life and his wondering about himself, and had his young man's ambitions. He revered his father above all other men, and remembered his mother with a lingering sadness; but Will, too, could hear her in the valley, even if Ashdla often did not.

"The Change is coming," he said softly.

"What is this Change?" Brierley asked. "Do you know, Will?"

"It's a change in the gifts, I think. Once the dragons were only two, male and female, light and dark, up and down, higher and lower, all the great opposites. Now they've taken on the character of the four elements, but that change occurred centuries ago, so long ago that some adepts thought the whole idea of Two instead of Four was only a legend. Two divided into four, and the air witches thought the four were completed, and that there would never be more than four. That started the big debates."

"It sounds like a vigorous time."

"Oh, it was. It was a new flowering of the shari'a, cut short by the Disasters and delayed these three hundred years, but I still believe it can happen, Brierley. Why not believe, given a choice? Maybe not in my lifetime, but there's always hope, always the new dawn. Maybe the true fault of Witchmere was to forget that cycles must end and begin again, not freeze at some point in the cycle. The air witches should never have tried to confine the gift according to their definitions. I wonder why they tried. Is there something about riding the storms that makes you wish for order in other things, some wildness in Soren that they couldn't bear? Or was their gift too intellectual, too separated from the heart?"

"Thora told me that they brought down the Disasters."

"With some help from the other adepts. It could have gone the other way, even near the end. They knew Rahorsum and his army were coming into the mountains to attack Witchmere: why did they stay and wait for him? Witchmere has endless tunnels, all kinds of doorways: they could have led the people to safety. We had hidden places in the upland hills, places hard to find unless you're shari'a: we could have held out for months until whatever had angered the duke had eased, as it might have. There had been friendship for a long while, after all, however wary: how did we lose that friendship so quickly, enough that they wanted to murder us all? Something happened to change it, I think, something terrible, and it was born of our arrogance and theirs. The Allemanii were not wholly at fault; we contributed, too." He shrugged. "Now we might have a new chance, maybe one that needs different choices. If the air witches do not rule, who should govern us? Who should make the decisions? I think you should."

"What, me?"

He smiled. "Lady Brierley of the shari'a. We'll make you a duchess."

"I don't want to be a duchess."

"We won't give you any choice on that, I think." Brierley made a rude noise at him, and Will grinned all the more broadly, teasing her now. "It will be a universal election, once everyone gets to know you."

"Not if I can help it," she said firmly. "Do you really think the shari'a still survive across the bay?"

"Maybe. Maybe they don't, and the Finding is only a daydream. Maybe we four or five, perhaps a dozen others, are all that is left—but even that could be a beginning. Even that could be a dawn. Ashdla wishes for the Finding the way it was promised in the books. I wish only for a beginning, and

I don't particularly care about its nature. I want something that fulfills the hope, even if it's not what we expect it to be, even if it's much less than we hoped. Sometimes you can hope for something so hard that you destroy its chance of happening—or never recognize what is given in its place. Sometimes, however we wish, the hope never happens." He looked up at her. "You miss Earl Melfallan, don't you?"

She grimaced. "I sense two paths, that's true. Basoul gets impatient with me."

"Don't assume it has to be two paths."

"Quite aside from all that, it's not respectable," she said uncomfortably. "He's married."

"Ashdla told Da about your baby."

"*What?*"

"She didn't really mean to: it sort of came out. Ashdla's like that. Don't worry. Da sat for ten seconds looking stunned, then smiled and said, 'Ah well, that's something to know.' He already loves you: you remind him of Mother, and somehow that has comforted him." He smiled and leaned his elbow on the arm of her chair. "Brierley, why do you think the rest of the world can't be as accepting as you are? Why do think that gift is confined to the sea witches? Isn't love everywhere?"

"I wish she hadn't told him."

"It's done now, and no harm. But you might be a little careful about Ashdla. She means well—surely you must know that—but Ashdla lives her life, um, rather directly. It's one of the few differences we have, that and how we wish for hopes. What's he like, your earl?"

"Restless. He worries more than he should, but for some reason he loves me. At least I hope he still does." She frowned slightly. "We sort of tumbled into love, not expecting it at all, and now I don't know what to do about it. Neither does he, I think."

"I've heard that love often happens that way, from my vast store of august knowledge, you see."

"You're only fifteen. You'll find someone."

"Ashdla doesn't want me to."

"Love is everywhere," Brierley said with a smile. "For love of you, she'll adjust."

"You really think so?" he said doubtfully.

"Why, do you have someone in mind?"

"There are a couple I like, really pretty, and they seem to like me. And they're willing to like Ashdla, too, and the more people in the world who love her the better. She doesn't have very many friends. We're both rather shy, like Mother was. I'm glad she has you as a friend."

"Sister."

"That, too." He smiled.

Far out on the lake, the Four rose together from the water, nodding their heads gracefully to each other. They spread their gossamer wings, catching every color of the dawn, and the water sparkled all around them.

"Just showing off," Will murmured. Brierley laughed. He took her hand and they sat comfortably on the porch and watched the dawn complete itself, then went together into the house.

Later that day the afternoon sunlight flowed through the small windows of Hinton Witt's house, lighting the thin dust drifting on the air of his office, a large room near the front of the house where the factor conducted the count's affairs in Flinders.

"That whole family has always been odd," Sigrid exclaimed, waggling her hands at her husband.

Hinton regarded his wife tiredly. When he had married Sigrid fifteen years ago, wanting a local connection for his new position as Count Charles's factor, he had liked his wife; but Sigrid had spent the time in between steadily eroding that early liking, harassing him about stupid things. He glared at her, but little deterred Sigrid on a tirade, and nothing added a better impulse than the Toldanes. He had never understood Sigrid's fascination with that family or the three or four others she had picked as her targets, and he liked it as little now.

"Nothing wrong with being odd, Sigrid," he said. "In fact, some might call *you* odd."

Sigrid dismissed that comment with another wave of her hand. "Emilie came home in tears! What Ashdla said to her! I just can't bear repeating it!"

"Emilie uses her emotions well. She'll get over it."

"And now this *stranger* woman is here! Who knows who she is? Who knows?"

Always the dramatics, Hinton thought irritably. Always the fascination with other folks' business. He sniffed. In the beginning Sigrid had praised that new family, especially the young man who had flattered her, but then the neighbors had sniggered and Sigrid had belatedly realized all might not be as she had thought. And so his wife had gone full circle, back to her outrage about Emilie's having been insulted, while the neighbors no doubt still laughed behind their hands.

"Nothing wrong with strangers, Sigrid," he growled. "Happen to be a lot of them in the world, and occasionally they drift through one place or another, even here at the Flinders Lakes." He reached under his desk and deliberately pulled out his flask of ale, then filled his cup on the table. Sigrid hated it when he drank ale, one of her high-and-mighty pretensions about a factor's proper behavior, and he saw her shake her head angrily at his lapse. For a hopeful moment he thought the provocation might divert her—but sadly not.

"You never listen to me, Hinton!"

"How can I help but listen, the way you din at my ears? I've important tasks to do—it's my duty as the count's factor. I don't have time to hear more of your dislike for Michael Toldane and any part of his business. Emilie gets what she deserves, and no doubt Ashdla had the right of it. And a relative visiting is not a crime. Give it up, Sigrid." He raised a hand as she opened her mouth again. "Enough! My dear wife, you're an incurable gossip, and I admit you have your uses to the count's factor in bringing me sly news, but there's nothing wrong with Michael Toldane or his family and his relations. He's a good and quiet man, does his work well, takes care of his children, and minds his own business. I wish you would, too." He bunched his eyebrows at her, then took a large draught of ale from his cup.

Sigrid put her hands on her hips and glared. For the next few moments, they fought a war of wills, her measuring his patience, him measuring her determination. When Hinton didn't yield, Sigrid shifted tactics, not that it'd do her any good. "Hinton, it's not just me ranting," she said, trying hard to sound sweet and reasonable. "I've never heard of Dani having a sister, and we both know Michael was an only child. So how could this Clara be a cousin? A cousin requires an aunt, and that means a sister, and neither Michael nor Dani ever had a sister."

"There are second cousins—and third and fourth and sixth and twelfth, and I couldn't care less if she's a cousin or a coot-bear. Give it up."

"It's an odd time in the world, Hinton," Sigrid wheedled, "with witches being found again."

"Supposedly found again: I don't listen much to High Lord affairs beyond those of Count Charles, and *he* hasn't bid me look for witches."

Sigrid flopped herself down in the chair in front of his desk and sighed gustily. "They found a witch, this Brierley Mefell, in Darhel." Sigrid rolled her eyes in pretended alarm.

"Wasn't proved," Hinton said resistantly.

"So you say. My brother says—"

"I know what he's been saying," Hinton interrupted. "And I haven't heard of any reward offered by the duke, whatever Jake is pretending; and I won't have townsfolk taking the law into their own hands, especially against the Toldanes." He wagged his finger warningly at Sigrid. "You tell Jake to stop that talk, or I'll lock him up for menacing, just like I did last time you two did your finger-pointing at our neighbors. And I'm not writing to the count about any reward. Give it up, both of you. There are no witches in Flinders, however you and Jake like the dramatics of looking for them. First you accuse that young daughter of the Mayhews, when everyone knows she just takes after her mother's craziness; then you're goggling and carrying on about poor Robert Sayer's stroke and how it took his speech, saying a witch had blighted him; and now you're poking into the Toldanes' affairs again. Leave it be."

"I still say you should look into it," Sigrid said stubbornly. "You're the count's factor, and you're supposed to investigate these things."

"What things? All I've heard is that the Toldanes have visitors."

"On top of everything else, Hinton! That daughter of his runs off into the woods and doesn't come back for days at a time, and sometimes the son disappears, too. Where does she go? Laurie Cosen told me two weeks ago that Ashdla wasn't there when she went by the Toldane house to visit— nor was this Clara. Where were they that day? What are they up to?"

"Sigrid—"

"It's your duty, husband." Sigrid glared at him fiercely.

"I do my duty, without much help from you, and Count Charles is satisfied. If I sent half the witch reports downriver that you'd have me send, he'd think me a madman and find some other man than me. And where would you be then? The only other trade I know is my father's fishing, and that would make you a fisherman's wife, Sigrid, no better than any other of the town women. You'd wear homespun like all the others, and find it hard to think yourself superior. Even *your* imagination can stretch only so far. There'd be no fine gowns bought upriver, no store of gold for other fripperies that you like, no dowry for Emilie. She'd be a fishwife, too, in her time, just like you." He jabbed his finger at her. "I'm warning you, wife. Leave it be! I've trouble enough."

"You haven't heard the last of this, Hinton!"

"Sadly, I've no doubt of that, but not today." His wife flounced up from her chair, threw open the door, and stomped out. Hinton sighed, then slowly rubbed his face. What a wife! What had possessed him all those years ago? If only he still had his youth, when women had looked his way, he might think of finding a better woman; but he and Sigrid were too much like barnacles on a boat bottom, stuck beside each other for life, to think of that now.

"It's not the strangers that trouble me," he told the empty room, "it's the damnable relatives I have, especially my wife."

He scratched his gray-haired head for several moments, wondering if he should threaten Jake personally, then drained his cup of ale to soothe his nerves. No need, he decided. Sigrid's brother talked large and often, just like his sister did, but usually it was just talk, a way to shudder about old legends and get attention from the other men drinking at the inn. The Flinders folk liked their tales about witches far too much, and Jake always found an audience willing to listen. In time Sigrid would give up harassing Michael's visitors, and she and her brother would pick on some other unfortunate in the town, making trouble, stirring things up.

But not today, he hoped. Hinton sighed again, shook his head, then turned back to his other business.

Sigrid stalked along the town street, her anger adding vigor to her stride. Why wouldn't Hinton listen? Why did he always roll his eyes, call her silly, treat her with such disdain? She was his wife! He should listen, as husbands should listen to their wives. Not that Hinton had ever listened that much: she had known at the time they married that he mostly wanted a connection to the town, a way to settle into the community. Marrying a local girl accomplished that purpose, with little tending needed thereafter. And Sigrid had made a similar good bargain, gaining the advantages of his rank, the good pay from the count, her position in the town above all over wives. And so they had tolerated each other— except on the topic of witches. On that subject Hinton never listened at all.

She passed through the market, ignoring everyone who

was there, and went up the lane to Jake's small house near the warehouses by the docks. He saw her coming through the window, and opened the door for her, then shut it behind her. "Well?" he demanded.

"I told you he wouldn't listen," she muttered.

"He won't even write the count to ask about the reward? Why not?"

"Jake, you don't know there's a reward. Brierley Mefell is dead. Everyone says so." Sigrid sat down in a chair and crossed her arms. "All you can talk about now is that reward. I'm tired of hearing about it."

Jake sneered. "I want the reward, Sigrid. I want out of this valley once and for all. I want to go to Darhel and find my fortune. Is that so hard to understand?" He pointed his finger at her. "You're the one who says the Toldanes have a witch in their house. So let's go get her and take her to the duke."

"You mean kidnap her?" Sigrid asked, aghast. "You can't do that, Jake! Hinton will—"

"You can come with me, Sigrid, and finally give up this sorry marriage of yours. You couldn't have Michael Toldane and you've been sour about it ever since. So fix it: find another Michael somewhere else—or don't find one and look to me for your fortune. I intend to acquire one. The duke always needs ambitious men."

"But I don't want to go to Darhel!"

"What? Stay here in Flinders with your bore of a husband? Your silly daughter who lets the young men use her, one by one, and thinks she's the winner? Or will you go down the river to Arlenn or even to Efe? Count Charles has his trusted men, has had them for years, and isn't looking for more, nor is the earl—and neither lord is interested in witches. The duke is, especially in this one."

"But she's dead!" Sigrid insisted.

"Maybe. Let's find out. Even if that one is dead, we can bring him another, this Clara." He bent over her chair and seized her arm, squeezing hard. "It's a good way to get the duke's attention. It's a way to get noticed, and there find our fortune. Why not, Sigrid? Why not seize the chance? She's perfect for the part, a stranger here, nobody knows who she is, wandering off in the woods, staring at the lake, acting strange—"

"Not that strange," Sigrid admitted, and firmly pulled out of his grip. "Not as strange as Ashdla."

Jake shrugged indifferently. "So we'll take Ashdla, too."

Sigrid jumped to her feet. "No! You mustn't! It will get Hinton in trouble!"

"What do you care?" he asked harshly, then smirked as Sigrid hesitated. "You don't even like your husband anymore, if you ever did. I know you, Sigrid. I've known you all your life, after all. You're tired of Flinders, tired of it all. Once you were different, but now you're sagging and blotched, fat and disliked. You know it's true."

"I'll tell Hinton!"

"No, you won't," he said smugly. "If you do, I'll hurt you. I'll hurt you like I hurt Mack Saunders, him who couldn't walk right for a full year afterward, and then that courier who came upriver from the count, the one I buried in the forest after I took his pouch of gold. I gave you some of it, you'll remember, and you were happy enough to see it. You never told Hinton what I did then, and you won't tell him about this."

"I couldn't tell him," Sigrid protested. "You'd have been arrested!"

"And Hinton would have lost his comfortable factor's rank and you'd have lost everything, too. Count Charles can't keep on a factor, after all, whose brother-in-law is a murderer. Oh, I knew all that when I told you—told you for a chance that might come in the future when I might need your help, a chance that's here now. And so you'll help me, Sigrid. You'll do everything I ask." Jake shrugged easily. "It's all for the best, Sigrid. We'll rid the world of a witch, and find our fortune in it."

"But Clara isn't—"

Jake smiled. "Isn't a witch? We find the truth at last. Despite all your yapping these past three weeks, you don't really believe it, do you? Do you believe in the shari'a at all,

Sigrid? Or has it been only more of the posing, the malice, the delicious thrill? With all those shari'a shrines in our hills? If a shari'a witch still lived anywhere, she'd live here—and so maybe she's Ashdla and Dani before her. Maybe it's true."

"You don't believe that either," Sigrid accused him.

"Ah, but I don't care if it's true or not. And neither will you, Sigrid—when you help me catch a witch, as you must." Jake bent over her chair, menacing her, and she cringed away from him. "You'll be sorry if you don't," he promised earnestly. "Trust me in that, dear sister. Believe me it's true."

Sigrid stared up at her brother in horror, her mouth sagging open in her shock. He meant this, she realized, meant to do it all. It wasn't just more of his boasting, his liking to talk about hurting people, of the fortune elsewhere he had only to claim, talk she had heard for years from her brother.

Jake's hand came down on her arm again, crushing with its pain. "Do you believe me?" he whispered, leaning close. "Say it! Say it now!"

"I believe you!" Sigrid gasped. "You're hurting me, Jake! Let go!" Jake released her.

"Good," he said, turning away. "Very good."

12

*D*erek Lanvalle took a long draught of his ale, emptying the glass, then gestured at the nearest barmaid to bring another. The girl was busy at the center table and didn't notice his signal, likely for the best. Derek slumped back in his chair and squinted groggily at the ceiling, trying to remember how many glasses of ale he'd downed this evening. First had come the large bowl of stew and a half loaf of the inn's excellent bread—he remembered having dinner. It was good to put food in the stomach before starting an evening of determined drinking, and Derek had always tried to be prudent. Prudence suited a spy, especially a duke's spy, and on occasion a spy's prudence meant living until tomorrow.

Five? Or was it six? He looked hazily at the empty glass before him, as if it might announce its number. Yes, he was sure it was six.

At a nearby table, three soldiers in the duke's livery matched coins for the next round, but had to squint hard to read the coins, each being as drunk as Derek. Poor vision led to rough words, and Derek carefully shifted his chair out of range as the fight began, earlier than usual, but that was part of the variety at the Hound and Dagger. The innkeeper quickly bustled toward the soldiers' table, his two large sons in his wake, and they seized all three for the tossing out of the door. Derek watched with interest as one son missed his aim and ran the soldier's head hard into the doorjamb. It was a solid *clunk*. Derek winced and shuddered in sympathy, but a few other customers raised their glasses and cheered. The next shove threw the lot out the door, to another general cheer from the common-room crowd. A firm slam of the door, a stolid march of owner and sons back to their station by the kitchen door, and it was over. Derek idly scratched his neck, yawned, and then raised his glass to his mouth.

Empty. Derek stared blearily at his glass. When did this happen? he silently asked the glass, but it had no answer, being a glass. Derek, you're drunk. Ah, well.

He'd been largely drunk most of the time for nearly a month now, starting that afternoon in the Lowyn inn after Brierley Mefell had escaped him, a determined drinking happily continued in Arlenn and Skelleford up the bayside coast, and diminished only moderately during the ship's voyage from Efe to Lim. Once he reached Count Toral's town on the strait, he had found another horse—he didn't remember quite how, and hoped he hadn't stolen it—and had then traveled south to finish his homeward journey to Darhel, taking his time on the road, swigging steadily from a long succession of flasks, and occasionally dismounting his horse to nap by the occasional tree. In truth, he didn't remember much of the ride, but at least he'd stayed on his horse—or so he assumed. At least he didn't have any bruises he couldn't account for, nor broken bones, the more serious problem in falling off a horse.

Once Derek arrived in Darhel, Derek's horse had contrarily taken him to this inn instead of the palace. The Hound and Dagger was a small inn that Derek knew well from earlier stays in the duke's capital, but it needed little in size to enjoy its ideal location. Eight streets up stood the duke's palace with its crowd of thirsty soldiers and clarks; eight streets down lay the river docks with as thirsty a crowd of river men, merchant's helpers, and the occasional farmer come to market who had strayed too far uptown. In the evenings the Hound's common room was always full, first for a good supper, then for the drinking and the bragging, the arguments, the tweaking of the barmaids' pretty rumps, the fights, the yelling, and then the dragging by the city guard as they hauled their choice of sodden customers away. It was a nightly show, one of great variety, and never quite the same twice. Derek enjoyed it.

He raised his glass to his mouth again. Empty. He frowned severely at the glass, then signaled to the barmaid.

"What can I get you, Derek?" she asked brightly as she reached his table. She was a pretty girl, a little plump but nice enough, and quite deft on her feet in avoiding the inevitable pinches as she moved among the tables, far too quick for Derek to try, not in his sad condition. Ah, well, he thought.

"Another glass, please." Derek pushed three coppers toward her, then added a fourth for her trouble. It gained him a happy smile, and he watched the extra coin disappear down her amply filled bodice. Sadly, she left, taking the bodice with her. The bodice returned quickly, but then left again before he could focus properly. Derek sighed.

He had sat in the Hound's common room for six nights now, seeking answers in a steady succession of ale glasses, but still had no solution to his dilemma. He knew his duty to the duke, knew his spy's duty to report what he had learned. *The witch is alive, sire, and hiding in Mionn.* Nine words, borne to the ducal ear, and the witch would die, her pursuit and death the duke's tool to ruin Yarvannet's young earl. Brierley had seen that possibility when he discovered her at the Lowyn inn, a spy in pursuit of a witch as his duke had bid him, yet she had healed Derek of the infection that would have killed him, using her witch's gifts, knowing what she did, knowing the risk.

You have a fair spirit, Derek Lanvalle, she had told him solemnly, her gray eyes mild and knowing, with a lilting loveliness to her gaze that haunted him still. *You honor your father's memory in that. What is your crime, Derek, to deserve death at my hand? That you are trusty to your duke, that you are deft in your skills as spy? Is loyalty evil? Is healing evil? What is your crime?* she had insisted. And she had smiled with a grace that stole his breath, then touched him with her witch's hands, taking the pain away, and had soothed him into sleep, to awaken renewed, healed of his wound. And she had done this, knowing he could kill her with nine simple words, and perhaps she had even expected him to try. Did she think that now, that he would say those words to the duke? Did she count the measure of her days of living until he did? Or had she known him better than he knew himself?

What is your crime, Derek Lanvalle? Or does it still await you in those nine words?

Fortune had given him the life of a spy rather than the knighthood he might have had, but he had done his best to serve his duke in the tasks given him, and had found a different honor in that. The honor of a spy, true, but not to be disdained. Duke Tejar had never understood that honor, thinking Derek only another of his bought men, a man who worked only for his pay, never for loyalty, never for honor. However the duke misunderstood Derek's reasons, it was Derek's duty to tell the duke what he knew. He knew that, and knew also that it was his honor to keep silent, a knight's honor valued by a spy never a knight, that he save her as she had saved him. That much he had decided in his tardy journey home from Mionn. But when had his duty and honor divided so badly? When had they moved these mountains apart? Perhaps when a witch's touch had upset the world.

If the duke found out that Derek had hidden this news from him, or, worse, if Derek actually lied to keep Brierley's secret, Duke Tejar would have no trouble naming Derek's crime—or its punishment. Such treachery to this Kobus duke could be fatal, given Tejar's nature as duke and lord. Yes, best to sit in the Hound and Dagger, wondering if the count was five or six or seven. Derek lifted his glass in mocking salute to his own dilemma, then drank deeply again of the smooth ale.

Then he thought he might lay his head down on the table, a most pleasant idea. Or he could start the endless journey across the common room to that opposite door, to the laborious step-by-step up the stairs, the reeling of half a hallway to his rented room: ah, but his bed beckoned, soft with rushes, a feather pillow for his head, there to sleep without dreams, to sleep and sleep and never wake. Derek closed his eyes wearily, his glass cradled protectively in his hands, and thought earnestly about his bed upstairs.

Six? Or was it seven now? he wondered. Yes, it must be seven. It was six last time, and one more makes seven. He had always been good at summing.

A hard jolt to the table startled him awake, and his glass tumbled on its side, splashing ale on his trousers and the floorboards. "Lanvalle!" a voice barked from above him, hurting his ears. Derek looked up blearily and matched the sergeant's face to the booming voice, a slow fitting of one to the other, then a name to the rugged face, another slow fitting.

"Hello, Albert," he said.

"Drunk, I see!" the sergeant barked at him, scowling down at him in deep disgust. Two hefty soldiers stood behind him, hands closed tightly on the hilts of their swords, their expressions fierce. An age or two ago, Derek remembered soggily, Albert Driscroll and Derek had shared a glass or two or five, trading tales and other lies, and at this very inn, too, a fact Albert now obviously chose to ignore.

"Sit down, Albert, and have a glass," he invited, then winced and slowly rubbed his aching ears as even his own voice hurt them. "I'm glad to see you, for sure, but must you shout?"

"Get up!" Albert barked. The sergeant scowled even more fiercely when Derek failed to leap to his feet, stiff at attention—something he'd never done for Albert before and why the man should expect it now, Derek couldn't fathom. Derek considered him a moment, then decided to hold his head before it fell off. A prudent man, Derek Lanvalle: anyone can tell you that.

"Get up, Derek!" Albert blared somewhere over his head, and Derek winced again. "They tell me you've been here six days, with the duke waiting for your report all this time. Ocean alive, man! Look at you! It's disgusting."

Derek raised his head and blinked soggily at Albert. "Six?" he asked, badly confounded. "I thought it was seven."

"Haul him away, lads."

A gloved hand seized Derek above the elbow and yanked

him smartly off his chair. Derek fell half to the floor and narrowly caught himself with one hand as he sprawled. More
rough hands grabbed him and hauled him to his feet. The
inn's customers turned to look happily at the commotion in
the corner as Derek now became part of the nightly variety
at the Hound and Dagger. Two of the river men even
cheered, raising their glasses in salute, and Derek smiled
crookedly back at them. Good lads. Always a good time at
the Hound and Dagger. Then the innkeeper rushed up like a
bull charging his field, his hefty sons in tow, and added to
the drama, but Albert waved him off. "The duke wants him,"
he growled. "Leave off, man. The duke's own business." The
innkeeper backed away, a bit too hastily for his dignity, but
the duke's name had power in his own capital town, especially this duke.

My duke, Derek reminded himself.

Albert's two soldiers dragged him roughly across the
wooden planking of the floor, not allowing him time to get
his feet in order, then dragged him into the street outside,
where five other soldiers waited. A whole squad, Derek
noted, and felt pleased by the compliment. Then muddy water soaked Derek's trouser legs as the two burly young soldiers dragged him onward through a puddle; with an angry
heave, Derek threw off their grip. "I'm not a bale of hay!" he
shouted at them all. Another soldier reached for him and
Derek smiled, then drove his fist hard into the man's face.
The head snapped back and both feet lifted from the ground
together, followed by a most satisfying arc through the air
and an enormous splash into a rain puddle. Derek laughed.

Wrong move, as Derek discovered an instant later.

They smashed him to the ground, piling their bodies on
top of him; then, after pushing his face firmly into the mud,
hauled him to his feet. Albert leaned forward and smiled into
Derek's face, a toothy smile of good cheer, then cocked his
fist and delivered a solid punch to Derek's midsection, blast-
ing out the air from Derek's lungs and, seconds later, the full
contents of his stomach. The soldiers dropped him disdain-

fully to let him spew, then, when he was done, grabbed him again and dragged him bumpily along the street.

"That was for your own good, Derek," Albert told him, as he stomped along beside him. "You didn't need that last glass of ale anyway."

"You'll get yours, Albert," Derek muttered. He was trying to keep up, but kept dragging a foot, first one, then the other, tripping himself on the cobblestones.

"Not from you, at least not tonight," Albert gloated. "And I'll take you on anytime, Derek: just name the place and time, when you're yourself again, that is. I like my fights fair, not hopeless pushovers. You'll thank me for this in the morning."

"What?" Derek asked.

"I'm arresting you," Albert explained cheerfully, "for refusing a sergeant's lawful order, you see. I told you to stand up, or don't you remember that? We'll ignore that punch into the puddle: no reason to lock you up for a month when overnight is better." Derek swore at him, and Albert tsked at his bad language. "You *want* the duke to see you now?" Albert demanded. "In your condition? I thought not. Come along, lads. We'll dump him at the palace gate."

And so it went, dragged up one street and then another, right to the palace gate. There Albert delivered him to the gate guards.

"He's yours now," Albert informed them. "Lock him up. I'll bring the charge sheet back later." Albert spat on the muddy street. "You've Ocean's blessing, I'm sure, Derek. Have a nice sleep." Albert beckoned to his soldiers and then stomped away.

"Haul him up!" a gate guard barked, loud enough to make Derek wince again. As they reached for him, he staggered sideways, avoiding their grabs, and found himself leaning on the gate wall.

"Leave off!" he shouted. "I'm here, aren't I?"

"That you are," the guard retorted. "So?" He was short and squat and ugly as a frog and likely knew it, with that no help to his temper either. Derek brushed mud from his sleeves, bent to brush at his muddy trousers, then straightened again to squint blearily at the man. He didn't know this one—probably a recent barracks promotion while Derek was away in Mionn. More to the point, the guard didn't know Derek.

"I'm here to see the duke," Derek muttered, brushing vainly at the mud. Albert's gesture was appreciated, but Derek was caught now and knew it. No reason to put it off, he thought groggily.

"Sure you're here to see the duke," the sergeant said skeptically, visibly amused by Derek's sorry lie. "Take him down to a cell. He can sleep it off. See the duke, indeed!" The sergeant turned away, barking a laugh as he shook his head.

"Hey, wait a minute!" Derek protested, as the guards moved toward him again, but these soldiers didn't listen to him any more than the others; and they grabbed his arms to drag him away. With a weary sigh, Derek stopped resisting and a few minutes later found himself shoved into a small, dank cell a level below the gate. The door boomed shut behind him, followed by a brisk jingle of keys and the retreating footsteps of the guards.

Derek looked around blearily at the oozing stone walls of the cell.

"Wonderful," he muttered.

He eyed the low cot standing against the far wall. It didn't seem too dirty, if he discarded the blanket, of course. Derek navigated the few uncertain steps across the stone floor, then gingerly laid himself down on the cot, a process of creaks and his own moans and a muffled squawk as his hand slipped and he nearly upended himself, face first, on the cell floor. "Ocean's breath," he whispered in mild shock, and then muttered more colorful oaths as he laboriously pushed himself up again and over onto his back. When he was done, his boots projected a full foot off the end and a wooden strut jabbed his flesh, but he wriggled himself into a more comfortable position, then lay there, staring at the ceiling.

Six? Or was it seven? It must have been seven, he decided. Nothing like this happens until I get to seven.

Derek closed his eyes, and felt the room slowly revolve around him in the darkness, a slow whirling that spun him away, around and around. The duke could wait until tomorrow, praise Ocean, thanks to Albert. When I get my hands on Albert again, Derek thought wearily, I won't pound him *too* hard, just a little.

Nine words. Words of importance, of duty and honor, of dilemma and betrayal. They formed themselves in their crooked letters against the darkness of his closed eyes and began a dance, a slow, sifting dance that mocked him, that jeered at Derek Lanvalle and his spy's honor. Derek groaned and laboriously turned on his side, banishing the words until tomorrow, and let the darkness spin him slowly away, around and around, away from the words, away from the duke, away from everything.

Mercifully, no one came to get Derek until late the next afternoon. By then the worst of his pounding headache had subsided, and he had ventured to eat a little of the meal brought him at noon. At Derek's insistence, a gate guard had brought him some water and a cloth, and he washed his face and hands, tried uselessly to repair the worst of the mud on his clothes, then decided a man was only a man and gave up. With a sigh, he sat down on the cot and held his head awhile.

He winced at the solid sound of guard boots tramping down the hallway outside his cell, then winced again as his cell door boomed open.

"Get up!" the guard barked rudely. He was a large, young man, dressed in a helmet too big for his limited head and a hauberk shirt far too small for his beefy flesh. The chain mail strained at his armpits and neck, and its pinch no doubt contributed to his mood. A soldier's lot was a hard life, Derek mused: few of them had a happy disposition.

Derek eyed the young soldier and considered starting another fight for its high enjoyment. One on one: at least the odds were better than last night. The guard thumped his hand on his sword hilt in warning; the small eyes glared fiercely through the helmet eyeholes. Derek eyed the guard's bulky muscles a moment longer and stayed where he was. Maybe when his head was better, he decided.

"Get up!" the soldier barked again.

"Why?" Derek asked mildly.

"The duke has summoned you!"

"So now we admit that I'm to see the duke?"

The guard set his jaw and glared. "Get up!"

Derek got up, without too much of a sway and a jerk, to his own pleased approval. When the guard reached to seize his arm, Derek coldly stared at him, daring him to try it, just once. The guard hesitated, then dropped his hand and stepped back. "Out!" he barked. Derek went out.

Up in the open air, Derek took a deep breath, then scowled at the gate sergeant, a different man than last night, but then a half day had passed and even gate sergeants had to sleep sometime. When the sergeant motioned to a guard for his escort, Derek shook his head. "I can find my own way." Without waiting for an assent, Derek passed through the palace gatehouse into the palace itself and joined the flow of persons in the hallways. His muddy clothes gained him several sharp looks, but no one tried to stop him. He did not drag his feet nor hurry overduly, and in time he reached the door of the duke's study on the second floor, a busy place with servants passing to and fro, many of them clarks with important papers, others mere servants abroad on their tasks.

"He's inside?" he asked the soldier standing duty outside the door, and got a sardonic look for his trouble. He and Richard had also shared a glass now and then, talking over news, and now the guard grimaced as he looked Derek up and down with little pleasure.

"What in Ocean did you get into?" he demanded.

"Mud." Derek made another vain attempt at brushing his trousers.

"That I can see. You were supposed to get here last night, Derek, not this morning, and certainly not looking like *that*. He's not pleased with you, by the way."

"I was detained. Ask the gate sergeant why."

"Hmph. I already did, and the duke knows about it. I suppose he'll forgive you as usual, Ocean knows why."

"You're a vessel of sympathy, Richard."

"You always get away with everything," Richard sniffed. "Duke's pet, I declare. If I did half the things you did—"

"Enough! So I'm here. Does that mean I have to listen to you?"

Richard shrugged. "Welcome back to freedom, you sodden mess." Richard shook his head, tsking a few moments longer, then tapped at the duke's door. When they heard a muffled answer, Richard opened the door partway. "Sire, Lanvalle is here."

"Indeed," Duke Tejar's voice rolled ominously. "He can wait."

"Yes, sire." Richard shut the door and smiled toothily at Derek. "Oh-oh."

"Go drown yourself," Derek suggested. "I'll be sitting over there." Derek pointed at a bench down the hall, and then put action to his words. He stretched out his legs in front of the bench and slouched, then wondered if he dared a quick trip to his room for some better clothes. He closed his eyes to think about it, but was jerked awake by the sound of his own rattling snore. At his post in front of the duke's door, Richard rolled his eyes in disbelief. Derek ignored him, but tried to sit up a little straighter.

A few minutes later, Richard stiffened to sharp attention as a roll of booted steps echoed down the hallway. Derek looked, too, and saw Sir Galbert Lydell striding quickly down the hallway, his boots crusted with mud, his traveling cloak no better. It was apparently a day for mud, Derek decided, although Galbert's seemed more honestly won. Long a knight in Duchess Charlotte's service, Galbert had been good friends with Derek's father and a boyhood hero to Derek, an affection Galbert had returned to both the father's sons. The older knight might have even cosponsored Derek's own knighthood had Daughter Sea not taken his father untimely with Plague and ended those hopes. Had Galbert been traveling, too? Where? Galbert glanced casually at Derek as he passed the bench, then stopped short in surprise. "Derek! Whatever did you get into?"

"It's a long story, Sir Galbert."

Galbert chuckled. "It usually is with you, son, but I'm glad you're back at Darhel. The duke will need you."

Derek straightened, caught by something in Galbert's tone. Was it triumph? "Why?" he asked sharply.

Galbert glanced up and down the hallway, then lowered his voice so none would overhear. "Well, that's really for him to tell you, not me, but our problems with Yarvannet may soon be solved. Melfallan's witch is still alive, and when we catch her, we'll catch Melfallan, too. You can help in that, Derek: he'll need your talents. Here now: you can't see him in that condition, Derek. I'll tell him I lectured you severely and sent you off for a bath." Galbert affectionately thumped him on the shoulder. "Scoot."

"Thank you," Derek mumbled, and watched in shock as Galbert strode toward the duke's door. Only later did Derek think he should have stopped Galbert before that door opened, before the duke greeted Galbert, his deep voice brusk with surprise to see him, before Galbert went in and the door closed behind him—how he could have stopped Galbert before it happened, Derek never knew, but surely he could have done something, something more than sit and stare in sick disbelief at the closing door.

Nine words, he thought in despair: he had hoped to guard those words, to find a knight's honor in that guarding when all else of that honor had been denied him by fortune—now a chance stripped from him.

Everyone had thought Brierley was dead: all had assumed, even the duke, that the duke's torturer, Gammel Hagan, had murdered her. Perhaps Hagan had killed her by accident in his dungeon play, and then had fled into hiding from the duke's fury. Or perhaps the duke, it was whispered by a few, had given the order to kill her, as Derek himself believed, and had assumed Hagan had succeeded in his task. But now the duke knew better and the hunt would begin, the hunt to murder a witch and undo an earl.

Nine words. Nine useless words. Derek repressed a groan and bent forward, covering his face with his hands.

~

Later that day Jared Cheney and Evayne Ibelin arrived in Lowyn, the southernmost village of Mionn's bayside towns, and wearily looked for the local inn, finding it a few streets up from the harbor. The Daystar had set an hour before, and now the Companion, too, had sunk behind the western peaks of Mionn's interior mountains, its twilight dimming into cool blues fading into indigo. Already a few stars winked in the east, and more would follow as the True Night fell, bringing its winter darkness. In front of the inn, Evayne reined up her horse beside Jared and leaned an elbow on the horn of her saddle, sensing that Brierley Mefell was not here and had indeed traveled onward. She felt a shiver pass down her spine. If the prophecy were true, Brierley was now traveling toward the Flinders Lakes, where Thora Jodann had left the Star Well. For three long centuries the air witches of Briding had awaited the Finding, and now the Four were bringing the last shari'a survivors to the Well, including herself. A quirk of fortune had recently brought her to Yarvannet to the earl's service, when she had thought it disaster at the time, an ending of hopes, and then came another eye's wink by fortune when Earl Melfallan had included Evayne in Jared's hunt for Brierley in Mionn. Why had the earl done it? she marveled. Had he been prompted by the Four? But how? Melfallan had no witch-blood, none that she could sense. But here she was, in Mionn at last against all accounting, traveling toward the Flinders Lakes and the Star Well that awaited her, that awaited all the shari'a.

"Well," Jared said tiredly, "we've arrived."

"It's better than another camp beside the road," Evayne offered.

"True."

Jared sighed, then dismounted and went into the inn to find the stableboy. Evayne looked around curiously at the sturdy houses of the Mionn town. Until a few short months ago, she had lived all her life in Briding, first with her mother in a small town south of Ries, the count's capital, and then later in the count's castle as one of his soldiers. At twelve she had learned sword craft from her father, Count Parlie's castellan, and so had found a new life for herself in Ries, a soldier's life, after her mother's death. Her father had never claimed her at a Blessing, nor even much admitted his liaison with the farm girl who, years before, had given him a daughter, but he had been kind enough to Evayne in his own rough way.

Odd, Evayne mused, that an air witch would have skill with the sword. That craft properly belonged to the fire witches, the guardians of the shari'a, but so it was, likely her heritage from her father as the air gift was heritage from her mother. When Count Parlie had sent her away secretly from Briding to escape the attentions of the rivermaster's son, her sword craft had won her new security in Yarvannet, security she had not really expected, and she felt grateful for it. She grimaced, remembering that lecherous, pompous young man, him and his friends who thought any woman fair game for their pleasures. They had boxed her in an alleyway one afternoon in the town, and all four had goggled when she drew her sword on them: one had nearly been run through, so startled by her attack that he barely moved aside in time. The rivermaster's son she had pinked in the shoulder, hardly enough to hurt him, but that small feat had landed her in a dungeon cell for a few months until Count Parlie and her father could arrange her escape. Odd chance that the son had chosen Evayne for his rape that day while prowling the town; odd chance that she had been the castellan's own daughter when he did. Odd chance—or perhaps not chance at all.

Odd, too, she thought, her first meeting with Yarvannet's young earl outside his tower study, and that the luck of the draw for guard assignments that morning had placed her out-side his door. More fortune, some might call it, but Evayne believed otherwise.

Had Brierley already reached the Flinders Lakes? she wondered. And when I arrive to join her, what will happen when four living witches again stand around the Well, evok-ing the magic that Thora Jodann left there? The ancient books in her Briding house, now lost to the fire she had set herself, had spoken of shari'a Exiles in the East, now wan-dering in those distant lands beyond the Eastern Bay, in catling lands. Would the Well summon them home? After three centuries of a slow defeat, the Finding would bring new hopes for the shari'a. But what hopes? Revenge upon the Allemanii who had nearly destroyed her people? Would the Exiles return with sword and fire to punish an old evil? Would they return at all? Or would the last shari'a in these ancestral lands, now held by the Allemanii as their own, abandon all that had been here and seek another destiny in the East with the others? Was war or exile all that the Find-ing might give them? Her books had not said.

Jared emerged from the inn and stopped by her horse to look up at her. "She's not here," he muttered in disappoint-ment. "The innkeeper's busy with customers and I couldn't ask yet, but maybe she and Stefan stayed here. She had to come through Lowyn. It's the only road from Airlie."

"Mionn is a very large place, Jared."

"True, but I was hoping—" Jared thumped his fist on his thigh in frustration. "We've got to find her and bring her home, Evayne. She's in danger."

"All the shari'a are in danger," she said. "It's how they live their lives."

Jared gave her an impatient glance, then tugged at his horse's reins. "The stable's around the back," he said. "The boy will meet us there."

Evayne prodded her horse with her heels and followed Jared around the side of the building, then helped unsaddle their horses and lift off their saddle packs. They then re-turned to the inn, where the loud-voiced but pleasant innkeeper, a man named Bart, showed them to a comfortable room upstairs. Jared threw his pack on the bed, and then sat down in a chair to pull off his boots.

Evayne looked around at the comfortable furnishings. "Well, Sir Jared," she said lightly, "at least we'll have a bed to sleep in tonight. No more blankets on hard, frozen ground."

"I told you not to call me 'Sir,'" Jared muttered.

"Why not?" Evayne asked curiously. "If I were a knight, I'd take pride in the rank."

"The only reason I'm a knight is—" Jared scowled fiercely. "Earl Melfallan took a liking to me, I guess, Ocean knows why. Or my uncle arranged it, thinking me suited to a knight's rank. Maybe it was both. I didn't know an earl liked people who talked back to him. It doesn't seem something a lord likes at all."

"What?" Evayne asked in surprise. "What did you say to him?"

"Well, I told him things about Brierley. I told him it wasn't right to take her to Darhel and put her in danger. And I told him it wasn't right not to tell the people who loved her that she's still alive. He didn't agree, so I guess I lost that argument. And because of *that,* I end up a knight." He pulled off a boot and dropped it on the floor. "My uncle thinks it's wonderful, of course. He even said it was inevitable."

"Maybe it was," Evayne said.

"Are you mocking me?" Jared demanded.

Evayne raised her hands. "Not at all, Jared," she said hurriedly. "You have every right to wish you weren't a knight, but I don't think you can do much about it now."

Jared shrugged and looked sour, then tugged wearily at his other boot. Jared Cheney had been quite content to be a blacksmith's son and nothing more, and would likely never quite accept his knighting, stubborn to the end. Evayne hid a smile. It was sea gift, that stubbornness. Jared was quite unaware of his witch-blood, but she had sensed the pulse of it when she had first met him. Although the shari'a gifts rarely manifested in men to an adept's full power, they subtly shaped a shari'a man's character: in sea gift, it meant insight into souls, a way of knowing things about persons that ordinarily one could hide, and, as in Jared, a sturdiness in his loyalties, a refusal to fail. Jared thought himself only an ordinary soldier from Amelin, and would have happily lived in that trade the rest of his life. Others might see little more than that stocky young soldier, that quite ordinary young man, but Brierley Mefell had seen more in him. Jared had told Evayne that they had been childhood friends: during her traveling with him, Evayne had discovered several of the reasons why.

Outside their room's window the wind rose in its howl, the advent of another hard rainstorm from the bay. Evayne listened to the wind and thought of Soren, who rode every storm, especially the fiercest. When Soren consented, Evayne rode the winds with the air dragon, hurtling through the sky, buffeted by the winds, enthralled by the rush and the power that Soren controlled as the storm bringer. Some Briding witches had distrusted the wildness of Soren's rides, had even avoided them when they could, but Evayne accepted the surrender of self and will that they required. In no other way could she be worthy of her gift.

She would have to tell Jared soon, she knew. By chance—odd chance again—they had met Countess Rowena on the road as she traveled to Yarvannet for baby Audric's Blessing, and so had learned that Brierley and Stefan Quinby had indeed left the wayfarer cabin high above Airlie, passing into Mionn. Even so, one night in their rough camp in the Airlie hills, while Jared lay sleeping, Evayne had taken flight with Soren to visit the hidden fortress in Witchmere's upland valley. Through her flights with Soren, Evayne had often visited Witchmere's underground chambers and hallways, seeking vainly for some sign of life, some flicker of light in the darkness, but all she had found was a tomb with its disintegrating bones. Once a great fortress ruled by the shari'a air witches, its caverns now echoed with emptiness, the only movement the slow patrol of guardian machines. On this most recent visit, she had found the traces of Brierley's visit to Thora's library—several volumes missing from the shelves, more damage to the disintegrating books on the north wall than she remembered from before. A mile down-valley from Witchmere's front gate, the wayfarer cabin still stood on the edge of its clearing, the cold white of snowdrifts piled against its wooden walls, a white heaviness of more snow on its roof. She had found the front window smashed, the marks of the guardian's fire apparent on scorched wood: why had the guardians attacked Brierley? It was a mystery that would wait until Evayne finally met Brierley Mefell—if they could find her.

Last night, again while Jared lay sleeping, Evayne had hunted the Flinders valley itself, but the Flinders towns had several hundred folk and, indeed, a number of young women with long, brown hair. Evayne had never seen Brierley Mefell, and met her usual frustration that Soren would not guide her hunting. He claimed limitation in his nature, more of the Four's refusal to help the shari'a adepts too much. Many times Evayne had often flown the Flinders valley looking for the forest witch who must live there, but so far her searches had been defeated. It was a lack in the air gift, being limited to sight when she did not know the person she hunted, and Soren would not help the lack, not even now.

And that meant seeking Jared's help, for he knew Brierley, and *that* meant revealing her shari'a blood to him. Although she liked Jared, she still felt reluctant to take the risk. She had learned to guard herself, to keep her silence with others, to refuse to hear their thoughts, lest her gift betray her by showing knowledge she could not rightly have. She had continued that habit with Jared during their journey, although she'd felt tempted to listen to what he was thinking, wanting to know more about him. But such reluctance had saved her life in Briding several times, and she had kept her caution, a prudent witch. If she told him now, would he believe her? Jared was a good man, dogged in his loyalties, devoted to his lords, his feet planted solidly on the earth, his determination fierce. It was like Jared to offer to find Brierley Mefell, with all the world to look in. It was like Jared to believe that he could do it, too.

"Where *is* she?" Jared fretted.

Evayne took a deep breath. "I think we should go to the Flinders Lakes. She'll go there." Before Jared could open his mouth to ask how she knew, she plunged onward. "The Star Well is there, and now is the time of the Finding. Basoul, the sea dragon, will direct Brierley to Flinders, as Soren has directed me, and so we should look for her there."

As Evayne spoke, Jared's mouth had slowly sagged open, as if Evayne had just brightly discoursed on the merits of purple horses.

"What did you just say?" Jared managed.

"What part do you need repeated?" she asked impatiently, then threw up her hands as he continued to gawk. She walked angrily to the bed, then began sorting through her pack. I have no skill in this, she thought in despair: I don't know how to talk to him. Why do I even try? Because of her need for a witch's secrecy, Evayne had always walled herself away from possible friends, had never dared to take a lover. When the others laughed and joked, she always stood awkwardly nearby, a stupid half-smile on her face. When they told their tales and invited her to share, she always held back, afraid to show too much. And so they all thought her cold-minded and arrogant, a hard-faced woman to avoid and envy, a woman to be excluded.

She had tried to be different in Yarvannet, had tried awkwardly to join in with the troop's camaraderie, but there found a new barrier in her gender. Count Parlie employed several women into his castle guard, and the castle troops were used to a female soldier, rare as one was; in Yarvannet she had been the first, odd again for a reason she could not change.

I can't do this, she told herself.

Jared cleared his throat, but Evayne refused to look at him. She unbuckled her sword and hung it by its belt on the foot-post of the bed.

"Evayne?" Jared prompted. "You know a way to find Brierley?"

So he had gotten the gist of it, she thought, and turned to face him. "I'd forgotten," she said wearily, "that you don't believe in witches, Jared. Forgive me. You don't even believe Brierley is a witch, even though the earl himself told you, and Brierley had told him. To you, witches are a fancy tale, little more." She spread her hands. "So how can I persuade you? How can I persuade you that you yourself have witch-blood? 'Nonsense!' you'll declare." She sat down on the bed and scowled even more fiercely at him. "You stubborn man."

"So it's finally out," Jared said with a slow smile. Evayne blinked in surprise.

"What did you say?"

"I knew you've been hiding something, but I thought it might be the reasons you left Briding."

"You did?" she asked uncertainly. "How?"

"Oh, the speculative looks, the words started but stopped, the refusal to tell me anything about yourself, although I've probably told you all about me. You don't share much of yourself, do you? I've been wondering why."

"I—"

Jared eyed her a moment. "Earl Melfallan told me to bring you along, but I don't know the reasons for that either."

Evayne shrugged. "Neither did the earl. I think something about me reminded him of Brierley. A perceptive man, your earl. If I didn't know better, I'd suspect him of having witch-blood—like you do." She narrowed her eyes at him in challenge, and Jared considered her for a long moment.

Finally he snorted. "I would have left Briding, too," he said, "the way you act." Was he teasing her? It was so hard to tell.

"Aren't you going to ask why I left?" she insisted, but only got a smile for her trouble. She glared at him. "Fine! So long as we go to the Flinders Lakes." Evayne turned back to her unpacking.

What did I say? Jared's thought dropped neatly into her

mind, and she sensed him studying her, distressed that he had upset her and wishing he could set it right. *Why is she angry?* It was like him she thought, to want the connections. It was like him, to believe the most unlikely things merely for the other's need in the believing. She stopped and leaned her hands on the bed, and felt the loneliness of all her life settle on her shoulders, to watch others laugh together, the simple joy of a walk in the town together, the knowledge that one was liked, even loved. Sea gift: how she envied him, those connections, that confidence in others and in oneself.

"I didn't mean to make you angry, Evayne," Jared said quietly.

"I didn't intend to make you angry either," she muttered, but would not look at him. "I'm sorry."

"So tell me," he invited. "I'm listening." Evayne set her mouth and upended her pack, dumping everything all over the bed. Jared sighed. "Brierley never told me, either, when she had to hide her witchery." He paused another moment as he watched her push her things around. "Evayne."

"What?"

"Tell me how we find Brierley. We can't hunt through all of Mionn, inch by inch: I realize that now. You obviously know a way, or you wouldn't have dared to tell me about yourself, especially that. I don't think you've ever told anybody about yourself, not the important things. Why not?"

"Telling gets you killed," she muttered.

"Not with me. So tell me."

Evayne turned to face him. "We can find her through my air gift," she said tiredly.

"Air gift?"

"One of four shari'a gifts: air gift is mine. But I don't know your Brierley, Jared, and so I can't find her without looking at every face, and even then I might miss her. I've spent years trying to find the forest witch in Flinders, but she eludes me. I know she has to be there: someone is guarding the Star Well, which I also can't find." She shrugged and sat down on the bed. "I'm not good at taking images from another's mind, and so I can't just borrow your memory of her face." Evayne scowled, but Jared seemed to accept the idea of mind invasion without much alarm—but no, he really wasn't listening to that, only to her, with all his attention focused on her face. "All in all, I haven't been much of a success at air witching," she admitted, "just like I've never been very good with people." She shrugged again. "I'm good with the sword."

"You certainly are." Jared had a half-smile on his face. "Better than I've ever seen. Who taught you?" Evayne hesitated, and Jared moved his hands slightly, trying to encourage her. "Who?" he said softly. "Tell me, Evayne."

"My father—he's Count Parlie's castellan, although he's been careful not to claim me. I'm a by-blow child, but he's watched over me since my mother was hanged."

"Hanged?" Jared blurted, aghast.

Evayne flinched, and Jared quickly moved his hands again, reassuring her.

"Sorry," he said. "Why, Evayne? Why did they hang your mother? I want to know."

Evayne hesitated, then gestured helplessly. It was an old grief: some days she managed not to think of it at all. "For murder. A neighbor in our village saw one of her seizures, like the one you saw take me in the castle courtyard, and she started watching us. We had a house up in the hills where the air witches kept our journals and the scrying tools. It was our retreat, a place to be safe, but one day Maron followed us there and got into the house." Evayne sighed. "She stole several things and would have shown them to the count's factor, but Mother caught her on the last slope into town and killed her with a knife. The murder was witnessed, and Mother barely had time to give me what Maron had stolen and tell me to run. I had to burn the house, you see, and everything in it before the village folk found it. And so I wasn't there when they arrested her, and then she wouldn't even see me in the dungeon. Three months later she was tried and hanged." Evayne's shoulders slumped. "I was nine years old."

"It wasn't something you did," Jared said, "and it sounds like your mother had no choice."

Evayne shrugged. "Maybe. After Mother was dead, Father brought me to Ries." She smiled slightly, although likely the effort was a travesty. "We share that, an important relative in the castle. I've never been sure how much my father knew about my mother's witchery; I took care to assume he knew nothing, and he played the same gambit, if it was a gambit. As it was, my father didn't know quite what to do with a girl, but I liked to watch him at swordplay and he saw my interest and began to train me with the sword. It's the bond between us, as much a bond that can exist between a gruff old man who really doesn't like women and a lonely girl who has to hide practically everything." Evayne sighed. "My father is a bloodthirsty man, Jared, and is proud to admit it. He enjoys violence, as some soldiers do, and I suppose I share that trait with him, if in a different way. When I ride the storms with Soren, the wildness is something I seize, as strongly as a soldier seizes his sword for battle." She eyed Jared carefully, but he seemed to be listening with interest.

"Go on," he prompted.

"I don't think you believe me about Soren."

"How do you know what I believe or not? I'm listening." He spread his hands. "See? I'm looking at you now while you're talking. Isn't that a clue?" Evayne tightened her lips, not liking the tease, however kindly he meant it. "And I'm talking back," Jared insisted, "saying to you, 'I'm listening.' Another clue. And you aren't as clever at hiding as you think, Evayne, at least not with me. So tell me more about air witches."

She hesitated. "Back before the Disasters, the air witches ruled the shari'a. They tried to confine the air gift, not liking its lack of control when Soren took them. Maybe that's what led to their mistake with Duke Rahorsum. They wanted to control everything, put reality into a neat, logical framework that never changed. If their descendants in Briding learned anything from the Disasters, it was that mistake. The storm takes control, not you." She shivered and smiled tightly at Jared. "The lightning flashes, *crack*, and the thunder could shatter your bones, if Soren were not with you. We fall screaming, he and I, shouting our defiance at the storm but still yielding. We fall and fall, down on the mountains, and might hit them—we come so close to striking ground. Then, a snap of his wings and we're climbing again, high on the storm."

"You can fly?" Jared asked uncertainly.

"No, I can't fly." She grinned crookedly at his expression. "I'm not completely deluded. But the mind can be seized, and that, too, is part of the surrender." She paused but Jared was still looking at her, his face interested, not angry, not hating. "Many of the Witchmere air witches never rode the storms, and thought themselves better for it. But the air dragon, Soren, is his own master, save only the storms he rides; and he will abandon those who deny him, refusing the whole of what he gives. Without passion, without the willingness to lose everything, the Sight cannot come, with its true dreams of the future. Nor can one hear the stars sing—they do sing, you know—nor sense the weather moving in from the ocean, changing, sliding ashore. You blunt the gift by trying to control it. I think your Brierley knows something of that, if she is truly an accomplished healer. To possess the gift, there must be risk. There is always a penalty for the witch's gift, always a risk of losing yourself and everything." She tipped her head and studied his face. "Are you following any of this?"

Jared smiled. "I'm trying. Brierley told me once that she could hear shell-stars think."

Evayne dimpled. "She probably can, but I'm sure my account has something of the same disorder of self-delusion."

"Well, it sounds unlikely, but who am I to say?" Jared grinned. He seemed to believe her, to Evayne's great relief, and his trust emboldened her.

"I need your help, Jared. When I search for a place, I can fly the terrain. But to find a person, well, there are thousands of people in Mionn, and I can't go one by one. My gift is one of vision, not of heart connection, so to speak. To search for a person, I need help. I need your memory of Brierley, and whatever help you can give me from your sea gift, Jared. A man's gift rarely manifests, but it's still there in subtle ways."

"And so how do I give you a memory and that, uh, heart connection?" Jared asked warily.

Evayne stood and moved another chair to face him, then sat down and held out her hands. "Don't be afraid. I've done this since I was a child, when I was taught by my mother. I have the gift. Do not be afraid. I won't let go of you."

"What do I do?" Jared asked nervously.

"Think about Brierley so that I can find her."

"Find her? Just like that?"

"Jared! I'm an air witch! I *can* find her, but I don't know her face. I arrived in Yarvannet too late and I never met her. I can't go one by one through every soul in Mionn. But you know her. It's our only hope to find her in time. If you can't trust me, there's no point in trying."

"I still can't quite believe Bri is a witch," Jared muttered stubbornly. "Nor you. Are you sure?"

Exasperated, Evayne dropped his hands. "Yes, she is. So am I. And so, brother, are you, although your gift will never rise because you aren't a woman. *We* are shari'a. Now is the time of the Finding, when the shari'a will be brought together and a new beginning made. The air witches of my line have waited for this for three hundred years. It *will* happen, but your stubbornness is in the way. If you love Brierley, you will help me, because this is the only way we will find her in Mionn."

Jared hesitated, then held out his hands. "All right," he said.

"You must trust."

"All right, I will trust—for her sake."

Evayne smiled wistfully. "For my sake, too, for this is a dream of our people, Jared. All my line has dreamed of the Finding, and we have ridden in search vainly, not permitted to make it come into being until now. I feel it, Jared. I feel that the time of the Finding is here. So come with me. Think of Brierley."

Jared put his hands firmly in hers and closed his eyes, not at all certain, but willing to try. Evayne sent out her call to Soren, and the dragon answered, folding time.

～✑

On a beach two children hunted for shell-stars, a boy nine years old, long and leggy, and a brown-haired girl as slender. They looked in crevices among the rocks, and laughed when the water splashed them, and the suns' light bathed them with its warmth.

"Brierley!" he had called as they raced each other on the beach, and she had turned, poised on her toes, her face filled with laughter.

Brierley—

Jared called out, yearning for her. Soren's wings snapped like thunder, bearing them upward with dizzying speed.

～✑

Another time, another place, a town street, and the suns' light beat down in its brilliance, casting Brierley's young face into harsh shadows.

"Why won't you talk to me, Bri?" Jared demanded in frustration. "What's the matter?"

They stood in the middle of the street, with Amelin folk walking by on either side. Her eyes filled with tears, but she said nothing to him, nothing at all.

"Why?" he cried in anguish, and then could not bear it and ran away from her, up the street as fast as his legs could carry him.

Brierley—

Jared's yearning swept them high above the bay waters, then inland over the mountains, each wingbeat a pulse of the heart, stronger and stronger as the dragon gathered speed.

It was another day, another time, when he had stubbornly tried again. "Why won't you talk to me?" he'd asked her, and heard the quaver in his own voice. "What did I do, Bri?"

Her mouth worked, but nothing came out as she stared at him mutely, her eyes filling with tears. He stood in front of her, his fists clenched. "Why?" he asked again, pleading with her.

But then Rob and his friends had come up behind them and had mocked her, calling her strange with an even stranger mother, and he had thrown himself on Rob, punching and rolling, getting the worst of the fight when all the boys had piled on top of him. And Brierley had run away, sobbing and hating herself because she'd abandoned him.

Brierley—

*Well, his arm is broken," the healer said, looking down at Jared in his bed with great disapproval. Jared's father scowled as fiercely, his mouth set in a firm line.

"I won't have you brawling, Jared," his father said. "How did this happen? Was it that daughter of Jocater Mefell again? Did she cause this fight?"

"No!" Jared protested. "It wasn't her fault."

His father shook his head briskly. "Well, we'll see about that. I'll talk to Alarson and get this settled."

"No, Father! It'll only get her in trouble! Please!"

"Trouble she deserves, I'll hazard." And his father hadn't listened, although he had tried to listen later, when it was too late. Twice more Jared had tried to talk to Brierley, but she had run away from him. He had given up then, and had seen her from time to time in Amelin as they grew up, and had never known what he had done to lose her.

Brierley—

There was a rush of air, and the thunder-snap of a golden tail, and suddenly Jared and Evayne flew high above a wide valley, its lakes sparkling in the suns' light. They fell, rushing downward with dizzying speed. *Do not fear,* a quiet voice whispered in Jared's ear, and he clung to Evayne, trusting that voice, trusting her. For a moment two blended into one, blurring self, blurring mind. *I am with you,* Jared told her. *I am with you,* Evayne replied, and it was the same thought, the same yearning, surprising them both.

Do not fear, a deeper voice rumbled, as thunder might rumble in the distance, bringing the storm.

They swept across a broad expanse of water, hurtling toward several houses along the lakeshore. From one of the houses Brierley stepped onto the porch, a cloth bag in her hand. A little dark-haired girl burst out of the house behind her and skipped down the porch steps, then turned and spread her arms wide, laughing. Brierley nodded, and the little girl ran off down the lane. Brierley followed, walking easily along the dusty path, her face turned toward the lake and the suns' sparkle.

Brierley—

Brierley stopped short, startled, when she heard his voice, and swayed as the wind buffeted at her clothes, tossed her hair, sweeping all around her.

"Jared?" she breathed. "Where are you?"

But the wind swept past her, rising high into the sky, soaring, tumbling, a golden mist bearing them away, a dragon hurtling high above the mountains, then descending toward the bay.

"Wait!" Jared cried out in anguish. "Bring her back!"

Evayne sighed, and suddenly she and Jared were sitting in the inn room again in Lowyn, hands joined tightly. Jared swayed in his chair, dazed, and she tightened her hands still more to steady him, then saw his eyes clear. For a moment they stared at each other in shock.

"We found her," Evayne whispered in astonishment. "Those were the Flinders Lakes, Jared. That's where she is."

"So why the surprise?" Jared asked dryly. "I thought we were all confidence." He chuckled at her expression. "That's called a tease, Evayne. It's about time you got used to it."

And then he leaned forward and kissed her soundly on the mouth, taking his time with it. She froze in surprise, and he took time with that, too, drawing her gently upward to her feet and pulling her firmly against him until she relaxed, and then kissed her awhile longer until he was sure she liked it.

"I think that was your first kiss," he said judiciously, teasing again.

"Why did you do that?" she demanded.

"Why not?" And to prove it, he kissed her a second time.

"Jared—" she said helplessly, not knowing what he wanted, not knowing why.

Jared smiled gently. "Have you ever thought, Evayne, that sometimes matters are easy? It's true—it really is. It doesn't have to be always walls, always loneliness. It doesn't have to be loss and regret, not all the time. If you wanted to convince me that witchery is real, you just did, trust me. And so I just felt like kissing you, and I thought maybe you might like to kiss me, too, and so we did." He smiled. "Don't worry: I won't push the kiss any further tonight, and not later if you don't want it." He paused a moment, looking down at her. "Or did I make a big mistake?" he asked wistfully.

"No." She took a deep breath. "I'll get used to it—"

" '—maybe,' " he finished for her, amused. "I heard the 'maybe,' although you were kind enough not to say it. Don't you like me, Evayne?"

"I like you very much, Jared," she said, trying to say it firmly and not quite succeeding, but Jared didn't seem to mind.

"Then that's a good start." He grinned. "Now you say, 'I suppose.' "

"I suppose," she retorted promptly, and pushed at him. "I have this problem with dares, Jared, just like my father does

Dare him to do anything and he will. Sometimes I'm the same: I'm warning you."

He winked at her. "I'll keep it in mind." He looked over at the tumble of Evayne's possessions on the bed. "What you can do now is move all that stuff you dumped. Just once on this journey I want a comfortable mattress underneath my bones." She hesitated, and it made him smile again. "I told you I won't try anything, not if you don't want it, and not tonight even if you do. I mean that." He drew his fingers down her face, a lightest of touches that made Evayne shiver. Then Jared stepped back, releasing her. "Next we'll be talking about one of us sleeping on the floor, a totally stupid idea. Let's not even get started."

Evayne smiled. "I don't want to be stupid either."

"Good," he said.

13

Count Sadon of Farlost greeted the new morning in a sour mood. He squinted out his bedroom window at the misting rain, the damp and dreary day, and felt irritated that the weather chose to match his mood. But then, what brightened his days now? With a muttered curse, he tossed the window curtain back into place and turned to glower at his bedroom. There was the wide and comfortable bed, two chairs for sitting, his desk with its drawer of papers, a wardrobe with his clothes: all of a lord's necessities, he supposed. A place to sleep, a place to sit when he tired of lying abed or standing about, a desk to keep things he thought important, fine clothes for his aging body: what more could a lord want? What more could any man want?

For a fleeting moment, Sadon wished he could climb back into that comfortable bed, pull the covers over his face, and seek a pleasant dream, something about sailing on the sea or riding a spirited horse on a summer day, something from his youth, before the bitter disappointments, before the long humiliation by Earl Audric, before the ruin of Farlost that was now descending through his son's folly. To sleep comfortably, warm and safe, away in a different world, where hope still found some being, to sleep and sleep, perhaps forever. He eyed the bed another moment and almost did climb back in, but Edmund would no doubt roust him out any minute now, bustling into the bedroom, throwing back the curtains to admit the daylight, calling loudly to his lord to wake, then slamming open the wardrobe doors to choose a suitable day robe to grace his lord's body. Ocean's breath! Sadon thought irritably. How could a man sleep through such a racket? No point in even trying.

I'm old, he told himself sourly, and sadly, it was true.

A knock came at the door, and Edmund put his head around the door-edge. "Ah, you're up, my lord," he declared cheerfully. "Good!"

"Ocean curse you, Edmund," Count Sadon muttered.

"And in a good mood, my lord. Wonderful!" Edmund crossed to the window and threw back the curtains, then turned to look at his count. They had been born in the same year, he and Edmund, and Edmund had been his nursery playmate, his young man's companion, his principal body servant in the decades since. Sadon saw the challenge in those old, knowing eyes, then sighed despite himself, and so earned himself a wide grin for the moment of weakness.

"May She blow you away," he wished Edmund.

Edmund smiled. "I thought perhaps the green robe today, my lord, the one with the embroidered sleeves."

"And drown you in a watery grave," Sadon added, menacing him further.

"Yes, my lord," Edmund said agreeably, then raised a prompting eyebrow. "The green robe?"

Sadon gave it up, and nodded. After all those years together, sadly, Edmund knew Sadon too well: none of his usual tactics worked. Each morning Edmund was determined to be cheerful, and cheerful he would be, however his count growled and glared at him. Edmund bustled to the wardrobe, opened the doors, and brought out the fine robe, an old garment and much-worn but still a favorite of both his and Edmund's. "Do you always have to be so cheerful?" Sadon complained.

"Yes, my lord. How's your headache this morning?"

"I don't have one," Sadon replied, realizing in that moment that it was true. Almost every morning Sadon awoke to the crushing vise of his persistent headaches. He blinked at Edmund in surprise, who blinked back. "It's true," he said, mildly amazed. "No, Edmund, I lack that usual excuse for cursing you. We'll have to rely on general principle."

"Yes, my lord."

Edmund helped him out of his sleeping robe and offered

fresh undergarments, which Sadon put on by himself. At least Edmund allowed him that measure of personal dignity—usually. "Meaning the general principle that I deserve it, I suppose," Edmund observed. "Still, it's an encouraging event, my lord."

"Be quiet, Edmund," Sadon suggested.

"Yes, my lord." Edmund proffered the green robe, slid the sleeves up Sadon's arms, then turned him around to do up the loops and buttons.

"I can do that," Sadon grumbled, trying to push away his hands.

"But you won't, it being my task, not yours." Edmund's deft fingers flashed through the loops, then straightened a wrinkle in one sleeve. "There! All done!" He brushed the fine velvet of the robe one more time, tugged the hem into better order. "We go through this every morning, you know," Edmund said. "Complain, complain. I truly think you need a good berating of me to meet the day."

Sadon smiled slightly. "Probably. And you let me do it, too."

"Of course I do." Edmund's eyes crinkled, a joke at Sadon's expense more than a servant should properly show his lord, but quite suitable to two old men of long acquaintance, both stuck with each other and having no way out of it, not anymore.

"Thank you, Edmund," Sadon murmured, as Edmund knelt to proffer the shoes.

"Always, my lord," Edmund replied quietly. Then the twinkle returned. "I'll go see to breakfast. You'll need a hearty one, my lord. I'll see to it!" And he bustled out of the bedroom.

Sadon blew out a breath, looked again longingly at his comfortable bed, then shrugged. Ah, well. Outside the window, the rain dripped and pattered onward, wetting the world.

⁓

By midmorning, the rain had eased its steady drumming on roof and land, leaving puddles everywhere. The clouds dispersed toward the ocean far to the west, and the two suns rose together higher in the sky, shedding their light in a bright dazzle. Farlost tended toward swampy ground, and the heavy rains of the early spring had not helped Sadon's problem of too much water and too little ground to hold it. After visiting his injured folk in the infirmary, Sadon put on mud boots and a warm coat, then tramped out with his field master to the new plantings, worried that the rain might rot the roots, but Farlost grain was hardy, used to the weather and overdamp ground, and all appeared well.

Sadon paused and squinted up at the suns. A few more days and the Companion would Pass the Daystar in the sky, worsening the storms for the next month. This rain was only the precursor of heavier rains to come, soaking the ground still more. He stamped his boot into the mud, testing the ground's firmness, then scowled as the ground yielded spongily.

"It's not too bad, my lord," his field master judged. "At least not yet."

Sadon grunted. "That's all we need this year, for the rains to drown the fields."

"The grain is hardy," the man said confidently. "We've had worse winters, and perhaps the spring will be mild." He, too, glanced up at the suns, now close in the sky. "They'll Pass in a week, maybe ten days, I'd hazard."

"Likely so. We need another drainage ditch." He pointed across the field toward the far fence, where a large sheen of water spread across the ground, another effort by this Pass to make Sadon's fields a lake. "There along the fence, I think, and maybe over there, too."

The field master squinted against the glare, then nodded. "I'll see to it, my lord."

"Good." Count Sadon turned back toward the manse and walked gingerly over the wet ground, cautious of his footing. The soil yielded inches at every step, clogging mud onto his boots, but he persisted doggedly. Nothing to be done about Farlost's mud, he reminded himself: it wasn't even worth the effort of a cursing.

With his attention on his feet, Sadon didn't notice the party of horsemen in the front quadrangle until he had nearly reached the gate. He stopped in surprise, then saw Lord Tauler's colors on the bannerman's staff. A half-dozen soldiers were tending to the horses; the others, Tauler with them—if it *was* Tauler now arrived—had already gone into the house. The horses and their riders were splotched with mud and wet in the bargain, if they had ridden since breakfast this rainy morning. Sadon unlatched the gate, then bit back his dismay as his head began to throb with the familiar pain. A few short hours this morning without the pain, a few hours to feel healthy and well, seeing to his folk, seeing to his fields: only a few short hours. He rubbed his temples hard, willing it away, and the settling vise eased slightly. His vision blurred, then steadied.

Not worth a cursing, he thought bleakly, neither my mud nor my head. He set his mouth and walked through the gate. The soldiers in the yard saluted smartly, and he nodded to them, then went into his house. Why was Tauler here? he wondered. His annual accounting wasn't due for another four months, and no message had come of war, fire, or death elsewhere in Yarvannet.

He found Lord Tauler standing on the rug in the front parlor, waiting for him. The younger lord turned as he heard Sadon's footstep on the flagging in the entryway, then bowed.

"What brings you to Farlost, Tauler?" Sadon asked suspiciously. "I didn't summon you."

"To speak with you, my lord. Earl Melfallan sent me."

"Indeed." Sadon threw himself into a chair, then winced as his head throbbed in response. "Sit, sit, sit," he said impatiently, gesturing at a chair. "Don't mind the mud: it's everywhere in this season." Tauler hesitated, then sat down. "And what message has the earl for me? No doubt his affront about my missing the Blessing? What penalty does he plan for Farlost now?" Sadon slowly rubbed his forehead.

"Nothing, my lord. How are your injured folk?"

"Mending. What do you mean, 'nothing'?"

"A lord's duty is to his folk. What else could you do but tend to them?"

"He's not angry?" Sadon asked, with honest surprise.

"No. Why should he be?"

"Earl Audric would not make those fine distinctions of the greater duty."

"Earl Melfallan does." Tauler leaned forward, elbows on his knees, and clasped his hands together. "My lord—" He stopped as a servant brought in a tray of glasses and a wine bottle. Sadon gestured the servant impatiently toward the table, then ordered him out of the room.

"And close the door behind you!" Sadon shouted, then waited until the door was firmly shut. He got up and walked to the table, poured two glasses of wine, and brought one to Tauler.

In his twenty years as Penafeld's lord and Sadon's vassal, Tauler had been a faithful lord to his count, cautious as he must be, but courteous when all the others had forgotten their courtesy and followed Audric's lead in their contempt. It had not always spared Tauler the edge of Sadon's temper, a fact Sadon always regretted after it was done, and perhaps because of that Tauler had not come often to Farlost in recent years. He knew Tauler disapproved of Landreth's excesses, had even dared to speak of them to Sadon, but Sadon would not hear it then. A man can be the worst of fools, he thought, when he drives away the best of his lords, even for the sake of a son. He looked down at Tauler's honest and rugged face, seeing the usual wariness, but something else there, too, then offered the glass of wine.

"You were saying, Lord Tauler?"

"Thank you, my lord," Tauler said, accepting the glass. He watched Sadon reseat himself in the other chair, then quirked his mouth. "You look tired."

"I'm old. It's not quite the same thing. But tired also, I suppose." Sadon stretched out his thin legs. "Tired to my bones," he admitted. "It's a day for regrets of many kinds. How are your wife and son?"

Tauler leaned back in his chair and cradled the wineglass in his hands. "Doing well. I may send Estes to the earl's court soon. He's of a good age for the polishing in his manners, and he certainly enjoyed this latest visit, although others did not. You haven't heard?"

"Heard what?"

Tauler's eyes narrowed with amusement. "How Earl Giles of Mionn humiliated himself at the Blessing. First he nearly got himself carried bodily aboard his ship at Melfallan's order, the way he'd been acting all week, but then he nicely put his hand into the poisoned Blessing basin instead. Burned his hand badly; fainted dead away with the pain." Tauler shrugged casually, then sipped at his glass. "Earl Giles is planning to take ship next week—after he's recovered a bit."

Sadon's mouth had dropped full open, and Tauler laughed. Sadon pointed an accusing finger. "You did that deliberately."

"Did what, my lord?" Tauler asked, still grinning.

"Never mind. Back up. Did what all week?"

"Count Toral's son killed himself in a fall from his horse, and the daughter's up for bidding as Lim's lady heir. Seems Giles wants Count Robert to be her bridegroom."

"But he's already married!"

Tauler lifted his shoulders, let them fall. "So? That's easily solved. It seems Earl Giles thought it might please the duke, who has to approve the lady's marriage, of course, if Earl Giles insulted Melfallan at every turn on his visit to Yarvannet, so he did. When Melfallan asked that the basin water be tested, Giles stalked forward and thrust his hand into the water. Sadly for him, it *was* poisoned."

"By whom?" Sadon demanded.

"Apparently the baby's manservant, Norris Mallory. Melfallan has him locked up in the dungeon, but he's not talking, not yet."

"Norris?" Sadon's head swam in shock, and the wineglass in his hand slipped from his fingers, tumbling to the floor with a wide splash of wine. Tauler jumped to his feet and crossed the floor in a single stride, then bent over him. "My lord? Are you well?"

Sadon clutched desperately at Tauler's sleeve. "Norris, you said? You're sure it was Norris?"

"Yes. What in Ocean is the matter?"

"Norris," Sadon breathed.

"You're not well, my lord. I'll fetch your servants." Sadon stopped Tauler with a jerk as he turned toward the door.

"No, don't." Tauler sank to one knee in front of him, staring at him with concern. Sadon smiled at him, a travesty of a smile. "I raised Norris, and sent him to Tiol with Landreth. His real name is Norris Dammarell." Tauler drew in a sharp breath as he recognized the name, and Sadon nodded wearily. "Son of Sir Malham Dammarell. Malham died in the battle with Earl Pullen, of course. When Audric reached Tiol and began hunting down the knights' families, Norris was only two days old, the youngest of their four. Lady Felice gave him to a trusted servant, who brought him to me. We were good friends, Malham and I, years and years ago when we were both very young, and Felice knew that I would protect her son for Malham's sake. She told Earl Audric's soldiers that her baby had died in childbirth and showed them what she claimed to be the grave, and so saved him by her lie. The soldiers murdered the rest of the family, including the lady." Sadon shook his head in bewilderment. "Why would Norris try to poison the baby? Unless—" He stopped short. "Perhaps Landreth used him to kill Earl Audric, too," he said faintly. "They grew up together, you see, and Norris worshiped Landreth for any kindness shown him. But why choose Norris? I never told Landreth about Norris's birthright—I told Norris only when he came of age, and he knows why it must be secret. Oh, how revenge would fit the reasons! But how could the duke use a fact he didn't know? And I can't believe it of Norris, even if he did know! Not Norris!"

"Are you sure Landreth caused Earl Audric's death?" Tauler asked quietly.

"No, I'm not sure. There have been hints in Landreth's letters to me, and he's said as much to the duke. His lie to curry favor, Tauler? A truth to gain a reward? Who can tell with my son? Perhaps Landreth wrote to Norris, doing the duke's bidding that he strike at the child as he'd struck at the grandfather. But I still can't believe that Norris would do such a— To kill a baby! To kill Yarvannet's only heir!" Sadon pushed Tauler aside and stood up as the enormity of the treachery finally penetrated, but he didn't know where to move, where to escape the ruin of Farlost, of everything in his life—a ruin that was deserved, fully deserved. All these years Earl Audric had been right in his contempt, wiser than Sadon. Sadon gripped his head as the vise crushed him, and bent forward, and might have torn out his hair, rent his own flesh, anything to push away the agony. Then he felt Tauler take a firm grip on his arms, push him forcibly back into the chair.

"Sit down," Tauler commanded firmly. "Sit, my lord," he insisted, as Sadon began to struggle, "or I'll do violence on you! I swear it!"

Sadon looked up and squinted. "Will you now?" he asked softly. "Violence on your liege lord?"

"Only when necessary, as always," Tauler retorted, and reached up a hand to caress Sadon's thinning hair, then rested his palm on Sadon's cheek for a fleeting moment before he pushed Sadon firmly down in the chair and made him stay. Sadon blinked up at him.

"I'm ruined," he muttered. "You mustn't take my side."

"No, you're not. Even with this, I don't believe so. I told you I bring a message from Melfallan. He wants peace with you, my count. He believes you were ill-used by his grandfather, repaid with contempt for your loyalty during Pullen's war. And he worries for Yarvannet if Farlost remains estranged. I asked to be the messenger, and I believe his intent is true." Tauler straightened. "I've watched this new earl for several weeks now. I wasn't sure of him at first, being Audric's grandson, but he's a different man, a different earl. Perhaps in time a great earl, greater than his grandfather."

"He arrested Landreth! How is that different?"

"Are you joking?" Tauler asked harshly. "Landreth was guilty of the rapes! I've told you before about his appetites, his carelessness in the willingness of the maid. Whenever he visited Penafeld, I had to hide my innocent girls from him, and even then I wasn't sure of their safety." Tauler grimaced with disgust. "He likes virgins best, you see, likes how he uses them when they're new to it. There, shout at me again when I tell you news you don't want to hear." Tauler turned and stalked back to his chair. "He's guilty, and Melfallan was right to charge him, not look the other way as High Lords often do when the nobility misbehaves. But you appealed it to the duke, and now Landreth is in Darhel to be used by the duke against Yarvannet."

Sadon winced. "I had to do something, Tauler. He's my son."

"Why?" Tauler spread his hands in anguish. "How long do you hope for your worthless son? How long do you menace Farlost by clinging to him? He's lost to you. He's betrayed Yarvannet and, if you're right about his using Norris, murdered our earl. Whatever Earl Audric's faults, he did not deserve murder by a treacherous hand. No lord does."

"Melfallan will—" But Tauler was firmly shaking his head.

"I don't know what he will do, but it's not what you assume. He thinks of wider issues, of Yarvannet, of all of us, not just revenge for his grandfather's death. The rumors have painted you as the murderer all these months since Audric died, but he hasn't acted against you. He didn't arrest Landreth to punish you; he arrested Landreth because Landreth raped those girls. One of them was only thirteen, and she'll never recover from the shock of it. She sits in a corner in the kitchen, staring at nothing, and the healer has no remedy. To Melfallan that young girl has worth. That girl must be defended, like all young commoner girls in Yarvannet, because he is earl, and no reason except that." Tauler clasped his hands tightly together. "I trust him, my lord. I didn't think I would, but I do. I haven't all my reasons in order, not to define them all, and I've wondered if my old romantic self has made me a fool, but—" Tauler bowed his head. "I trust him, and I am faithful to you, as always. And so I've come to ask you to come to Tiol to see him, to talk with him."

"Even after this?" Sadon asked in protest.

"Especially after this. It's your land at stake, my count, and Landreth is not your land. Farlost's folk are your land, and I am your land, and you are a worthy count, whatever your doubts about yourself." He opened his hands in a mute appeal and stared at Sadon, waiting.

Sadon raised a shaky hand to his head. "I need wine," he said faintly. "Will you get it for me, Tauler?"

"Of course."

In a few moments another glass was thrust in Sadon's hand, and Sadon drank thirstily, draining the wine in one long draught. Then he closed his eyes. "My head hurts," he complained. He heard Tauler's soft chuckle. "Well, it does." He squinted up at Tauler bending over him, then patted Tauler's arm. "It always hurts—well, not always. It didn't hurt this morning. It certainly hurts now."

"Perhaps you should rest."

"That never helps. Nothing helps the headaches, curse them." Sadon drew in a deep breath, then blinked wearily. "So he has impressed you that much."

"Yes."

"Have a care, Tauler. Go much further and you might be willing to lay down your life for him, as any sworn man must do." He patted Tauler's arm again. "I never say it much, but I know your loyalty to me has always had that depth. I haven't treated you well, not as well as I should, but I've always trusted you, as I trusted your father, as unlikely as that may seem to you."

"I've never doubted it," Tauler said stoutly, then smiled at Sadon's skeptical expression. "Well, perhaps an occasional fleeting moment, from time to time—" Sadon snorted, and Tauler tightened his grip on his sleeve. "For the sake of the trust, my liege, will you not listen to me? Come to Tiol. Take the chance."

"Such a slight chance, it seems."

"Still, a chance." Sir Kaene had said the same, Sadon remembered, but he hadn't listened. Tauler's gaze was steady and unafraid, and that honesty finally persuaded him, for reasons he could not define, not at all, but in this moment he did not need reasons, only Tauler himself.

"Yes," he said, nodding. "I will come. I believe I must show the earl a letter." He nodded again, more to himself than to Tauler. "Yes. And I will see Norris and find the truth, wherever it lies."

~

Melfallan rattled up the flight of stairs from the stableyard, then took a quick detour past the kitchens. His passage made a distinct bow-wave among the servants in the hallways, as it always did when he popped into view when they weren't expecting it. "Your grace!" they exclaimed, one after the other, and made their hasty bows, like birds ducking into water, one by one, as they fished. Melfallan nodded to every bow and hurried onward, making his wave until he reached the Great Hall. The stewards, busy with preparations for the next grand meal for the gentry, stiffened in surprise as he burst upon them, gawking that an earl was suddenly there. If he moved fast enough, he reminded himself, he'd be out of the room before they finished their bows.

He found his aunt in her comfortable bedchamber, directing her lady-maids as they packed her traveling cases. Axel lounged nearby in a chair by the window, watching the busy activity, and smiled in surprise as Melfallan entered the room. "Hello!" he caroled.

His voice made Rowena turn.

"Do you have to leave?" Melfallan asked wistfully.

"I have a county to rule. Why? Do we have another crisis?"

"No." Melfallan kissed her cheek. "I just don't want you to leave. Why can't you stay a few more weeks? We'll pamper you with compliments every day."

Rowena dimpled. "I'm not *that* vain, but, no, I must return, however you tempt me." She shook her head briskly, then pulled down his head for a kiss. "Now, I must go see the baby one last time, and then we must leave to gain a good start on the day. Perhaps soon you and your family can come to Carandon and stay a month, even two."

Melfallan smiled at the wistful tone in her voice, and knew as well as she how unlikely that wish, while Tejar was duke. He winked at Axel lounging in the chair. "Perhaps when Axel gets married, as he surely must."

Axel made a face. "I don't like girls," he announced, and made another face for emphasis. "Girls are stupid."

"That opinion will change, my son," Rowena advised severely. "It happens to all young men: get prepared. But surely not that long, Melfallan."

"Surely not," he agreed, and wished it so, as did she.

⁓

Later that afternoon came a more welcome departure, although Melfallan couldn't admit that to anyone. Earl Giles walked beside him down the wharf, cradling his injured hand against his chest. Lady Mionn and Daris followed in his wake, as did half the gentry of the town, all a-gather to see Earl Giles safely away. The earl's men on his ship were busy with the ship lines and bringing the last of the trunks aboard, making ready to set to sea. It would be a long voyage along the coastlands back to Mionn, a good four weeks' sail when done leisurely, which Earl Giles no doubt planned to do. Melfallan watched as Saray kissed her mother's cheek and embraced Daris, and then gave a greatly enthusiastic hug to Robert. As she approached her father, he waved her off irritably.

"Mind my arm, daughter. Don't be bumping it."

"Yes, Father," she said meekly.

Earl Giles faced Melfallan, his feet squared solidly on the wharf, very little expression on his face. Melfallan bowed courteously, received a gruff nod in return.

"A good voyage home, Earl Giles," Melfallan said pleasantly, and actually meant it, although not for the better of possible reasons.

"A good life to your new son and your land, Earl Melfallan," the earl replied, no doubt in a similar vein, then turned and walked up the gangway onto his ship, his wife and elder daughter and son following in his wake. Arm in arm, Melfallan and Saray watched the sailors warp the lines. Earl Giles's ship moved slowly back from the wharf, then eased into the harbor water, making for the harbor point and the sea beyond. Saray's fingers pressed hard on Melfallan's forearm, holding him firmly, as they watched the ship sail away. The large ship with its white sails weathered the point and moved out of sight behind the rocky outcrop, vanishing from view. Melfallan waited until the last timber of the ship's stern had vanished, then turned to his wife. "Well, they're gone. Is it a relief?"

Saray smiled. "A small one," she admitted, shaking her head. Standing on the dock in the view of everyone, he kissed her soundly, and then together they walked back to the castle.

Two days later, well into the afternoon, Sir James found Melfallan in the library, studying a book of maps. Melfallan looked up as his justiciar stopped in front of his table. "A rider just arrived," Sir James said. "Count Sadon will be here tonight."

"Was there any more to the message?" Melfallan asked.

"Only that. What are you going to do?"

Melfallan leaned back in his chair and glanced idly at the clarks in the room, all busily bent over their tasks. The afternoon light struck down in golden beams through the high windows, sparkling on the drifting dust in the air. A maxim there, but for the life of him, Melfallan couldn't find it. He blew out a breath and looked back at Sir James. "It depends on him, I suppose. At least he's come. I hope that's a positive sign."

"Maybe," Sir James said skeptically. "Perhaps he comes only to rant and rage against the Courtrays." For thirty years Sir James had dealt with Count Sadon's temper, to his great impatience with the irascible lord; and in his heart, Melfallan knew, Sir James believed that Sadon had indeed murdered Earl Audric, despite the lack of proof. A just man, Sir James had struggled with his own bias, and regretted that he failed. Melfallan grimaced in sympathy.

"So how do I win him, Sir James?"

"He'll be happy to hear his son will likely live," Sir James said sourly.

"I know you've had your battles with him, Sir James, and I also know you think Grandfather was too harsh. Could your opinions go further, that Grandfather was unjust?"

Sir James scowled. "I suppose," he admitted. He pulled out a chair and sat down. "But I warn you that if you pardon a rebellious lord, you only ask for more trouble later."

"Perhaps." Melfallan shrugged. "Even most likely."

"Whatever his faults, Melfallan, Duke Rainalt did speak some truths about the High Lords. Don't ignore *all* his precepts." Melfallan grinned at him, and earned himself an even fiercer scowl. "You have a gift in rule that you must use," Sir James insisted, determined to lecture. "I should not be there when you meet with him; he and I have too great a history of quarrels. No, this is between you as liege and Sadon as vassal, one-on-one. Tauler may try to help, but—"

"It's still up to me. I know. I certainly have a good motive: the last thing I need is an invasion from the north and rebellion in the south. But I'd like it to be more than a simple practicality about current facts, that if the facts were changed, nothing would be offered. I'd like to offer more, for justice's sake. Count Sadon has been ill-used by the Courtrays."

"And may have murdered your grandfather. Don't forget that."

"And if I have to forget it, Sir James?" Melfallan asked him candidly. "Could you accept that decision by your earl? And not with any plan for later retribution, after this crisis with the duke ends, however it ends. A fair offer, not to be betrayed. Forgiveness for a murderer, for the sake of Yarvannet. And we may never know the truth of it, one way or the other."

Sir James scowled unhappily and considered for a long moment, giving Melfallan that grace, then slowly nodded. "I worry for Yarvannet, but I do not worry about you, Melfallan. Past a certain point measured by logic and careful thought, one must trust." He smiled. "In the end it always devolves to the trust of a sworn man, however Duke Rainalt wished otherwise."

"I agree." Melfallan thought a moment. "I just hope I have the right instincts, say the right words. I hope I have a margin of error."

"Tauler will help."

"But it's still up to me." Sir James nodded. "Do we ever reach a point," Melfallan asked wistfully, "where all problems are solved and matters become easy?"

"Of course not, son, but we can always hope our foolish wishes. There's no law against that."

Melfallan chuckled.

⁓

Full darkness, spangled with stars, had fallen by the time Sadon and Tauler reached Tiol. They rode side by side along the crest road leading to Yarvannet Castle, a half-troop of soldiers in their wake. The many windows of the castle glowed with light, and bright watch fires burned on the battlements, making shadows of the soldiers who stood evenly spaced along the upper walls. At the gate more soldiers straightened on the alert, and their captain called out a challenge.

"Farlost and Penafeld," Tauler called back. "We are expected."

The man, a grizzled sergeant, stamped forward, his hand

on the hilt of his sword, his eyes suspicious. Then he recognized Tauler, glanced at Sadon. There was a hesitation, Sadon noted sourly, before the man bowed to him. "Count Sadon," he murmured. Another pause. "Welcome."

"Thank you," Sadon said wryly. This sergeant had been Audric's soldier before he was Melfallan's, and all of Sadon's greetings at this castle over the past thirty years had been much the same—the effort to hide the surprise, the pause, the pause again. Sadon repressed a sigh and looked up at the battlement above the gate, blazing with torches, then looked to the left toward the ocean. The murmur of the surf filled the air, with moving water and wind on this high bluff that ruffled cloak edges, teased at the skin with a delicious coolness. The hard bite of winter was easing into the turbulent spring: the surf pounded far below. The sea, he thought, and closed his eyes, smelling the salt on the wind. *I forget the sea too easily.*

Tauler heeled his horse forward, and together they rode through the gate, the half-dozen soldiers rattling in their wake. The inner courtyard led to a cobbled tunnel and the stableyards, and there Sadon dismounted, stiff from the day's ride, and handed the reins to a stableboy. The boy nodded jerkily and then suddenly smiled up at him, lighting his face. How old was he? Twelve? A short, dark-haired boy, quick with his hands. The boy bowed again, gracefully enough. "I'll take good care of your horse, my lord," he promised. "My name is Gramil: ask for me if you need him soon."

"Excellent," Sadon said. "I'll do that." Another smile, brilliant in the torchlight, and the boy was tugging hard at the reins to get the horse started, then hurried him away.

Perhaps I fail to notice these smiles, Sadon thought. *Perhaps I just don't see. More than you realize,* Tauler had told him. He took a deep breath, then looked up at the star-filled sky. *And perhaps, too, Mother Ocean lends a little ease I don't deserve, a kindness unexpected. The last in my days before the ruin? Or a new beginning, these signs, these small signs—my faithful Edmund and his determined cheer, my* good lord Tauler, this boy who doesn't even know me? Could it be?

"My lord count?" Tauler touched his elbow, startling him slightly. Old men tend to drift, Sadon remembered, and I am old.

"Yes?" Sadon blinked at him.

"I think you are very tired, my lord. Here, lean on me if you wish."

"I *am* tired. And I will lean on your arm, Tauler, not too much, but a little." He grasped Tauler's forearm and together they walked across the cobblestones. After a few steps, Sadon nearly stopped, half-turned. "The soldiers—" he began.

"I've already given the orders. Tend the horses, find a space in the barracks."

"Ah." Sadon blinked wearily. He hadn't heard it. "Good."

"This way." Tauler led him into the covered walk that led to stairs, then a broad hallway near the kitchens. A steward appeared, all solicitous, and guided them to guest quarters on the second level, a well-appointed room with a wide, comfortable bed, lamplight and a brazier, a broad table, a bench, a wardrobe. Sadon look around in confusion: he'd never been given so fine a room. Indeed, his usual rooms were across the castle on a lower level, awkwardly positioned by a busy hallway near the storerooms.

"Is this my room?" he asked the steward uncertainly.

"Of course, my lord. Have you eaten dinner?"

"Yes, on the road."

"Then wine, and perhaps some small cakes to refresh you." The steward, an older man with gray hair and a finer quality of clothes, perhaps the chief castle steward himself, bowed and then hurried away.

Sadon looked around the chamber again. There was even a window. He took a few steps and peered out, but could see nothing in the night outside, of course, only his own reflection in the glass. He studied his face a moment. I *look* tired, too, he thought, and scowled that he did. Then Sadon caught

Tauler watching him, and the wry smile on Tauler's face widened.

"Not your usual rooms?" he asked.

"Hardly. You know they're not." Sadon walked a few more steps to the bed and fingered the fine velvet spread, then sat down in the chair by the bed and looked around again, bewildered and too tired to hide it, not that he needed to hide it from Tauler, he supposed. "This is too much," he complained. "Your hope torments me, Tauler."

A discreet knock came at the door, the servant returning with the wine, of course; but it was Earl Melfallan who walked into the room when Tauler opened the door. Sadon blinked at him for a long moment, startled, and then struggled to rise from his chair. "Your grace," he said, trying to bow gracefully and not managing it well.

"Count Sadon," Melfallan said in his clear voice, strong with youth, a youth Sadon no longer had. "Please reseat yourself. You've had a long ride."

"He *is* very tired, your grace," Tauler said. "And I have not persuaded him." Then Tauler smiled down at Count Sadon, and something in his face brought sudden tears to Sadon's eyes. He muttered a curse and rubbed at them.

"Smoke from the lamps," he muttered.

"Of course it is," Tauler said dryly. "Show him Landreth's letter, my count." Tauler had read it on the road, and had not seemed surprised, only sad. Sadon treasured that sadness for his son, another gift from his good lord Tauler, another gift.

Melfallan sat down in a nearby chair and looked at him, not with contempt or anger, but with a slight smile, waiting. "Letter?" he prompted.

"Not yet," Sadon protested, looking up at Tauler. "I have to explain—" He shot a glance at Melfallan, whose expression had not changed. "I didn't order your grandfather poisoned."

Melfallan nodded soberly.

"But Landreth may have," he blurted. Sadon rubbed his eyes with his hand, then looked wildly around the room.

"Norris was a knight's son I saved from your grandfather's soldiers. Landreth would use his gratitude and devotion, use him like a tool to be discarded after he bent it. And now Norris has tried to poison your son?" Sadon blinked rapidly. "Or so Tauler has told me—"

Melfallan nodded again, his expression now grave.

Sadon closed his eyes, unable to meet those solemn eyes, those youthful eyes, clear and strong and measured.

"Count Sadon," Melfallan said quietly. "Did Tauler tell you that I wanted peace between us? That I felt my grandfather repaid your loyalty with undeserved contempt?"

"Yes, he said that," Sadon muttered. He heard Melfallan rise, and opened his eyes and looked up, startled, as Melfallan loomed over him. Melfallan then knelt on one knee before his chair, the position one took to swear a feof oath, as Sadon had knelt to Melfallan some months before. "I ask your pardon," Melfallan said earnestly. "And to win that pardon, I believe you."

Sadon stared at him, shocked. "Do not kneel to me!" he protested. "Get up! Get up!" Sadon grasped his arms, urging him upward, but Melfallan resisted the pull.

"Not until you give me your pardon."

"And not until you get up!"

Melfallan relented and got to his feet. When he had re-seated himself in his chair, he laughed softly. "We never had a chance to talk, Count Sadon. You would come to the castle, angry and bitter, and fight with my grandfather. All I saw were the tantrums, the shouting, the bitterness. But Tauler has told me that is only part of what you are, and I choose to believe him, too." He put his hand on his breast. "I must have peace, for Yarvannet's sake, for war is coming, Count. But I must have peace to gain justice, too, to heal an old wrong, one against you."

Sadon stared at him, gaping, and heard Tauler's low chuckle. Now they were both laughing at him, it seemed, and he found enough spirit to glare at Tauler.

"I told you so," Tauler said and grinned.

"Shut up," Sadon said crossly.

"Show him Landreth's letter, my lord," Tauler prompted again. Sadon sighed and reached into his tunic pocket, drew it out, then hesitated. Abruptly he thrust out the letter to Melfallan, and felt it taken gently from his hand. Then, to Sadon's surprise, Melfallan simply laid the letter on the table, and turned back to him.

"What does it say?" he asked quietly.

"Duke Tejar has promised Landreth your circlet, and they may invade Yarvannet in the spring."

Melfallan nodded. "That's not a surprise. Should I read this letter, Count Sadon? Or can I make a gift by giving it back to you? You must advise me." He smiled, and the smile lit his face, like the stableboy's smile, exactly the same. Sadon looked around at Tauler, who shrugged.

"He means it," Tauler said smugly. "And I told you so."

"So you keep saying, to my displeasure, Lord Tauler." This time Tauler laughed out loud, a booming hearty laugh that likely Sadon deserved. Sadon glared at him, then sighed his defeat. First Edmund, now Tauler: he must be losing his vigor of rule. Yes, that must be so. "You tempt me," Sadon said to Melfallan, and heard the defiance in his own voice, defiance he didn't mean to be there. Can an old man lose all flexibility? Could he never change his ways again? He looked at Tauler in despair, saw the smile still there.

"Tempt?" Tauler asked. "You were saying, my lord?"

Sadon hesitated, then focused with difficulty on Melfallan. Ocean, he was tired! "You tempt me to ask even greater favors. A rash young earl, to trust too much."

"So some have said, no doubt, and I have worried about it. Am I rash in trusting you?" Melfallan lounged back in his chair, shrugged. "Tauler doesn't think so, and I've already chosen to be rash by trusting him. At some point I must trust my lords, and perhaps the beginning with you is by giving my trust first, in the hope of earning yours." Melfallan hesitated, as if he might say more, and slipped his poise as he hesitated, only slightly. The breath he drew next was uneven, the smile slightly forced, and Sadon suddenly knew that this meeting was as hard for the earl as it was for him, that Earl

Melfallan, too, was uncertain. How easy it would be to thrust away his kindness, the offer of loyalty! To indulge the temper, smash everything to ruins, as he had done too often in his long years. He met Melfallan's eyes for a long moment, and then breathed deeply, filling his lungs to the bottom, and closed his eyes a brief moment. When he opened his eyes again, he quirked his mouth.

"I am old and tired, young earl. The dreams of my youth are long battered into the dust, or so I have believed. A lord's life is hard on those who cling too much to what should be. We must deal with reality as it is, the political books say, not spin daydreams about the ancient West and its heroes. We must be crafty in our deceits yet hold out a pretense of great virtue, and find no contradiction between the outer and inner man. Ah, you know the text, I see. Well, of course, you would: Earl Audric would have failed in his teaching had he excluded Duke Rainalt. But despite those wise truths about the reality of rule, I have tried to be a good lord to my people. And I meant my feof oath when I swore it to you."

Melfallan nodded slowly. "I remember when you promised your oath to me, Count Sadon."

"And believed then that I had killed him."

To his surprise, Melfallan shook his head. "That came later, and even then I had no proof. I still don't. We may never know who murdered my grandfather. I may have to accept that." He looked at the letter on the table, then abruptly picked it up and offered it to Sadon. "Take it, my lord."

Sadon made no move to comply. "Read it," he countered softly.

Melfallan scowled at him, and then stubbornly put it back on the table. As he did, they both heard Tauler's soft sigh of exasperation, and Melfallan and Sadon grinned at each other in the same moment. "You're hard on your lords, Count," Melfallan accused mildly. "Lord Tauler is standing over there, scarcely able to breathe in his anxiety, and you're being difficult again."

"Contention strengthens a lord," Sadon retorted loftily. "Read the text."

Tauler snorted, marched over to a chair, and sat down. He crossed his arms over his chest and glared at his count, ably enough to match Sadon's own skills at the art. Sadon twitched his fingers at him, then looked back at Melfallan.

"Did Norris try to poison my son?" Melfallan asked quietly.

"I don't believe it. I have considered it for four days, ever since Tauler told me about the suspicion, and I don't believe it. Not Norris."

Melfallan took in a deep breath. "It's more than a suspicion, but I don't believe it either. I saw him every day in my son's nursery. You say he's the son of one of Pullen's knights?"

"Sir Malham Dammarell. He held lands near Amelin and died in the Carbrooke battle. Your grandfather murdered the rest of the family when he reached Tiol, including Norris's lady mother. I could have raised Norris to hate the Courtrays, but I didn't."

Melfallan nodded wearily. "I loved my grandfather. I thought him a great earl, and he was my suns and stars as a boy, the ever-oak in my life. But now, in these months since I have became earl in my own right, I have faced questions about him I had never considered, and I've found I have different answers as earl than did my grandfather. The nature of treachery, for instance, both by definition and the extent of its proper punishment."

"I didn't order Audric's death," Sadon muttered desperately.

Melfallan smiled, confounding him, then picked up the wine bottle and slowly filled a wineglass. "Wine, my lord? It should warm away the rest of the chill. Our Yarvannet nights are still cold." He offered the wineglass and Sadon took it, then Melfallan filled two other glasses for himself and Tauler. "I've also had to consider the nature of trusting." He set the bottle back on the table, handed a glass to Tauler, then drank from his own. "Thirty years ago, my count, you handed my grandfather an earldom, and he repaid that favor with constant and withering contempt. Perhaps the two, treason and trust, should balance each other in the scale. Another of those political texts, one I like better than others. For the wrong done to you, I choose to believe you. Perhaps I will find it my fatal mistake in time, but trusting, too, has its scale. Tauler speaks for you, begging my understanding, and him I chose to trust sooner than you."

"And Landreth?" Sadon asked in a whisper.

"If Landreth returns to Yarvannet," Melfallan said grimly, "the duke will expect me to try him for treason and hang him, giving him the excuse he needs to invade Yarvannet. It will start the war. You know this." Sadon nodded. "And so I must spare him, not for love of you, Count Sadon, but for love of Yarvannet. Let's hope your son stays north. But you, Count Sadon, must choose another heir. I will never enfeoff Landreth with Farlost, but I'll give you the privilege of choosing another young man to succeed you."

Sadon sighed, and knew he had to accept it, and indeed, knew it to be wise by any measure of the political texts. He had known for years, but had never admitted, even to himself, that Landreth was not suited to rule. He considered, and then looked up at Melfallan. With what was perhaps his usual perception, a fact to consider later, Melfallan promptly frowned. "Don't say it," he warned.

"Norris is nobly born," Sadon said, a slow smile building on his face. "Another wrong to be righted, I think. A chance for both inner and outer virtue, your grace." Tauler covered his eyes with one hand and groaned audibly.

"No," Melfallan said.

"I consider him, in a way, another son." Sadon decided to enjoy himself, especially with the way Tauler was behaving right now. "Whatever conditions you wish." He paused and looked over at Tauler. Now the Penafeld lord had his head in his arms on the table, a bit of playacting Sadon found partly amusing—but only partly. "Tauler, stop that. Look up at me: that's better. Our earl is more perceptive than you, a fact that surprises me greatly, given your longer years of rule. We have made our peace, he and I, foolish as we both are in our trusting." He quirked his mouth as Melfallan could not quite hide that moment of relief, that small effort to hide it. Sadon spread his hands. "I am earnest in this. If you give Norris back to me," he said, and placed his palm over his heart, "I will see that your will is done, that your intent is observed in all points." He let his hand fall and looked at Melfallan pleadingly, all anger gone, all pretense vanished. "I cannot believe that Norris had any hand in this, but will you forgive him," he asked softly, "even if he had some guilt in it, for whatever reason he chose? Landreth I cannot ask for," he added, his voice breaking slightly, "but perhaps, since you are balancing the scales, perhaps—"

Melfallan hesitated, considering the request with a grave courtesy that lifted Sadon's hopes still more. Yes, he is different, Sadon thought: could Tauler be right about the whole of it? Could it be? Melfallan sighed. "Some lords would call me a fool for offering peace to you, Count, but I do. Most would expect me to kill for the killing of my grandfather, if only to protect myself from similar plots. One never trusts, if one is a High Lord. Mercy is suspect and invites treachery. Harshness makes your vassals fear you, and fear is a good thing." Melfallan stood up and began to pace. "But I have a problem, my lords. When I look out on Yarvannet, its harbors and coastland, its good and trusty folk, I find a division between such lordship and the land I call mine. Yarvannet deserves better from me." He gestured at the window and the unseen harbor below, the dark hills rising beyond it, invisible in the night. "To possess such a land, mustn't you be worthy of it?"

He turned to face Sadon again. "So I will parole Norris to you, as you have asked, Count Sadon," he said formally. "There may still be a trial, of course, and there will be terms for his parole: we can discuss them later. Perhaps we will find the real traitor who did this, and clear Norris's name beyond question: I hope so. More importantly, Count Sadon, I, too, offer you peace between us. I offer the trust you deserve from your liege lord, and his seeking of your counsel, and the giving of honors owed to a lord's sworn man. I offer this for the wrong done to you by my grandfather, and"—he paused to study Sadon's face for a moment—"and for other reasons, many of them dealing with yourself. But I cannot forgive Landreth. He is lost to you."

Sadon nodded reluctantly. It was true; it was just. Even an old man must see reason when it is presented, for the sake of his folk. He nodded again, and accepted it within himself as well.

Melfallan sat down again with a gusty sigh. "Perhaps, as your next item of counsel, my lords, you might suggest how I explain all this to Sir James. I'm really supposed to ask his advice first before I parole a prisoner."

Tauler chuckled. "After a lord passes a certain point in his rule, your grace," he said quietly, "a good justiciar, as Sir James is, understands."

"You really think so?" Melfallan turned and smiled at him. "Brace yourself, Lord Tauler. I'm also going to enfeoff you as Count of Penafeld. You'll lose a vassal, Count Sadon, because I need better security on my Airlie border."

Tauler gawked in open surprise, his jaw sagging. He then stood up abruptly, and simply sat down again—more a collapse than a sit, Sadon judged, and gave a wheezy bark of laughter at Tauler's expression. He heartily wished he could say, "I told you so," but he hadn't known, not at all, and so lost that pleasure. Serves you right for your meddling, Tauler, he thought fondly. Oh, serves you right! If Earl Audric had done this or, worse, appointed one of his foreigner Tyndale knights as Penafeld's new count, Sadon might have launched a war on his earl, a disaster for the land, a rightful penalty for Audric's treachery that would have been utterly wrong. He closed his eyes a moment, thinking of the deaths and fire, the ripping apart of Yarvannet that he would have made, convinced he had the right to do so. Your blessing, Mother Ocean, that Audric did not think of it. Or perhaps he did, from time to time, and my blustering and outrage all these years protected us, for Audric would not dare with me. But Melfallan did dare, and was right to do this for Yarvannet's sake, and not at all to spite Farlost, as Audric would have done it. Sadon felt his hope surge again that Melfallan might truly be different as Tauler thought he was; and that through this young earl Yarvannet would find its safety, perhaps even greatness to rival all other lands. Perhaps with this earl a sworn bond might be kept true and not feared for its foolish trust. Could it be?

Melfallan picked up Landreth's letter and held it out to Tauler. "He won't take it back and I won't open it, so perhaps you might keep this letter safe for us, Count Tauler. Consider it your first act of rule as Count of Penafeld."

Tauler hesitated, then took the envelope from Melfallan's hand and slid it inside his tunic. "And if I decide to burn it?" he asked softly. "This letter was crafted as much by the duke's manipulations as by Landreth."

"That's part of the entrustment," Melfallan said. "Do as you will." He leaned back in his chair and took a sip of wine, his eyes on Sadon again. "Do you understand my reasons?" he asked. "Do you accept them, Count Sadon?"

Sadon nodded. "Tauler will be a good count for you, as good a lord as he has been to me." He chuckled at the open relief that filled Melfallan's young face, relief the earl could not quite hide and likely wished he could, as any prudent lord must. But then, Sadon thought wryly, he does not know me very well, not in the essence—not yet. As I do not know him, but am learning.

Melfallan nodded his thanks. "If I march north through Carbrooke," he said lightly, "I'd rather not tempt you to repeat history by choosing duke over earl, Count Sadon, to the ease of both our minds."

"Are you marching north?" Sadon demanded.

"Not at the moment." Melfallan bared his teeth at both his lords. "This isn't entirely my lordly virtue, you understand, wanting justice and righting old wrongs. I need a safe border into Airlie, Tauler, and I need Farlost loyal to the Courtrays. Without those two things, those critical strengths that you both are to me, Yarvannet may be desperately weakened, and we cannot be weak, not now."

"Will you start the war, your grace?" Sadon asked bluntly.

"No," Melfallan said. "But Duke Tejar will start it. It's only a question of when."

"And why," Tauler added.

"Yes—and the excuse."

⁓

The hour was late but Melfallan took Count Sadon and Tauler to see Norris, whom he had moved to the infirmary near Marina's quarters. Although still drifting in and out of consciousness, the young man seemed to be recovering under Marina's constant care. When Sadon stepped into the room, Norris was awake and smiled wanly, recognizing him.

"My lord," he quavered weakly.

Melfallan watched as Sadon quickly crossed the room and took the young man's hand. I really shouldn't be this surprised, Melfallan thought wryly. All I ever saw was the temper: I never saw the rest of him, this count that Tauler loves, although even Tauler might not admit the fact that far. "How is he tonight?" he asked Marina.

"I still worry for him," she admitted. "He is not improving as quickly as I wish, but he is not losing ground." She blew out a breath, then glanced at Tauler, clearly wondering why both lords were present in her sickroom.

Count Sadon had pulled a chair from the wall and sat down beside Norris, then looked around. "How did this happen?" he demanded. "How was he injured this badly?"

"He was caught saddling his horse in the stable," Melfallan said heavily, "and four of my soldiers beat him and came very close to killing him when they did. First someone had poisoned my grandfather, then this attack on the baby—emotions were high that day, my lord. His bruises are fading now, but Marina says his head injury persists. He drifts in and out." As he spoke, Norris closed his eyes and seemed to fall asleep. Melfallan sighed.

"Will he live?" Sadon asked huskily.

Marina smiled, reassuring him. "I think so, my lord, but it may be a long recovery. I will care for him: don't worry."

Sadon smiled at the kindness in her voice, and carefully placed Norris's hand on the bed, then just as carefully replaced his chair by the wall. "I'd like to sit with him tomorrow if I could."

"Of course," Melfallan said. "I intend to parole Norris to Count Sadon's care in Farlost," Melfallan told Marina. "Can he travel soon?"

"Oh, not yet, your grace. He is quite ill."

They exchanged a look, and he saw the wistfulness in her careworn face. *Brierley would not be as limited in what she could do. Brierley's gift promised hope for Norris once she returned to Yarvannet and could tend him, but once it was known Brierley could heal such a desperate wound, how would the other High Lords react, thinking that one of their own controlled—or so they would think—such a witch's power? I must think about those other facts, too,* Melfallan reminded himself. *I must think clearly, for her sake and mine.* "But he improves?" he asked anxiously, wanting Marina's reassurance again.

She nodded. "Yes. He grows stronger each day and, mostly, my lords, he has not died. This type of injury either kills quickly or not. I'm more worried about damage that may persist, even after he recovers, but I cannot test that yet, not until he regains his alertness."

Sadon turned. "His mind might be damaged?" he asked in alarm.

"We don't know that yet," Marina said firmly. "His youth is a benefit, Count Sadon. It is too early to know, and hope is as likely as loss."

Sadon nodded, trying to accept it, then contrarily retrieved his chair again and sat down beside the bed. "Actually, I'd like to start the sitting now," he muttered.

"Whatever you will, my lord," Melfallan replied easily. Count Sadon turned and looked at him, and the naked gratitude in the old man's eyes made Melfallan pause. *We never* knew him, he thought—all he needed was the trust, something Grandfather never allowed, never ventured. Only that. "Sit as long as you like," Melfallan assured him. He glanced at Marina, smiled at all the questions in her eyes and shook his head, then took Tauler's elbow and guided the Penafeld lord out of the room.

"Well, *I'm* surprised," Tauler remarked, as they walked along the hallway. "It's always good to have a naked hope acquire some clothes."

"I won't be ragged by you, Tauler," Melfallan said. "Give it up." Tauler snorted his amusement. "I need more wine. How about you?"

"Decisively, your grace."

"Then let's go find some."

14

$\mathcal{T}$he next morning Brierley watched the lake through the front window, then heard footsteps within Michael's bedroom, and a moment later his door creaked open. She turned her head and smiled at him, and his face lighted.

"So now you're up?" he rumbled pleasantly.

"And so is Megan, although Stefan is still slothfully abed." Michael glanced around the room, then looked at the closed doors of the twins' bedrooms, hunting his children. "Will is fishing," Brierley helped him, "and Ashdla is gathering something in the forest. Iverway moss, I think, although what she plans to do with it eludes me. She asked me to go with her, but Stefan's not up yet and I wanted to listen for Megan."

"And you're feeling a bit abandoned, are you, sitting here by the window?" She chuckled and shook her head. "Have you had breakfast?" he asked.

"Yes, Michael."

"Well, I haven't, to the empty feeling in my stomach. Lying abed too late has its pleasures, but a drawback, too." Michael opened one of the cupboards by the sink, and she sensed his mild frown and the thought that went with it. "I could go to the market," she suggested. He turned quickly, his eyebrows rising in surprise, and she shook her head at him reprovingly. "Now, Michael, you know I can read your thoughts. The twins might be limited, but I am not—and neither is Megan, I warn you."

"Even Dani couldn't do that," he admitted. "Takes some getting used to, if I ever will." He smiled warmly. "Well, since you're offering, we need fruit and cheese."

"Surely bluestripe, too."

He sniffed at her. "You'll know all my secrets in time, that I can see. We can't afford bluestripe, as I keep telling my daughter, for all that she and I love the meal." He fetched down a small jug and lifted its top, then shook out several coins, counting them carefully.

Brierley sighed. "It's hard to keep us in addition to your family, I know. I don't want to be a burden on you, Michael, but we've already given you all the coins we had left."

"My customers don't always pay their accounts on time, that's a fact. And I'm grateful for what you've given, and you're not to worry about it, Brierley. The forest is all around us and the lake at our front door, and we won't starve. Here." He walked to her and held out five small coins. "I'm liking the spring apples, the small, sweet ones. Bring me a dozen of those, and we're even, your burden and my small hoard of coins." He paused, his hand outstretched, and looked down at her face. "How like my Dani you are," he murmured, and then blushed. "Ah, sorry, lass. It's not fair to burden you with my feelings."

Brierley shook her head and smiled. "She is the ruffle on the lake, the voice in the wind. She is everywhere here, Michael, and I'm sorry you still grieve, but you have chosen a good comfort. My gift runs to persons and does not bless the land: hers did, hers and all who lived here before her. I can feel the power in the valley, and it's more than the Well: it is Dani's spirit."

"You truly believe that?" he asked in surprise. "I sometimes wonder at my own fancies." He looked down at his large, square hands. "I sometimes wonder if I imagine a foolishness, and what that promises for my good sense and the safety of my children."

"Why can't it be true? Can you name a reason why not?"

"No, nor can I name a reason why it's so."

"I call that a fact to choose as you will." She grinned at him, and he suddenly grinned back, then dropped the coins into her palm, making it a small ceremony.

"And perhaps a small melon or two," he suggested hungrily, "if the money's enough."

"Definitely a small melon, perhaps two. I'll take Megan with me to spare your watching her."

"I'm not burdened with watching the little one," he protested. "She reminds me of when the twins were small."

"I'll take her anyway. I look for every chance to run off some of that energy, if only to tire her out for sleeping earlier tonight than later."

"A worthy goal, I agree." Michael sighed. "Lively she is, your little one, enough to tire all the rest of us, that's the truth. Who's this Rasheen she talks about? I haven't heard of any child in the neighborhood bearing that name."

"Ah—" Brierley stopped, and frowned as she wondered how to explain a fire ghost. The last few nights, as best Brierley could understand, Megan and Rasheen, with Kaare's help, had begun decorating Rasheen's castle, with much planning of draperies and furniture and roses outside the door.

"Perhaps it's a witchly thing?" Michael guessed. "Along with her seeing Jain the fire dragon and greeting the chairs each morning?"

"Something like that." Brierley grinned, then decided to worry. "Has she been prattling about Rasheen to the other children?"

"I don't think so. She was talking to me yesterday when no one else was out in the stable. Actually, I think she was talking to the black mare, not me." He frowned. "In fact, I'm sure of it, that good beast being far more interesting than me. Don't be long now at the market, or we'll worry."

"I won't be. Let me go call Megan."

Stefan awoke slowly, warm and comfortable beneath his bedcovers in Michael Toldane's spare bedroom. Through the closed door, he heard a murmur of voices and a clattering of

pottery. He turned his head slightly and saw the rest of the
bed was empty, the usual state of affairs here in Flinders
upon his waking: Brierley was up early again, as was
Megan, while Stefan lay lazily abed. In Carandon he acted
far more dutifully, up every morning to charge about his
tasks for the countess, but here—here he found lying abed
far too long a pleasant substitute, no doubt to his moral de-
cline. I should get up, he thought sleepily. He yawned
hugely, then closed his eyes again. Good morning, Stefan, he
thought, and tried to return to his pleasant dream about
Christina.

That last morning in Carandon Castle, his wife had set
down bread and cheese for Stefan's breakfast and seated herself across from him, then bent to give their little boy a kiss
as he clung to her skirts, wanting attention. Christina gave
the boy a wedge of cheese and a second kiss, prompting Stefan to say he needed kisses, too, being badly neglected. His
pretty wife had tipped her head to the side, regarded him a
moment, then shifted herself around the table into Stefan's
lap, where she kissed her husband soundly.

"Is that better?" she asked, smiling down at him.

He pretended to consider. "Moderately," he decided.
"Give me another, love, so I might feel less forlorn." She did,
and then gave him a third kiss for good measure, long and
sweet, and Stefan had heartily wished it was time to get into
bed instead of being out of it, and had said so. And she had
laughed at him, her dark eyes dancing.

He stretched lazily beneath his bedcovers, happy to think
about her, then yawned as the dream slipped away to wherever dreams went when they left a man. On that last day in
Carandon he had expected a simple day's journey into the
eastern hills to take Brierley back to the upland cabin, then a
journey back again on the next day, to return to his wife and
children and his comfortable duties as Rowena's liegeman.
How much time has it been since that last morning? he
thought wistfully, then counted the days and weeks on his
fingers. It had been the twenty-second day of Yule, that last
day—what was today? Ah, the last day of Swords, over two

months since he bent down from Destin's saddle to kiss her, and had thought a single day, only that, would pass until he kissed her again. Not so. He sighed.

The countess had entrusted Sir Niall Larson, her Mionn courier, with Brierley's protection at the cabin, and had intended that in the spring Niall would take Brierley and Megan into Mionn for their safety; but Niall's sudden death in a snow-slide had shifted that charge to Stefan. He had done what he could do to protect Brierley and the child during their journey into Mionn, although Brierley had insisted on sharing that task when it came to the larger charge of protecting Megan, and truly they had become friends. He put his hands behind his head and idly studied the rough planks of the bedroom ceiling. Had he met the measure of the task? Had they truly found safety here in Michael Toldane's house? He wished so, but guessed that his wishing might not have the truth behind it. Brierley didn't think so, however happy she'd been here the last few weeks with the twins and Megan and all the friendly town.

Ellestown was an Allemanii village like other villages, filled with pleasant and curious folk; and they reminded him greatly of the Airlie folk, generally happy, none truly in want, proud of their valley and vaguely disdainful of all other places not as fine as their Flinders home. Most of the Flinders folk had accepted their visit to their cousin Michael, for so they had been described. Even so, the weeks spent with Brierley had taught him a different attitude toward the usually friendly world he had always assumed, one of hiding and secrecy, with lives at stake in that secrecy. And the duke likely still hunted Brierley now, hoping to use her against Melfallan.

Stefan's worry flicked a steady beat against his mind for his boyhood friend who was now a lofty earl, for Brierley and Megan, for his countess. A deadly battle between the High Lords now shaped in the future, and Stefan found himself at the center of it, a mere steward's son who had risen to a position of trust through Rowena's favor, and was now charged to defend Brierley with his sword and whatever counsel he could offer her. One mistake and all might be un- done, like one stone beginning a rattle down the mountain. One mistake and he might never kiss his Christina again, if the duke's men found them in Mionn.

During their weeks in the cabin and the weeks of travel, and now this month in Flinders, he had partly entered into Brierley's shari'a world, so different from the Allemanii's. An Allemanii might find ease in each day, without danger to one's confidence in living, but a shari'a lived in constant fear of discovery. An Allemanii knew a tree to be a tree, and a cloud a cloud, and thought the world reasonable. For a shar- i'a witch, the day had different shades of meaning, of things perceived to which Allemanii eyes were nearly always blind. Her world was not an Allemanii world, but one built from her gifts that colored life differently. He greatly suspected that Brierley could hear thoughts; certainly Megan could. It was one detail Brierley had not actually admitted to him, not really, likely from a lifetime's caution, although she had al- lowed him to read her shari'a books and help as he might with the fire ghost who had afflicted Megan. What other wonders did the twins know? Peas in a pod, those two, dark and slender and quick-footed, seeming no more than ordi- nary young folk but also witches in secret, and not Brierley's type of witch, but another. The explanations had been vague, from both the twins and their father, and he had not pushed the matter, content to help as he could in the stable and watch Megan run on the lakeside.

He drowsed onward until he felt a small weight settle on his stomach, and he opened his eyes, mildly startled. Jain neatly closed his wings and regarded him pertly with eyes faceted like jewels, his smooth-scaled sides flickering with tiny flames of blue, red, and green. Greatly daring, Stefan reached up to caress him, and the flickering flames bathed his fingers with a mild warmth, lilting to the touch. The sala- mander seemed altogether real, Stefan marveled, not only to sight and thought, but to touch, by what magic he couldn't begin to hazard. He ran his fingers down Jain's sleek side, touching him more boldly, and the dragon indulgently tolerated the caress.

Good morning, Stefan, Jain said, his thought as clear as spoken word, an oddity that still made Stefan marvel. In the beginning Stefan had not believed Brierley's explanation about Megan's odd conversations with someone who wasn't there, nor Megan's sighing complaints about when he truly wasn't there, a doubling of nothing that could blot a parent's mind but was easy enough for any young child. His little boy had recently acquired a similar invisible friend, a goodly knight who rejoiced in gallantry and busy adventures, who required a seat at the dinner table and an occasional sharp warning to give room for the knight to pass through the door. Stefan had thought Jain nothing more than Sir Martin, his boy being nearly the same age as Megan. Or so he had thought: in a father's usual world, a little son's invisible friend stayed invisible. Jain had not.

"Are you now the morning bell for the castle?" he asked lazily.

Get up! Jain commanded.

Megan's head popped up beside the bedside as she stood on her tiptoes to see him, and Stefan then suffered the jouncing as Megan climbed onto the bed and onto him. Jain moved aside and watched from a nest in the bedcovers. Megan poked Stefan's chest imperiously. "Time to get up, Stefan. You're a lazybones."

"Am I, dearling?" Stefan yawned. "What time is it?"

"I don't know." Megan shook her dark curls vigorously. "I don't tell time yet."

Jain fluttered to the foot-post of the bed and cocked his small head. *I do: it's ten o'clock,* he supplied, then put on a smirk. *Time to get up, Stefan.* Stefan retorted by closing his eyes and making a rattling snore.

Megan promptly poked him again. "Wake up!" she demanded. "Mother and I are going to the market. Do you want to come?"

"What are we buying?"

"Why does that make a difference?" Megan asked, puzzled.

Stefan thought a moment and realized he hadn't an answer, the usual problem with Megan's questions. In Carandon, his boy put him to the same test every day, and it was only a matter of time before Christa plagued him as well. He hoped his little daughter at six would be much like Megan, bright and lively and into everything. He thought she might be. "I have to get up and wash and shave off my beard and eat breakfast—"

"We'll be gone by then," Megan said, disappointed. "We're going right *now*."

"Then I guess not." He spread his arms wide. "Give me a kiss, sweetling, and off with you." Megan happily complied, struggled a bit to get off the bed, and landed with a huge thump on the wooden floor. And then she was gone, and Jain with her.

Stefan stretched hugely, and then regretfully got himself out of bed. Sad to say, he had found he liked a life of sloth, although he tried to help Michael in the stable when he could and twice went fishing with Will. He shook his head at himself. No discipline, Stefan: what's wrong with you? He twitched the covers back over the mattress, making it neat, and then found fresh clothes among those hung in the bedroom closet, and poured water into a basin to shave. Ten minutes later, he emerged back into the world by opening the bedroom door.

No one was there.

He found Michael in the stable, as usual, and helped the big blacksmith repair a wagon harness, then went out when Michael asked to feed and water the horses in the paddock. Michael had two horses, a gelding and a pregnant mare, and the two had made friends with the other three. Somewhat predictably, Friend, Megan's quiet mare, still ended up at the bottom of the horse hierarchy, picked on by everyone, including Michael's two. Stefan took some time scratching Friend's ears as she whiffled in the bucket for the last few shreds of oats, then petted her sleek neck. The black mare twitched her ears agreeably. A pleasant beast, like all horses in the essence. He leaned on the top railing of the paddock fence, watching Destin wheel around the paddock, showing off, and then reminded himself about sloth and its slow creep. He carried the bucket back to the stable, where Michael found more tasks for him to do. In another month or two, Stefan thought cheerfully, he'd have learned enough of the blacksmithing trade to hire himself out as a blacksmith apprentice, truly a step up in Stefan Quinby's career.

"Tired of all the chores, I think," Michael rumbled pleasantly.

"I have a different life elsewhere, Michael, but not different enough that I can't appreciate yours. It's a good village and a good house, a good family, and a good man at the center of it."

Michael straightened from the forge and smiled. "And a good man to guard a witch."

"My lady bid me do it, and I'm happy to do so."

Michael frowned and looked beyond Stefan at the sky. "How did it get so late? Has Brierley come back with the young one? Have you seen her?"

"No."

"Neither have I." Michael put down his stone hammer and stalked past Stefan out of the stable, then marched up to the porch. Stefan followed him: the parlor was empty, and a quick push on their bedroom door showed that room empty as well. Their eyes met.

"I'll go look for her," Stefan offered.

Michael nodded. "And if you see my twins in town, send them home right away." He squinted and thought a moment. "I've no shari'a gift, of course, but I feel uneasy this morning, Stefan, more than usual. She should have been back by now."

"I agree." Stefan lifted his jacket off the peg by the door and left the house.

⁓

Stefan walked the half-mile to the town market, passing the dozen houses on this side of town. He didn't hurry, but still moved briskly enough, and once he arrived at the market began a long hunt up and down the market lanes, where the stallmen still did a quick business in fish and fabric and other wares, for all it was past noon and most of the townsfolk had finished their marketing and gone home. He saw no sign of Brierley, and finally stopped in the middle of the lane, puzzling. Had she gone for a walk in the forest? Taken Megan to the lakeshore? When he saw the factor and two soldiers turn the corner at the end of the lane and change course toward him as they saw him, he felt a sudden dread that they might be bringing bad news. He walked to meet them.

"Master Hinton," he began, "have you seen—" The factor gestured abruptly to one of the soldiers with him.

"It's him. Take him into custody, Shane."

"What?" Stefan stared at him, and then stepped back as the two soldiers advanced on him, his hand falling instinctively to the sword he didn't have, not here in Ellestown, not in his role as cousin come to visit. The two soldiers seized him roughly. "What is this?" Stefan demanded.

"You're under arrest for harboring a witch. Since it's a hanging charge, I'd advise you, young man, to keep your silence. These men are witnesses, as am I, to whatever you choose to admit."

"Harboring a—" Stefan gaped at the factor, then struggled as the soldiers forced his hands behind him and quickly tied them fast. "I don't know what you're talking about. Who is my accuser? This is absurd. I don't know any witches!"

"You fit the description in the duke's orders," Hinton said wearily, "and Count Charles has ordered all persons who fit the description to be sent down to him at Arlenn, and so you're going downriver. I told you to shut up, Master Jacoby. You might take my advice." He signaled to the soldiers, and Stefan was quick-marched down the lane, to the interest of the stallmen and the few customers left in the market. Stefan thought about fighting, but with what? What orders by the duke? What description?

Where was Brierley? Stefan tried to swallow his sudden

fear for her, then looked around, too, for Megan. Had they taken Megan, too?

No use in asking, he realized, not of this no-nonsense factor. Numbly, he walked onward. When they reached the factor's office near the lakeside, the soldiers muscled Stefan into the room. Hinton sat down in his chair behind his desk with a weary sigh, then fussed with some papers on his desk. He nodded to Stefan to sit in a chair, then glanced at the soldiers.

"Keep up the search," he said. "I want both the woman and the child." Stefan let out a soft breath of relief despite himself, but Hinton was focused on the soldiers and didn't hear that betrayal.

"Yes, sir." The soldiers went out.

"What description?" Stefan asked quietly. He had heard Factor Hinton was a fair man, gruff and perhaps too quick to find guilt before the evidence was had, but perhaps he was open to reason. Perhaps.

Hinton scowled, then found a paper in another stack, and held it up to his face, squinting: "Long, brown hair, pale skin, skinny, gray eyes, age nineteen to twenty, recent arrival. It describes the lady you're with, Master Jacoby. Where is she?"

"I don't know. I was looking for my wife in the market. This is an outrage! Is this how the Flinders folk treat visitors to their valley?"

Witt squinted at him. "Puff all you want, whoever you are. I've orders from my count to hunt any strangers, and the woman fits the description of the witch the duke is seeking. I'm the factor here, and so I'm ordering your arrest."

Stefan struggled against his bonds, but it was hopeless. Hinton eyed him with faint distaste. "It's a shame, I suppose. The townsfolk had liked you, you and your wife and pretty little girl. Too bad she fits the description. Too bad I'm the factor of this town, trusted with its care. Too bad Count Charles has ordered you taken downriver, but that's the way it's going to be. If it all works out, come back and continue your visit; you'll be welcome."

"Surely you're joking! After this outrage?"

Hinton shrugged indifferently. "Your choice, should it come to that. Now sit there, and be warned there's nowhere in this valley you can go and not be found. We keep a good eye on outsiders, even ones who claim to be family of our own and so win a place among us they don't deserve. If you are witch-kind, Mionn will not be merciful, believe me." Hinton rose and went to the door, then went out. A moment later a soldier stepped in, his hand on the hilt of his sword. Stefan got to his feet, not knowing what he intended, and the soldier drew his sword in a flash.

"Sit down!" he ordered brusquely.

Stefan sat down slowly. In Ellestown, he reminded himself, the folk believed in witches, were courteous enough to outsiders, but they knew the line between the stranger and the accepted. By this duke's order, Stefan had been abruptly shoved across the line and beyond, at least for now.

Where was Brierley? Stefan might still talk his own way out of this mess—he had always been good with words—but Count Charles might easily remember him from the Darhel court, when both he and the countess had visited there—if they met. If they did, then all of Stefan's clever words would not help, would not help at all. Robert Jacoby might visit the Flinders valley and none would remark overmuch, but Stefan Quinby did not belong in Mionn. He was well-known to the High Lords as Countess Rowena's trusted liegeman, and Rowena was the aunt and political ally of Earl Melfallan, himself the High Lord who had recently championed a witch in Darhel, to the duke's displeasure. Count Charles would have no trouble, none in the slightest, in connecting those three facts. What would he do then?

Where was Brierley? Stefan worried. Where?

⁓

Michael lifted his head sharply, then leaped to his feet. When he threw open the front door, he saw Megan stumbling toward him, sobbing frantically. Two children were following in her wake, demanding anxiously to know what was wrong. Michael scooped up the child and spent a few moments soothing the others, then sent them home.

"Not to worry, children! All will be right!" he called, and carried Megan into the house. Megan clutched at him hysterically, her sobs racking her body. When a few soothing words had no effect, Michael sat down in his chair and slowly rocked her to and fro, his face buried in her dark, curly hair. "There, Megan," he murmured. "There, sweet child." Not knowing if it would do any good, he tried calming his mind and "sending" comfort at her, however that was done, and whether it was time or his closeness or some comfort she took from his mind, Megan's sobs slowly diminished. She clutched less frantically at him, but still cuddled close. "Megan?" he murmured.

"I—I—I can't hear Mother! I can't hear her! She told me to run and the man hit her with a stick and carried her away!" Megan's voice rose to an aching wail. "Mother!"

"Where did this happen?" Michael asked soothingly. "Megan! Listen to me, child. When did this happen?" But Megan only sobbed more violently, then suddenly, from one breath to another, she stopped. Her head jerked around toward the window—or was it the table?—and she seemed to listen intently. Then, after a large sniffle, Megan looked up into Michael's face.

"Jain says I must be brave," she quavered. Megan drew her hand across her tearstained face and then took a deep breath. "I can do that."

"Jain?" Michael glanced around the room and saw nothing. "The fire dragon?"

"He's outside the window." She pointed at the panes, where Michael saw nothing but the lake and a low branch of the tree beside the house. "Can't you see him?"

"Ah, child, no, I can't," Michael said.

"Oh." Megan turned back to him, her small face distressed. "Jain says you—" She looked back at the window. "What?" She seemed to listen again, and Michael looked again at the empty window, wondering if indeed a fire dragon stood outside, and yearned to see. "Jain says you must leave Flinders and take the Well with you," Megan said in a singsong voice. "Stefan is arrested and Mother has been taken captive, and the Four have decided—" She frowned ferociously. "You're going too fast, Jain!"

"Just be patient, child," Michael said. "I'm listening and will hear it all."

"All right." Megan took in a shuddering breath, then listened, her gaze fixed on the window. "The Four have decided it is time to intervene, and will no longer stand aside. If the cabin is discovered, all here may be lost. Save yourself, Michael. Take the twins and me to the cabin above the lake, pack the Well, and leave Flinders. Go to Yarvannet." Megan turned back to face Michael. "That's all. That's what he wants to say."

"But about your mother and Stefan?" Michael asked.

Megan's face crumpled. "That's all he said!" she cried in distress. "I don't know!" Michael held her close as she began to cry again, her hands tight on his sleeves. Then he set her on the floor and held her in front of him.

"Remember what Jain said about being brave?"

Megan nodded, tears running down her face.

"Then we'll both be brave, won't we?" He waited for Megan's tentative nod, then squeezed her shoulders encouragingly. "Then I want you to be a tower of courage, sweet child. It's fire gift, according to the books, that kind of courage. I admire that courage, and I know you have it."

"But what about Mother?" Megan cried. "She's hurt! The man hit her and I can't hear her anymore!"

"I don't know the answer. That's part of the bravery, right? Not to know?"

Megan blinked, took in a shuddering breath, and then nodded more firmly. "It's part of the brave?"

"Yes."

"Then I will be brave." The small chin firmed, and a grown man armed with sword and shield might have quailed at the fierce look that entered the child's eyes. Fire gift,

Michael thought, and hugged her quickly. Against such gifts, how could all the world prevail?

"We need to pack things. Can you help?" Megan nodded.

Michael sent the child into the bedroom for the pack cases, and then stepped out on the porch, hoping to see the twins. At the far end of the lane, he saw the factor's men approaching, the suns' light winking on their helmets. He stepped back into the house, slammed the door and locked it, and then moved quickly into the bedroom and caught up Megan. He shoved the leather case back into the closet, then shut the closet door. No time for pack cases, no time at all. With Megan under one arm, he climbed out of his own bedroom window, then remembered to shut the window behind him. "Can you call the twins?" he asked Megan.

"Maybe. Where are we going?"

"To get the horses and then go into the woods."

"Oh," Megan said. "Why?"

He set Megan on her feet and knelt down to bring his face close to hers. "Because it's time to run, Megan," he said earnestly. "It's time to seek safety. They'll come here next, and we mustn't be here when they do. Do you understand?"

Megan nodded. Michael kissed her, then got to his feet and held out his hand. Megan's fingers curled tightly around his.

Michael opened the gate to the paddock and whistled softly to his mare and colt, hoping the other three would follow their friends, and then jogged across the paddock to the opposite gate. The mare came trotting up, her ears swiveled forward in interest, the others coming after. He opened the gate wide and let the horses canter through, and then closed the gate. He caught the mare's halter and tugged at her, then scooped up Megan and ran down the forest path into the woods, the other horses following in their wake. After several hundred yards, safely out of view of the house, he slowed to a walk and led the mare off the path through the trees. Many years ago he had cached supplies in the woods nearby, a prudence at the time he hoped he would never need, and had regularly visited the cache to check what he had stored there. Spare clothing, water, tack for the two horses, trail food: it would be enough.

A mile from the cabin, he turned and looked back, but the house and lake were fully obscured by the trees. Likely he'd never see that view again: he should have turned earlier if he wanted the look, he thought, but it was done. He put Megan down on her feet, and she looked up at him solemnly.

"Do you want me to call the twins now?"

"If you can. Tell them we're going to the cabin."

"I'll try."

Michael sank to his haunches in front of her. "It's important, Megan."

"I know. They aren't good at hearing, but I—" Her head turned and she pointed. "Will is that way, down by the lake, and he's coming now. He heard me." She turned and pointed ahead into the forest. "Ashdla is that way, but she's not listening. If we go a little bit that way instead of your way, we'll meet her."

Michael let out a great breath of relief. "Good, child," he said, nodding. "Good." He rose slowly and took in a deep breath; for the first time he truly believed they might escape. Running pinned their guilt, of course, but in the current times innocence would be hard to keep for certain. He loved his Flinders folk, but he knew their ways for gossip and witch tales, and he'd not risk his children in the trusting. He looked down at Megan. Nor this sweet darling with her odd ways, he thought. The ancient shari'a had revered the fire witches, the rarest of the adepts, and likely understood them not at all. He had as little understanding, but he would keep the trust he had promised her. These three of his own he had safe. But what of Brierley?

He looked back up the trail and hesitated. Truly, indeed, he could rush away to where she was now, wherever that was, and try to make a rescue. At the least, he could rush into town and hunt for her in the market, and there be caught by Hinton's men, whatever had set this into motion. He could demand Stefan's release—and his own by then—with likely little result, if in fact the witch hunt had begun. Dani had feared that hunt all her life, and Michael had learned the fear of it, too. But these three, his twins and Megan, he had safe; he wasn't man enough to save all and knew it. He bowed his head in shame, hoping he had Brierley's forgiveness. He took Megan's hand, tugged at the mare's lead, and walked onward, deeper into the forest.

Will could move faster than Michael and the horses, and his boy quickly caught up with them a mile farther along. He had brought his catch of fish, and Michael thought to tell him to leave the fish behind, but decided on prudence and let Will pack the fish with the rest of the supplies they found at the cache.

"When did you put this out here?" Will asked in surprise.

"Have kept it for years, son, hoping it wouldn't be needed. It is needed now. Put a saddle on two of the horses, the tall gelding and Megan's black mare, I think. We'll put Megan on the mare; those two understand each other and it will help the child." He smiled at Megan, who stood nearby, her face forlorn, her dark eyes huge. "Although I can see she is very brave." It won him a tiny smile in return, and Michael marveled again that a child could win a heart so easily, with a quick smile, a laugh, her wondering at every marvel in the world that let a man see those marvels all over again through her eyes. He bent down to her and felt her small arms come around his neck, and then lifted her onto the mare. "We'll finish up the packs and put them on the others."

"Yes, Da."

"Where's your sister?"

Will promptly pointed off to the left. "She's coming now. Amina warned her."

Michael blew out a breath of relief. "Thank Ocean we have that gift of yours, Will, and a forest dragon to help. I hadn't really counted on it, hadn't thought of it, but it will help us get to safety now."

"But—" Will stopped and closed his mouth firmly.

"But what of Brierley? Yes, I know, and I worry for Stefan, too. I don't like the choosing, my boy, don't like it at all."

"If you choose it, Da," Will said loyally, "it must be right."

Michael smiled at him sadly. "Then why, dear boy, do I feel I'm wrong? Why do I feel I should charge off to the rescue? Why do I feel I'll regret this day the rest of my life?" He shook his head briskly. "But enough of that: it doesn't change the choice. Let's move on."

They finished packing the other horses, and Michael swung up into the gelding's saddle. Will mounted their mare, riding bareback in front of her packs, and they moved onward. Ten minutes later, Ashdla ran into the glade they were crossing, and Michael pulled her up onto the horse, in front of him, then kicked the gelding into a trot. Ashdla craned her head around him to look at Will, then looked up into Michael's face. She turned around as much as she could and wrapped her arms around him, pressing close. He kissed her forehead and felt her trembling against him.

"Amina says we need to take the Well with us when we leave," she whispered. "She says she'll show us how to pack it—but how do you pack a well, Da?" Ashdla's chin quivered. "And we're to take Brierley's Thora book, and three of the others at the cabin. She says the townsfolk will find the cabin this time and burn it."

"Does she now?" Michael said heavily.

"She says they're already talking in the town about us, that the factor is hunting a witch in Flinders and that he's arrested Stefan and is looking for Brierley. A few are already saying that we must be witch-folk, too, because we said they were relatives. Amina says we must leave Flinders and go to Yarvannet if we can. She says we have to go now through the mountains."

Michael sighed. "Jain said the same to Megan, and so we will, if we can."

"But it was supposed to be the Finding," Ashdla protested, her voice heavy with tears. "It was supposed to be the beginning again, the renewal of all the shari'a. And, oh, Da, I'm worried for Brierley. What if they burn her? What if we've lost her forever?" Michael held his daughter close as she sobbed brokenly in his arms.

———

They reached the forest cabin near dusk, a difficult ride along the last few miles of the narrow ravine. Finally their father bid the twins to dismount, and Ashdla walked beside Megan on the black mare, trying to cheer her. The child huddled within the cloak Michael had wrapped around her, and perhaps she had fled to her dream world that Brierley had said was her sanctuary. Ashdla patted her leg encouragingly, but Megan did not respond.

She shared a worried glance with Will, then watched their father carry Megan into the house. At the door, he turned. "I'll pack what we can of the cabin. You go to the Well and see what might be done there. Perhaps the Four will help you."

"They will, Da," Ashdla said. "Amina promised us." Michael nodded heavily and then carried Megan into the house.

"Come on," Will said, and led the way along the side of the ravine. The light was fading fast with the Daystar's setting, and Will looked worriedly up at the darkening sky, then suddenly stopped short. Ashdla nearly walked into his back, so suddenly did he stop.

"What?" she demanded, then looked up where he was looking, but saw only the first stars winking in the darkening sky.

"Today is Pass," he said. "Today is one of the days the lines on the Well always move." He turned to look at Ashdla, and his face was bereft. "If the air witch had come, today Brierley could have made the Finding."

"We don't know it had to be one of the quarter days, Will. That's not in the *Lists of the Change*."

"It's still tradition."

"Nuts to tradition." Ashdla took his hand and held it tightly. "I've decided I'm on your side about everything. Why is Megan so quiet, Will?"

"I don't know."

"Will we lose her, too?"

"Not if I can help it. She's our sister now, like Brierley was—*is*," he added, correcting himself fiercely. "We'll both watch out for her. Promise?"

Ashdla nodded, and together they walked onward toward the Well. Their footsteps echoed hollowly in the tunnel leading to the Well, and there they found Amina waiting for them. The forest dragon flowed along the northern wall and half into the next, as much within the wall as upon it: in the darkness, she seemed little more than a gleam of dark emerald eyes, a flash of her green tail, a flexing of gold claws. *My children,* she greeted them solemnly.

Ashdla looked helplessly at the solid stone of the Well and the four unmoving shades who guarded it. How did one move a Well? Or move shadowy figures that could not be touched?

"Da is finding the books you said we needed," she said.

I know. They are necessary.

"But what about Brierley?" Ashdla asked tearfully. "What about the Finding?"

Basoul watches over her, dear one, as I watch over you and Will. Do not be anguished; not all is lost, not yet, even for her. And it is still the time of the Finding. That is still true, if we Four act to preserve what we guard. Perhaps we risk all if we do; perhaps we risk even what we are, but we will take the chance. You can help, both of you.

"How?" Ashdla cried. "How can we help *you?*"

I will show you: watch me.

Amina began to circle the full circumference of the Well, blending in and out of the walls. As she moved across the lines engraved into the walls, they flickered in pattern to her movement, then began to glow, filling the Well with their light, first green, then gold and blue, and finally, first as pinpoints of flame that crackled to life, the reds of fire.

"Look!" Will breathed, pointing at the Well. As one, the four shades bowed to each other with solemn dignity, then straightened and stood still again. Then, on the forest witch's shoulder, the hawk turned its feathered head and eyed the twins with lively interest; beneath her skirt hem, the ferret twitched its nose, its black eyes gleaming. The forest shade visibly took a deep breath and lifted her head, her face shadowed within her hood. She looked at the twins and smiled, moving her hands slightly in welcome.

"Oh," Ashdla whispered, and clung hard to Will's hand. Amina restlessly circled the Well, moving still faster, and now Soren had joined her, the dragons flickering green, then gold, from line to line around the walls.

"I am Isanna," the forest witch said in shari'a, her voice almost a melody. "I was first to guard this Well."

You are the ward of the Well, Amina replied solemnly, and Isanna bowed low.

"I am ward," she agreed.

These two are of your line, Soren said.

"Not the boy," Isanna disputed.

Even the boy, Soren insisted. *He is a male twin of your line: it was predicted.*

Isanna's dark eyes studied Will gravely for a long moment. "Not the boy," she decided flatly. She bowed her head and grew still, ceasing to breathe, ceasing to live, and both hawk and ferret grew still with her. The two dragons slowed their movement and then stopped, and Ashdla sensed their dismay as they looked at each other.

"What happened?" Will demanded. "What did she mean, 'not the boy'?"

The Change begins in the dawn, a new voice suddenly intoned, ringing hollowly through the chamber, and Ashdla gasped as another dragon took misty shape on the eastern wall, a dragon she did not know. He was brilliant, pearl white with golden claws, and his pale eyes flickered with all the colors of the dawn, ever-changing, ever-moving. Will stood transfixed, then sank slowly to his knees as if his legs could not hold him up.

"Will!" Ashdla cried. "Are you all right?"

Welcome, brother, Amina greeted the stranger, her mental voice hushed with awe. *It has been too long that we have awaited the Change.* But then the new dragon faded back into the stone, vanishing both from sight and mind, and Ashdla felt the surge of the dragons' disappointment, and of Will's.

"Come back!" Will pleaded, and Ashdla could not bear the longing in his voice. She knelt beside him and put her arms around him, hugging him close.

"He'll come back," she whispered, although she knew no such thing, had no such certainty. "I know he will," she said fiercely. Will sagged loosely against her, then turned his face to her. "I know it," she told him. Will took a deep breath, then another, and finally nodded.

But he did *appear,* Soren insisted. *Will is truly a witch of the Change, as I have told you all many times.* Ashdla belatedly realized she'd missed part of an argument, one that did not include the twins at all. Instead, Amina and Soren glared at each other across the chamber, each rustling wings with irritation.

But I don't hear his new voice in the East, Amina protested. *Perhaps Night has finally emerged to join the Star.*

That was not *the night dragon, Amina,* Soren retorted aggressively. *And Will is not a night witch. Rather, he is an opposite, a witch of the dawn, of the beginning of the light, not its end.*

Will and Ashdla looked at each other, perplexed. "Why are they arguing about you?" Ashdla whispered. "I thought the Four knew everything."

"Maybe not," Will whispered back. "It doesn't sound like it."

Will was born with forest gift, Amina insisted, then sniffed audibly and flicked her tail-tip.

Soren made a rude noise, not at all polite. *And born with air gift, as I have also told you, and together his gifts make the dawn. This new Voice comes from Will as a witch of the Change—the Change in the West, not the East.*

There cannot be two Changes, Amina insisted.

Why not? The two dragons glared at each other, with no sign that either intended to yield.

"I have a question," Will said into the pause, and both dragons swiveled their heads to look at him, then blinked. "Who was that?"

Amina wrinkled her snout. *We're not sure,* she admitted ruefully.

I'm sure, Soren offered.

Be quiet.

Whatever Isanna's reasons, Soren said, undented by Amina's glare, *she won't recognize Will as a forest witch. Ashdla must move the Well by herself.*

"But I don't know how to move the Well!" Ashdla protested.

Isanna will help you, Amina reassured her. *Do not fear, my children. Basoul led the making of this Well and the future it holds, and she thinks we can move it to safety. The stones themselves are unimportant, as is this cave, this place. Even the shades are only an image created by the Well, not true inhabitants of this cavern. What counts is the device Thora left here, and that, we can move. Basoul is certain of it. And we can argue later, Soren.*

I'm still right about Will.

Later, Amina said firmly. Again the two dragons began to circle the well, invoking the lines of power, and once again the shade of the forest witch stirred to life, as before. "I am Isanna," she said solemnly. "I am ward of this Well."

Answer her in shari'a speech, Ashdla, Amina instructed. Again, both dragons slowed their circle, then faded mostly into the walls, watching. *Follow your instincts, and do not fear.*

"I am Ashdla, a witch of your line," Ashdla said bravely to the forest shade.

"Greetings, my daughter." Isanna bowed low, and Ashdla copied her, trying not to sigh her relief too loudly.

Ashdla straightened and hesitated, wondering if she should bow again. *Probably not,* Will sent, trying to help.

You don't know any better than I do.

True. He nodded, encouraging her.

"We need to move the Well, Isanna," Ashdla said earnestly to the shade. "It is in danger."

Isanna considered for a long moment, then nodded. "I hear you, my daughter. Walk around the Well, a half-circle from Fire to Forest, and then look down at the stones of the Well." Ashdla glanced at Will, then paced the half-circle as directed. As she approached Isanna, the forest shade moved aside and pointed downward. "See the bottommost stone? See that its corners are square, not rounded?"

Ashdla nodded. "I see it."

"Speak my watchwords aloud after I chant them. Be very careful with your intonation." Ashdla glanced at Isanna with alarm, for her voice was grim with warning. "I am the ward of the Well, daughter, and my warding you must pass if you are to move the Well. Beware: I am dangerous." Isanna then raised her hands, palms upward.

"Ta'lata arbil-sin!" she chanted solemnly.

Ashdla listened carefully to the tones, noted the breath of a pause between the words, then raised her hands. It was the ancient chant speech, more complicated in its intonation than most chants, but a pattern she understood, a pattern she could sing.

"Ta'lata arbil-sin!" she echoed. *The forest calls to the sea,* the words meant. Across the chamber Will mouthed the words silently as she chanted them, and she then saw him nod. He was better at chant, she remembered, better than she was, and she took courage from his approval.

"Bay'rasi ma, Hirdaun matun!" *And the sea answers; the Four hear.*

Again, Ashdla chanted the words in perfect mimicry. She saw the bottom stone move slightly, then slide to the side.

"Sofan'i a-be'rit!" Isanna sang, her voice rising strongly. *In the East is the Promise!*

Ashdla gasped as Patterns flared into life on the cavern walls, the Patterns of forest and sea, air and fire, new patterns yet old, old patterns yet new, the cycle of life, the meaning of the world. The Patterns seized upon Ashdla, binding her, and she laughed in exaltation.

"Sofan'i a-be'rit!" she sang back in triumph, then lowered her hands, knowing she had done it right, knowing it to the core of her being. The four shades flickered, then vanished, as if they had never been.

"The wall lines are gone, too!" Will exclaimed in surprise, but Ashdla did not look to see, instead looking down at what Isanna had yielded to them.

Within a small cavity at the base of the Well's stones, she saw a boxlike device made of crystalline rods, each a few hand-spans in width. For a moment her eyes saw a dragon in the flickering pattern of the rods, then a castle with many turrets, an ever-oak spreading its branches over a stream, a crouching leopard, each pattern shifting to the next as light moved from rod to rod, an odd ghostly fire of blues and greens. Then the light faded, and the rods became only themselves, yet another pattern. Ashdla blinked, slightly dazed, then knelt to look more closely at the crystal device, but the light did not return.

Amina sighed. *You've done it, Ashdla. Remove it carefully.*

"I can touch it?" Ashdla asked.

Yes.

Ashdla reached and carefully drew out the crystal device. When she looked up, both dragons had left. "We'll need a blanket to wrap around it," she told Will. "Or a box might be better."

Will nodded. "And let's take the things from the altar, too, while we can." He shrugged unhappily. "We can never come back to Flinders, Ashdla," he said bleakly. "You know we can't, not with the hunt starting again." He hesitated, pain in his face. "I think we should burn the cabin."

"No!"

"What if the townsfolk find it this time? What if they find the books and journals? We can't take them all with us, but we don't dare leave any behind. Even here in Flinders, the shari'a are mostly thought a legend, a threat long dead. What if the Allemanii have *proof* we still exist? What will follow us to Yarvannet, if we can get there, when they know for sure? And if we are discovered for what we are, what will happen to the Finding?" Will set his mouth grimly. "I'm not going to force Da to say it first, not when it means burning what belonged to Mother before it belonged to us. We will say it first so he doesn't have to. Do you agree?"

Ashdla swallowed hard, then nodded, knowing he was right.

"Then let's go do it now," Will said, "while we still have the courage. We don't have much time, not if we're to get safely away."

"Safely," Ashdla echoed hollowly. "A simple word, but not easy to find now, Will. Not easy at all."

Will pulled her close against him and kissed her, then led the way out of the cavern.

15

*B*rierley awoke slowly in darkness, at first aware only of an enclosed space, a gurgling sound of water very near at hand, the creaking of wooden timbers. Her body felt sluggish—*sleepweed,* her healing gift told her, even as it attacked the semipoison, melting its influence like a slow drip of water through her veins. Her hands could not move, she realized then, and she felt the rough scratch of hemp against her wrists. Rope, she thought groggily. But why am I bound? She struggled with the question and had no answer. Other aches and pains appeared, one by one, as she fumbled to assemble the messages her senses brought to her. More sounds: a chuckling sound of water, splashes, a soft swoosh of water on wood. And motion, carrying her forward rapidly. But why water? She puzzled another moment, and then moved on. Vision: all was darkness. She blinked her eyes open and shut, but the darkness remained. Was there a touch of gray? She couldn't tell. She lay on her side on hard wood, her knees drawn up, her hands pulled behind her. Smells came then: dust and moisture and—and cloth and wheat and a slight scent of mold.

Where was she?

She tried to rouse herself as the sleepweed cleared further, and then finally sensed the injury to her head, feeling its dull ache of deeply bruised flesh, the drawing down of fractured bone, the sharp edges of pain in the cuts in skin. How? One moment she had been walking down the market alley, and the next— Where *was* she? How had she been injured? Had she fallen? Confused, she probed at her own injury, exploring the fracture, the bruised brain-flesh, as she had probed at others in her Callings, only this was herself—

She assembled the injury at last, finding the whole of it, and her eyes flew open in alarm. *Danger!* The blow had crushed part of her skull, driving bone inward, to bleed into crevices, to kill the brain with that slow, fatal seepage—but in those few instants close to death, her witch-gift had eased the danger, mending flesh, shifting bone, mending, rejoining, while she lay insensible. Brierley closed her eyes wearily, and focused her healing gift on her broken skull, continuing what instinct had begun while she might have died. Had they meant to kill her? If not, would her death have come so carelessly, so ineptly, were she anything else than what she was, a healer witch?

In Yarvannet she had tried to heal her own occasional fevers, with indifferent success as always with fever, but she had never suffered such a grave injury as this. Her witch's instinct guided her and she yielded to it, both guided and guiding. Curiously, the Beast did not appear to menace her at this healing, and its beach remained distant. Why? she wondered groggily, and would have laughed at herself, and did, hearing the single, gasped croak that echoed oddly in the enclosing darkness. Always why, Bri, she thought hazily, always another why, with no end of whys.

The whys assembled themselves around her in the darkness, floating in infinite progression, and expanded steadily to fill all that might be, pressing at her. With an effort she banished them, and floated alone again within the darkness, enclosed within herself as she lazily traced each line of fractured bone, each bruised artery, the damaged flesh of her upper brain, mending what had been broken. Had the blow landed but a few inches lower on her skull, she sensed, striking at the parts that prompted breath and heartbeat, she would be dead now. The gift could not have acted in time, not in the few short minutes left to her after her heart ceased its beating, her lungs ceased to draw in air. She thought lazily about that other future narrowly averted, that chance doorway to death her feet had somehow passed by, and wondered why the fear of it seemed so distant a question— But no whys, she told herself firmly. In this place the whys will

drown me. She drifted, focused upon her task, then drifted
still farther and slept.

～

Voices woke her, muffled and indistinct, somewhere above
her head. She heard a measured tread of a foot on wood,
then a passage of steps directly overhead. More words, and
she reached out with her witch-sense to catch those words
and touched the two minds above her.

Sigrid Witt sat on a bale of hemp by the boat railing, her
mind prickling with anger, and she glared at her brother as
he sat at the tiller at the stern of the boat. They were on the
river, on Jake's riverboat, descending the rapid currents toward the distant bay, a journey of eighteen hours at this season with the river running so high. Brierley sensed hours
gone by, several miles passed, enough for both her captors to
feel bored and ready for a quarrel.

"I told you, she's safely asleep," Jake said irritably, returning Sigrid's glare. "I gave her the sleep tonic I got from the
midwife."

"And I told you *not* to give it to her. You hit her too hard,
Jake, and sleep tonic on top of a head injury—" Sigrid threw
up her hands. "Even *you* should know that. She's no good to
us dead. All she'd be is a stranger in Ellestown with nothing
proven. And then where is your *reward?*" she spat. "The
count's message to Hinton didn't say anything about a reward. Why didn't you let Hinton—"

"Shut up, Sigrid. Maybe you didn't tell me all the message."

"I did, too!" Sigrid glared at him in frustration. "You
didn't need me to come! You didn't have to force me to do
this."

"Yes, I did. There's a woman to have the tending, and so
you're here. I told you I'll give you some of the reward; do
your thinking about that. Now shut up and watch the river for
any snags ahead."

Jake's strong hands shifted the tiller smoothly, guiding
them across the river as the current changed toward the other

shore. The wind blew strongly in his face, heavy with moisture, and he scowled at the building storm clouds in the sky ahead, his weather's eye measuring the time before those clouds brought worse winds and a pounding rain. Time enough to pass the first rapids, he judged, perhaps even the long gorge. Past those dangers, the river flowed quickly but smoothly down to the count's port town. They would be thoroughly wet when they arrived by the morning, but time enough, he decided. He shrugged again, more to himself than to his sister, who had not relented her glare.

"We could take the body to Darhel," he said mildly. "They'd recognize her there."

Sigrid snorted. "It's two weeks to Darhel overland through Lim, three by the river. She won't be recognizable by then."

How odd, Brierley thought, that no emotion follows that thought of a rotting corpse, nothing but calculation and greed, as if Brierley were a sheep's carcass ready for market, or a fat, shining fish piled on other fish for the viewing. Perhaps to these two she was little more. In Jake she sensed again an odd flatness of emotion, an utter lack of empathy with other people that she had occasionally sensed in others: such men thought all folk saw the world in grays, that all pretended to see more, as Jake pretended. Such men eventually killed, as Jake had killed, and might kill frequently, as indifferent and gray to the lives they ended as they were to all else. She shivered, and knew that Jake truly hadn't cared how his blow had landed, and still didn't care.

Jake shrugged again at his sister. "So we send a messenger and have them send somebody here to look at her."

"It's still three weeks to get there and back again." Sigrid shook her head angrily. "You hit her too hard, Jake. If we lose the reward because of you, I'll take it out of your hide."

"So we pack the body with ice if she dies. Leave off, will you? We got her captured and she's now stowed below, out like a snuffed lamp. And when she's out, she can't use her witchery on you. Did you think of that? Or do you just *say* she's a witch, Sigrid, and don't really believe it? What was her fault, after all? That she's pretty and Michael Toldane took her into his house? He'll never look your way, Sigrid."

"Shut up." Sigrid looked away at the river, her jaw set.

Jake smirked, knowing how well he had hit his mark. Although they were siblings near in age and raised in the same house, he and Sigrid had never really liked each other, despite their mother's urging. Now that their mother was dead these long years, neither really tried anymore. It was more pleasant to quarrel, their snide bickering safe within the blood bond neither could change. And so they picked at each other, happy to wound the other's feelings, with delicious resentments when the courtesy was inevitably returned. Jake knew his sister disliked her husband, the count's factor, despite the rank it gave her among the biddies in town. No, Sigrid had pined for Michael Toldane these twenty years, her shy girl's liking for him turning sour, into a sense of life cheated, for reasons unknown and bewildering. It amused him that she still hoped, a hope she never admitted, not even to him.

Jake allowed Sigrid to simmer for a few minutes, then needled her again. "Assuming she's really Brierley Mefell, that is," he drawled. His sister stared more determinedly at the water, as if the trees on the opposite bank were a fascinating vision, or the chevron of teal arrowing across the sky brought some hidden message. "If she's not," he added, knowing she was listening however she pretended she wasn't, "I hope you'll have a good explanation for the corpse. Don't you think for a moment I won't tell Count Charles it was your idea."

"Shut up," Sigrid snapped.

"Or the duke himself, if it comes to that," Jake said, enjoying himself.

Sigrid said nothing, but had clenched her jaw hard enough to turn the flesh white. Jake smiled more broadly, but, too bad, Sigrid wouldn't look around at him and see the smile. Jake shrugged. Sigrid knew the dangers of their plan, just as he did, but five hundred livres—surely the duke would give that much, maybe even more—had tempted Sigrid as much as him, however she protested. Six years' income in a single cache, and honor in it, too, finding a foul witch for the duke's stern justice: Jake mused again about what he might buy with his share. Yes, his life would change if they had indeed caught a witch.

Was this girl the witch the duke so eagerly wanted? Or did that really matter? Was it necessary that she be alive? He idly turned the choice over in his mind, the death or the life of the helpless woman below in his riverboat's storage hold, testing one choice against the other for the best advantage to himself.

Brierley shuddered at the coldness of his thinking, and twisted her wrists uselessly inside their ropes. Her hands were bound, but could she sit? Careful of her tender head, Brierley slowly maneuvered her body inside the tight space of the hold, using a shoulder for leverage on a bale, a steady push of her boot on a box. Finally she achieved sitting, and felt her head swim with the effort. She panted slightly, propped against the softness of a bale. The sleepweed still dragged at her muscles, relaxing them too much, but her thinking was more alert.

How had they known she would be at the market? Or did they see a quick chance and take it? She briefly touched Sigrid's mind and found the second answer was the truth, although the two had planned their assault for a fortnight, crouched over their table, whispering to each other, until the count's message had arrived, prompting them into action. The count's factor had no hand in the plot: Sigrid had not dared to tell her husband about Jake's plan, and so had not. This taking, then, was not official. Brierley had that much time, this passage of the boat down the river to the count's port, to turn her fortunes.

But how? She twisted her wrists again, but they were firmly tied. The darkness of the hold was profound. She squinted against the blackness before her, trying to find some light. A slight gray there in the high corner, she thought, a faint outline of a rectangle barely sketched against the darkness—perhaps the hold door to the deck above. Tentatively, she reached out a boot to prod at the boxes and bales around her, then reached with the other boot, finding the borders of her enclosed space. She had scarcely enough room to turn around, but enough space to stretch out on the rough decking. A coffin-sized space, she thought, ready for the burying.

Stop that, she told herself briskly. No one is dying here today—or tomorrow either.

Yes, she should have until tomorrow morning, assuming they left her safely stashed in their boat hold, which they might. Although horse and riverboat alike took several days to ascend the river to the Flinders Plateau, as she and Stefan had ridden that road for those days, the passage downward went far swifter on the fast current of the river, even still swifter when the riverman knew the river well, as Jake did.

A boon to me, she thought wryly, that he is confident. An incompetent boatman on top of all else might be unconquerable. She struggled against her wrist ropes until she panted, but got herself nowhere. Jake tied good knots.

Brierley gasped as the boat swayed hard on the current, and she felt its gain in speed. On the deck overhead, Jake stood and grasped the tiller firmly in both strong hands as the upper course of the river's rapids approached. Deftly, he guided his boat into the broader part of the current, then pulled hard to starboard to weather the first boulders on the right bank. A measured pace of several breaths, and a strong heave to port, riding the river's speed, pulling broad, sweeping curves on the current. Brierley almost forgot to breathe, and was not at all as confident as Jake was: Sigrid make a squeaking noise as one looming boulder passed scarcely three yards from the boat's side, but Jake knew the depth had been measured by Mionn river men centuries before, however Sigrid gasped and doubted him. Jake also knew all depths were rechecked each summer by the count's river men, every rock charted and warnings given of the changes, and so he knew the rocky face of this huge boulder plunged fifty feet to the riverbed, straight down, with no protruding rock to seize his keel. More dangerous were the low rocks near the left bank, where the river shallowed, and he steered a wary distance from their hidden threat. As he passed the last of the shallows, Jake nodded to himself and braced his feet for the next turn.

Brierley leaned against the sway of the boat, trying not to be thrown on her face with no hands to save her. Finally, she braced one foot firmly on a bale, the other on a sturdy box, wedging herself as best she could. The movement of the boat grew even more violent as they reached white water among closer rocks, with splashing and spindrift on either side that whipped through the air. On each side of the river, the riverbanks steadily rose in height, first mounds of grassy turf, then piles of large stones, and finally the cliffs of the gorge. Steadily, calmly, Jake guided his boat through the main channel of the river, a channel he knew well even in the spring floods.

The sound of rushing water echoed between the cliffsides, magnified in its sound until all seemed a roaring. Amid that roar, Brierley sensed Sigrid's fear, a fear she sternly repressed as best she could, lest Jake see it: unlike her brother, Sigrid was no waterman and had never pretended a liking for it. She sat white-knuckled at the railing, for all she knew her brother's skill at boat handling on this river, for all she had journeyed downriver with him a score of times over the years, going to market in the count's town while her husband delivered his annual reports to Count Charles. For all that, she held on hard to the railing and counted every yard of the mile through the gorge. Only then did she loosen her grip, take a shaky breath, and brace herself for her brother's taunt if he had seen her fear. But no taunt came—for once. Cautiously she looked around at him.

"Best check on her," Jake suggested, his hands shifting grip smoothly on the tiller. "Bale might shift and smother her." He smiled tightly as Sigrid hesitated. "Afraid she's awake? Maybe you believe in witchery more than I'm thinking."

"As if anyone cares what you're thinking," Sigrid declared. "I certainly don't." Sigrid stood, then walked the few paces across the deck to the hold hatch. A slide of the cover latch, a heave on the heavy wood, and light cascaded into Brierley's hold. Those few seconds' warning gave Brierley time to slide down and curl on her side again, back to the position in which they had left her. She closed her eyes, carefully quieted her breathing. I'm asleep, she told herself. She heard the clump of Sigrid's boot heel on the ladder stair, the woman's soft grunt as she climbed down the half-dozen steps. A rustling of skirts, a darkening of the light beyond Brierley's closed lids as she stooped, then the touch of her fingers on Brierley's neck, hunting her pulse.

"Hey, Sigrid!" Jake called, his voice a shout. "Is she still alive?"

"Still warm!" Sigrid shouted back, then nudged Brierley with her foot. "Are you awake, mistress?" she hissed. Another nudge, then a sharp kick into Brierley's hip. *I'm asleep,* Brierley told her silently, adding a subtle mental pressure that the thought be believed—but not too much, she cautioned herself: sometimes, if she were incautious, the other caught her at her suggesting, as Captain Bartol had that morning in Natheby an age ago.

Not this time. "Well, sleep onward," Sigrid muttered. "At least you're alive." More clumping of boots a few steps to the stairs, the heaving of the corpulent body up the ladder, and the hollow thud of the hold cover. Light vanished again, and Brierley opened her eyes, no closer to her freedom than before.

In Gammel Hagan's dungeon, she had faced Hagan's chasing of her with his knife around the big table, with the only key to the door safely inside his pocket. Compared to that, this should be easy. Isn't it? She tried working at her wrist bonds again, then strained her fingers into cramping trying to feel the shape of Jake's knots. Useless. She sighed and closed her eyes a moment, grateful beyond thinking that Megan had escaped. She had only herself to save. And my baby, of course, she reminded herself, my baby inside me, my precious baby. Brierley bit her lip hard and struggled harder against her bonds. With her hands free, she had a chance—what chance, she didn't know, but surely a chance.

She leaned weakly against the soft bale at her back and scowled at the darkness. Yes, when a future daughter wrote her history of Brierley Mefell, the wondrous Brierley Mefell, this adventure would definitely be included—but how would it end? She felt a wave of dizziness and blinked groggily, then a growing dread as if a terrible future moved toward her. The danger sang through her nerves, that warning, that approaching future self she could only dimly perceive. Danger! Danger! She gasped with her fear.

A teakettle sigh, a flicker of shifting flame, then a bright flare that threw light into every corner of the hold. Sheathed in flickering flames, Jain fluttered to her shoulder and quickly rubbed his head against her cheek. *Don't be afraid, dear one,* he soothed. *I have found you at last, and Basoul is near.*

There is danger coming! she thought in panic. *I cannot get my hands—*

Turn around. That is easily fixed. Brierley struggled to sit up and felt a brief flash of heat by her wrists, then felt the hemp rope give way. *There: all fixed,* Jain announced.

Where is Megan? Brierley asked anxiously, and raised her hands to her face.

She is safe with Michael, Jain said. *Do not be anxious. Amina and Soren will help the twins save the Well, and Evayne now travels upriver toward you.* He snorted in dismay. *This is not how we planned the Finding, and even I am concerned that we must act in the world. It is against our nature and we may dare too much.* He rubbed his head against her cheek again, cool flame that soothed and did not burn. Brierley slowly rubbed her wrists, gingerly touched the bump on her head, then sank back again on the soft sack of wheat. Her head felt strange, and for a moment the salamander faded back into the darkness. *Brierley!* Jain called urgently.

"What?" she gasped, jerking awake. "What is it?" Jain walked up her chest and put his snout inches from her nose, studying her, and she blinked back at him groggily. Then the salamander turned his head and looked beyond the wooden wall of the hold.

I hear darkness seeping into her thought, Basoul. Is that the danger she hears? He listened a moment. *Then it must happen now! We can't wait until nightfall. We can't wait at all!* Jain rustled his wings in high agitation, and then pressed close to Brierley, crooning. *Hold tight, beloved. We are with you. We are always with you.*

Brierley stiffened as the Calling swept over her, a Calling for herself as death neared, its impending future and its end, closer now, desperately close. Danger! Danger! She stifled a scream. Overhead she heard Sigrid's own shriek of fear, felt Jake's shock of disbelief. She swung her head to look, too, through wood and bales to the front of the ship, but her own eyes saw only the dimness of the hold; but through their eyes above, she saw the massive serpent's head rise from the river a quarter-mile ahead, its eyes an opalescent gleam, and felt the thrill of their terror as the gomphrey lashed toward them with its great tail, churning the water with its endless coils. The gomphreys in the Eastern Bay were no benevolent companions of ships, as they were in Yarvannet's Western Ocean: here the great sea snakes hated men, Ashdla had told her, and often attacked the fishing boats that ventured too far abroad at sea. Only rarely did the gomphreys enter the rivers, and never one this large.

With an oath, Jake swung the tiller hard toward the shore, already knowing it was too late to reach safety. "Brace yourself!" he shouted to Sigrid. "Grab hold of something!" But Sigrid only stood on the deck, her hands thrown to her face, screaming and screaming. "Sigrid!" he cried out, then abandoned the tiller and lunged toward her, taking her down to the deck. Brierley felt the impact of his elbow bone on wood, gasped with his pain, and then struggled frantically across the hold, trying to reach the ladder. She could hear the gomphrey itself now as it boomed its shuddering voice against the river bottom, and she sensed its intent to smash the small boat in front of it, to smash it to timbers. It lashed its tail more fiercely, sliding through the cold river water with mounting speed, and hurtled toward the riverboat.

"No!" Brierley screamed, and threw herself frantically forward toward the ladder. "No!" she screamed in her despair.

Brierley, Jain called desperately. *Wait!*

The world exploded around her. Wood broke in a rending crash, shearing, splitting, tearing, followed by the roar of river water. A flood of cold water crashed on her, forcing her to the deck, then lifted her bodily and smashed her into a box, then against hard wood—and suddenly nothing but water was beneath her, water that pushed hard at her, spinning her downward toward the bottom. She had not thought to take a breath of air, had not thought in her terror, and now her body wanted air, burning her throat like fire, convulsing her ribs to gulp in the air that was not there. She kicked frantically with her feet, but the fast current only spun her downward toward the river bottom, spinning her round and round.

Something buffeted her from below, then curled firmly around her body and bore her upward toward the light. She gasped in air as her head broke the surface, then suddenly was drowning again, struggling for air. She beat weakly at the huge serpent's body wrapping around her, all sense leaving her as she began to die. But in the next instant her head was again above the water and she coughed and sputtered, then managed a small breath of precious air. The gomphrey crooned encouragement, cradling her within its coils. She coughed rackingly, spitting water, and still could not breathe in enough air.

Do not panic, Basoul said gently, crooning to her. *Listen to me, my own, my beloved. I am with you, and I will never let go.* The gomphrey lashed at the water with its tail, bearing her away from the tumbling wreckage of the boat. Brierley flinched as she felt Sigrid's head smash against a rock at the river bottom, smashing bone, cracking open the skull. Swept along helplessly by the current, Jake was now drowning, too, his strong arms losing their strength as he struggled, his lungs filling with water. *Let them go,* the gomphrey commanded firmly. *They are not yours to save. Do not listen to them die. Brierley!* Groggily, she obeyed. The turbulent water battered at her, chilling her flesh, and she became dazed with it. Black fell on black as her vision failed, then suddenly there was water and bright sky again. She lost her grip on the gomphrey's slippery scales, nearly sinking under the water, but it caught her firmly, and then lashed even more strongly toward the nearing shore. *I hold you safe,* Basoul crooned. *I am here.* Brierley laid her face against Basoul's scaly skin, unmindful of the icy water that splashed into her face, unmindful of everything.

On a distant shore that only she and Basoul understood, the Beast rose strongly from the surf and lunged onto the sands, seizing Brierley hard with its oily tentacles. The massive, beaked head rose above her, mouth agape to plunge down and rip and tear. It roared in triumph at its prize, gloating, its single, wide eye bent upon her. Brierley struggled weakly within its grip, and knew she had no escape this time, not this time. In the far distance she heard the starchild shriek in mortal pain as the Beast began to kill her child. Brierley sobbed and pushed vainly at the coiling limbs that surrounded her, pressing, gripping, drawing her onward. *No!*

She felt the scrape of gravel on her knees, then felt herself pulled onto the riverbank. Basoul coiled herself gently around her and pressed close. Brierley cried out as she felt the first convulsion in her womb and heard her baby cry out in fear. The starship her child sailed staggered, its gossamer sails tearing, its timbers crumpling, and it began a slow fall toward the nearest sun, falling helplessly.

Let her go, Brierley, Basoul said heavily, her mental voice sodden with pain. *You cannot save her.*

I will save her! Desperately Brierley struck out at the Beast that towered over her, and flung herself away. She scrambled up the sand of the beach toward the small child who cowered there, her face stark with fear of the Beast that now stalked them both.

Do not! Basoul commanded in panic. *Do not risk yourself!*

She's my daughter! She's all I have left of Melfallan! I won't give her up. I won't! Brierley gathered the tiny child

into her arms, staggered to her feet, and then fled from the
beach into other times, other lives.

⁓

In another time, another place, there once had been new love.

On a narrow street in Ries near the harbor, Brierley
looked up into Dram's handsome face and smiled at him.

"I'm called away to Duke Luke's war against Airlie," he
insisted, "and have only this day before I leave. Surely I can
ask for your company to stroll through the town."

"And how does one lead to the other, your war and my
company?" she teased. Dram grinned at her and boldly offered his elbow, and she hesitated. A witch must not love,
she knew, but how could she resist the love shining in
Dram's eyes? How indeed? Shyly she slipped her hand under his arm, and felt him pull it possessively against his ribs.

"Good," he whispered.

And so they had strolled along the street that day, that last
day she had with him, for he had never returned from the
Airlie war. Never again had they walked the streets of Ries
in Briding, watching the folk pass to and fro, the ships in the
harbor, the flicker of waves against the piers. Never again,
and the emptiness sighed between them.

⁓

In another time, another place, there once had been love become grief.

"But it cannot be Plague," Brierley murmured feverishly,
plucking weakly at the bedcovers as she fretted. "Not for
me." The Plague loosed long ago by Witchmere struck only
at Allemanii, not shari'a. It could not be Plague, even here in
Mionn.

Her husband bent anxiously over her bed, his face etched
with worry. Had he slept at all this long day and night while
she lay in childbed? Had he hovered near her bed as their

baby died during the birthing, a son who never took a breath, never stirred, only lay limp and blue and dead?

"What did you say, beloved?" His hand pressed on hers. "What did you say? Speak to me again, oh, please!"

She felt the bleeding begin again as another artery dissected, filling her womb with blood and gushing into the sheets, a slow emptying of her veins that no one would stop. The midwife shoved her husband aside and tried to help, but no one could help, not even herself. *I cannot fight fever and this bleeding, not both,* she thought weakly. Brierley threw her arm across her eyes as the Beast rose from the sea, and she died when it seized her and tore her to pieces.

In another time, another place, there once had been despair and death.

"We've trapped you now, witch!" the duke's soldier shouted behind the screen of trees. "You can't get away!"

Brierley ran onward, the brush catching at her skirts, the tree branches whipping at her face. *Why do I try?* she asked herself, catching back a sob. *Who can save me? What use?*

She stumbled to a stop in a small glade of the forest, her chest heaving, and looked one more time at the bright sky overhead, at the brilliant leaves of the trees, dancing in the suns' light, then calmly turned to face the men who hunted her.

The first one burst into the glade and shouted in triumph as he saw her. Brierley braced herself as he ran toward her, her death, her Beast, and then gasped as he roughly seized her and threw her hard to the ground. "Bring the rope!" the man shouted. "We've got trees enough here for the hanging."

Two other men, then four more, ran into the clearing, one carrying a coil of rope. Brierley closed her eyes as they dragged her upward. She staggered as they pulled at her, forcing her toward an ever-oak on one side of the glade. The rope was put over her head, its rough hemp scraping at her flesh, and then they were dragging her upward, choking out her life. Frantically she tugged at the noose around her neck, trying to pull it away from its burning grip on her breath, and they laughed when she did, and rejoiced as she slowly strangled.

Their laughter became a blazing roar, the triumph of the Beast as it surged toward her across the sand. It struck out with its talons, and seized her with its jaws to rend and tear, but she would not scream, not this time, not this last time. Its horrible stench filled her senses, and its hatred of life shuddered through her soul, and she yielded to its hatred, and gave up all hope, and died on that branch, that rope.

In another time outside of time, in another place of no existence, there was now fear.

Brierley ran across a wide wasteland, her tiny child in her arms. The suns' light was a harsh glare, bringing no warmth to the world, only affliction. Bodies lay all around her, grotesquely distorted in death, bodies upon bodies without number to fill the world. Some had died of Plague, their bodies swollen obscenely, their skin blotched. Other had died in battle, their heads crushed, their sword wounds gaping. Others, the women, had died in pain and in loss and in regret. Still others, the children, had died in confusion, and all lay unmoving on the Plain of the Beast. Behind her the Beast called its obscenities, wooing her with its threats, promising her defeat. Brierley held her child closer and ran onward through the bodies, not looking back.

I will kill you! the Beast promised.

Brierley ran on, dodging with sure feet around the corpses. Her child clung to her desperately, her arms holding tight around Brierley's neck, her breath sweet on Brierley's cheek.

I will murder you!

Far ahead she saw a white pavilion standing on its cliff above the sea, gleaming in the suns' light against the uncertain gray of the sky. Her breath coming hard, her hands tight upon her child, she ran toward it, the Beast closing on her heels. She could feel the heat of its breath, hear its panting behind her.

A dozen selves, a dozen lives: Brierley drew strength from them all, from each time and place, and welded them to the Now to save her child. In a distant future at a distant ford, Peladius cried out to Thora as the sword pierced him, and Thora wept. On a distant Airlie battlefield, Dram moaned as the final spear was thrust into his heart, and his beloved wandered the streets of Ries, bereft. A Mionn castellan mourned, never comforted. Thora lay down on her bed in the sea cave, weary beyond living, and listened to the sea for a time, then yielded herself to death, wistful that she might see Peladius again but despairing she would not.

Believe! Brierley now cried out to the world, denying the Beast, invoking the future. *Believe!* Brierley cried out to all who would listen, all who loved, all who lived.

Believe! Thora cried out with her, and all Brierley's other selves cried out their hope, a healer's shout of defiance at the Beast, the Beast who was Death, and whom Brierley now defeated.

Brierley burst through the ring of white stones surrounding the pavilion, and leaped up the steps, her child in her arms. Her foot stumbled on the topmost step, and she heard the Beast roar in triumph. She darted frantically aside, and its lunge missed, achingly close. Its claws caught her skirt, ripping it, but she pulled free and ran into the safety of the pavilion. In the coolness within, a still pond of water blazed with the light of the stars. Brierley staggered to its edge and fell to her knees, and heard the Beast roaring outside, terrible in its anger.

"Believe," she whispered. She wrapped her arms around her child and slowly rocked her, back and forth, back and forth, as her breath slowed, her heart eased its pounding. "Believe, little one," Brierley murmured, and smiled as her tiny child clung to her. She kissed the small face and cuddled her, then listened to the Beast as it prowled, unable to get in.

Brierley awoke suddenly on sand, the current near the river shore plucking at her sodden skirts, where she lay half in and half out of the water. She raised her head and looked blankly up at the small cliff that fronted this bend in the river, the jumble of trees and brush at its base. With a moan she turned over and looked at the river, but saw nothing except the rushing water and the other shore. Jake's boat had vanished, even its wreckage, as if it had never existed; and the gomphrey had vanished, as if Basoul had never existed. The suns were setting beyond the mountains, and a deep velvety darkness built itself out over the water, reaching for her. The darkness shifted slowly toward her and settled over the beach, masking all in shadow. Brierley tried to stand, but her arms shuddered as she tried to lift herself, and her legs would not hold her. A second try brought more progress, giving her a body-length's lurch forward up the riverbank. On the third try, she managed several steps before she fell.

She felt the pain then, deep in her womb. She tried to sit, then felt her unborn child begin to die. No Beast came for it, no shuddering roar, no gloating, only a slow wavering of the child's presence—then nothing. *No!* she screamed silently. She had no strength to give her child, but tried nonetheless. The pain struck again, a great wrenching at her bowels, and she felt herself begin to bleed. *No!* She managed to get to her knees and then hunched over. *Don't,* she wished, *please don't.* She felt an answering flicker from her baby, nothing more. But the pain faded into the past, where outside of time Brierley had fled the Beast, and then time moved forward again, slowly at first, then quickening, yielding the future. The small, glowing spark within her strengthened, flickered, then lived.

Brierley looked groggily around her, at the empty sand, the empty river, the night-filled sky. Something was not right with her arm: she could feel a lancing pain as the cracked bone ground its edges together. She looked down at it with perplexity, confused. I should heal my arm, she thought vaguely, and reached for her witch-gift—and found nothing. She blinked in surprise, and could not understand.

Once before, her witch-sense had deserted her and vanished for several weeks, and the loss had felt like this emptiness, as if she fumbled in a dark cavern, amid a silence curiously blank and unmoving. And even afterward, after her gift had returned to her as mysteriously as it had left, a difficult healing usually depressed her witch-sense for several days, as if her mind retreated to heal itself. She frowned, trying to understand, but still could not.

She was utterly alone. She huddled on the riverbank sand for a time, cold and shivering, then tried to regather her strength, however that might be done. Her broken arm began an insistent throb and the pain worsened steadily, distracting her thoughts. Thunder now rumbled in the distance, and then the rain began, first a smattering of raindrops, then the slow, insistent fall of cold rain. Brierley struggled to her knees, upended her face into the sand, then tried uselessly to stand, and finally crawled as best she could toward the nearby trees. That thirty yards exhausted her, but she reached the nearest tree, then the large bush behind it. Gratefully, she crawled under the slight shelter of the bush and lay down on the rough bracken beneath it. With a soft groan she pulled her knees to her chest and wished uselessly for warmth, and huddled against the storm.

~

Jared and Evayne arrived in the count's town of Arlenn at the suns' setting, wet and irritable. They asked three times for directions to an inn, only to get lost in the winding, dark streets near the harbor, but had finally found a small establishment a street up from the docks. The mist from the harbor stole into every crevice, and the bed was damp, its mattress lumpy, with a faint odor of mold. They had tried lying down on the bed, but after half an hour both had unrolled blankets from their packs and chosen to sleep on the floor, a hard bed, true, but not that different from every bed but one on this journey. Jared had left a small lamp burning on the battered chest of drawers, and a thin sliver of light shone under the door to the hallway, giving a dim illumination to the room. Although tired to his bones, Jared couldn't sleep and neither could Evayne. It did not improve their tempers.

"Have you ever been in love?" Jared asked.

"No. Why?" Evayne said resistantly. "Are you offering?"

He grinned at her, got a sour look back. He had seen every variety of Evayne on their journey, and had liked them all. Sometimes she was bold and sassy, other times withdrawn and bitterly lonely, hiding behind her walls, but usually somewhere between, never quite the same woman twice. He thought she liked him, too—in fact, she had dared to say so in Lowyn, even if he hadn't managed to wheedle her into admitting it again. He knew she tried to trust him now, tried so very hard, but it wasn't easy for her. Now she was tired, as was he, and not in a good mood, but he liked that Evayne, too. He liked all the women she was. Jared wrinkled his nose at her. "Just collecting information. Would you be interested if I did offer?"

"Drown it, Jared."

She turned over and put her back to him.

"Hey, I'm not that lout, the rivermaster's son," he protested. "I've been polite—most of the time."

Evayne rolled over on her back and looked at him sourly.

"Well, it's true," he insisted.

"Is there a purpose to this conversation?"

"You could be polite, too," he pointed out.

"Is there?"

"Maybe. Have you ever had a friend, Evayne, a real friend? Or has it always been lonely for you, knowing what you were and having to hide it? Your father doesn't seem that warm of a person, torrents of blood and all that, and never claiming you as his daughter. And I think you still miss your mother, and I think you blame yourself for her death, and I think you're worried for the Finding, that you might arrive too late."

"You think lots of things." Evayne sighed and put one hand behind her head. "I could say something cutting and shut you up."

"I'm not that easily shut."

"I've noticed," she said dryly. She quirked her mouth, then considered. "Well, I could ask why it's important for you to know."

"That's nicely cutting."

"I think so, too. Or I could tell you to shut up and go to sleep."

"That, too," Jared said comfortably. "Too bad I'm not sleepy."

"Neither am I." She sighed. "I'm sorry, Jared."

"For what?" he demanded.

"I'm sorry to disappoint you," she said, suddenly shy with him again, an Evayne he liked very much, the most of all. "I'm sorry I'm not very good at being a friend—and whatever else you're wanting of me."

"Nonsense." She sighed and he knew he still hadn't persuaded her. Ah, well, he thought. "So do you want to get back on the road?" he asked. "Dirt would be softer than this floor."

"Suits."

Jared pushed off his blankets and got up, then began repacking them into his saddlebag. "I think you like me," he said smugly.

"I think you think I'm unhappy, only I'm not." Evayne sat up and hugged her knees.

"I think you don't know what I think."

"I'm an air witch. I know everything." He wrinkled his nose at her, and she grinned. He paused then and smiled down at her, liking the grin, but after a few moments she couldn't bear his smile and looked away, flushing slightly.

"Not to worry, Evayne," he said softly. "Not to worry about anything." After a moment she nodded.

They looked for the innkeeper in the common room, but he was busy in the kitchen, and so they piled their saddlebags in a corner and sat down at a table next to them. Jared signaled the barmaid for ale while they waited, and she soon brought them two large glasses. Evayne stretched out her long legs under the table and eyed the room.

Near their table several fishermen sat in their leather smocks on a long bench, enjoying a glass before they went home. "Efe has sent messengers to all the counts," one fisherman said. "Duke's orders. This Brierley escaped, or so the duke says, and he thinks she's somewhere in Mionn." Jared looked quickly at Evayne, then casually leaned forward over his glass, his head turned to let his ear catch the talk more easily. Evayne promptly copied Jared's casual posture and looked elsewhere around the room, her expression bored. "The soldiers are searching for her in Arlenn and Lowyn," the man continued, "and the count has sent word upriver to Flinders, too."

"Why would she come to Mionn?" the fisherman's friend scoffed.

"Better than Ingal, believe me. The duke wants her life."

"And fitting that he does," another man said assertively. "We can't have that old menace again, those witch-women with their evil wishing and harm to the folk. Stamp them all out, I say."

"But what if she's innocent?" one asked. "What if your granddaughter got accused by some biddy in the town who doesn't like her? It always starts that way with women's gossip. How do you prove she's *not* a witch?"

"Won't be my problem," the first man sniffed. "My granddaughter isn't a witch."

"So you say. So prove it." He sat back in his chair and crossed his arms, then put up his chin in challenge. "Prove to me she isn't a witch."

The other man sneered and quaffed another long swallow from his mug. "I've got better things to do, like taking my ship out before the new storm rolls in."

His friend snorted. "I'd say the duke has better things to do, too."

The first man thumped the table softly in warning, then

leaned toward his friend. "Not so loud," he hissed. "The duke has ears everywhere."

"So does Earl Giles, and I'll take the measure of our earl anytime over Duke Tejar." Heads swiveled toward him, but he kept his chin in the air, looking around the room. "And I dare any good Mionn man to say differently!" The bravado earned him a few muttered cheers, but others shifted their chairs cautiously to put their backs to him, then found much interest in their ale.

Evayne nudged Jared's elbow. "Let's get out of here," she said softly. Jared nodded and rose, their glasses forgotten, and they soon found the innkeeper and settled their account with him. Within ten minutes they were riding on the main street up from the harbor. When they reached the crossroads on the far side of town, Evayne kicked her horse into a canter, and soon the harbor lights fell far behind them, finally winking out behind the trees at the first wide turn in the Flinders road.

The next morning, after a cold camp in a forest glade beside the river, they came upon a party of men toiling over the wreckage of a riverboat. They rode by, eyeing them curiously. Jared felt a sense of dread, as if time had run out, and they stopped briefly to hear the news from the chief of the party, who had little interest in them but the same courtesy as all the Mionn folk. Evayne and Jared walked their horses onward until the next bend in the road and then increased speed. During the next four miles the darkness settled, making the road hard to follow, but Jared did not want to stop, did not want to waste the hours of a night camp.

"The road's footing is getting dangerous," Evayne warned.

"We can't stop."

In the growing darkness, he saw Evayne's immediate nod. "I know. I feel it, too."

They pressed onward, although the horses occasionally

stumbled in the starlight. After another mile, Evayne suddenly reined up her horse and looked across the river. "Wait!"

"What is it?"

"Oh, blessed Four! It's Brierley!" She pointed across the tumbling waters. "Over there under the trees. I can barely hear her—she's injured or sick." Jared promptly heeled his horse toward the river, and Evayne quickly snatched at his reins. "Are you mad? The current's too fast!"

"Born a boatman, were you?" he snapped back. "I thought you claimed yourself only as witch or soldier. If Brierley's over there, I'm going. You can stay here."

Evayne yanked hard on the horse's reins, bringing the horse around abruptly. "That's not fair, and not worthy of you, Jared. What good does it do her if we both drown? Let's find some kind of ford where we can cross, some shallow place where the horses can keep their feet on the riverbed."

"If there is such a place."

"Let's at least look. Please, let's not quarrel, not now. If there's no place to ford, then we'll swim—and drown."

Jared opened his mouth for another sharp retort, and realized she was right. "Hells," he swore, and saw the answering flash of her grin.

"You're so predictable, Jared."

"Thank you. Did you see any place behind us?"

"I wasn't looking."

"Neither was I. Wonderful. Let's scout a bit upriver."

They rode a half mile and found a shallowing in the river, as best they could tell in the darkness. A short, grassy bank led down to the river's edge. Jared leaned low over his horse's neck to look at the ground and thought he saw wagon tracks, a single, parallel groove that might be a dozen other things. He swung off his horse and knelt, fingering the firm mud of the track, then straightened and handed the reins to Evayne. "I'm going to try to wade across. It's shallower here."

"And how can you tell that?"

"I don't care. I'm going to try it. You wait here."

"Please?"

"Of course," Jared said absently. He walked gingerly down the muddy bank and found more tracks: something had come out of the water here. Perhaps it was a ford, but he could see no details on the opposite bank of a path or landing space. He waded into the water and gasped at its coldness as it tipped over the tops of his boots, then pushed forward, struggling to keep his balance against the strength of the current. A dozen yards from shore, the water swept him off his feet and he went under briefly, then bobbed again to the surface, spitting water. In Yarvannet he had been a good swimmer, and he struck out with a strong kick, and hoped that no rocks jutted downriver to smash him under. He swam as hard as he could, lifting one arm, then the other, kicking hard at the water, and in a few minutes grated one boot on the riverbed. The current nearly up-ended him again as he tried to get to his feet, but a few seconds later he staggered up on the opposite bank, shivering violently.

"I'm across!" he shouted back across the water, and heard Evayne's answering shout, then set off along the riverbank, hunting downriver.

It was a hard half-mile, with tree roots tripping his boots, branches slapping him in the face, rocks tipping beneath his feet. Twice he fell, bruising his knees on the smooth rocks on the river shore, but got himself up each time to labor onward. "Brierley!" he called. "Brierley!"

This way, a deep Voice sounded into his mind, and Jared jerked to a sudden stop, his eyes widening in alarm. He looked around him, and then turned quite around in place, hunting the person who had spoken. He had never heard such a voice, not from any mortal man, and his skin prickled. He saw no one. *Jared, my son,* the Voice said then, and Jared gasped with the sudden yearning that rose up within him, for what he could not say. *Come this way.* Jared stumbled onward, faster and faster, for all it risked a bad fall, and then pushed into the forest lining the bank.

A blue light shimmered within the trees ahead, as if the Companion's light had descended to burn brightly as a flame. He stumbled over a tree-root and caught himself on the tree bole, then struggled through the brush, and finally stepped into a small clearing among the trees.

I am Basoul, the dragon said softly, arching her long neck to look down at him. *And you are mine, sweet Jared, trusted and true.*

Jared tore his eyes away from the dragon's gaze and saw Brierley lying within the embrace of the dragon's forelegs. Her head hung limply across the blue-scaled hide, her hair cascading over her face. *She is here, and very weak. She attempted too much,* Basoul added softly, *as is her way—and yours, Jared.* Basoul lowered her head protectively and wound her tail around herself and Brierley, then closed her eyes with a sigh. *How can I do less?*

"She's alive?" Jared asked anxiously, fearing that she was not.

Yes, she's alive.

"Uh, are you real?"

Yes—if one bends a few definitions of the Real. He heard the smile in the answer, and grinned.

"You're beautiful," he breathed. "More beautiful than anything I've ever seen." The aquamarine eyes glowed, and Jared felt light-headed and swayed slightly. How long he stood looking at Basoul, he never knew, but finally he shook himself and set out to find wood for a fire. He had a small blaze going when Evayne arrived with the horses. She came on foot, pushing through the brush, the horses following on a long lead, and was as wet as he, her dark hair dripping, her clothes soaked. Evayne stopped abruptly as she stepped into the clearing, as had he, then bowed gracefully to the dragon, with great solemnity.

"Basoul," she breathed.

My child, the dragon answered, nodding her head.

"It is the time of the Finding," Evayne said ecstatically, her hands clasped at her breast.

It is—or may be. Brierley is desperately ill. She is the key-stone to the Well, and the Well itself is imperiled by a townswoman's greed. Others must deal with the Well: here we have one to be healed.

"Yes, Basoul," Evayne said meekly.

"I'm making a fire," Jared said. Evayne nodded and turned to the horses. Together they quickly made a rough camp among the trees, and Evayne left briefly to check the river.

"There's no one in sight," she reported when she returned. "We should still shield the fire."

"Right." When the fire was burning hotly, Jared approached Basoul, stopping two yards away, then craned his head to look at Brierley lying limply in the dragon's embrace. Basoul extended her neck and nudged him slightly on the shoulder. *I will watch the river. She will be as safe in your arms.* In the next instant the dragon disappeared, and Brierley lay curled on the cold ground in front of him. He knelt beside her and gently gathered her into his arms, and brushed her hair away from her face. "Brierley?" he whispered, and shook her slightly, but she did not respond. Evayne sank to her heels beside him.

"I know nothing of healing, Jared," she said desperately. "It is not my gift."

"I'm not a healer, either, but we can keep her warm at least. What's wrong with her, I wonder? Has she been in the river? Her clothes are wet. How did she get here?"

Evayne shook her head helplessly. "I don't know."

Jared tipped Brierley's face toward the firelight and saw bruises on her cheek and neck. Her face was pale and drawn, and for a moment he saw death in her face, its muscles slack. He shook her slightly again and called her name, but still she did not respond. "Put together some of the blankets, will you?" he asked Evayne. "And that spare cloak in your saddlebag."

Jared laid Brierley down gently on the ground, and then began unbuttoning the buttons on her bodice, blushing

slightly as he did. But surely her wet clothes weren't helping, he told himself, and she would be warmer near the fire.
With difficulty, he removed her wet dress, chafed her arms
and legs with one of the blankets, then lifted her and carried
her next to the fire. Evayne had made a bed of brush and
blankets, and Jared wrapped Brierley warmly, then sat beside her, wondering what next to do. Finally he simply took
her hand into his and sat wearily, watching the light flicker
across her face.

"Don't die," he whispered. And then, because it seemed
right to do, he found his saddlebag and then the earl's letter,
and read it to Brierley as she lay there, wrapped warmly in
the blankets. Although Melfallan had not forbidden Jared to
read the letter, likely forgetting that instruction in his haste,
Jared's curiosity had failed him barely a week into his journey, and so he had found, to his joy, that Brierley had won
Melfallan's heart, and much was explained about Melfallan's
urgency to find her. She deserves an earl, he had thought, and
had decided the whole matter perfectly right, and had not
changed his mind since. "He says he loves you," he whispered and took Brierley's hand, then glanced at Evayne, who
had long since closed her mouth in her surprise.

"I couldn't tell you everything," he said defensively.
"Sorry."

"I'm not complaining," she said quickly. "But how do you
feel about it, Jared? You love Brierley, too."

"Me? Well, of course I do, but don't you see how fine it is,
Bri and the earl? I'm happy that she's found someone."
Evayne shook her head slightly. "What?" he demanded.

"I will admit from time to time," Evayne said, "that I
don't know everything. You surprise me."

"Why? Can't a man and woman be friends without being
lovers? I've loved Bri since I was a boy and never stopped
doing it. Does that mean I have to frown and fret and complain if she finds someone else? When it's an earl, and especially an earl like Melfallan? Is that loving? I don't think so."

"And from the moment you knew about him," Evayne said
with a smile, her face half-shadowed by the night, "you were

never jealous, not for an instant. It's like you, Jared."
Evayne's smile turned wistful. "And likely you're as little
proud of that as you are about your knighting."

Jared frowned at her. "You aren't making sense," he
grumbled, and heard her chuckle. "None at all."

"If you like."

⁓

Brierley woke slowly in Jared's arms in the rough camp bed,
and blinked in surprise as she saw his face near hers.
"Jared?" she whispered. He opened his eyes and blinked
back a moment, then smiled with relief.

"There you are," he said in immense satisfaction, then
raised himself on one elbow to look down at her. "There
you are," he repeated, and caressed her face. "How do you
feel?"

"Where am I?" she asked, and looked vaguely around her,
then sighed deeply with the effort of the words. All was guttered out, every part of her witch-sense. When she heard
movement behind her, she started in alarm, and then saw the
slim woman sitting up in another camp bed near the fire.

A fire. She gazed at the flames a moment, dazed, then
looked again at the woman. "Who are you?" she asked, and
her voice broke weakly.

"This is Evayne Ibelin," Jared said. "She's an air witch."

Brierley looked back at Jared, confused, and could not
comprehend. "A what?"

"She can't hear my mind-speech, Jared," the woman said
worriedly, and something rippled in her voice, something
important. Brierley felt a shiver pass down her spine, but
didn't know why. "She can't hear me." The woman sounded
confused, even worried. Why? She struggled with the question for a moment, then closed her eyes and sighed wearily,
then drifted away again. So tired. When she awoke, the night
seemed colder.

"Are you awake again?" Jared whispered and touched
her face.

"Who is that other—"

"An air witch, as I told you. She was coming to the Finding. Earl Melfallan sent her with me to find you, my own 'finding,' if you will." He smiled. "That's a joke, Bri."

"You know about—"

"What Evayne has told me about it, but it's far above me, I think. All I wanted was to find you, and now I have. Are you feeling better?" he asked anxiously.

"Everything's strange, Jared."

"What happened, Bri?" He shook her slightly. "Bri?"

"I sent you away," Brierley mourned. "My mother feared for my safety. I was never allowed friends, especially someone like you."

"I know that now," he whispered. "I think I always knew it. Don't be sad, Bri. Everything's all right."

"I sent you away. I ran away when you needed me."

"That's long ago." He caressed her face. "Don't fret."

"And then the boys hurt you, after I ran away."

"Actually, you should have seen Rob," Jared said cheerfully. "He was worse than me. I pounded him. He was always a bully, and he still is. Have you seen him recently? He's fat, I mean really gross, with his paunch hanging out and his buttocks quivering when he walks. He's got three chins and huffs when he bends over—as much as he can bend, that is. Revenge comes in many ways."

"Does it?" Brierley asked, confused.

"Fatter than me, at least. Where have you been living all these years? Earl Melfallan thinks you have a cave somewhere."

"He told you that?" Brierley asked uncertainly. "How does he—" She stopped and closed her eyes a moment, baffled beyond thinking.

"Never you mind," Jared said, gathering her close to him. "Never you mind." Safe in the comfort of his arms, Brierley drifted back into the darkness.

Bright sunshine, a touch of a cold breeze. Water chuckled nearby. Brierley opened her eyes and found herself in a different place, high in the mountains. She lay comfortably under blankets on the ground, and a horse stood nearby, watching her as it chewed, its jaw moving from side to side, ears flicking. She stared at it in surprise, and it stared back amiably, then bent its head for another mouthful of grass.

A slim, dark-haired woman walked into her view, carrying an armload of dry branches. She dropped her load on the ground, and then smiled in surprise at Brierley. She was tall and lithe, dressed in riding leathers, a sword hung from her belt, and she seemed familiar. "You're awake again!" she said. "Good!"

"Who—who are you?"

"Evayne. Don't you remember?"

"Evayne." Brierley frowned, then looked vaguely around at the cliffsides and the everpine. *This wasn't where I was,* she thought, and could not make the fact fit anything.

The tall girl sat down beside Brierley, folding her legs comfortably, then sighed. "This wasn't what I expected, but at least we found you. Nor did I like moving you, but where could we find a safe place in Mionn now?" She gestured broadly at the valley. "This is one of the high passes above Airlie, Brierley. We've been traveling for three days." She pointed beyond Brierley's head. "Two passes over is Witchmere. Can't you feel it?"

"I can't feel anything." Brierley craned her head to see, but saw only more trees and yellow rock, and the effort exhausted her.

Evayne bit her lip. "Soren says I'm not to push you. He says you've shut down your witch-sense to shield your baby, and that the Four will guard. We're not to worry, but to ride easily with you, not too much each day."

Brierley sighed deeply, then closed her eyes.

"Brierley?"

Water dripping against stone, a sighing darkness. Brierley hunted through the caverns for Megan, but could not find her anywhere. *Where are you, Megan?* she called in anguish, to be mocked by nonsense voices drifting on the hollow air. *Where are you?*

She heard the slither of tentacles nearby, the sigh of bloated flesh, and ran.

Where are you? she sobbed, as she stumbled from one hallway to another, wanting Megan, but there was no one here, no one living, not anymore. *Why am I alone?*

"I love you, Brierley."

Melfallan?

She stopped abruptly, thinking she had heard his voice, but there was nothing, no one. He was lost to her, and she wept. She leaned against the stone of the corridor wall, then slid weakly down to sit. Far in the distant blackness, the voices mocked her again, dead voices, dead memories. "Have I died?" she wondered aloud, and her words echoed hollowly away into the blankness, then boomed back at her, shouting. Brierley covered her ears in fright. *Don't!* she pleaded. *Please don't.*

"Brierley," said a soft voice, and the echoes did not boom at her. Brierley looked up blearily at a girl with aquamarine eyes, a girl tall and slim and dressed in blues and silvers. The girl held out her hand, beckoning. As she moved her hand, the cavern walls dissolved and rebuilt themselves into a row of columns, glowing white under the starlight above. She sat next to a pool of dark water in which stars shimmered in rhythm with the sound of the surf far below.

"Where is Megan?" Brierley asked, bewildered, and looked around her in amazement at the white columns, the smooth, dark water of the pool.

"Megan is safe," the girl said, sitting down beside her. Brierley leaned against her shoulder and sighed, not knowing whether to believe, not knowing too many things. Slender arms came around her and held her close. "You are safe, too, as safe as I can make you."

"Basoul?" Brierley whispered in despair. "Is it you?"

The girl kissed her forehead and held her even more closely. "Yes, it is I. Where are you wandering, Brierley?" she asked sadly. "Do not wander too far. Oh, please don't."

"Where are we?" Brierley again looked around at the pavilion columns, the pool of unmoving water. "Where is this place?" She struggled against Basoul's hold and pulled away, then staggered to her feet, not knowing where she was going. Where was Megan?

"Brierley!"

~~~~

The starship flowed gracefully on the shimmering light, mounting the stars. The light sparkled on the crystal lines that confined the sails, tempering their power. Brierley watched, transfixed, as the ship plunged toward a nearby sun, then lifted its prow and turned easily toward another star shimmering bright blue against the blackness.

"Can you hear the music?" a child murmured.

"Yes, I can."

A small hand clung trustingly to Brierley's skirt, and Brierley looked down into the star-child's depthless eyes. "The twilight is rising," the girl said softly. "Can you see it, Mother?"

"Yes, child."

"It will be a new beginning, a new song," the girl said confidently. "And all will be right again." She raised her other small hand, feeling the wind, and smiled.

~~~~

Brierley and the star-child wandered the world together, finding Amelin and its narrow streets, then a high tower room in Tiol where Melfallan sat studying a book, another castle room where Lady Saray sat at her stitchery. They lingered near the beach before the great sea stones, listening to the surf play itself upon the sand in moving melody. In Natheby Master Harmon straightened from his stoop over his plantings and squinted up at the sky, not liking the look of the clouds this morning, but spring was here now and all would be fine, no doubting that. He listened to his boys shout as they ran, and smiled.

At Flinders again they watched Lake Ellesmere shimmer in the suns' light, the wind stirring the grasses of the meadows, a sibilant hush that never ended. The suns rose slowly into the sky, the Companion leading the dawn, and the world was filled with their healing light. Far out on the lake, two dragons rose from the waters, necks entwined, shimmering red and blue. Beside them a golden dragon spread its gossamer wings and cried aloud to the dawn, and was answered by a murmuring voice sounding within the forest.

We are with you, daughter.

"I know you are," Brierley murmured.

Brierley lay comfortably beneath her warm blanket, a scent of sweet brush tickling at her nose. She rubbed her cheek against the rough weave of the blanket, content.

"But she hasn't spoken for four days," Jared's voice said worriedly, somewhere nearby, somewhere— Where?

"You have to trust, Jared," another voice replied. "We're almost to Carandon now. She can rest there, refind her strength."

"But you aren't sure of that, Evayne," Jared accused.

"No," the other admitted. "No, I'm not sure," she said sadly. "I'm not sure of anything, not anymore. I wish I was. I'm sorry."

"That's not your fault, Evayne. I'm just worrying about Brierley. She seems a little better."

"I hope so."

The voices faded into a murmur, and Brierley listened to the trees rustle all around her, warm beneath her blanket. The air rose up the Airlie hills, teasing with cool fingers at her face, reminding her of—what? The problem perplexed her a moment, but she could not find the answer, not now. Sleep, she told herself drowsily. Sleep and be healed. She sighed and closed her eyes, then slept.

16

*D*erek Lanvalle lounged on the wall beside the palace entrance, watching Albert give instructions to the guards coming on duty, the last of his sergeant chores for the day. Albert's brother had a farm across the river, and their younger sister lived with the brother, and Albert was intent to make Derek his brother-in-law. Each time Derek came home to Darhel from his spy's travels, Albert rowed him across the river to see the sister, with heavy hinting to and fro. The girl was pretty enough and Albert was a good friend, and the sister loved Albert and indulged him the hinting, and Derek indulged, too; and only Albert didn't know it would never happen. Derek liked Cathe, and she liked him; but Cathe knew Derek would never be a farmer, and a farmer is what she wanted, whenever she finally found him.

In truth, as pleasant as her household might be, Derek would rather go hawking. He looked up at the blue sky with its tatter of white clouds, and thought about the pleasures of the sport: riding abroad on his horse, launching the bird, watching it spiral upward to a dizzying height, then the swiftness of the strike. In Derek's boyhood his father had often taken him hawking, teaching Derek and his older brother that nobleman's sport for such times as Duke Selwyn might ask his castellan and his young sons to join his own hawking party, a sport the old duke had loved as much as Derek's father had. Derek remembered how it was before the Plague took his father and brother, before Daughter Sea took Duke Selwyn, too, and had elevated a different kind of man to duke. Derek's life wholly changed then, although it took some years for Derek to realize it. He no longer hoped for any gentleman's rank, no longer expected a knighthood, however excellently he served his duke. Tejar chose other rewards for his kept men.

Derek often thought wistfully of a gentleman knight's honors that might have been his: fortune had instead made him a spy, not an ignoble calling, true, and Derek's talent for lying, also a truth, had made him a good spy, good enough to survive this current period of the duke's displeasure. For a week Derek had lounged around the palace, eating well and sleeping late, and taking prudent care to stay out of the duke's sight. The unaccustomed leisure had become tedious, especially since Derek didn't dare put as much as a chin-whisker inside another inn. Even a spy can be spied upon, and Derek suspected that Tejar knew exactly what Derek was doing each moment of the day. After all, the duke's servants were everywhere, watching everything, and most probably that careful watching included Derek. Maybe not, he thought, but best not to test it. And so he had lolled and lazed and stuffed, until he felt he might tear up the marble floors with his fingers for the boredom of it all. Derek looked up at the windy sky, its clouds scuttling high across the Daystar and thickening steadily. If Albert didn't move things a bit faster, they'd be rained on by midafternoon.

Well, at least it would be an event, Derek thought. The thought did not cheer him.

He yawned, then blinked his eyes several times to wake up. Ocean alive, he thought, I just got up an hour ago. If this goes on, I'll end up sleeping the clock around. The palace servants will goggle and turn to each other, mouths amazed. Whatever happened to that spy? they'll ask, shaking their heads and tsking. Oh, he's still sleeping, the others will answer, nothing new.

Derek's next yawn nearly cracked his jawbones, and he determinedly pushed himself off the wall to a more upright position, one that required some attention to standing erect. Can a man fall fast asleep while standing? he wondered. Surely one would sag a little, even pitch forward in a heap, and surely the limp fall to the pavestones would wake him up—a help there in getting awake again, if rather hard on the knees. He watched Albert give one last instruction to the senior guardsman.

Albert turned and stomped over to Derek. "Ready to go?" he asked cheerfully.

"Do we have to?" Derek retorted.

"Now, none of that, Derek. Slothful you are. You can help row the boat: it'll keep you fit. If you don't, I fear, you'll get fat with a double-chin and a stomach far too large, a rump even bigger, and everyone will point and snicker when you waddle by." He looked Derek over, inspecting him for the first signs of fat and the fate that would follow.

Derek glared. "You're a hard friend to have, Albert."

"You're worse, and in truth I don't know why I put up with you at all. Come on: you need some exercise. I've got the horses down at the inn stable."

Albert turned and led the way. Derek followed, amiably enough, his eyes flicking over the folk in the street, the wagons, a half-troop of soldiers that tramped by. At the inn he waited outside as Albert went in to find the stable groom, and so saw Stefan Quinby and the troop of the duke's guard turn the far corner of the street and march toward him. He instantly recognized the stumbling figure among the soldiers. The last time he had seen that young man, Derek had been tied in a chair in an inn room in Mionn, thinking the witch he had discovered must kill him.

If Stefan is captured—he thought in sudden alarm. And the duke's own prisoner! He looked beyond the soldiers but saw no other party come around the corner, no second party conducting a young woman, pale and slender. He pressed back against the inn wall into the shadow of the eave and watched the soldiers' party tramp past him.

Stefan's eyes were bent on the ground and he had a halting stagger in his walk that suggested a dazed mind as much as painful bruises beneath his clothes: he had been badly beaten. His face was a ruin, with one eye swollen shut and the other not much better. Why did they beat him? Derek wondered, shocked by Stefan's appearance. Stefan's chains clanked as he walked, and Derek bit his lip as one of the soldiers shoved him roughly. Pushed hard off-balance, Stefan nearly fell to the cobblestones, but another of the guards caught his arm and pulled him along, half-dragging him. Although the duke was sometimes a brutal man, most of his soldiers were not: to treat a prisoner this roughly meant deliberate orders to do so, or at least that there had been an effort to escape, probably the latter.

Derek turned his head to look again down the street, but saw nothing except the normal foot traffic. Was there another prisoner coming on the next ship and the overland ride from Lim? And what would the duke do with Brierley Mefell if he had caught her? Derek abruptly wanted very much to speak to his duke. He gave Albert the courtesy of a quick glance through the inn door, didn't see him, and hurried after the guard party that was conducting Stefan to the palace.

He found Duke Tejar in his study on the third floor near the family suites. Richard stood guard as usual outside the doorway, and bristled at Derek as he approached, for all the man recognized him and knew him well.

"I want to see him," Derek demanded.

"You don't have an appointment."

"So now you're a steward, insisting on appointments? Come on, Richard: announce me."

Richard hesitated, shrugged, then turned to rap on the door with his mailed hand. A muffled shout came in response, and Richard opened the door partway. "Derek Lanvalle is here, your grace, and wishes to see you. I told him he didn't have an appoint—"

"Send him in," Tejar barked from within the room. With a tight, triumphal smile, Derek pushed past Richard and confronted his duke.

Duke Tejar sat behind his wide table littered with papers, a glass of ale at his elbow, the remains of a brief meal on the side table. He looked up as Derek entered and scowled. "So?" he demanded.

Let us be bold, Derek thought, and took a deep breath, then strode across the carpet and sat down in one of the ornate chairs fronting the desk. He crossed one leg over the other. The duke's eyebrows lowered ominously and Derek stared back defiantly.

"So?" Tejar repeated, his tone softer, and Derek saw a glint of approval in the duke's eyes, quickly gone.

"I've paid my punishment for a week now," Derek announced. "I've eaten three fine meals a day, four when I could get an extra, slept until noon, behaved myself admirably, and not once have I touched a taste of ale. I'm sorry I got drunk like I did. I'm sorry I embarrassed you, if I did. You know that I hate failing you, sire."

"Swilling ale in that ramshackle inn isn't a solution," Tejar huffed, then waved his hand dismissively. "Nor is stalking into my study, insolent and outspoken. Tell me, Derek, why didn't you find the witch in Mionn?"

"I didn't know she was in Mionn. Is she?" Derek carefully controlled his expression as he waited for the answer, reminding himself to breathe normally. Tejar had a shrewd gaze and knew him too well. He had never dissembled with Tejar, wanting to serve him as his father had served Duke Selwyn and find his honor in that. For that service Derek had excused the duke's excesses, his temper, his easy cruelty, and even his frequent misunderstanding of Derek's motives in serving him, thinking Derek worked only for his pay like too many others in the duke's service. That earlier devotion and its attendant lack of practice at lies could easily betray him now, as did all habits that become part of a man's purpose, and thus send Derek off to the fate that surely awaited Stefan. Stefan Quinby was Countess Rowena's favored liegeman, and the duke's hatred for Airlie's countess was well-known. He would kill Stefan without a twitch of his eyebrow, even a quickening of his breath, and then use the death to destroy Airlie's countess. Derek saw the confirmation of that predictable intent in the pleased expression on the duke's face and in the confidence of his gestures—indeed, in his easy forgiveness of Derek's lapse. "Sire?" Derek prompted, taking the risk.

"She was in Mionn. She's dead now." Derek didn't catch

what next Tejar said, although he knew he'd missed something in the next few seconds. He blinked.

"Dead?" he asked faintly.

"Drowned in a river." Tejar shrugged indifferently. "The word came from Count Charles with the ship's captain this afternoon, along with his prisoner. Too bad. I had hopes for a witch trial to pin Melfallan, but instead, still to the better, I've got the liegeman who was traveling with her, Rowena's liegeman, and the clear proof of the countess's treachery in that fact." Tejar smirked. "Let Rowena try to explain *this*. I'll disenfeoff her and then, by Ocean, I'll hang her, and hang her son to boot."

Oh yes, Derek thought dazedly, the duke is quite happy.

"How do you know it was Brierley Mefell?" he asked, clinging to that hope.

The duke shrugged. "I sent notices to Mionn to look for her, and Count Charles found her in Flinders. The boat cracked up as they were bringing her downriver. Too bad, as I said, but at least we found her and I'll find some way to use that against Yarvannet. Not that I don't have a tool to use already." Tejar smiled and shook his head. "Garth's lady was most useful in pointing the way."

"I don't understand, sire," Derek said carefully.

"I sent Sir Galbert to Yarvannet to talk to her, and she's the one who confirmed the witch was alive. Got it from Melfallan's own lady wife. Ironic, don't you think? Lady Joanna has sent me several letters in the past few months: it seems she doesn't like Melfallan at all, and so Galbert pinned her. But how to use it, I wonder? Should I expose Lady Joanna's treachery and get her husband disenfeoffed? A new and untried marcher lord in the lands next to Briding would open the way for the march to Tiol in the summer. Or, hmm, should I turn it into Saray's treachery and finally break that alliance between the earldoms when Melfallan divorces her and ships her back to Efe? Ah, but Earl Giles will storm and rant at the insult. I might send a spy to Mionn just to watch and bring me a report." The duke actually rubbed his hands in anticipation. "What? You don't believe Lady

Joanna would betray her earl? You underestimate Sir Galbert—and perhaps the lady herself. Here: look at this."

The duke shuffled among papers on one side of his desk and extracted a single sheet of paper. "Galbert made her write it down. A nice touch, that, but Sir Galbert always was deft." Derek took the paper and looked at it.

I, Lady Joanna of Carbrooke, attest that Lady Saray told me that the witch Brierley Mefell is alive; Earl Melfallan himself told her so.

"But it doesn't say Mionn." Reluctantly, Derek handed back Lady Joanna's note to the duke.

"Didn't have to," the duke said gruffly and slipped the note under the cover of other papers on his desk. "I sent notices everywhere except Yarvannet and Airlie—all I needed was the certainty she was alive so that the threats produced her, not made me look like a fool all over again. But it makes sense. Where else could she go but Mionn? Airlie was too dangerous, and she couldn't go back to Yarvannet. Count Toral wouldn't hide her in Lim, and Lady Margaret of Tyndale wouldn't dare, and I hadn't a sniff of her in Briding, despite the extra men I sent there to watch Count Parlie. But whatever—" He casually waved his hand. Yes, the duke was very pleased. "The best part of that note, you see, is that it implicates Melfallan. I have him now where I want him. And I have a task for you, now that you are properly humbled, my good Derek." The duke smiled and nodded, pretending a joke, pretending good camaraderie with his spy, his trusted man, a man now quite forgiven. "A delicate task, one suited to your talents," Tejar added, openly flattering him now. "Go to Yarvannet and find out why Melfallan's own wife betrayed him. I want that fact."

A tiny corner of Joanna's note protruded from beneath the papers that concealed it. Derek forced himself to look away and focused again on Duke Tejar.

"Maybe Lady Saray didn't know she betrayed him," he suggested. "Surely Lady Joanna hasn't confided to the earl's own lady that she's been writing to you."

"Likely not," Tejar agreed. "Her stupidity is one of the

possibilities. Find out for me, one way or the other. Hmph. You'll need some money, I suppose."

"And extra for bribes," Derek suggested, and watched Tejar stand up and walk to the chest on the wall near the door. The duke sorted through the keys on his belt, looking for the small key to the money chest he kept there, his back to Derek. Derek leaned slightly, reached out his arm, and tweaked Joanna's note from the stack of papers, folded it, and slipped it inside his tunic, all while Tejar was busy with his key. The next moment Tejar opened the chest, took out the money box, and brought it back to the desk.

If Derek had mistimed his quick movement, misjudged the duke's peripheral vision, he had just cooked his own goose in her grease. He watched, his face carefully schooled to polite interest as the duke sat down with a soft grunt, worked his key in the lock of the money box, and flipped open the lid. "What amount?" the duke said. "Two hundred livres?"

"That will be ample, sire. I'll bring back what I don't use."

Tejar nodded absently and counted out a hundred silver coins, then pushed them across the desk toward Derek. "Bring me the news I want to hear, Derek. If you need help, talk to one of the castle cooks, goes by the name Gillan now. He was once a soldier in the duchess's service, and has performed quite well the last few years, if rather independently. He's the one who poisoned Earl Audric last spring, and Galbert says he had a hand in the attempt on the infant, too, none of that on my orders, of course."

"Of course not, sire," Derek said obediently, not believing it for an instant. "Gillan, you said?"

"Formerly Hugh Bachet." Tejar considered a moment. "Besides the news about Lady Saray, learn what you can about Count Sadon. That's a wound in Yarvannet's side I want to help fester. I want the timing right with both father and son when I send Landreth back to Yarvannet. Send regular reports about Farlost. Hugh knows the usual route."

"Yes, sire. I won't fail you." It was an easy lie, easier than he expected, but Derek had made his choice weeks ago when a witch had touched him, and through the touch had saved him. Now all it needed was to play the token to its success.

Derek stood up, bowed to his duke, and then walked the several steps to the door, opened it, went out, returned Richard's hard glare measure for measure, and strolled onward down the hallway, conscious of the slight scratching of Joanna's letter against his chest. Did it rustle? He placed his hand on his chest and puffed out his cheeks, as if a bit of dinner had risen in the gorge, and subtly shifted it around his ribs to a safer position. No one bothered to notice, but Derek was very cautious, far more cautious than his duke had been just now.

The duke had said too much, too happy with his satisfaction to guard his words with Derek as he should, even if Derek were still his trusted man. Duke Tejar was a prudent lord, usually cautious, even with a spy in his service for eight years, a successful spy who had brought him several tidbits the duke had found most useful. There will be war in the summer, Derek now knew, and the duke's own agent, a cook named Gillan, once Hugh, had poisoned Earl Audric, and Landreth would be coming to Yarvannet to prompt Farlost's treachery. Perhaps later Duke Tejar would remember all he had revealed and frown; perhaps later the duke would send another spy after Derek to spy on his spy, or perhaps not.

At the next turning of the hallway, while palace servants bustled past, Derek looked to the right, where the halls would take him to the stables, where a horse awaited him to carry him to Yarvannet. He looked left, where the halls led through many a turning and descending stair to the dungeons deep beneath the palace. He smiled slightly, paused yet another moment to savor the moment, and then turned left, striding down the hall.

Halfway there, Derek detoured toward his rooms. He took care to stroll along the smoothly polished stone floors of the palace, aware of the servants bustling in the hallways, each with bright, alert eyes. In his room he packed two bags, one for himself and one for Stefan, and then hefted them to his shoulder and went out again, closing the door behind him. He paused a moment after he did so, then shrugged.

For you, he thought, to the pale and slender witch who had spared his life, and in that short meeting had changed all that Derek was. The duke had killed her, as surely as if he had waved his hand and caused that boat wreck. The duke had pursued her throughout the lands, intending to use her as a tool, nothing but a tool, to ruin Yarvannet. The duke had murdered Yarvannet's old earl, and now would seek to murder Earl Melfallan with war and treachery—a man Brierley had admired, a man of whom she had spoken with such confidence, such trust. The moment Derek had decided his fate was not this moment, not this last time he left his room in this palace in his duke's service—nor when he had stolen Joanna's letter nor packed these bags on his shoulder. When Brierley had reached out her hand and touched him, healing his desperate wound, she had won him as a knight in her service, although he was no knight and she had no service left to offer. Sweet mistress, he thought sadly, Ocean give you peace. Derek walked onward, away from his life as it was, into another.

Another hallway, a descent of stairs. At the turning above the stairway to the dungeon, he put down his packs in an alcove, then paused a moment to choose his disguise. He looked down at his clothes, measuring the man they suggested, fine enough but not fine enough to be a lord, yet not a soldier or farmer either: ah, yes. Lord Dail had just acquired another clark, another of the few hundred such servants who swarmed the palace. He rummaged in his pack and pulled out Lady Joanna's letter and folded it into quarters, then folded it again into eights. It would do as the distraction: the guard wouldn't be conscious long enough to read it.

He straightened and put on the clark, then walked down the last set of stairs. A single guard sat at the front table in the hallway, an older man with grizzled hair and the reddish nose of the habitual drunkard, the usual type given service in the dungeon, being no good for anywhere else. Derek saw only him, as he expected. The guard looked up blearily as he heard the footsteps, then scowled.

Derek swaggered up to his table, young and arrogant and privileged, the better man because he served Lord Dail, the duke's trusted counselor, not a hungover guard who sat dozing in this pit of a dungeon. He looked down his nose at the guard and sneered. "I'm here to see the new prisoner," Derek said. "Lord Dail had ordered several questions."

"If you work for Lord Dail," the man retorted, squinting up at him, "you know there are procedures."

Derek smirked and held out the paper. "Of course there are. I'm glad you remembered."

The guard took the paper suspiciously and began to unfold it with slightly quaking hands, all his attention on the simple task. He never saw the punch coming. His head snapped back, his body came off the chair, and he flopped down hard on the floor. Derek bent over him and took the dungeon keys from his belt, repocketed the letter, and then seized the man's collar. He dragged the guard to the nearest cell, then quickly flipped open the grate on the door— empty. Another half a minute and the guard was inside the cell on the cot, tied nicely with his own belt. Derek covered him with a blanket before he left: no reason to risk a chill.

He locked the cell door, then listened anxiously for any sounds from above. All he needed was a few minutes to find Stefan and move him, for whatever might come later. Their escape from the palace was by no means a guarantee, however well Derek knew every twist and turning of the palace underlevels. As boys, Derek and his brother had played in these dungeons, and like dungeon mice knew every secret way. May Mother Ocean lend the help, he wished earnestly.

He ran quickly up the stairs for the packs hidden behind the turning, and then returned as quickly. He flipped open the guard book on the table. "Stefan Quinby of Airlie," the book read, the last notation. "Liegeman to Countess Rowena. Charges: harboring a witch and treason." Hanging charges, Derek thought, as he had suspected. That notation promised a countess's downfall and a new lord for Airlie. Who among the duke's men would it be? Bartol, the duchess's bastard nephew? One of Lord Dail's sons? Tejar had a dozen lordlings among whom to choose. He remembered Rowena's pleasant capital city with its smiling people, and thought how that would change when Tejar put a favored toady into Rowena's place, a lord to gouge coins from every source, to punish any resistance, to do the duke's bidding without question, to take and never give.

Cell Sixteen, the jail log said, the next floor down. Derek hefted the packs and descended to the next floor of the dungeon, cautious in case he might find another guard there, but the stair and hallway were empty. He unlocked the door with the dungeon guard's keys, swung it open, and there was Stefan, blood newly dripping off his face. Had they beaten him again? Or had they failed to catch him when he tripped? Stefan looked up dazedly, and his defiance shifted to open surprise.

"What are *you* doing here?" he blurted, recognizing Derek as easily as Derek had known him. "Are you the torturer now?"

"So you remember me," Derek grunted. "Good." Derek quickly crossed the floor and pulled him to his feet, a bit rough in his haste. Stefan has been very ill-used. He had a black eye and other fading bruises, with enough variety in their fading that Derek guessed Stefan's resistance had steadily provoked his guards. Stefan wavered on his feet as he stood, one hand cradled protectively against his chest. A broken finger perhaps, but Derek would not test that now. Stefan blinked dazedly at Derek, and nearly swayed right off his feet. Derek grabbed his sleeve and tunic to stop the fall, then pulled Stefan's arm around his neck. "The more you fight them, Stefan, the more they hit you. What did you do? Try to escape?"

"Yes," Stefan mumbled, then resisted as Derek tried to move him toward the door. "What are you doing?" he demanded. "I'm not going anywhere with you, spy."

"Shut up. I'm rescuing you." Stefan still resisted the pull, on the brink of another wild struggle that had won him nothing but bad bruises. Derek shook him impatiently. "If you want your life and the life of your countess, come with me."

"Why should I trust you?" Stefan protested groggily, and still would not come.

Derek eased him back on the cot, then glared down at him. "Do you have a choice? Put what thought you can together and answer."

Stefan thought about it for a groggy moment. "My head hurts," he complained tiredly. "All right. She trusted you, more than I would."

"She did?" Derek asked, startled.

"I never did understand why. Haul me away, Derek." Derek helped him to his feet, being careful about moving him. Despite his care, he heard Stefan moan in pain as Derek turned him unwisely.

"Sorry," Derek muttered, and tried to hold him more carefully. "This way, Stefan. We haven't much time."

Derek helped him down to the stairs at the far end of the hallway, and they descended another level, and then another level still. The light grew dimmer, for the lamps were not as carefully tended on the lower levels, sometimes allowed to burn out for a week before some boy came around with new oil. At the end of the long passageway on the bottom level, Derek leaned Stefan against him and fumbled for the keys. One fit the cell door and it creaked and groaned as it opened, dust sifting down. How long since someone had slept in this cell? Years? Derek hoped so.

"My head is strange," Stefan muttered. "I can't think."

"Just hold on a moment," Derek encouraged him. "Come in here."

"Why?" Stefan asked suspiciously.

"I'm coming in, too. Just go in, Stefan. I have to check upstairs and bring the bags, and then I'll return." Stefan didn't move. "So stand where you are, and when you fall down, I won't be here to catch you."

Stefan frowned. "Why are you doing this?" he asked, and sounded genuinely baffled.

"A witch's touch, a mercy given. How could you have been with her all those weeks and not know?"

Stefan blinked at him. "She said you had a knight's heart."

"She did?" Derek blurted, then blinked at sudden tears that smarted and burned. Sweet mistress! Had she known him that well, known him better than he even knew himself? Or had she trusted, simply because she chose to give the trust? He dragged his sleeve across his face. "Will you fall or go into that cell, Stefan?" he asked, with no patience at all.

"All right, all right." Stefan reached out an arm for support, and Derek helped him into the dusty cell, then lowered him onto the rough cot against one wall. The leather sank alarmingly beneath Stefan's weight, but the cot managed to hold itself together. Then Derek left Stefan, moving quickly.

He took a lamp from the wall and retrieved the bags, then checked for blood drops on the stone floors and stairs, finding a few but not many. On the lowest level, they had left footsteps in the dust, and he quickly pulled a tunic from his bag to retrace his steps, erasing what trail they had left. Now, he thought, pausing a moment, how to play it? A door stood locked on the second level, and he knew it led upward to the stables. How that door tempted him now, but Stefan was too weak and the search would come too soon for safety. With a muttered curse, he pulled out the warder's keys and hunted a key for the door. If it were unlocked, perhaps even left slightly ajar, the search would go elsewhere, or so he hoped. He looked up as he heard a shout above, then quickly unlocked the door and pulled it slightly ajar. Then he ran down the stairs again and locked himself and Stefan into their dusty cell.

Stefan was still awake, and now eyed him with renewed suspicion. Derek sat down on the floor beside him, not trusting the cot to take more than one man's weight. He moved the wick-key on the lamp, raising the light slightly. "Did they break your nose? It looks like it. How's your head?"

"It's still there," Stefan muttered weakly, and tried to push Derek's hand away when Derek turned his face closer to the lamplight.

"When were you beaten, Stefan?"

"Which day did you have in mind? I got sunk the moment Count Charles recognized me. Maybe he thought shipping me off to the duke would please Earl Giles, or maybe he just didn't want the trouble of explaining me. And how could he explain? He didn't know I was in Mionn, but get the duke to believe that." Stefan blinked and tried to focus again on Derek. "Let's see, the poundings. I tried to run in Arlenn and they beat me up then, and then later on the ship after I tried to go over the railing, and then in Lim—Count Toral helped with that—" His voice trailed away. "My head hurts," he complained.

"Stay awake, Stefan."

"Why?" Stefan asked resistantly.

"Ocean alive, man! I'm rescuing you. Hasn't that penetrated yet?" Derek opened one of the travel bags and drew out a water bottle and cloth to wash away the blood on Stefan's face.

"Why should you rescue me?" Stefan said, shoving his hands away.

"Because I want to," Derek said in exasperation, "if you won't listen to the other reason. Now shut up and do as I say. We'll hide until nightfall—or longer if you need the rest. I think you do."

"And go where?" Stefan asked, more mildly. Derek wetted the cloth and gently dabbed at Stefan's bruised face.

"Stop complaining. I'd take you to Carandon, but it would be unsafe for both you and your countess. The duke will have his soldiers on the Airlie road within hours; we'd have little chance. I thought instead we might go to Yarvannet. I have something Earl Melfallan must see, and other news he should hear." Stefan frowned at him in bewilderment, then closed his eyes wearily and gave it up. When his face was cleaned of most of the blood, Derek helped him lie back on the cot, then covered him with a blanket from the packs.

The noise above their heads rose to a great hubbub, with running feet and muffled shouts. Derek listened anxiously, but none came down that last flight of stairs, not when they found the upper door ajar. More shouts, a quick rumble of feet, and then nothing.

He felt Stefan's eyes on him and looked at him, saw the wry smile. "She said that we might be friends in different circumstances," Stefan said faintly. "Perhaps we've found them."

"Who? Brierley?"

"She said that when I told her we should have killed you for her safety. She said you had a knight's honor and would have a hard choice now. I guess you've made your choice, Lanvalle. My thanks." He reached out his hand and waited until Derek took it, then closed his eyes, slumping back on the cot.

"Is she truly dead?" Derek asked.

"I'm not sure. The count's men said so, and I fear it's true. A boat was wrecked and bodies were found. Everyone is assuming she is dead. Jain hasn't come to tell me differently. But of course he can't—Megan isn't here. Jain never leaves her, you know."

"Jain? Megan?" But Stefan was asleep.

Derek sat next to him by the cot, his hand on his chest, making sure that Stefan still breathed, and he hoped that no blood vessel had broken in his brain when the duke's men had beaten him. He hoped Stefan wasn't dying, and that this crazy rescue would work. Eventually a man could cast all his lot into one path—an ironic choice if it then fails, yielding nothing while the man has lost everything else. The darkness of the cell surrounded him, illuminated only by the gleam of light from the shielded lantern. As a caution Derek turned the lamp still lower, then bowed his head and began their long wait.

A knight's honor: had she truly thought that of him? If Brierley had thought it, perhaps it was true.

～

"No, your grace! Not like that!" Philippe exclaimed, aghast.

"What?" Melfallan demanded, then stood impatiently as

his body servant untied the laces on Melfallan's tunic, then did them up again. "A knot is a knot, Philippe."

"Only to the ignorant, your grace," Philippe said with spirit. "There! All done!"

"Did you just call me ignorant?" Melfallan looked down at himself and truly did not see much of a difference, even if Philippe had. "I don't believe it. You just wanted to fuss over me as usual."

"Yes, your grace," Philippe murmured, then took Melfallan's silver circlet from its case on the dresser and offered it solemnly. "Count Parlie's courier is waiting to see you and Sir James. You should wear this, too. After all, the count is an important ally: it will not do to offend him." Philippe tsked at the horrible thought.

"Am I supposed to put that on in some special way, too?" Melfallan asked dryly, taking the circlet.

"I'm sure Earl Giles thinks so." Philippe's old eyes twinkled. "But I suppose plopping it on serves just as well, your grace." Melfallan promptly took Philippe's dare and plopped it, then grinned as Philippe rolled his eyes. "You're hopeless," Philippe mourned.

"But you keep trying, Ocean knows why. What's it been now, Philippe? Twenty years you've been trying to teach me proper dress and manners, ever since I was five. Isn't that when you were put in charge of my nursery?"

"You were two, not five." Philippe straightened a small wrinkle on Melfallan's sleeve, then brushed off dust that wasn't there. "That makes it twenty-three years, not twenty, ever since your mother in her despair called upon me for help, and now almost twenty-four years, your grace, with little sign of improvement. This won't do." He stepped back and smiled with pride. "You look truly an earl!" he announced.

"I'm relieved you think so," Melfallan retorted. "Some mornings I really worry about that, Philippe, maybe so much I'll make myself ill. Think about it: I could lie in bed all day long and not have to get dressed at all. I like that idea: let's do it."

Philippe shook his head and sternly tsked. "As I said, hopeless." Melfallan winked at him.

He heard quick footsteps in the outer hallway, and a moment later Saray came into the room, a silken nightgown in her hands, its weave so delicate it would hide very little when she wore it. She held it up for him to see, then jounced it slightly, making the fabric shiver. "How about this for tonight?" she asked. "Not that it will stay on me too long, I'm sure," she added coyly, batting her eyelashes. Philippe froze in place at her words, and now slowly reddened with embarrassment, not knowing whom or what to look at.

"Saray!" Melfallan protested. "Not in front of Philippe!"

Saray pouted her lips. "Oh, I'm sure Philippe knows all about what happens between us. All the castle knows." Saray held up the nightgown to her body and moved her hips enticingly, almost blatantly. "Oh, how I wish bedtime were here," she crooned.

Philippe made a strangled sound and abruptly fled the room.

Saray turned in surprise and watched him go. "What's wrong with him?" she asked, genuinely startled.

Melfallan angrily snatched the nightgown from her hands and tossed it on the dresser. "You shouldn't say things like that in front of Philippe," he told her. "He's an old man who's never married—he doesn't know that much about women, not that way. And he's very prudish, very correct. And you come in here, flaunting that indecent gown and acting like that—"

"Indecent!"

"Hells, Saray, the thing's practically transparent."

"Well, I'd think you'd like it!" she flared back. "If you had your way, I'd be naked all the time. Isn't that what you told me, try to be natural?"

"Not in front of Philippe!" He gestured angrily. "And I didn't mean that kind of natural, and you know it."

He watched, his heart sinking, as Saray deliberately chose to misunderstand him. Likely Saray had wanted this fight for some time, for once not pretending all was sweetness and light, for once letting him know how she really felt about her own brazen behavior in the bedroom, the sexual passion she hated. In a sudden flash of understanding, Melfallan realized that Saray had wanted him to reject the carnal woman Lady Joanna had urged Saray to become. By responding to her advances, as Saray saw it, Melfallan had told her that she had failed him previously as wife, that Saray as she willed herself to be had not been enough for him—and so he had gravely insulted her when he had meant to be kind. He now saw the hurt and anger in the flash of her eyes, the proud lift of her chin.

"Saray—" he began, appalled by his mistake, and reached out to her. Saray flinched and quickly stepped backward, then tossed her red-haired head, wanting her quarrel and determined to get it.

"Then I should be unnatural, I suppose?" she threw at him. "Make up your mind, Melfallan. Clothes or no clothes, every night or not at all. Let me know when you decide." And then she snatched the gown from the dresser and stalked out.

Melfallan sat down in a chair, and was still sitting when Philippe came back. His old beloved friend stopped in the doorway and hesitated. Melfallan saw Philippe consider the usual breeziness, the teasing, the happy pretense of taking all aghast. After another moment Philippe instead came into the room and knelt down awkwardly on one knee in front of Melfallan's chair, then bowed his head in shame. "I'm sorry," he quavered.

Melfallan laid his hands on Philippe's bony shoulders, then bent and kissed him. "It's not your fault, Philippe. Don't think that."

"But—"

"No." Melfallan shook his head. "It's not." He patted Philippe's shoulder. "Come now, get up," he insisted. "What do you think you are, a lord swearing fealty?" he asked. "What a pretension! What an outrage! This won't do."

Philippe looked up and smiled sweetly. "I don't need to swear fealty to you," he said. "It's quite unnecessary: you

won my heart the first time you toddled into my arms,
Melfallan, and have never lost it."

"And you think I don't know that? I know it every day.
Come now: this floor is too hard on your old knees."

Melfallan stood and helped Philippe to his feet, then
brushed lint from Philippe's shoulder that wasn't there and
straightened a wrinkle. It won him another smile, a nod, and
for the moment that would have to be enough.

After Philippe had gone, Melfallan set his mouth hard.
This time Saray would not get the excuses he always gave
her, he vowed. This time he would wait for the apology from
her, not the other way around, and if that apology never
came, so be it. I mean it, he thought.

~

If Saray looked for him, whether to continue their quarrel or
to pretend nothing had happened, nothing at all, she would
look in his tower study or Sir James's office, and so Melfallan went elsewhere. As he mounted the stairs to the battlements, he sighed as he remembered Parlie's courier,
patiently waiting, as couriers were often forced to wait. It
seemed his recent habit to keep couriers waiting, if two were
enough for a habit, and now Sir James was waiting as well.
He walked through the upper gallery, with its tall cloister
windows. The rain chattered against the windowpanes, a
soft, comforting sound. He paused a moment to listen. The
Pass rainstorms always persisted through the month named
for the event, sluicing down on the fields and harbor, turning
the roads into mud, the fields into damp stumps of grass.

Rain—he'd forgotten about the daily rains. He'd get wet,
very wet indeed, out on the battlements. Melfallan hesitated
and then stubbornly walked onward, nodded to the soldier at
the doorway, and went out into the open air. Rain misted
across the harbor below, shifting in broad curtains across the
water. Out to sea the rain clouds clung near the ocean's surface, blending air and water into a near-seamless slate and
blue. As he stopped by the battlement wall, the rain pattered

on his head and shoulders, then seeped cold fingers inside his collar and tickled its snaky paths down his skin. Melfallan scowled at the sky and folded his arms across his chest, then glowered down at the harbor.

What do I do? he asked himself, and for the first time seriously considered divorce, a decision that would be as much political as emotional. The emotional side he knew too well, for he had struggled for years to understand his wife, only to be baffled again and again. Saray could be sweetness itself, openly devoted to him for all to see, a gracious and laughing creature that men envied as his wife. She professed to think only of him, to want only what he wanted, and often it had seemed true. They had shared the grief of three children lost during pregnancy, and they had rejoiced when Audric had lived, coming as closely together at that time as they had ever been. At the Blessing only a few weeks ago, Saray had stood proudly with him as he claimed their son, and they had shared a fragile peace at that time, even though she knew then about Brierley.

Is it my fault? he asked himself. He had always assumed it was, and certainly his love for another woman put him solidly in the column labeled "Betrayer." His brief affair with Brierley at the cabin hadn't been his first, nor the second nor third—only the first affair that had genuine significance in his marriage, and likely Saray had sensed the peril. If nothing else, her instincts were excellent. Saray knew precisely how to manipulate her husband—not with cold indifference, not with a purpose to use the other, but to protect herself. She had learned those skills in Mionn, where her unhappy family had deprived her of love, and she used them now, as instinctively as a falcon used its wings in effortless flight. Saray used her pretending as a shield, designing reality as she wished it to be. Perhaps in her deepest heart, she still believed she did not deserve to be loved.

He had found her that day in her chamber, working on her stitchery, and she had told him her options, gravely considering what she should do. Somehow she had then confided in Joanna, likely because Joanna was the best among her noble lady friends, someone who genuinely liked her, someone who did not mock or ignore or deny Saray the perfection she wanted. And Joanna had given her this idea about Saray the Seductress, a role Saray did not play well: Saray certainly knew that, and so had turned her option to her own ends. Melfallan had been put to the test, but not the test Joanna had intended: Saray had wanted proof of her husband's love, and then had designed the test to make him fail. If he had rebuffed her, it would have been proof he wanted Brierley more. When he responded, the denial was just as bitter. Saray had made it so, and probably didn't realize she had.

What more can I do? he thought in frustration. What else is there to try?

She may never change, he knew now, and looked up bleakly at the sky. Had she deliberately chosen her moment today, knowing Philippe would be there with him, knowing how easily she could humiliate Philippe with that revealing gown? Philippe was a vulnerable man, an old fussbudget who enjoyed his frets and poses as much as Saray enjoyed her own, and a man always shy with women, who likely had never tried to court a woman in his whole life, and a man Melfallan loved above nearly all others. Perhaps Saray had miscalculated that last point and got more of a quarrel than she expected: to Saray, servants were usually furniture. Probably so. But that she wanted a quarrel, that was clear.

Now what is the test? he asked himself, for surely there was another test in the making. Saray always used their quarrels to make him come to her, to bring her assurances, to gain her regret. That, too, was clear. What is the test?

Does she want me to go to her humbly and beg her forgiveness, then tell her that she is lovely and seductive and wanted, and take her to bed for a night of wild passion? Or do I go to her humbly and beg, then tell her she is lovely and seductive, but admit that sex should have its limits? Do I apologize for wanting her? Do I beg her forgiveness for my lust? Do we then solemnly agree that Saray was right all along? If I did all that, would I pass the test? Or not?

What *is* the test? If I choose the first, will I find the second was the right answer? If I choose the second, will I find it was really the first? Who can know? Perhaps even Saray didn't know—at least until Melfallan chose, so that Saray could name the other.

He closed his eyes wearily and sighed deeply. No more, Saray. I don't want to play games, not anymore. I married you that lovely summer nearly seven years ago, and I meant to love you all my life. Does that mean I must keep to that vow, no matter what has happened since? Does that mean I must, even when you never allow me to win? Are promises disposable? He thought not. Other men might choose differently, but he would change as a man if he broke his promise and divorced her.

And what of Audric? As heir to Yarvannet, their son must be raised in Tiol. Although not explicitly stated in the Charter, all the High Lords expected it, and to arrange otherwise could affect Audric's right to accede. Yet he doubted Saray would stay in Yarvannet after a divorce, even to stay with her son. Stay in the court where the other noble ladies could mock her? Stay and watch Melfallan perhaps marry another woman, perhaps even Brierley, that commoner nothing of a midwife? Even life in her father's court, as bleak and empty as it would surely be, would be better than that. Melfallan sighed, and knew he had found his answer, not in the need of his lands nor the rightness of a promise kept nor even in his own heart, but in Audric. Melfallan's own mother had died when he was three: he barely remembered her, and had always keenly felt the loss. He would not inflict his son with that same grief.

A simple answer for once, he thought, and took a deep breath. For once, simple.

But what of Brierley? he thought, then sighed and bowed his head, and the rain dripped down his face. No, not so simple. Not simple at all.

⁓

Saray was waiting for him when he returned to his chamber to change his clothes. "You're all wet!" she exclaimed in surprise. "Why did you go out in the rain, Melfallan? What foolishness! Here, let me help you."

"And none of it happened, of course," Melfallan said tiredly. He stripped off his wet tunic and tossed it on the floor, then opened his wardrobe door.

Saray stopped abruptly in her bustling. "What?" she asked.

"Oh yes, 'what?' It's always 'what,' one after another, and nothing gets solved."

Saray bit her lip. "You're angry at me because I embarrassed Philippe."

"Good guess, Saray."

"If I apologize to Philippe," she asked meekly, "will you forgive me?"

Melfallan looked at her and saw the regret—for what? For hurting Philippe? He doubted it. Maybe it was another lady rule about not overly abusing the servants, or, far more likely, the mainstay of never displeasing one's husband in any way whatsoever. He sighed. "I always forgive you, Saray. Why don't you notice that?"

"Maybe sometimes you shouldn't, to teach me a lesson."

"I don't want to teach you lessons. But, yes, it would be good if you apologized. More importantly, if you don't like Joanna's type of sex, you should say so. Don't set up tests for me. Don't force me to pretend along with you."

"You don't like it?" Saray quavered. "I thought—" She broke off and looked away, heat rising into her face.

"Not when you don't, and I know you don't. I didn't marry Joanna—I married you. You don't have to change into somebody else. When did I ask you to do that?"

Saray had paled, and he could not bear the stricken look on her face. He turned back to the dresser and pulled open a drawer, found a new set of hose.

"I'm sorry I failed you," she whispered abjectly.

Melfallan repressed a groan and leaned a hand on the dresser, as if it might prop him up with a strength he needed, then made himself turn around to face her—but Saray was gone. He heard the patter of her footsteps in the hallway, quickly fading, and thought to follow, then decided against it. After all, what more could he say? What else might make a difference? He didn't know, never knew. He slowly rubbed his face with his hands, then continued the task of changing his clothes.

Count Parlie's courier was fat and bald and a happy man, especially when swilling someone else's wine, as he had apparently spent the last happy hour. He saluted Melfallan with his cup as Melfallan walked in, then belatedly thought to get up and bow.

"Your grace!" he said, bowing a second time. "My name is Edward Sonns. I bear a message from Count Parlie of Briding." Edward looked around and found his pouch on the floor, then produced a letter from its bowels, and bowed again as he presented it.

"Thank you, Master Sonns," Melfallan said, and glanced at Sir James. His justiciar had that patient look Sir James always wore when his patience had nearly run out, but apparently Sir James's irritation had aimed itself at the courier, not at his earl for being late. Melfallan sat down and began to untie the ribbons on Parlie's letter.

"May I have more wine, good sir?" Sonns asked, holding out his cup to Sir James. His tone suggested, however mildly, that Sir James, Yarvannet's justiciar, primarily existed to do that courtesy of pouring wine when Edward Sonns needed it, but then likely anyone would have suited, given a necessary proximity to the wine bottle.

"Absolutely not." Sir James firmly pushed the wine bottle farther down the table, out of the courier's reach.

"Is he really drunk?" Melfallan asked curiously.

"No. It's playacting." Sir James sniffed reflectively and crossed his arms. "Parlie sent him to find something out, and I'm trying to find out what it is. So far I haven't made any progress. He's as deft at hiding things as his count." Sir

James looked at Sonns with little favor, got a happy, drunken smile in return. Sir James sniffed again, unimpressed. "Sonns is Parlie's principal spy," he told Melfallan. "He usually lurks around Darhel to sniff out Tejar's news. Now he's lurking here and I want to know why." Sir James pointed accusingly at Sonns. "You're not leaving Tiol until I do."

"Really?" Sonns asked, visibly amused. "Will you throw me in your dungeon?"

"If necessary," Sir James promised.

Sonns sat up a little straighter. "On what charge?" he demanded.

"Spying." Sir James gave him a wintry smile.

Melfallan unfolded Parlie's letter and glanced through the first page, then looked at the second. "It's not in the letter, Sir James. The duchess is ill, the duke is surly, and nobody likes Count Toral of Lim, and at the end he asks about Evayne Ibelin, a nice touch. There's caution here: something has happened in Darhel to make Parlie careful about saying too much to us, something that affects Yarvannet—but not directly?" He studied the courier's face a moment, but the man was smooth as glass. "Perhaps affecting Airlie?" he guessed, and saw the slight reaction in the shift of the eyes.

"*What* about Airlie?" Sir James pounced.

"I'm not here to bandy words," Sonns declared loftily, "or play guessing games."

"It's either that," Melfallan told him firmly, "or sit in my dungeon, Master Sonns. We'll put you in a cell that lets the rain leak in. The nights are still cold enough to make the puddle freeze, but if you keep your feet up on the cot, you shouldn't have a problem." He smiled.

"You wouldn't really lock me up, your grace?" Sonns asked cautiously. "Tell me you won't."

"I really would," Melfallan replied. "Out with it, Sonns. What did Count Parlie send you to say to me?"

"I'm to say my news *after* I decide I should say it." The man puffed out his chest, posing. "Those were my instructions."

Melfallan tossed the letter on Sir James's table, then stood up. "Parlie likes his games, and maybe he likes yours, but I don't."

"No, wait!" Sonns raised his hand, stopping Melfallan as he headed toward the door. "Don't leave, your grace." He sighed, then gestured his surrender. "All right, all right. I was sent to tell you that Count Charles of Arlenn has arrested Stefan Quinby, the countess's liegeman. The duke plans to charge him with treason, and intends to use the charge against Countess Rowena to disenfeoff her. The count sent me as soon as he heard the news, thinking you should be warned."

"Arrested? How long ago?" Melfallan demanded.

Sonns squinted. "A good two weeks now, I suppose. This Quinby might be hanged already, if the duke's justice is swift."

"What was the specific item of treason?" Sir James asked quietly.

"Witch-harboring, if you can believe that." Sonns snorted. "I swear our duke grows more odd every year. First that matter with his torturer killing a prisoner, and now he thinks he's got another witch running around in Mionn."

"Was anyone else arrested?" Melfallan asked, trying hard to control his voice.

"Not that I heard." Sonns tipped his head to the side and put on a baffled look, so much like Count Parlie's own dissembling that Melfallan knew Sonns lied. There *was* other news, and Parlie had chosen to withhold it. But for what reason? Melfallan traded a puzzled glance with Sir James. "Why do you ask?" Sonns said.

"Just wondering." Melfallan managed a shrug, a tight smile. "Please tell the count we thank him for his news, Master Sonns." Melfallan picked up the wine bottle and set it in front of Parlie's spy. "Enjoy yourself."

"Thank you, your grace." Sonns nodded and smiled, then tipped the bottle to pour wine into his cup.

"By the way," Melfallan said, "what *did* Parlie send you to find out?"

The spy paused in his pouring, then carefully set the bottle back on the table. He sighed, looked up at Melfallan, and squinted. Another sigh, a wave of the hand, and all of it a game. Sonns cleared his throat, then sighed again. Another wave, another sigh, and then the spy relented, if he truly did. How to tell? This spy was clever, as all Parlie's spies would be clever, most clever indeed, like their count. "The count wants to know," Sonns said reluctantly, "if this Quinby was guarding your witch, the witch Hagan supposedly killed. If so, it's Yarvannet that might be disenfeoffed. Even a count as friendly as Count Parlie must think of his own safety." Sonns spread his hands and smiled, embarrassed, but what else could a prudent High Lord do? What, indeed? Melfallan tightened his lips. "Count Parlie told me to be honest if you were clever enough to ask."

Melfallan nodded grimly. "A nice bit of flattery: tell Parlie I appreciate it. And tell him his honesty obviously now comes in degrees." Sonns blinked in surprise. "You know something else. I want to know what it is."

"I've told you all I know, your grace," Sonns professed.

"The Hells you have. I get enough games from the duke— I don't need Count Parlie adding another measure, not if he wants to keep our alliance. Consider that threat before you answer, Sonns, and then think of your lord's real interests. Was anybody else arrested?"

"No, your grace, I swear!"

Melfallan slammed his fist on the table. "Tell me!" Sonns flinched hard enough to drop his cup, spilling the wine in a spreading pool.

"You had better tell him," Sir James advised. "There are certain facts you don't know, that your count doesn't know, and you do your count a disservice now. I'm warning you."

The courier's face abruptly changed, losing the happy cheer, the pretended stupidity, and finally revealed the true man, cold and shrewd. Sonns eyed Sir James for a long moment. "What facts?" he demanded. Sir James snorted. "All right: my news for your facts."

"No," Melfallan said flatly.

Sonns shrugged, considered another moment, then shrugged again. "As you will. There's more to the rumor. It's said your witch drowned in Mionn. A boating accident, as she was being sent to the duke by Count Charles."

Melfallan stared hard at the courier, trying to comprehend, but the understanding eluded him. The courier had said certain words, words with meaning, as words always had meaning, but he might as well have spoken total nonsense.

"Dead?" Sir James asked, appalled, then looked quickly at Melfallan. Parlie's spy promptly noted the look, perhaps gathering a useful fact, a fact to carry to Count Parlie, Melfallan's clever ally who had told his spy to hide the fact that Brierley had died.

Melfallan got to his feet and walked out.

A while later, Melfallan found himself in his bedroom again, sitting on his bed. He looked around dazedly at the bedroom walls, the window, the dresser with his clothes. How did I get here? In truth, he didn't remember. He put his hand to his head, dazed, and his fingers touched his circlet. Wearily, he got to his feet and returned it to its case, then closed the lid. Did I go anywhere after I left Sir James? He frowned, trying to remember, and thought that he had.

He shivered convulsively and belatedly realized his clothes were wet, soaked through again. But I changed my clothes, he thought, bewildered, and looked down at himself. I remember changing my clothes. How had he gotten wet again? He remembered standing on the battlement in the rain, watching the harbor below, then the broad ocean, thinking about divorce. But that was earlier— Melfallan shook his head, utterly confused. He closed his eyes a moment, trying to remember, then gave it up and began to pull off his wet clothes a second time.

"I don't believe it," he whispered hoarsely. "I don't believe she's dead," he insisted, but the words sounded hollow in his ears, achingly hollow, as if their truth would drown him, as it might. "I won't." He found more dry clothes in his wardrobe and struggled to put them on, a task suddenly hard to do, but he managed to pull on a shirt, the trousers, find a new pair of boots.

He heard Saray's footsteps in the outer hallway, and a moment later his wife bustled into the room. "Oh, there you are!" she said brightly. She held up the silken nightgown she carried, dangling it happily. "I thought I'd wear this one tonight. Do you like it?"

"What?" Melfallan blinked at her. But—but this had already happened, too, he thought, even more bewildered. He fumbled a moment as he stared at her. "Yes, that's very nice," he managed.

"Good." Saray beamed at him, and then, abruptly, she wasn't there. Again.

Melfallan raised a shaky hand to his face, and wondered if he was losing his mind. Maybe he was. Maybe now that he knew, the resonance would kill him, the penalty for loving a witch too much.

"I don't believe it," he whispered defiantly. "I won't."

_I_t was late now, long after the suns had set. Melfallan wandered through the hallways of his castle, not knowing where he was going. Occasionally he was greeted by a servant and nodded in return, or a soldier stiffened in salute as he walked by. No one stopped him as he descended the stairs to the Great Hall, nor when he descended farther, into the dungeons. At the end of the lowest cellblock, a level empty of the guards, a heavy, iron-bound door opened onto a winding stair leading downward, a secret stair. The staircase plunged through the rock of the headland, descending flight by flight, winding through hard stone. The sounds of the castle diminished as he descended, and his footsteps rang hollowly on the treads. At the end of the stair, he emerged at the base of the headland into the open air, then descended a final series of stone steps to the beach. Far across the water stood a row of sentinel, rocky islands, with the wink of distant lights that was Amelin.

No one had followed him. Odd that they would leave him alone today: perhaps Sir James had given orders. Melfallan sat down on a low footstone of the headland, and bowed forward over his knees. The cold wind ruffled his hair and clothing, chilling his flesh.

How do I go on if it's true? he asked himself numbly. How do I go on now? All his grand purpose in reuniting the shari'a in Yarvannet, becoming their protector, would vanish. All his reasons for rule, his hopes for independence from the duke, the prosperity of Yarvannet, the safety of his land, his son, might be gone. He knew dimly that he was still in shock, and his thoughts were sluggish and useless.

He raised his head and looked out at the cold sea. He must

not be thinking clearly, he knew, but in truth he hardly
sensed himself thinking at all. There is that wave, there is
the starlight on the water, the distant shadows of the sentinels, the winking of Amelin's lamps against the night:
surely all had some meaning, but he could not find it. The
cold wind ruffled his hair more firmly, then flapped the
collar-end of his tunic against his cheek.

How?

Perhaps I am dead, too, he thought vaguely. Perhaps death
is like this, a lonely beach and a dark sea, where all appears
as it was, but is not. He watched the waves move near the
shore and grew fascinated by their slow surge, imagining the
cold depths, their oblivion. The starlight moved upon the
water, gathering shape, and from the waves arose a sparkling
figure, the hazy shape of a dragon with glittering eyes. It
spread its gossamer wings and bent its head toward him.
Melfallan. Its voice resonated in his mind like the slow surge
of the ocean, deep and insistent. He groaned and covered his
face with his hands.

No, he wished at it. Not without her. When he looked up
again, the sea was empty: he was alone. The starlight
sparkled idly on the waves, moving with the ocean's slow
surge. Tired beyond thinking, Melfallan curled up on the
sand, huddling against the chill of the night.

$\sim$

He stood on the narrow beach far south of the castle headland near Brierley's cave. Fifty feet from shore, the rocky
sentinels of great sea stones, remnants of a sea bluff long
eroded, loomed in the darkness, a dull flicker of waves at
their base. The stars again glimmered on the water, moving
sparkles that shifted uneasily with the incoming surf. The
sea wind buffeted his body, cold and harsh, and he swayed
under its impact.

"Fair lord?" a voice said behind him, and it was Brierley's
sweet voice, lilting and soft.

Melfallan closed his eyes in his agony, and would have

fallen to the sand had her hands not caught his arm and held him. "No," he breathed, and pushed hard at her, making her stagger backward. He tried to stumble away, but the Everlight quickly seized at him again.

"Melfallan, don't!"

"Leave me be!" he cried. "No! No!" He tore at her hands, breaking their grip, and shoved her away. "No!"

"Melfallan!" the Everlight called, her voice panicked, but he would not look at her and threw off her grip again. "Wait!" she cried in despair. "Wait!"

"No!" he shouted. "Not anymore." Melfallan stumbled to one knee, staggered upright again, then began to run. His feet pounded on the sand, his arms pumped, each stride carrying him away from her, away from the truth he did not want, could not bear. Like a beast on the prowl, that truth pursued him, panting at his heels, growling its fury, its claws ready to tear him apart.

"No," Melfallan sobbed, and ran onward.

~~~~~

On a nearby shore in another's dream, near the cove with its sentinels of tall stones, a red-haired figure, a young girl who had not yet lived, stood bereft on the beach, swaying in her grief. She faced the sea and lifted her arms pleadingly.

"No more," she cried out to the night. "I want no more. Take my existence and end me." The sea moved slowly, rising and falling with a hiss of foam, but did not answer. "End me!" she shouted at the Four. "You let them create me, give me life, for *what?* To wait all these centuries, to hope this foolish hope, to endure the loneliness, the grief—" Her voice failed, and she shook with a sudden violent rage, then sighed deeply as it left her just as suddenly. Her hands fell uselessly to her sides, and she sat down abruptly on the cold sand, then buried her face against her knees.

"What is the use?" she whispered after a time. "The Allemanii take everything, murder everything, and now he will not hear me because I look like her, because I am her in too many ways, not myself, not anything different. If truly all is lost, I become his tormenter, and so he, too, is lost to me." She sobbed, then wiped her face with the back of her hand and looked out again at the ocean. The waves climbed the sands, one upon the other, a dim flash of foam in the darkness.

"Where are you?' the Everlight called out to the night. "Where are you for me? Not for the shari'a, not for him, but for me! You made me, a device, a machine to be used, but you allowed me to live too long. You gave me time to learn to love. You let me learn to hope. Why? Where is my fault?" She buried her face against her knees again and sobbed. "I hate you," she whispered.

You cannot hate, a deep Voice answered gently. *It is not in your nature to hate.*

The Everlight raised her head and looked around her, then saw the star-sparkles gather out on the waves near the shore, moving, shifting, and then rising up from the water, outlining the graceful shape of a dragon's head. Basoul floated toward the shore and then slowly emerged on the beach, her glowing eyes fixed on the girl watching her.

"I do hate you," she said defiantly. "I hate you all."

You wish to be ended? Are you sure?

"Yes!"

Are you sure? the sea dragon said more softly, her eyes intent. The Everlight hesitated. *I make no promises,* Basoul said adamantly. *Only hope against all reason, a chance set against near certainty of loss. Can you give that, my daughter?*

"Daughter? Since when do you claim me as daughter?"

As of now—and earlier, when you did not know it. My child, is hope ever ended? Is not hope an act of will, what we choose, what we believe? As Thora, you knew this—how can you have forgotten?

"But Melfallan will not hear me, and Brierley is dead! What hope is there now?" Her question was a cry of anguish.

Basoul said nothing, only waited. The Everlight looked up at her, trembling with the chill of the night wind, and then took a shuddering breath. She reached up to push back her hair, brushed the tears from her face, then crossed her arms and sat lumpily on the sand. "No promises," she said. "That is a hard rule, Basoul, very hard."

And Basoul smiled, a wash of love and gentleness suffusing into the Everlight's mind, a gift the Everlight owned herself and had often given to her daughters, a gift first learned from Thora herself. The Everlight smiled wistfully in response.

Do you wish to be ended?

"No," she answered, and bowed her head in defeat. "I will hope and I will love, and take the pain that comes with both. I will live without answers, without a future, but I will live, Basoul."

And by that, Everlight, you gain your soul. The Everlight looked up in astonishment, and the dragon nodded. *Be reborn, my daughter, and live as all the witches you have tended. Be one of mine, dear one, a sea witch walking the roads to heal, and I will be with you. But for now, if you are willing, continue this life a little longer, for Brierley is not dead, but alive. She will need you.*

"She's alive?"

Yes. Parlie's courier brought a false report, sent too soon from Arlenn. She is injured but is now on her way home.

"But Melfallan has to know!" She surged to her feet. "He thinks she's dead!"

Melfallan makes his own choices now, and meets his own test of hope.

"No! You don't understand, Basoul! He won't want to live without Brierley, and he is deciding that she is dead. I know it! Why else would he run from me? He will believe that he killed her and will hate himself. What of the resonance he shares with her? Not even you Four understand that bond—not even you know its limits. I know his depth of will—what if Melfallan wills himself to die now, Basoul? Any sea witch can will herself into death when all hope is gone, as Thora did: are you sure he can't? Are you *sure?*"

Basoul sighed, then looked away a moment at the broad ocean, then to the distant headland beyond the cove. *I already tried to tell him,* she admitted ruefully. *I shouldn't have, but I did, for his sake. There are rules, you see, rules that we Four are breaking now—first to save Brierley on the river, then to save the Star Well, perhaps now to save Melfallan from his own fear. What will be the consequence? Will we Four destroy by our disobedience what we wish to save? Or is it finally time, I wonder, to yield and give up all our hopes?*

"Are you asking me?" the Everlight demanded indignantly, and put her hands on her hips, angry now. "What happened to 'no promises, Everlight,' and your test that won me a soul? You can't have it both ways." She stamped her foot emphatically. "Will you, won't you? I'm tired of it! Who cares about your rules? Melfallan is in danger! That stupid courier played his games and by that convinced Melfallan it was true! Had that man only said it outright, Melfallan would have doubted its truth, but Parlie hid it from Melfallan because Parlie believes it and so plays his treachery, plays his two-way games. I swear, Basoul, if that count dares come to Yarvannet, he's in danger, too—from me!"

My child— Basoul began.

"No! I won't listen! Tell him now!" She spread her hands pleadingly. "Oh, please, Basoul! I fear for him, how I fear for him! You must tell him, Basoul! Please! You must try!"

Basoul sighed, then nodded her surrender. *I will try.*

⟅⟆

In his nightmare Melfallan now stood on a battlefield, the suns' light hot on his face, the air filled with the stench of death. All around him lay the remains of the armies, his own and the duke's, and nothing stirred. Puddles of blood linked the swelling bodies of horses, of men. Already hawks circled overhead, ready to descend for the feast. Melfallan swayed dizzily, looking at the sky, and then looked down, knowing what he would see.

Her chest was sheeted with blood, the stain still spreading slowly across the fabric of her bodice. Her long hair lay spread across the mud, her eyes were half-open and glazed. Melfallan dropped his sword from nerveless fingers and knelt on one knee beside her, and moaned as he felt Brierley's face. Still warm. Indeed, she moved slightly as he touched her—or was it his desperate wish?—but then the expression changed in her eyes, a light gone out, followed by a stillness of the face and body too profound for living.

Why did you kill me, Melfallan? Her voice spoke sadly in his ear, in his heart, in his soul, then drifted away on the hot, still air, passing into silence. Nothing moved around him, nothing breathed. He was alone. Melfallan took her slender hand into his and wept, great racking sobs that pierced him to the soul, sobs that would not heal, would not end.

Melfallan. The deep Voice resonated in his mind, insisting at him. Melfallan shook his head, and clutched harder at Brierley's hand, enough to crack the slender bones. *Melfallan.*

"Leave me alone," he pleaded in a whisper.

See me, the Voice ordered sternly, compelling him. He resisted, groaning. *See me.* Unwilling, Melfallan lifted his head. Once, in a dream, he had seen the forest dragon, green shadow among the branches; now another of the Four appeared before him, blue-scaled and flashing silvers, her form shimmering with the movement of waves, the fall of water, so much the essence of Brierley that he gasped. *I am Basoul,* the vision said quietly.

"No!" he cried, and lunged to his feet. He staggered a few steps, then sank to his knees again and groaned, hiding his face in his hands.

Dear one, you will reave your soul with this grief, Basoul said sternly. *Do not test your will against the resonance, or it can destroy you. Stop this: stop this now. Brierley is not dead.*

"She is! Look at her!"

This battlefield is an illusion, a dark dream that haunts you, dear son, but it is not real. Thora did not die on Peladius's battlefield, only you, and Dram's beloved did not die on your later battlefield in Airlie—only you, dear one, only you. Do not remember your prior deaths, Melfallan: it is perilous. Do not let them seize you.

Melfallan shook his head dully. "You aren't real—you're just my stupid wish."

I am real; Brierley's death is not. Why do you believe it? Basoul asked sadly. *Count Parlie does not know for sure; his courier brought you only a rumor. Why do you believe, Melfallan, that life must inevitably lead to loss, that love cannot endure? Why do you believe that the ancient honor of the West cannot win against the malice of the High Lords? That Duke Rainalt's sly treacheries must prevail? Why? Why must your doubt in yourself lead to this?* Basoul paused. *Dear son, look at me.*

Melfallan raised his head slowly, then leaned back on his heels and looked up into the dragon's brilliant eyes.

I loved you as Peladius, Basoul said wistfully, *and I loved you as Dram and as Brierley's brave castellan. I have loved you since the beginning, and I love you now. You are highly favored by the Four, Earl Melfallan Courtray, and we will protect you, not only because Brierley loves you, but for your own sake. The Allemanii brought with them from the West an ancient honor: despite all that has happened in your politics, that honor remains. It will bind two peoples who should never have been divided. It will blend with the Change to bring a new flowering for two peoples, not only one. I believe that, as I believe in you.*

Melfallan took a deep breath, then tried to straighten his shoulders. "Even Thora despaired, Basoul."

In one of lifetimes, that is true—Thora lost everyone she loved and suffered the near-destruction of her people: even the strongest of souls can fail briefly under such griefs—but her despair was answered, my son. She lived again, as did you, and she lives now. The future is not set.

Melfallan frowned, struggling to understand. He looked around him and saw the battlefield with its death for a moment longer, but then it faded, becoming instead the beach by the sea stones, and it was night, not day, and winter, not summer. The waves rushed up the sand, making delicate traceries of foam, and the cool air filled with the sea's voice.

Is this not a better dream? a Voice spoke from the air all around him. *Here is peace, my son. Here is memory and hope, past and future, the endless turning of living.*

Melfallan took in a deep, shuddering breath, then heard soft footsteps on the sand behind him. He turned and saw the red-haired girl with the braids, the green eyes and freckles. The Everlight smiled and held out her hand. "I think it is a good night for walking on the beach, fair lord. Do you think so, too?"

"I want her home, Everlight," Melfallan said with a sigh. "It grows too hard."

The Everlight knelt beside him on the sand. "Perhaps soon? We can always hope it will be soon."

He looked at her earnestly for a long moment, then pulled her to sit beside him, wrapping his arms around her. He pressed his face into the softness of her hair for a moment and sighed again, and yielded. "Yes, I suppose we can," he said, then smiled at her, this lovely red-headed girl who had come to grace his life more than he had ever expected, had ever hoped. "Hope is an Everlight's gift."

"And the gift of the Four." She laid her head on his shoulder, and together they watched the starlight sparkle on the sea.

"Soon," the Everlight whispered. "I believe it will be soon." Her fingers tightened on his forearm. "I believe it, fair lord."

Melfallan smiled, then kissed her. "Perhaps I can believe because you believe, dear Everlight," he said. "Is that foolish? That one person's believing can be enough for two?"

"Not foolish at all," she answered and caressed his face. "I am sure of it."

When Melfallan awoke at the base of the headland, curled up by the rocks, the night was the same, as were the soft movement of the waves and the cool touch of the air. He took a deep breath, and then sighed in his exhaustion. "The future is not set," he whispered stubbornly, then for a time watched the waves, one by one, mount the sandy shore, and closed his eyes again.

It was Philippe who found him, one person in Melfallan's life who did not need answers, who never demanded that Melfallan explain himself. Apparently Philippe had sighted him from the stair and had retreated briefly into the castle, for he brought a warm blanket and insisted that Melfallan be wrapped up in it, then produced a soft pillow for Melfallan's head and insisted on that, too, with both pillow and head in his lap.

"What's this?" Melfallan asked wryly, looking up at Philippe's face. "Am I supposed to spend the rest of the night down here?"

"Do you want to?" Philippe retorted.

"Not really."

"Then don't. After all, you're the earl. You can do anything you want." Philippe crooked a wry smile. "Or so I've heard." Philippe tousled Melfallan's hair, as he had often done when Melfallan was young. "By the way, everyone is looking for you."

Melfallan groaned. "No," he protested and covered his eyes with his hands. "Don't tell me that."

"They're even searching the town," Philippe informed him briskly, "rousting folk out of their beds, poking into stables, opening every closet in case you might be inside. Sir James told them to stop, but nobody is listening."

Melfallan slowly rubbed his eyes and sighed. "Hells," he muttered.

"Exactly. They did the castle thoroughly first, of course, but only I thought to look down here. That stair was always your escape when you were a boy. Your grandfather had quite forgotten it existed, and I never reminded him." He paused. "Can I help, Melfallan," he asked softly, "with whatever is wrong?"

"No, it's better now. Thank you, Philippe."

"Of course, dear son. Always."

Melfallan watched the stars twinkle in the cold, dark sky for a time, and then stirred himself to sit up. "Well, I suppose there's no avoiding it. Let's go help them find the earl."

"Oh, surely not yet," Philippe protested. "Lie down awhile longer." Melfallan hesitated and looked at him. "For my sake," Philippe insisted. "Ten minutes more, time to listen to the night and the sea, time to remember when you were very young, such a fine young boy, growing straight and strong, into everything in your mischief. Your grandfather despaired at times, but I never did." He spread his hands pleadingly. "How many years has it been since I had this pleasure? Truly I have missed it." Melfallan hesitated another moment, then lay down again, his head in Philippe's lap. Philippe tucked the blanket neatly around his shoulders. "Good," he said with satisfaction.

"Ten minutes," Melfallan murmured sleepily and yawned.

"Twenty," Philippe amended softly, and waited until Melfallan had drifted again into sleep. The twenty minutes stretched to a full hour before a soldier thought to explore the old stair and found them. Philippe briskly sent him off to tell Sir James, then sat through the remainder of the night with his earl safely in his arms, watching the night sea and thinking of years long past and a young boy he had loved more dearly than his own life, and still did. When the first glimmer of the Companion's rising colored the eastern sky, to be followed soon by the brilliant light of the Daystar, he woke Melfallan.

"Wake up, your grace," he murmured, shaking Melfallan's shoulder. Melfallan stirred, blinked sleepily at the dawn, then gave Philippe a reproving look. "It's morning," Philippe said, rather unnecessarily.

"That I can see for myself," Melfallan growled. "Shame on you, Philippe."

Philippe grinned, quite unrepentant, and helped Melfallan to his feet and folded up the blanket, and together they climbed the long stair back to the castle.

⁓

In Airlie the Companion's blue twilight suffused the top edges of the distant mountains east of Airlie's grassy plains, beginning its dawning, but the golden glow of the Daystar already tinged its blues and lavenders, spreading a strengthening light across the land.

Derek reined up his horse and looked back at Stefan, and got only another scowl for his trouble. Stefan's face was still a mess—he'd need a healer's tending for the broken nose that hampered his breathing—but he could now sit his horse without swaying enough to fall off, to Derek's relief. Stefan's wobbly walk had helped two drunken friends get outside the palace walls, and a quick dodging into dark shadows and the theft of two horses from a sleeping farmer at the market had completed their escape from the duke's city, but twice on that first night's road Stefan had nearly fallen off his horse. Derek had finally fastened him to his horse by swinging up behind him and holding him on, to Stefan's irritable complaints, but a day's rest in a small bunching of trees by the river had brought improvement, as had the cold bath when they forded the river at a shallows. Since then they had avoided the roads, striking directly across the plains on the other side of the river, and so far any search parties had been but distant black specks riding in the wrong direction.

"We should go to Yarvannet," Derek insisted again.

"We're going to Airlie," Stefan said firmly. "In fact, we're *in* Airlie, Derek, in case you haven't noticed." Stefan set his face stubbornly, an expression Derek had found irritating when first he saw it in Tejar's dungeons. "I have to report to the countess," Stefan insisted.

"Your sense of duty is gratifying, Stefan."

"Ho-ho. Like you really believe that." Stefan shook his head, then winced an instant later. "Ouch," he complained. "Listen, Derek, your news for Melfallan is important, but I have to warn the countess. Do you really think my escape, and thank you very much by the way, is going to stop the duke? I'm the excuse he needs to disenfeoff her. He hates her, and he's already tried to kill her using Heider as his tool. Now I'm the tool, charged with witch-harboring and treason, and with Airlie directly beholden to Ingal, he'll invoke the Charter. I have to warn her. Can't you see that?"

Derek heeled his horse forward. "Hells," he muttered.

"Besides, she'll give you a reward."

"Do you think that's why I did it?" Derek said, rounding on him angrily. "For gold coins or a fine horse, like any paid man?"

Stefan blinked in surprise. "No. I don't think that at all. In fact—" Stefan stopped and looked up, his eyes widening. Derek looked, too, but saw nothing in the sky or on the grasslands, nothing but the growing dawn.

"What is it, Stefan?" he asked in alarm.

"Where are they?" Stefan asked the empty air, then looked to the left and pointed. "Those trees?" A mile off, near the river, Derek saw the dark shadow of a small grove of trees, one of several scattered groves dotting this part of Airlie's grasslands.

"Who are you talking to, Stefan?" Derek demanded. Had the man's injuries unhinged his mind?

Stefan paid him no attention at all. "Is Megan all right?" he asked the blank spot in the open air, ten feet up and two feet to the right. Derek studied the spot: empty. Stefan tipped his head and seemed to listen, nodded happily, then gave a sudden whoop of joy, badly startling his horse and Derek's in the bargain. Derek spent a few hasty moments battling his horse while Stefan continued to babble at nothing. "She *is*?" Stefan exclaimed. "Oh, thank blessed Ocean! Where is she? At *Carandon*?" Stefan shouted, and pumped his fist in triumph.

Both horses sidled violently at the noise, giving Derek another few busy moments, first to make a firm yank at his own horse's reins, then a hasty grab at the other's bridle before it bolted. "Tell Megan to wait for me!" Stefan shouted, another noise the horses didn't need. Derek gritted his teeth and nearly upended himself off his horse as he grabbed again at Stefan's reins, catching them this time.

"Stefan!" he protested. "Stop shouting! Or at least tend your horse!" Derek grunted hard as a determined jerk by Stefan's horse slammed Derek's chest into his saddlehorn, then dragged him half around in his saddle.

"Oh." Stefan returned to the living and deftly controlled his horse with a sharp tug at the reins, a touch of his heels to its flanks. "Sorry, Derek."

"Have you lost your wits?" Derek asked furiously.

Stefan grinned and waggled his finger tauntingly. "Of course, and so will you. You're stuck now, Derek. You had to play the hero and rescue me from Duke Tejar, you with your knight's soul, and now you'll never get loose. That's what happens to any knight who champions a witch, when he finds the whole world has changed." He pointed across the plain. "Over there, camped under some of those trees, are some people who want to meet you. Let's go see them."

"Who?" Derek demanded.

"You'll find out."

Stefan laughed and wheeled his horse, then set off at a gallop, racing across the plain. Derek stared after him a moment, dumbfounded, then cursed vividly and dug his heels into his horse's sides to follow.

⁓

Brierley heard a rustling in the room and opened her eyes. She lay in a comfortable bed, and the ceiling was vaulted stone, with a touch of a cool breeze through a nearby window. She turned her head slightly and saw the sunlight striking down through the grilled panes, a golden shaft of light that caught her and held her for a long, exquisite moment: all the world lived within that light. Then someone moved again in the room, and she turned her head toward the sound.

Countess Rowena bent over her bed, smiling, and laid her smooth, pale hand against Brierley's face, letting it linger a moment. "So you're awake again." Brierley blinked at her, then smiled faintly in response. "And you know me today," Rowena said with satisfaction. "That is very good, a fine improvement. Here, drink a little from this glass." She slipped her arm around Brierley's shoulders and lifted her, then brought the glass to her mouth. Brierley drank obediently, content to look at Rowena's face as she smiled at her. She remembered that smile: it was good to remember smiles. She swallowed several times and then sighed against the glass, raising a vapor. Rowena took the glass away, laid her gently back on the pillow, and then put the glass on the side table.

"Do you know where you are, dear one?" she asked.

"No—" Brierley's voice was little more than a croak. She frowned at the odd sound, tried to clear her throat to make it better, and then became distracted again by the shaft of sunlight striking down into the room from the window, dust motes swirling in the golden light. The dust sparkled, tiny motes of light dancing on the day.

"Brierley." Brierley blinked again, and looked back at Rowena. The countess bit her lip a moment, then shifted her shoulders in mild resignation. "Well, I suppose it's enough today that you know me." Rowena took Brierley's hand and pressed it. "Dear child, be easy. Have no cares, no fears. I will guard you fiercely." She paused, studying her another moment. "You do know me, don't you?" she asked, mildly uncertain.

In another place and time, beyond the window, behind the air, a sea lark swept the ambit of a sickroom, crying defiance, crying comfort, as Rowena lay dying of her wound and her grief for Jonalyn, a witch she had loved. It was not right that Rowena, brave Rowena, should die, she remembered. It was not right.

"Brave Rowena." Brierley smiled and pressed Rowena's hand, liking the touch of the lady's cool fingers.

The countess dimpled. "Am I?"

Brierley blinked, confused. "What?"

Rowena shook her head briskly. "Well, never mind that. You are safe in Carandon, high in my castle in a secret room. Do you understand that?" Brierley nodded slowly, her eyes on Rowena's face. "You've been here three days now, very ill, after a journey lasting two weeks from Mionn. Today is the fifteenth of Pass. Do you understand that, too?"

"Caran—?"

"Carandon. Does your arm still hurt? Nigel says the cracked bone has healed."

"Arm?" Brierley struggled to understand, then gave it up and sighed. She looked again at the golden light falling from the window, entranced again by its loveliness. She heard the countess sigh softly, felt a squeeze on her fingers, and then the countess left her, not going far, just to the table across the room, where she did something that clinked glass and made a sliding sound.

"Rowena?" Brierley called anxiously.

She turned, and Brierley noticed for the first time that the countess was dressed in an elegant green gown tied with a golden lacing at the bodice and waist. Her blond hair was tied up with a green ribbon and a sparkle of a jewel, and more jewels winked at her throat and one wrist. Truly a fine lady, Brierley thought happily, content to look at her. Rowena tipped her head, bemused, when Brierley said nothing further, and then crossed the floor back to her bed.

"Yes?" she prompted, her eyes twinkling, then tipped her head again to the side. "Now, what kind of lovely smile is that, my Brierley? What is it that you're seeing in me today?" Brierley laughed softly, liking to look at her, and Rowena chuckled in return. "I like you silly as much as I like you sensible, I think," Rowena said, "although I'd feel relieved if the sense outbalanced the other, at least more than recently. But your smiles, my Brierley, however I earn them, are jewels on my breast." She bent to kiss Brierley's forehead, and then went away again, back to the table. Brierley sighed, wishing she had not. She moved comfortably under the covers, feeling the slide of smooth sheets over her legs, and the blankets were a comforting weight, holding her firmly in the bed.

Brierley heard a harder sound, a clunk and a scrape, then saw the swing of a door beyond the countess and then Jared came into the room. He stopped short, staring at Brierley, then grinned ear to ear. It was a morning full of smiles, Brierley decided lazily.

"She's awake!" Jared said exultantly.

The countess turned toward him. "And she knows me." She turned her head farther and looked at Brierley. "Who is this, Brierley?"

"Jared," Brierley said obediently. "We hunted shell-stars on the beach." She smiled at her friend.

Both Jared and Rowena looked at her for several moments, but it was true what she had said. Brierley looked back. The countess tsked and took the bottle Jared was holding in his hand. "And she knows you, too, Jared, however the manner that she gives it. What is this?"

"Another potion from Master Nigel. He said she should drink it, uh, twice a day." Jared scowled. "I think it was twice. Uh, I think— Ocean alive, my lady, I've forgotten. You'll have to check with him, I fear." Jared walked toward Brierley, then backtracked a few quick steps to a nearby chair, and dragged it to her bedside. Brierley watched him as he sat down in the chair, then watched more as he looked back at her. They watched together for several moments, both with solemnity, a mutual task.

Finally Brierley pointed at the window and the golden light streaming down into the room. "The light is singing," she said. "Can you hear it, Jared?"

"I will if you say so," Jared said promptly. "Does light sing?"

"Doesn't it?"

"You're the witch who knows, not me."

"But you're shari'a, too, Jared! Jain said so."

"Jain?"

"Megan's salamander, the fire dragon. He said that you

have witch-blood." She smiled ecstatically. "I never knew. I thought I would know any other shari'a, but I never knew about you. Isn't that funny?" She regarded him a moment, considering. "Sea witch, I think, like me. Yes, I think so. The page of the inner world, the hunter of the peace between persons—both of us." She paused. "What's the matter, Jared?" she asked, confused by the distress in his honest face.

"Uh—"

Rowena had joined him by the bed, and both of them looked at her. Brierley lifted her hands to her face, touched her nose. Still there. Why were they staring so? "What's the matter?" she asked plaintively.

Jared turned his head to look up at Rowena. "My lady—" he murmured.

And then Brierley understood and reached out her hand to him, and waited until he took it in his. "I could say don't mind my nonsense, but you'd worry anyway. It's true, Jared, but we can put it on the rack and let it dry."

"Rack?" Jared asked cautiously.

"Like a fish in Yarvannet, readying for market," she explained. Jared looked at Rowena again, peas in a pod with their slight frowns of worry, and Brierley sighed feelingly. Best she not talk at all if this happens. She looked instead at the window and the golden light, Jared's hand firmly in hers, sighed again, and then closed her eyes.

She drifted then, like a sea float bobbing on the gentle waves, having no direction, having no cares. By a distant shore the Companion's light shimmered on the water, dancing in broad bands of lavender and blue, and all the world was filled with music. On a high cliff a white pavilion gleamed in the semidarkness. Brierley stepped across the firm sands of the shore, then slowly climbed the stone staircase carved into the rock, step-by-step, ascending to the top.

Within the pavilion the pool lay there, still and dark beneath the starlight. Brierley sank down beside it and trailed her fingers in the cool water. She sighed and smiled, then arranged herself comfortably on the smooth flagstones and listened to the sea far below. The Voice was there, calling to her in the suns' light, in the endless murmuring of the surf. She smiled. *I love you,* the Voice said, and it was true. Brierley nodded happily. "Yes, I know."

When she awoke again, Jared was still sitting by her bedside. Perhaps he had left for a time, or perhaps not. Did it matter? she thought lazily and smiled at him.

"Who am I?" he asked, an answering smile tugging at his lips.

"My friend Jared." Jared raised her fingers to his lips and kissed them, then held her hand tightly.

"I'm a knight now," he announced with some pride. "Sir Jared Cheney."

"You are?" Brierley goggled.

"Melfallan knighted me. I don't know why, but he did it. Maybe my uncle asked him to do it."

"Or maybe more than that," she judged.

"Maybe." Jared shrugged. "Do you know where you are?"

"Carandon."

Jared beamed. "Good. I've been worried about you, the way you faded out on the way here. You weren't in very good shape when we found you."

"I remember that."

Jared nodded. "It was a long road over the mountains, and hard to keep you warm. Sometimes you talked, but not to us; sometimes you looked—lost, and I couldn't find you, wherever you had gone. But we had to get you out of Mionn, Bri. The duke was looking for you." He reached inside his tunic and brought out a folded paper. "I brought you a letter," he said shyly. "From the earl. I don't think you remember me reading it to you before." He studied her face for a moment. "I can see you don't. Do you want me to read it to you now?"

"Please." Brierley smiled at him.

Jared unfolded the paper and cleared his throat. It says, 'Dear Brierley.' " He pointed at her. "That's you." Brierley lifted an eyebrow, and Jared cleared his throat again. " 'I've met your Everlight,' he says."

"I know that," she said promptly.

Jared hesitated. "Uh, good. Anyway, he also says, 'Or perhaps she is Thora Jodann, your dream-guide. Or perhaps it is all pure fancy, as a way to dream of you, my love.'" Jared stopped again. "Ah, a clue. You deserve an earl," he added with satisfaction. "I asked Evayne what an Everlight might be, and she told me. You really have one of those in your cave?"

"Yes."

"And Evayne told me about Thora Jodann, too, so that's all right." He rustled the letter and resumed reading. "He says then, 'She showed me your cave and journals, and we—' He breaks off there. I don't know why. Do you?"

"Do I what?"

Jared bit his lip. "Well, all right. On the next page it says, 'My love, I miss you.'" He grinned. "Another clue." She smiled back at him, and Jared again busily cleared his throat. Brierley chuckled, and he laughed back, then determinedly put his attention again on Melfallan's letter. "'I worry that you might fall out of love with me while we are parted: such matters must be tended carefully, I know, as a farmwife tends her fragile herbs in a box through the winter. Aunt Rowena told me—I hope you aren't angered I spoke with her—'"

"Not at all," Brierley said, and looked around for the countess, but she wasn't there. Brierley frowned slightly, confused, then looked back at Jared, who was biting his lip again. "Don't worry, Jared."

Jared nodded slowly. "I hope you get sensible again really soon," he said earnestly.

"I'm working on it."

"Well, good. Anyway, here's the rest: '—that we should let fate carry us to where it will, but I don't accept that. Nor will I tell myself that I should, even if you disagree. I hope you don't disagree. I worry that you might hide yourself away, thinking it saves me: you have great skill in your eluding, and I might not be skillful enough to find you. I want you home in Yarvannet, Brierley, and I now doubt our choice that you live elsewhere. You would be safer here. You must come home, and soon.'" Jared folded up the letter. "He didn't sign it, but he gave it to me and told me to find you." He held out the letter to her and she blinked at him, then he stood and tucked it under her blanket. "It's your letter, Brierley, not mine. Here, put it in there."

"All right." Brierley lifted the edge of the coverlet and looked at the letter where Jared had put it. "It's there." Jared sat down and folded his hands on his knee, then gave a great sigh.

"I told you not to worry," she reminded him, then lifted the coverlet slightly to look again at the letter.

"That's easier said than done. At least you're better than you were." He watched as Brierley pulled out the letter and unfolded it.

"He gave this to you?"

"Brierley—" Jared said in anguish, then stopped.

Brierley carefully put the letter back in its safe place and held out her hand to him. "My lovely Jared. Do you forgive me for running away from you that day when you fought the other boys? Do you forgive me?"

"Long ago." His strong fingers closed tightly on hers.

"Then forgive me my foolishness now, and do not worry. It is a long road home, and we are almost there, aren't we? When I am a little stronger, we will ride some days and then find a boat on the river through Penafeld. Isn't that right?" she asked uncertainly.

"Yes."

She nodded. "And then we will ride on the river and then we will be home."

"Yes, we will." Jared hesitated. "The healer says that you're going to have a baby. Is it the earl's?"

"Yes, she is. Are you angry?"

"Why would I be angry? We already went through that— don't you remember? No? Well, I think it's wonderful. What are you going to name her?"

"Rowena," Brierley said, then frowned slightly. "At least that's my idea now. I've had the worst time trying to think up the right name. Do you think he'll be happy?"

"Who? Melfallan?" Jared smiled. "I think he'll be surprised, and then be very happy. As I said, you deserve an earl, and Earl Melfallan almost deserves you, as good a lord as he is." He stood and bent to kiss her forehead. "Now rest. Put all your attention on resting and get well. And then we'll go home, Bri."

Brierley closed her eyes obediently, and after a time heard Jared quietly leave the room.

Home, she thought sleepily, and smiled as she drifted into sleep again.

Home.

～

Jared came often to Brierley's sickroom high in the castle, determined to cheer her, and on the fourth morning brought Evayne with him. The tall, dark-haired girl hesitated in the doorway, as if she wasn't sure if she was welcome, for reasons Brierley couldn't guess. Her witch-sense was still guttered out, leaving her with only eyes and ears to guess at reasons, a skill not much practiced in her life, considering.

"Come in," Brierley encouraged her, beckoning with her hands. Evayne stepped into the room and stopped, then stepped forward more bravely as Brierley beckoned again. Jared brought two chairs from the wall and set them beside the bed.

"Do you remember me?" Evayne asked, as she sat down.

"Vaguely, I fear, but that is easily corrected." She smiled. "You're the air witch."

Evayne glanced at Jared. "Yes, I am."

Brierley nodded. "We will be sisters, you and I." She wrinkled her nose. "I'm sorry that I am silly, but soon I should improve and you can think better of me."

"But your sea gift should have healed you by now!" Evayne protested. "And you still can't hear my mind-speech. I just tried to use it with you before, and you didn't hear me."

"Mind-speech?" Jared asked cautiously.

Brierley waved her hand at him. "More witch stuff, Jared. Get prepared." She focused again on Evayne, finding it harder than she expected, but then, she was silly. Not to worry. "My witch-sense is gone. I can't hear anything. Perhaps that's why I'm silly. Do you think so?"

Evayne's eyes widened in dismay. "You've lost your gift?"

"No, I've just mislaid it for a while. Not to worry." She closed her eyes and sighed. "Is this really Carandon?"

"Yes," Jared assured her.

"Where are Stefan and Megan?"

There was a long pause. "We don't know," Jared admitted. "We only found you, and didn't dare go through the Flinders valley, not with everyone out with arrest warrants and looking for witches. We took another track into the mountains, one that Evayne knew from her, uh—"

"Flights," Evayne provided briskly.

"Right, those," Jared mumbled. "A flight is how we knew you were in Flinders. I don't know how Evayne did it, but I saw you come out of a house by the lake. A little girl was with you. Was that Megan? The girl you found in Darhel's kitchens?"

"Yes, she is. I heard your voice, Jared. I thought it was a fancy."

Jared nodded. "I saw you hear me, but I thought the whole thing was a fancy."

Brierley opened her eyes and smiled at him, then looked at Evayne, but Evayne was looking at Jared. She sighed, and wished heartily that things would start matching up soon. "Has Michael left Flinders, Evayne?" she asked. "He would know the danger. Did they get away?"

Evayne frowned in confusion. "Michael?"

"Michael Toldane: he's the twins' father."

"Twins?" Evayne now looked totally confounded.

Oh my, Brierley thought.

Evayne still frowned at Brierley in obvious confusion, odd for an air witch who knew everything, and Brierley decided to frown back, just to match. "Why don't you know?" she demanded. "I thought you knew everything."

Jared made an odd, snorting sound, then covered his

mouth with his hand for a moment, for reasons Brierley couldn't guess. It made Evayne look at him again, another good matching, one she approved. "How do you know that she knows everything?" Jared asked.

"Doesn't she?" Brierley blinked at him.

Evayne looked down at her hands, pale, slender hands, deft and quick. A wave of color spread up her neck into her cheeks, the other part of Evayne, the shyness to counter the boldness—a painful shyness, Brierley sensed, enough to cripple if it continued much longer, as it might while Evayne watched her hopes fade, one by one, and the silence grew, having no answers. "How old are you, Evayne?" Brierley asked curiously.

"Twenty-three." Evayne looked up.

"I'm nineteen. You're a sword-fighter?"

"Yes." A touch of defiance in the answer, as if Brierley might find fault in Evayne's choices.

"That is a difficult skill." Brierley nodded solemnly, although she knew little of such things, as she once had known little of Melfallan's politics and most of the remainder of the world, all the while thinking herself well informed. "Are you good at it?"

"Yes." Pride now, the chin lifting, the gaze level—then, abruptly, the shy glance toward Jared, the looking down at the hands. A deep wounding there, Brierley sensed, and more than one wound, and none of them of the body, only of the spirit. Brierley sighed and closed her eyes, abruptly exhausted by the new stirring of her witch-sense come too soon.

I wonder if she's always this pale? Evayne's worried thought intruded. *Is she turning ill again?*

"No, I'm all right," Brierley murmured. "I'm always this pale."

"You heard me!" Evayne blurted, sitting up straight in her chair, and Brierley winced at the noise. "You heard my thought! She did, Jared!"

Abruptly Brierley's witch-sense vanished, like a frightened mouse driven back into its nest. Stay there, Brierley told it firmly, and hoped it would obey: it was too soon. How she knew, she couldn't hazard, but that fact she knew. Too soon. She rubbed her face slowly with her hands, then lowered them to the counterpane and scowled fiercely at Evayne. "Not so loud," she complained.

But then her witch-sense stirred again, reaching out gladly to another place in Rowena's castle, a hallway near a hidden gate next to a stairway leading upward. Another voice came, one she knew, and it was ecstatic in its joy. *Mother!*

Brierley gasped. "Megan!"

Brierley! came another voice, a voice rippling like moving leaves in the suns' light—but no, not one voice, but two as one, as those two were always one in the essence.

When she heard their voices, Evayne had leapt from her chair to her feet, her eyes widening, then looked wildly at Brierley. "Who—?" she gasped.

"It is the Finding, beloveds," Brierley declared, spreading her hands in triumph. "What you sought, Evayne, and what they guarded in Flinders, what Thora gave us to believe: it begins at last." Brierley laughed, then laughed even more merrily when Evayne could only gawk at her.

"Believe!" Brierley insisted. "It is the answer!"

~ 18 ~

$\mathcal{T}$he season had progressed into the month of Swords, the second month of spring. The storms of Pass had now subsided, and the night winds no longer lashed the coast and the forest above the bluffsides. Instead flowers appeared in the grass between the tree boles, and birds called to each other in the branches, and the weather warmed. In the early morning the Companion rose first in the east, shedding its blue twilight across Yarvannet, tingeing every wave and leaf with a sparkling sheen. Two hours later the Daystar followed, completing the dawn as it rose above the coastal mountains and adding its warmth to the land, and all was flashing bright on the surging sea.

On this morning Melfallan spared little attention to the beauties of the season as he urged his horse to greater speed along the coast road. His half-troop of soldiers tried hard to keep up, but Melfallan wanted all speed. He touched his heels to Glaeve's sides, and the stallion responded, stretching his legs still more. The suns' light beat down in all its brilliance, and the trees flowed by on both sides of the road, with flashing glimpses of the sea to his right as Glaeve pounded onward, striking his hooves proudly as he galloped.

"Your grace!" the sergeant called behind them. "Wait up!" Melfallan looked around and grinned, then spurred on Glaeve all the more. And so they chased him, his brave soldiers, all the way to Amelin, no doubt cursing him under their breaths, for all he was their earl.

Outside Revil's manse, Melfallan threw Glaeve's reins to a stableboy and mounted the outer stairs, then pounded on the wooden door with his fist. A few seconds later a servant swung the door wide, ready to berate the noise, but stopped short when he saw Melfallan. "Your grace!" the man declared in surprise.

Melfallan stepped in and pulled off his gloves, then swept off his cloak and tossed it at the servant. It was an elegant toss, although not exactly ending as Melfallan intended: still agape in his surprise, the servant moved too late and so got draped. Melfallan frowned distractedly at the squawk, then looked beyond the servant and saw Revil on the stair.

"Where is she?" Melfallan demanded.

Revil tsked, shaking his head "My message said to come after nightfall, Melfallan, when it's dark and nobody will notice. It's called strategy."

"*Where?*" Melfallan bellowed.

Revil pointed behind him up the stairs. "Up there, in the room you sleep in when you visit me." Revil stepped aside neatly as Melfallan charged past him up the stairs. "And hello to you, too, cousin," Revil said drolly, then followed.

When Melfallan swung open the door, she looked up and smiled, and it was her smile and her eyes and her face, truly hers. He stopped and looked at her in amazement, only vaguely aware of the others in the room. And then Revil was there beside him in the doorway, saying something, and somehow the others left and Revil left with them, shutting the door behind him, and still Melfallan could only look at Brierley, unable to move.

"I love you," she said softly, and held out her hand.

"Is it really you?" he asked, and held his breath for her answer.

"I heartily believe so." And the smile was back, her lovely, entrancing smile that had caught his heart and would hold it forever. "I'm home."

Melfallan still would not dare move: if he moved, he knew, she would vanish like a dream, like all the other lovely dreams these long past months, leaving only the empty day to follow, another day without her, until the night would come and he could find her in his dreams again. Weeks ago Rowena had sent her courier with the joyous news of Brierley's safety, and he had waited impatiently until Brierley could travel the rest of her journey home. Time and again he had thought to travel to her, crossing the leagues by river and horseback to Airlie, but had forced himself to wait, however his heart demanded what his good judgment would not allow.

Brierley tipped her head to the side and waited a few moments, then stood and crossed the steps between them. She reached to touch his face with her hand, and he sighed and closed his eyes, then sighed more deeply as the hand moved, caressing him, but still he could not move, could not believe.

"Whatever is the matter, Melfallan?" she asked, her voice rippling with amusement.

He opened his eyes, and Brierley was still there, standing before him. "Is it you?" he asked, and held his breath again for her answer.

"Yes, it's me. What's wrong? Are you silly, too?" she asked in dismay. "How did that happen?"

"What?" He frowned down at her in confusion.

"What?" she replied, mocking him, then slipped her arms around his neck. "I think you should kiss me. Yes, I do think you should." And so he kissed her, long and sweetly, then kissed her a second time, and then a third. She clung to him.

"I saw you dead in a dream," he said huskily. "I killed you, Brierley."

"Not at all," she said. "It isn't so."

Melfallan sighed and buried his face against her hair. "I'm glad," he murmured, then held her tightly. "You're all right? Rowena sent that you had been injured."

"I'm all right now—mostly. I'm still a little silly, but not to worry. All is fine now."

He looked past her at the empty room and frowned, then turned to look at the closed door. "There were other people here. Who—"

"Several you will meet later, but for now, beloved, there is only you and I. True? I won't share you with anyone, not right now, as I told your cousin." She kissed him lightly. "I have missed you, more than I could imagine I'd miss anyone."

"It's really you, Brierley?" he doubted, and she tsked,

shaking her head, then laughed up at him, and it was her laugh, her joy—and his.

"Yes," she said firmly.

⌇

Beyond the windowpane the night sea made its rushing sounds, sibilant whispers against the darkness. Beneath their bedroom window, the wheels of a solitary cart rattled on the cobblestoned street as it passed the manse, followed by a low murmur of voices. Melfallan lay in the comfortable bed with Brierley beside him, and turned his head to look down at her face, shadowed in the darkness.

She was more fragile than he remembered, and he had wondered if he should stop what he later started in bed, but she had insisted, and the combination of his hesitation and her fragility had made their eventual joining sweet and prolonged, an entirely different way to have sex, he decided afterward, and a way he intended to repeat. He had thought about it drowsily as he lay next to her, trying to define the differences, and she had teased him about it, reading his thoughts as likely she always had, then had teased him further when he decided to comment pompously about the rightful privacy of a man's thoughts. She only laughed at him, as he had well deserved.

"Nothing you can do about it," she told him firmly, and it was true.

"Are you awake?" he whispered.

"Um."

He kissed her forehead, content, then watched her face in the light from the window as it shifted when a watchman walked by with his lantern, calling the hour. Brierley stirred slightly, and then reached up and pushed at his face with her hand. "I can't sleep when you're looking at me," she complained sleepily.

"Good," he said, and tightened his arms around her. She rubbed her face slowly on his shoulder, then walked her fingers down his stomach, lower and lower, and he held his breath, but she contrarily marched them up again. He sighed despite himself, and heard her chuckle.

"That's not fair," he complained.

"Where's that rule, fair?" she teased.

"Why don't you do it again and see what happens?"

"I have a secret to tell you," she said.

"Secret?" he asked indulgently. "What secret?"

"First I want to know what you'll say before you say it."

"Excuse me?"

"I want to know what you'll say before you say it," she repeated, and he heard the breath of another chuckle. Brierley lifted herself on one elbow and looked down at him, her face silhouetted against the dim streetlight from the window. He felt the touch of her long hair on his chest, and reached up to caress her.

"Why is that a problem," he asked, "that you have to know what I say before I say it?"

"Perhaps it might be better not to have you say it," she judged. "On the other hand, you're going to know eventually." She sighed. "It's just that I wanted this time as it is. So perhaps I won't ask what you'll say." She kissed him and lay down again, then laughed to herself.

"You sound like the Everlight with its puzzles," he complained.

"What?"

"I have a secret, too," he told her smugly. "I'll tell you my secret if you'll tell me yours."

"I already know your secret," she said. "Basoul told me. You've met the Everlight, however that was done. Did it show you my cave?"

"Yes."

"And the journals?"

He held her closer to him. "Yes."

"Then you know all about me now—except my secret, of course."

"What secret?" he insisted.

"I won't tell you."

Melfallan pressed his face against her hair and breathed in

her scents as he slowly caressed her. "Perhaps I can persuade you," he whispered, and moved his hand to her breast, then pulled her even more tightly against him.

"Yes, perhaps so," she agreed in a murmur. "Yes, do."

The Companion's dawning now shed its blues and silvers into the bedroom, touching everything with a shimmering light. Another cart rattled on the cobblestones below, and the voices were more brisk, greeting the beginning of another day. In their bedroom Brierley sat nude at the end of the bed, brushing her hair, and smiled as Melfallan frowned in confusion.

"A forest witch?" he asked. "What's that?"

"*Who's* that, not what," she corrected primly. "Remember the book in Witchmere? Four kinds of witches, Melfallan, and maybe more to come with the Change. Evayne is the air witch."

"I thought Evayne is a soldier."

"She's both."

Melfallan bunched his eyebrows, pretending to think hard as he counted. "With the baby, that's five witches," he announced. "We are enriched."

"Actually six: Will Toldane is also gifted. And there's more, Melfallan: both Jared and Stefan have witch-blood. Jared is a sea witch like me, and Stefan is a fire witch, as much as men can be witches when they're not twinned."

"*Jared?*" Melfallan blurted.

"*Stefan?*" she mocked him. "Let's include both in your shock and be fair." She waved her brush. "I never knew about Jared. I thought I was wholly alone here, yet there is shari'a blood in the commonfolk, especially here in Yarvannet, or so the dragons say." She shook her head, tsking at herself. "Part of maturity is finding out things you don't know, a host of things you'd never guess. Don't you think so?"

"I suppose."

"You can do better than 'suppose,' I think." She paused in her brushing and looked at him soberly. "Will you do me a favor?"

"Anything," he said promptly.

"Some would call you besotted," she reproved, shaking her head at him. "What's that, 'anything'?"

"Anything," he repeated firmly. "You look very nice when you're naked. Why don't you come back to my end of the bed?"

She sniffed at him. "I will—in time—but I want you to be serious now, Melfallan. It's a serious favor." She waited until he nodded. "I want you to trust Derek Lanvalle when you talk to him today. He has news for you that you must know and believe."

"But, Brierley, he's the duke's spy!"

"Not anymore, if he ever truly was in his heart." She sighed. "Derek has looked many years for something he has never found, but he can find it with you—if you allow it. He risked everything to save Stefan, and the duke will try to kill Derek for his treachery when he finds out, which he will. It is more than the shari'a who now need your sanctuary." She smiled wistfully, and tipped her head to the side. "Will you do that for me, because I ask?"

"If you wish it, yes, I will."

"Good," Brierley said with satisfaction.

"Why don't you come back to my end of the bed?" he repeated.

Brierley eyed him severely. "I think you're distracted, your grace," she advised. "This won't do. What would Sir James think?"

"On the contrary, I am quite focused, dear heart, and right now I don't care what Sir James thinks." She smiled and resumed brushing her hair. "If you don't come up here," he warned, "I'm coming down there."

"I don't believe you," she scoffed. "It's not so."

He laughed softly, and heard her answering laugh, a musical sound, and the laughter was another way to love her, one of a hundred ways to discover now, one by one. "I love you," he said.

"Yes," she answered happily, "I know."

⟋⟍⟋◝

In time the dawn completed itself, and the Daystar's mellow golden light filled the room. As Melfallan sat down on the bed to pull on his boots, he heard the happy shrieks of Revil's little daughters below, then Revil's own laughter as their father chased them up the stairs and down again, a noise as loud as a stampede of cattle. Melfallan smiled, then looked at Brierley standing by the window. She felt his look and turned.

"There will be war this summer," he told her soberly.

"War over me?" she asked sadly.

"No—war would have come for other reasons. Perhaps it's part of my times, however those fortunes are determined. Perhaps it could have been stopped, but that chance is likely gone now. I accept that, and will do my best."

Brierley sighed softly and bowed her head. "There will be many deaths."

"A healer would think of that first. It suits you, my love." Melfallan stood and went to her, then entwined his arms around her waist. She leaned back against him, and together they looked out the window at the harbor. "We'll have the advantage: Tejar has to bring the war to me. He'll come by sea, of course, but the main thrust will be by land, either through Carbrooke or Penafeld."

"It will be Carbrooke, I think," she said soberly.

"Why do you think so?" he asked in surprise.

"Part of Derek's news for you, news he learned in Darhel."

"Garth?" Melfallan asked sadly, and wondered if he would ever truly know a man's heart without risk of mistake, if he would ever have more than his faithful one or two.

"Not Garth," Brierley reassured him. "He is true to you.

No, it was his lady, a foolish woman jealous of you, and not intending great harm."

Melfallan closed his eyes and sighed. "That route should help Rowena, at least at first. To attack through Penafeld, Tejar must first invade Airlie, and she would fight back, whatever the cost to Airlie—for your sake as much as mine, perhaps even more." He shook his head. "I worry for her: if I win the war, I can declare Yarvannet independent of the duke, a free earldom beholden only to itself, but Airlie has only wide meadowlands between itself and Ingal. The real loser in this war may be Airlie. And who knows what Mionn will do?"

"Mionn is not your concern, not any longer. There will be war, but not war everywhere as you had dreaded. Earl Giles will have a choice, not the necessity. And Rowena is clever in her politics, far more clever than you are. She has strength more than you know." She turned in his arms and looked up at him. "The course is set, my love. You have seen it coming; you have prepared as best you can. A swimmer sometimes should not fight the surf, but yield to it, finding his strength within its surge. The future is not set." She set her mouth firmly. "In the end the good must prevail: we can will that truth into being, committing all that we are, and trust in the future—as Thora trusted."

"I asked the Everlight if one's belief could be enough for two." He kissed her lightly. "It's true, I think. Whatever I lack in my believing, perhaps you can give."

She smiled and turned back to the window. In the street below, more people walked briskly in the morning, busily about their affairs, and another cart bumped noisily along the cobblestones, clattering and creaking with its heavy load of market goods for the wharf. In the distance a fishing boat with white billowing sails moved slowly, wending the estuary to the sea and a fine morning's catch. "We have to talk about Saray," Brierley murmured reluctantly.

"Not today," he protested. "Please don't."

"But soon."

"I don't have answers about that," he said in anguish, and she turned and looked up at him in concern. "All I care now is that you are home and safe. That's all I can think about, all I want to think about. Don't say that we mustn't—" Brierley stopped him with her fingers on his mouth.

"Now what would I say?" she asked him. "That I can give you up? It's not possible, Melfallan. That you can give me up? Worse still. Whatever happens, we will be together." She smiled wistfully. "It is fated. Basoul says so."

Melfallan sighed and relaxed, then took a shaky breath.

"The future is not set," she whispered, pressing close to him. "Basoul told me that, too. I believe it now."

"Then it must be true," he said, smiling down at her. "A dragon knows everything."

"No: that's Evayne who knows everything."

"What?"

Brierley laughed softly. "Get prepared, Melfallan."

"Get prepared for what?"

"I won't tell you," she said. "It's a secret." She shook her head, tsking, and would not tell him—at least not yet—and so he kissed her, and then, for good measure, kissed her again.